THE
TRAITOR'S
GATE

THE TRAITOR'S GATE

The Nowhere Chronicles

BOOK II

SARAH SILVERWOOD

Indigo

For Tim Lebbon and Mark Morris, my first buddies on this adventure of writing. Thank you for everything. One for all, and all for one!

The right of Sarah Silverwood to be identified as the author of this work has been asserted by her in accordance with the Copyright, Designs and Patents Act 1988.

First published in Great Britain in 2011 by
Gollancz

This edition published in Great Britain in 2012 by
Indigo
An imprint of the Orion Publishing Group
Orion House, 5 Upper St Martin's Lane, London WC2H 9EA
An Hachette UK Company

1 3 5 7 9 10 8 6 4 2

A CIP catalogue record for this book
is available from the British Library

ISBN 978 1 78062 065 7

Typeset by Deltatype Ltd, Birkenhead, Merseyside

Printed in Great Britain by Clays Ltd, St Ives plc

The Orion Publishing Group's policy is to use papers that are natural, renewable and recyclable products and made from wood grown in sustainable forests. The logging and manufacturing processes are expected to conform to the environmental regulations of the country of origin.

www.sarah-silverwood.com
www.orionbooks.co.uk

THE MAGI'S PROPHECY

Nine there are, and standing side by side
Linked by Love, Truth, Freedom, Hatred, Pride –
Their blood, it is the river's ebb and tide.

Here are two reflections of the same,
The dead bones of the one, the other's frame –
The Magi see the unravelling of the game:

This, their Prophecy.

The dark man comes to rule the new Dark Age.
His door admits those too who come to save.

Travellers from without, within
Bring honour, valour, hate and sin.
Light and dark and shades of each,
Will move through voids, the worlds to breach.

When life and death are bound in one,
The balance of all will come undone,
And love, the greatest damage cause
And forge the war to end all wars.

Eternal stories held unready shall bring
Black tempest, madness, and a battle for King.

The Magi cannot see the Prophecy's end,
Perhaps the Order of Travellers will defend.
Perhaps the stories will hold strong and clear,
The damaged keep us from the abyss of fear.

Don't fight these tellings: their passing must come,
But prepare, both worlds, for that which must be done.

When one plus one plus one is four.
All the worlds shall wait no more.

THE STORY SO FAR . . .

On Finmere Tingewick Smith's sixteenth birthday, during his annual visit to Orrery House, he finds a strange old man in a secret room who appears to know a lot about him. He's hauled out by his guardian, Judge Harlequin Brown, who declares it high time Fin learned more about his life, and his strange one-year-here and one-year-there existence, split between two schools and two best friends.

Before the Judge has time to fully explain Fin's enigmatic background, he is murdered, stabbed through the heart with a golden double-edged sword, and with his death, Fin and his two best friends, Christopher Arnold-Mather and Joe Manning, are thrown into the middle of an adventure. The Storyholder, who holds the Five Eternal Stories within her, and thus safeguards all the worlds, has been kidnapped, and the teenagers must travel into The Nowhere, an alternate London, and find Fowkes, a long-lost Knight, to help rescue the Storyholder. She is in the hands of St John Golden, the Commander of the Knights of Nowhere, who has turned from the path of good to bad. He believes the stories will make him the Dark King, talked of in the Prophecy handed down by the long-banished Magi.

Fin wants revenge for the murder of the Judge, but he also hopes to learn something about his unknown parents – he was found in a cardboard box as a baby on the steps of the Old Bailey, here in The Somewhere, as our world is known, the only clues to his parentage a knitted blanket and a ring.

Now it's beginning to look like his father might be Baxter, a long-dead Knight, for Fin has discovered it was Baxter's ring left in his cardboard box on the steps of the courthouse sixteen years before.

During their quest, Fin and his friends are helped by a Nowhere girl called Mona, who joins them to find Fowkes, meet the cursed Prince Regent, push a Knight called George Porter down a bottomless well, and fight the Black Storm that threatens both worlds.

Finmere manages to save the Storyholder from the Incarcerator Prison, but she's had to bite off her own tongue in order to keep the stories secret from St John Golden. Christopher has accidentally discovered that his father is in league with Golden, and to make up for his father's evil acts, undergoes a ritual with a Magus which costs the Magus his life and Christopher more than half of his own lifespan. The result of their dark magic is a potion that allows three of the Knights, Aged by Travelling between the worlds, to become young men again. The boys return to Orrery House in time to help in the fight against Golden.

After Golden is defeated and the Black Storm disperses, Fin – who still has no idea who his parents are – takes the recovering Storyholder to where he has hidden the blanket found with him in his cardboard box – for that is where she had hidden the Five Eternal Stories. As they pour out in stripes of colour, only three of the five find their way back inside her. The final two – the red and black – instead go into Finmere's friend Joe.

And here in The Somewhere's London, Justin Arnold-Mather, his own treachery undiscovered, is preparing for his next dark move.

PROLOGUE

The smell of blood, sweet, warm ... everywhere. The air was thick with it under the sludgy stink of life. The air was ... familiar. It had been such a long, long time that sometimes he didn't even remember who he was. What he was. Tongues and teeth and heat flashed behind his eyes. He shuddered. He wasn't there, not anymore. That nightmare was over. He'd clawed his way back. His torn and bleeding fingernails were testament to that.

Blood.

So sweet.

His mouth watered as he wandered through the dark, cobbled streets. It was night but unlike where he'd been, there were lights here. Lights, and life, and laughter. The human sounds hurt his ears and tugged at his heart as his feet shuffled along the dirty road. He squinted in the yellow glow of the gas lamp. Everything was familiar: not quite home, but almost. He thought he might be crying; it was all so confusing. He'd been gone for an eternity. He thought perhaps he'd half-become one of them, he'd lived like them for so long. He'd eaten like them. If he wasn't crying then he thought he should be.

'Night, Albert,' the young woman called as she stepped out into the street right in front of him. He ducked into a doorway and peered cautiously round the side of the rough stone.

A disembodied arm, cut off just above the rolled-up shirt sleeve, waved the girl off.

'Night, Tilda. See you tomorrow.' A man's voice, with a soft East End London accent.

1

London. That's where he was. Of course.

'I'll be sharp.' The young woman smiled over her shoulder.

The pub door closed and he heard the hard squeal of a metal bolt being drawn across it.

Blood.

The girl's blonde hair shone in the light from the pub windows, the curls carefully styled so they still fell neatly onto the collar of her coat, even after having worked behind the hot bar all evening. She was pretty, and her low heels clicked on the stones as she passed him and turned down the narrow alley opposite.

Blood. He smelled blood.

His feet slithered after her. It was night after all. And his tongue was growing.

PART ONE

ONE

If the ground floor of Orrery House was always slightly too warm, the third floor was a virtual sauna. Jarvis had hung up Fin's jacket downstairs, and as soon as the door was shut behind him the teenager stripped off the thick sweatshirt and long-sleeved top he was wearing over his T-shirt to keep him warm against the icy December blasts; in Orrery House they were definitely surplus to requirements.

His face was still flushed with heat as he looked around. This had been Simeon Soames' room. It was less than two months since Fin had come to shave that old man's face, just one of the old boys who filled the house. It felt like a lifetime ago – but time was a funny thing, as everyone around him was so fond of saying. Simeon Soames was no longer confined to a wheelchair by the Ageing, and he had moved out to a flat close by. Whole new worlds had quite literally opened up for Finmere since that night, his sixteenth birthday, though they hadn't stopped Ted and Fowkes packing him back off to Eastfields Comprehensive for the remainder of the term. That had been an abject lesson in how time could slow itself down when you least wanted it to. Fin hadn't needed to do any Travelling to find that out. Still, school was done now, and the holidays were here. It was Christmas and there were two whole weeks before he had to think about Eastfields again.

He tugged the stiff window open slightly, allowing a small, sharp breeze to cut through the oppressive heat, and stared out at the dark evening. Fairy lights twinkled on the trees and bushes that lined the square, and through one of the windows opposite – the offices of some bank or business – he could see a large, heavily decorated Christmas tree. The colours were simple, just red and gold, nothing too gaudy for a work environment, and the tree was strung with pearls instead of tinsel, but it was beautiful all the same. Normally the sight of any Christmas tree was enough to make Fin smile – a blend of holiday excitement and festive good cheer – but this time he found there was also a tiny kernel of sadness mixed up in all that traditional warmth.

He looked down at the ring on his middle finger and the jewel that glinted at its centre. Even in the short time that had passed it was fitting more snugly than when Harlequin Brown had handed it over. Another sign that he was growing up. Funny, he'd always thought that when you got older you got more answers, but that didn't appear to be true. His world was still full of questions. He still didn't know who he really was, or where he'd come from. If only the Storyholder—

'Your sword's under the bed.'

Fin jumped slightly at the sudden intrusion on his thoughts.

'You know, for if you want to visit Joe. And your friends. And there ain't no reason you shouldn't 'ave it when you're 'ere, is there?' Ted smiled from where he stood in the doorway. 'And it's good to 'ave you 'ere, Fin. For Christmas. It really is.'

'Thanks.' Fin smiled. The old man was no longer a once-a-year-almost-stranger, and the strange bond between the boy and man had grown into something strong. Until he knew anything different, Ted was the only family Fin had, as close as, anyway. It *was* good to be at Orrery House for the holidays – the first he'd ever spent there – but it also felt like another sign of the changing times, and as much as his old life frustrated him, sometimes Fin couldn't help but be afraid of where his new life might lead him. Ted, dressed in his nightwatchman's uniform, looked just the same as ever, though. There was always something comforting about seeing Ted.

'How have things been?' Fin asked. 'Is everything okay now?' The past few weeks at Eastfields had not only gone by tediously slowly, but he'd had very little information about events in The Nowhere. It was as if, now that his adventure was done, he was expected to just slip back into school life as if nothing had changed. How was *anyone* supposed to do that? Especially as Joe hadn't been there to keep him company.

Thinking of Joe, Fin's heart tightened he felt slightly ashamed. What was he whining about anyway? He'd dragged his two best friends into the madness of his strange life and neither of them had come out unscathed.

'So-so,' Ted said. 'Fowkes is Commanding the Order now. I think Harlequin would have approved of that.' The old man's eyes softened at the memory of Judge Harlequin Brown, Fin's erstwhile guardian, and Fin gave him a small smile. He wanted Ted to know that he felt the Judge's loss too.

'Joe's still with the Storyholder. They're 'aving some problems getting the stories out of 'im, but they'll get there.' Ted's smile was kind. 'Things could've been worse, you know, Fin. You did good – we *all* did good.'

Fin crouched down and pulled the heavy double-edged sword out from under the single bed. The metal was warm, and he felt the familiar tingle running through his veins. Ted was right, of course: things could have gone a whole lot worse. St John Golden was beaten, lost in the Incarcerator Mirror, and the Knights were regrouping. For the moment the Black Storm had disappeared. So why did he have this feeling that perhaps they were all celebrating a little too soon? And was that feeling coming from the black space behind the locked door in his mind? He was tired of it, whatever it was. The Christmas holidays were finally here and he fully intended enjoying them with his friends, his *family*, the Knights of

7

Nowhere, and all those who had helped them in their fight against St John Golden and his gang. If *they* weren't worried, when they knew far more about all this Somewhere and Nowhere business than he ever would, then why should he be?

Fin lifted the sword and turned it this way and that, catching the soft light in the room on the edges. It felt good in his hands, and he had to fight the urge to slice open a doorway to The Nowhere. His fingers tingled. The sword was as eager to be used as he was to use it.

'One of the finest, that sword,' Ted came further into the room and let the door shut behind him, 'and you're a natural with it, that much is clear. You'll make a fine Knight one day, Fin, and that'll make this old man very 'appy.'

The ruby embedded in the hilt winked at Finmere, and the boy looked from the sword to the ring on his finger and back again. At the centre of the black and gold ring sat a sparkling jade-coloured stone. Unlike everyone else who wore both sword and ring, his two stones were different colours.

'I wonder where Baxter's sword is,' he said, the thought slipping out of his mouth before he could stop it.

'It'll turn up when it's good and ready.' Ted leaned on the desk beside the bed. 'These things 'ave an 'abit of doing that. My guess is the Storyholder's got it safe somewhere. She'll give it back when she thinks the time's right.'

'I wish mine matched, that's all. Like all the others.'

'But you're not like all the others, mate.' Ted smiled, wrinkles creasing his face as he did. 'So maybe everything's exactly as it should be.'

Fin put the sword down next to his holdall on the bed and shook the tingles out of his fingers. Nothing felt like it was as it should be. He wished that niggle was as easy to shake away as the sword's tingle.

'Is Fowkes here?' he asked.

'No, 'e's over at The Rookhaven Suite. Got a few things to

8

do.' Ted's eyes darkened slightly. 'But 'e'll be along later to say 'ello. You know, if all 'is business gets done.'

Finmere wasn't surprised. He got the feeling that Fowkes didn't like him very much, and he wasn't sure exactly why. Sometimes he caught the Knight looking at him oddly out of the corner of one eye, and it felt like Fowkes *chose* every word he said to Fin, rather than just talking to him naturally. It was weird. Maybe Fowkes just didn't like that Fin had Baxter's ring. After all, they'd been best friends, back in the day. Still, whatever it was that made Fowkes act odd around him, Finmere was pretty sure it wasn't his fault, and that made it worse, because he didn't know how to make it better. Grown-ups were hard work. He was happy to stay a teenager for a while longer.

The strains of 'God rest ye Merry, Gentlemen' drifted through the open window and both Finmere and Ted stared out. The small Salvation Army band had taken up position in the square and were singing at the door of Orrery House. The brass instruments blew the wind aside as they blasted out the tune and the singers – many much older than the true ages of the men they were singing to – held up sticks with old-fashioned lamps attached. Watching them and listening to the soft blue notes of their carol made Fin feel happy and sad all rolled into one.

'They come every year,' Ted said quietly. 'There might be no sign outside, Fin, but some folk knows we're 'ere.'

Fin almost smiled. Outside, it was nearly Christmas, a time of good cheer. Why couldn't he feel that?

'Jarvis will be getting some mulled wine and 'ome-made mince pies ready to take out to 'em. Why don't we go and give 'im an 'and?' Ted's kind eyes twinkled. 'I could use a mince pie and a drop o' something warm meself. And then of course we've got the tree to decorate.'

'I didn't see a tree.' Fin's mood lifted slightly.

'We was waiting for you. There's always a tree. Who doesn't

9

'ave a tree at Christmas? What kind of thinking is that?'

Fin smiled, and this time he felt it in the pit of his stomach.

'Unless, of course,' Ted said, 'you're too old for decorating a Christmas tree—'

'You can never be too old for that, Ted. You going to help?'

''course I am, son. Now let's go before that lot out there eat all the pies.'

Grinning, Fin followed the old man out into the heat of the third-floor landing and towards the stairs. He glanced over at the inconspicuous little alcove behind which, not so long ago, he'd found a secret room. Where there had been a vase of lilies then now stood an arrangement of holly and berries. Fin wondered what would happen if he reached out and moved it. Maybe later, he thought, as they took the spiral stairway down into the heart of the house. It was Christmas, after all.

TWO

'At least they brought you back in an unmarked car,' Mr Arnold-Mather said dryly as he watched the tall gates at the end of the drive swinging slowly shut. He closed the front door and turned to face his son. 'It could have been worse. The police, at least, don't wish to embarrass me.'

Christopher favoured his father with an unfocused glare and headed into the kitchen. 'It doesn't matter,' he called over his shoulder, aware that he was slurring his words slightly, 'the man in the off-licence recognised me. Well, he called me "that bastard politician's son". I presumed from that he must know you.'

He drank a glass of tap water, aware of his father watching from the doorway. His stomach rolled and his throat burned. The combination of alcohol and cigarettes made him feel sick, but he was going to keep going with it until he got used to them. He'd only drunk four bottles of beer, but that was enough to leave him with a dull headache once the initial buzz had worn off, and although he was way past the 'two cigarettes and whitey' stage, any more than three or four left his chest feeling tight and sore.

'Why are you doing this, Christopher?' His father's voice oozed disappointment and irritation. Christopher did his best to hear some sort of care in it, but failed to find any. That didn't come as any great surprise.

'The sergeant said you were demanding a bottle of vodka,

and smoking in the shop.' Arnold-Mather's eyes were cold. 'It's almost as if you *wanted* to get arrested.'

'There's no flies on you, Dad.' Christopher leaned back against the sink and crossed his arms. Just looking at his dad made him angry in ways he couldn't even put into words. It was like a river of rage flowing constantly through his veins. He'd thought when he'd gone through the ritual with the magus that it would somehow make everything better, but it hadn't – everything was worse. His dad still had that smug, superior smile on his face, and Christopher still couldn't bring himself to tell anyone about the cigarette case. Not that there'd been anyone to tell. Fin had been sent straight back to Eastfields, and he'd gone back to St Martin's. What was it with adults that made them think they could just turn the world on its head and then expect you to believe that school was important? Like he even *cared* about school any more ...

'Where's Mother?' he asked, a small twinge of guilt adding to the nausea roiling his insides. His mother was kind. She was a good person. When he'd been suspended and sent home from school a week early, the only option left at St Martin's for a boy who insisted on sneaking out every night and rabble-rousing, he'd seen the hurt and confusion in her face. *Where was her good boy?* that face said. What was he supposed to tell her? That he was still there, somewhere deep inside, but that he'd done something good that he couldn't feel good about? Or that she was married to someone who was prepared to kill to get what he wanted? To tell her that would mean that he'd have to admit that to himself, and worse, he'd have to tell Fin, and Fowkes and the Order. What would they think of him then, the son of a ruthless bastard?

He would do his best to discredit his father, to do what damage he could where possible, but he couldn't bring himself to confront him with what he knew – and that made Christopher dislike himself even more.

'She's at church.' Justin Arnold-Mather looked as if he'd

forgotten he even had a wife. 'They've got a carol service on tonight. She's doing whatever it is she does up there.'

'Getting away from you, probably.'

'What is it, Christopher?' His eyes narrowed slightly. 'What is it that's made you so angry? You've been different ever since you ran away from me after that school trip to the House of Detention.'

Christopher stared at his father. He felt a small knot of fear tangled up in his insides. This was a game they were playing. There was no way that his dad still believed they'd been on a valid school trip – even if he hadn't known all along that the Doorway was there then, he had to by now. In fact, his dad knew *everything*, it turned out. He'd *played* Christopher.

Well, now *Christopher* knew something no one else did. 'Teenage angst, Dad,' he said. 'There's a lot of it going around.'

'Not like this there isn't,' Arnold-Mather said thoughtfully. 'You've gone from straight As to not bothering in the space of a few weeks, and as for all the rest of it ...' His right shoulder twitched, as much of a shrug as he could bring himself to make. 'St Martin's will expel if you keep this up, the Headmaster has made that quite clear. And that,' he said, 'would break your mother's heart.'

The well-chosen words pricked like a dart. Christopher didn't like letting his mother down; he didn't like seeing that pain on her face. But what was he supposed to do, just play happy families and ignore everything he'd discovered his father to be?

'You'll throw your life away if you carry on down this road,' Mr Arnold-Mather said. 'Is that what you want?'

The irony almost made Christopher laugh out loud. Much of his life was gone, but he hadn't *thrown* it away. 'I don't know what I want,' he said finally. That was the truth.

'We should be standing together, you and I.' Arnold-Mather took a few steps further into the room. 'Father and son.'

Christopher watched him warily. What was he suggesting –

13

that they join up in whatever nefarious plans his dad might have for the Order? After everything he'd done? Or maybe he thought that Christopher was as power-hungry and heartless as he was? What would his father make of the sacrifice he'd made? Call him a fool, probably. Perhaps there was a kind of revenge in that.

The buzzer saved him from having to say any more and as his father answered the gate intercom by the kitchen door Christopher splashed cold water on his face. He didn't feel good at all.

'And you are?' Mr Arnold-Mather spoke into the machine. He listened for a moment, then said, 'I see. And you want to talk to me about Christopher?'

There was another pause. Then he said grudgingly, 'Well, you'd better come in then.'

Christopher could feel his father's eyes burning into his back.

'What now?' Behind him, Arnold-Mather's words echoed his son's thoughts.

What now?

'Merry Christmas,' Christopher muttered. 'Merry bloody Christmas.'

London's streets were always busy, but as Fin wove his way through the crowds with Ted there was barely space for them to walk side by side without being jostled this way and that. Last-minute Christmas shoppers filled the pavements, using their bags full of as-yet-unwrapped gifts as weapons against the wave of on-comers. Those dressed in suits strode equally purposefully towards their offices, knowing that the days would be filled with staff parties and after-work drinks. The crisp air was filled with the anticipation of good times, and although it was freezing, the sun shone down from a cloudless blue sky.

'Where are we going?' Fin asked, lengthening his stride to

keep up. Ted might be due to retire, but he didn't show any signs of slowing down. When they'd left Orrery House half an hour earlier, the old man hadn't given him any clues as to their destination, except to say that he thought it was a trip Finmere might like to tag along on. Which was fine with Fin: getting out in the fresh air might be just the thing to clear the lingering sense of trouble he couldn't shake.

His first night at Orrery House hadn't done anything to set him at his ease. Fowkes hadn't appeared, and he'd only seen Lucas Blake in passing – although at least that Knight had given him a cheerful wink before disappearing into Freddie Wise's room. After decorating the tree, Ted had gone off to his job as nightwatchman at the Old Bailey, and Fin had eaten his supper alone, down in the basement kitchen. For a house that was supposedly full of people he'd barely seen anyone, and when he'd asked the butler what they were all doing, Jarvis had just looked at him like he was some kind of mental and said, 'They arrive tomorrow – the selected,' before disappearing off to do whatever it was he did all day. That had left Fin none the wiser – not that that was any surprise. The one certain fact in his life was that Orrery House would always raise more questions than it would ever provide answers.

Left to his own devices, Fin had gone back up to the third floor and moved the vase of holly out of the alcove, but to his disappointment no secret doorway appeared. Instead, he was left staring at the painted plaster. A cautious exploration of the rest of the house had revealed no evidence of anything interesting, so by nine-thirty he was back in his room, lying on the narrow single bed with a book and pretending it wasn't at all weird to be sleeping there.

Needless to say he didn't have a very restful night. For a house dominated by apparently very elderly men, there was an awful lot of shuffling along the corridors at night. Day and night didn't seem to mean much to the Knights of Nowhere, retired or otherwise – but time was a funny thing, after all.

''Ere we are.' Ted suddenly stopped, halfway along one side of Russell Square.

'Here?' Fin looked around him. As far as he could tell they weren't anywhere overly exciting.

Ted tilted his head. 'Use your eyes, Fin mate. Blimey!'

Fin did as Ted had instructed him and looked around. Ted had brought them to a halt outside a green hut that stood alongside the railings that enclosed the square's garden. Its painted panels shone glossily, and there were three hanging baskets bright with winter flowers of some sort beside the open door. How had he not seen it? He remembered Judge Harlequin Brown pointing out how much of the city people missed by not looking up at the buildings every once in a while – so how much of London did Fin miss by being so lost in his own thoughts all the time? He looked at the hut again. It was a strange thing: completely out of place, and yet totally belonging where it was, all at the same time.

'What is it?' he asked at last.

'It's a cab shelter – you know, for taxi drivers. There're thirteen of them. Some might say that's an unlucky number, but luck's a funny thing – it can go either way. There ain't lucky or unlucky numbers; that just ain't true. But there *are* special numbers, and thirteen's one of them.'

'Like sixteen, then.'

'That's right, like sixteen.' He paused and lit a cigarette. 'And eleven. That one can be a funny bugger too.'

'So what's so special about cab shelters?' Fin had never heard of them before. 'What's the point of them?'

'That's two different questions.' Ted exhaled a long stream of smoke. 'Most people would say that *the point* of 'em is to give your 'ard-working cabbie a place to rest up and grab a cup of tea or a bacon sarnie – or maybe on days like this an 'ot chocolate – without 'aving to find somewhere to park up and pay a meter. Why're they special? Now, that's a different question.'

16

Fin didn't interrupt. The air was cold, and his freezing nose had reached the stage when he was sure that it was about to start running uncontrollably, as if even his snot was desperate to get somewhere warmer, but he just sniffed hard and shoved his hands deep into his coat pockets. Ted had a way of sharing extraordinary things in the most ordinary way, and Fin had a feeling something was coming up now.

'Cabbies've got the Knowledge. You 'eard of that?'

Fin nodded. Everyone in London knew about that: Black Cab drivers had to take an exam on it before they could get their licence. 'They have to know all the streets in London or something, don't they? Or at least the middle of it.'

'Six-mile radius of Charing Cross, to be exact. That's the official Knowledge. But some drivers – and you'll always find 'em 'ere – they 'ave' – and he tapped the side of his weather-beaten nose – 'they 'ave *the* knowledge.'

Fin sniffed hard. His nose was definitely running now. 'Sorry, Ted, but you've lost me.' He gave up and ran his sleeve across his face.

'Wake *up*, lad. *The* knowledge – about us.' He threw his cigarette down and ground it out. 'You ever need to get a message to me, if you're stuck in the city and don't know where to go or what to do and you don't think the Old Bailey or Orrery House are safe, then you find one of these cab shelters and you wait. When a cab parks up, you check and see if it 'as a small sticker in the bottom left-'and corner of the windscreen – if it does, then the driver *knows*. You pass a message on through 'im, or maybe 'e'll give one to you. That's 'ow *the* knowledge works.'

'They know about the *Order*? *The Nowhere*?' Fin's eyes widened as he looked around at the cabs that were weaving their way through the traffic circling the square. Ted's words might not have done much to allay the gnawing sense of wrongness in his stomach, but the idea that there were

17

strangers cruising the streets of the city who shared his secrets was slightly comforting.

'They don't know everything,' Ted said, 'but they know enough. And anyways, everyone knows cabbies are far more interested in talking than asking questions, and that suits us just fine.'

'Shall we go in and get a hot chocolate then?' Fin stamped his feet in an effort dispel some of the numbness that was spreading up from his toes.

'It ain't for us – we ain't cabbies. You got to know your place, Fin. No, we'll just wait out 'ere, and then when we get back to the big 'ouse, there might be a surprise waiting for you. Stop you being so bored on your 'olidays.'

Ted winked again, and Fin smiled. His life was full of surprises, most of which seemed completely unsurprising to Ted and the Order. What could this one be?

'So, what are we waiting for? A message?'

As he asked the question, three sleek black cabs drew up in a line in front of them. Fin peered at the window of the first. Down in the corner, almost out of sight, was a small black and white sticker. He could just about make out a sword at the centre of it.

'Oh no,' Ted answered, 'this is better than that. We're not the only ones waiting at the shelters today. Simeon Soames 'as gone to Chelsea Embankment and 'arper Jones is at 'anover Square.' He drew himself up tall and nodded at the drivers. 'We're 'ere to meet the selected – new blood, Fin, new Knights to rebuild the Order.'

Doors opened and the taxis, whose engines hadn't even stopped running, drove away, leaving their cargo on the pavement: three young men, each with a small suitcase at his side.

'Are you Ted Merryweather?' the closest to them asked. He was tall, with a shock of ginger hair nesting on his head, and he wore thick-framed glasses. 'I'm Alex Currie-Clark.'

'So you are, me lad.' Ted grinned. 'So you are.' He nodded to the other two. 'And you're the twins, Benjamin and 'enry Wakley. Glad to see you're not identical. Life's confusing enough without people going around looking 'xactly the same as other people.'

The twins were both sandy-haired. One smiled back, his eyes twinkling with adventure; the other stared seriously at both Ted and then Fin himself. No, Fin decided, these two weren't identical at all.

'Right then,' Ted rubbed his hands together, 'let's get you back to Charterhouse Square. There's a lot to be done before the Initiation Ceremony tonight.'

The young men fell in step behind Ted, and with Fin in their midst they formed something of a bundle rather than two pairs as they headed back through the biting air. Fin was still slightly short for his age, but his head at least reached the shoulders of the three men. He no longer felt like a child – they weren't *that* much older than him, after all.

'Which one of you is which?' he asked, his nose running again.

'I'm Henry,' the twin with the grin said. 'That's Benjamin. He was in the Army, hence that serious expression – although he was always the serious one, even before that explosion exploded his eardrum. Bloody good at sport though.'

'Is this my CV?' Benjamin asked, casting a sideways glance at his brother. 'Shall I tell yours?'

'No need.' Henry winked at Fin. 'I like to think of this as a fresh start.'

'I was in the Army,' Currie-Clark chimed in. 'Well, the Territorial Army, really. I was thinking of trying out for the real thing – or maybe the Navy – when my current government contract ran out. But then – well, this came up.'

'Government contract?' Henry asked.

'Just computer stuff. You know.' Currie-Clark shrugged it away, but Henry's eyes were sharp. 'You're some kind of techno whizz kid, aren't you?' he asked. 'Like a hacker?'

'We don't actually like to use that term, and I've never done anything illegal but—'

'I bet you could make a lot of money with a skill like that.'

'Little brother,' Benjamin said, 'fresh start?'

The lighter-haired twin laughed, and Fin liked the sound.

'"Little brother". Two minutes off the mark and I'll always be the youngest.'

Finmere let the men creep slightly ahead of him as he listened to their banter. He felt somehow older than the three of them – well, Currie-Clark and Henry Wakley, anyway. He'd already learned that the downside of the excitement of an adventure was that adventures invariably caused damage, and these two didn't yet know that, he suspected. He watched the stiff spine of the man in the middle. Benjamin Wakley was different. He knew, Finmere was pretty sure of that.

THREE

'Well, that went better than I'd expected,' Lucas Blake said, spinning the steering wheel and yanking the car somewhat sharply onto the main road. 'Sorry, out of practice on this driving lark. Been a while.'

'I can see that.' Christopher gripped the handhold above the passenger door, but it was more for show than out of fear – he *trusted* Lucas Blake. Blake was just one of those people. You couldn't help but trust him. And right now he was just glad to be away from the stifling atmosphere of his austere family home.

'Your father took it well,' the Knight continued. 'I expected him or your mum to object to you spending Christmas away from home. I thought we might only get you for a couple of days, rather than the whole thing.'

'You don't know my father.' There were layers of truth in that sentence that made it sound more maudlin than Christopher had intended. He looked over at Lucas Blake's handsome face. He was every bit the hero that Christopher knew himself not to be. In the moment of silence he could feel the awkwardness between them. It wasn't a surprise: everything valuable came at a price, and Blake knew Christopher had probably paid a high one for his own returned youth. Ted and the Knights had tried to prise out of him – gently, of course – how he'd paid for the Magus' miracle, but he hadn't said much, just fobbed them off with vague answers, and they hadn't pushed. He guessed they figured he'd tell them in his own time. He wondered if they'd appreciate the irony ...

Lucas Blake littered the silences with talk as they sped into central London, filling Christopher in on what had happened since they'd found the Storyholder. The Order was being rebuilt, new Knights recruited, Fin had gone back to Eastfields Comp, but Joe had stayed with Tova to try and get the stories to reunite. What Christopher didn't already know he'd pretty much figured out already.

'I thought you'd all forgotten about me,' he said at last.

'Forgotten?' The car swerved slightly across the lane as Blake stared over at Christopher. 'How could we *forget* about you? We just thought a bit of normality would be good for you after everything.' He steadied the car. 'Well, not all of us, actually – Ted said that *normal* changes with knowledge, so everything was different now, but the old boys disagreed. Plus, you've got a family and everything and that makes it tricky. Joe's on a sports scholarship course as far as his mum's concerned.' He glanced over at Christopher again, keeping the car straight this time. 'But we've been keeping an eye on you.' He paused, then said quietly, 'Looks like normal's not working out so well at the moment.'

Christopher stared into the wing mirror. A black car had been behind them nearly all the way. Perhaps the Order weren't the only ones keeping an eye on him. He wasn't surprised. His dad must have been rubbing his hands together with glee when Lucas Blake rocked up at the door. Lucas led to Fin and the Order – and they were far more interesting to Mr Arnold-Mather than having his own reprobate son home for the holidays.

'Not working out so well?' A range of recent misdemeanours sprang to mind. 'You could say that.' He smiled over at Blake, but the expression was thin. Blake watched him intently and in his eyes Christopher thought he could see the first signs of a serious mind behind the man's devil-may-care exterior. Whatever Lucas Blake was thinking, it was beyond

Christopher's understanding. He might have shortened his own life expectancy, but it hadn't made him grow up any quicker.

'Nothing in the future is definite, you know, Christopher,' Blake said. 'Even the certainties can change.'

'Now you're sounding like Ted.'

'I don't know who that should scare more, me or him.' He grinned. 'It's *Christmas*! Let's go and see if we can find some fun to shake the melancholy out of your bones. You're back with us now. Anything could happen.'

Christopher couldn't help his spirits from lifting slightly as they wove their way towards Clerkenwell, despite the thing he'd done, and the anonymous car that dipped in and out of the traffic behind them. Blake was right: he was heading back to Fin and Joe, people he belonged with, and anything could happen.

The night had been quiet in The Nowhere, and now the damp grey of dawn crawled into the room. Beneath where Joe was sitting the Archivers continued moving and filing the truth vials, sorting them into a system only they understood. Joe never went into that vast hall, but he liked to know that the Archivers, strange as they were, were all up and busy. He didn't like the nights. They were too still. His head hurt at night – the stories talked to him then, and nothing they said was pleasant. Sometimes they were so loud he couldn't hear his own thoughts, and what *he* wanted and what the stories wanted would get confused. No, he didn't like the nights at all.

He liked the pure white of the Storyholder's apartments, though. When he'd first gone there, with Fin and the others, he'd been almost intimidated by the starkness, but now he got it: the stories had too much colour in them, and the white was relaxing. He sighed. It was hard enough having two of them inside him – he couldn't imagine carrying all five stories for all those years like Tova had. He liked her. She'd been kind to him, even while she had still been recovering from her awful injury. She wanted to make him feel better. So why was he just sitting here and doing nothing to help her?

They were supposed to be meditating – like they did every day, all day, to the point when Joe would kill to just kick a football around and have a laugh for half an hour. Unlike football, Joe wasn't very good at meditation. His attention span had never been the greatest before this, but now he found it even harder to empty his head and concentrate. Maybe the red and black stories weren't the best ones to have inside you – he got that impression, anyway. He didn't like to admit it to anyone, but they were changing him: he was angrier, that much was obvious – angry that the colours had gone into him and not Fin, and at the same time angry that no one wanted him to keep the stories. If they'd gone into Fin, would that have been different? They all trusted Fin. *Finmere* was somehow special.

Joe let out a long sigh and ran his hand over his hair. Tova wasn't meditating. She was sick. Beads of sweat had formed along her hairline, and though she had a temperature, her skin was deathly pale. She was lying twitching on the vast bed beside him. At some point in the last hour she'd slipped from deep concentration into a feverish sleep. For a while Joe had pretended that he hadn't noticed – he'd tried to tell himself that he didn't know why he'd done that, but that was just a lie. Lies were another thing that came easier these days.

He'd been ignoring Tova's sudden sink into illness because despite the headaches and the colours and the thoughts he didn't understand that came in the night, part of him was hoping that if she was sick, the other three stories would come out of her into him, instead of the other way round, and then he'd feel better, once they were all in the same place. The stories *should* be together – it was terribly, *terribly* wrong that they were split, both he and the Storyholder agreed on that – but why did it have to be *her* they belonged in? Wasn't *he* special enough?

Anger flared slightly, and he swallowed it. This wasn't like him. It *wasn't*. He wasn't that flipping complicated. He'd certainly never been a liar. He touched her small hand and her burning skin cooled his thoughts and he was back to being plain old Joe Manning again. He wanted the stories gone. He wanted to go back to Eastfields Comp. He wanted to see him mum for Christmas. He didn't *want* to be special.

A fresh bead of sweat burst into life on the Storyholder's face and he caught his own reflection in it. *What the heck was he doing?* Tova was sick – his *friend*, a woman he cared about. He squeezed her fingers and then stumbled over to the door, his legs numb from so much sitting still.

'Tova's sick,' he announced, and Fowkes, who was dozing in an armchair, was on his feet in a moment.

Joe followed as he pushed past the teenager to get into the bedroom. 'What do you mean "sick"?' Fowkes asked quietly.

'I don't know.' Joe was awash with his own shame and uselessness. 'We were meditating. I opened my eyes because I couldn't get into it and saw she was sweating.'

The Storyholder looked sicker than she had minutes before. Her face was all blotchy. Fowkes crouched by the bed, but before he could touch her, Tova's eyes flew open and her hand gripped his wrist, so tightly he winched. She gasped.

'Tova?' Fowkes said, 'Tova? What's the matter?'

Joe stared, his mouth half-open. The Storyholder might not be able to speak, but her eyes were almost screaming out her fear. What was she scared of? He'd never seen her show anything but a quiet strength. Was it *him*? Was she afraid of him? No, he decided, he was the only person who was scared of him, at night, when he sometimes felt he wasn't himself any more.

The Storyholder's eyes darted from Fowkes to Joe and then back again, desperate for them to understand her meaning.

25

'Pen,' Fowkes growled. 'Paper, quick!'

Joe grabbed Tova's pad and pencil from beside the bed and thrust them into her sweaty grasp. She started scratching out words so hard the paper was nearly punctured, and her hand was moving so swiftly it was almost as if the words weren't coming consciously, as if something were talking through her.

REDEYESBLACKTONGUEREDEYESBLACKTONGUERED-EYESBLACKTONGUE

She dropped the pencil and collapsed back onto the sheets, and within seconds, the red patches on her face had begun to fade, as if the fever had passed out from her into the words on the pad.

Joe and Fowkes both stared at the paper. 'What does it mean?' Joe asked, eventually.

'Probably nothing.'

'Yeah.' Joe thought that Fowkes needed to brush up on the delivery of his white lies. 'Probably nothing.'

They sat and watched her fever fade as she slept, and Joe was quite sure it wasn't just his eyes that kept drifting to the cryptic, creepy message on the crisp, white paper.

FOUR

It was almost ten p.m. when Ted closed the door of the Oval Room and faced the men gathered there. A plate of icing sugar-dusted mince pies sat on the long table and Jarvis moved from place to place pouring coffee into the small white cups beside each of the Knights. Simeon Soames, Lucas Blake and Harper Jones looked almost out of place, their youthful appearances contrasting with the wizened faces of their peers, but they were all dressed in their Initiation gowns, and Ted felt a glow of pride at all that the Order stood for, notwithstanding the Ageing, and that was tainted by only a small ache of sadness that Judge Harlequin Brown wasn't there to see this day.

'Where's Fowkes?' Cardrew Cutler asked, icing sugar settling on his upper lip as he bit into a warm mince pie. 'Haven't seen him all day.'

'He's with the Storyholder and Joe Manning,' Harper Jones said. 'He'll be back in time.'

'He spends too much time over there.' Freddie Wise took a neat sip of his coffee. 'That whole situation was too costly the first time round. He'd be best to leave well alone.'

'Now that we have new Knights he'll be able to,' Lucas Blake said. 'None of us can deny that those two need watching over, and it's not as if we've been overflowing with able bodies.'

'Bit harsh, mate,' Cutler cut in.

'No offence intended, but you know what I mean.'

'Trust me,' Jones said, 'I'd rather be baby-sitting those two than trying to get to grips with the Old Bailey. It's been a long time since I studied Law.'

'So, the new Knights.' Cutler looked up at Ted. 'All ready, are they? How many have we got?'

'Not sure they're ready yet, but then, which of us ever was, eh?' Ted grinned. New blood coming into the Order: it was like fresh beginnings, made him feel very nearly like a young man himself. 'We've got six. A good bunch I think.'

'Six is a good number,' Wise said thoughtfully, one hand twisting the end of his walking stick. 'With Fowkes and these three, that'll give us ten strong Knights.'

'True,' Cutler's word was muffled as he swallowed his last mouthful, 'but it's always better to have a couple of reserves. You know, in case any of the buggers end up like us.'

'Let's just look on the upside for now,' Simeon Soames said. 'Freddie's right. Six is a good number. And they're good men. Better to have six good ones than ten mediocre.'

'What about the lad, Finmere?' Cutler asked. 'Is he coming to the Initiation?'

''e'll be there,' Ted said, 'and Christopher. That one's got 'imself into a bit of bother recently. 'e needs to be around us for a while and I won't 'ave no arguments this time.' He sniffed, and waited for protest, but none came. 'I've told 'em to go over to see Joe. Fowkes'll get 'em back in time.'

'That was a good idea,' Jones said. 'They need each other, those three. I don't know if it's just me, but I get the feeling they're all held together in some way. Maybe the best way to heal them after everything they went through is to keep them together, now that things are back to normal?'

'Is it just me,' Wise's dry voice cut in, 'or are we all congratulating ourselves a touch quickly? Does anyone else suspect that things still aren't quite right?'

The Knights around the table stared at him, and Ted, watching them, could see more than one guarded expression.

Freddie wasn't alone then. They were all ignoring a vague sense of unease.

'Well,' said Cutler as he reached forward for a second mince pie, 'I have been having a funny feeling in my water recently, but to be honest that really could just be a funny feeling in my water. Bladder ain't what it was.'

'The stories are split,' Blake said, 'that's all. Bound to make things feel a bit weird.'

'But why haven't they gone back?' Wise's sharp eyes narrowed. 'Does no one else wonder about that? Never in recorded history have the stories been held by two people, and never by a person Somewhere born.'

'She's still weak, that's all.'

'She's not that weak, not any more.'

'Has anyone else noticed this?' Soames asked.

'Noticed what?' Ted said.

The young man was staring at a spot on the table. He frowned, his blond hair falling into his face. 'Has it always been like this?'

'What are you on about?' Cutler asked.

'Look.'

Ted moved round to the other side, Freddie Wise a second or two behind him. He leaned over Simeon Soames' shoulder and stared. Even after pulling his glasses on, it took a couple of seconds to see what was bothering the Knight. A tiny hairline crack ran from the corner of the table towards the centre, zigzagging sharply through the grain of the wood.

'It is an old table,' Harper Jones said, quietly. 'Maybe it's just wear and tear.'

'Maybe it is just the table. You know, the outer casing,' Cutler added. 'Could be nothing to worry about at all.'

'There's only one way to find out.' Ted looked at Jarvis, who went over to the light switch by the door and pressed the hidden multi-coloured button below. The centre of the long conference table rolled back to reveal its true identity:

a map of all the worlds. This time, none of the men gathered looked at the layers of moving living Londons in front of them; instead, all eyes scanned the surface. After a few moments, Ted looked back at Jarvis and the cover rolled back across the map.

'Not just my bladder then,' Cardrew Cutler said eventually, breaking the silence.

'This is not good,' Wise said. 'This is not good at all.'

Ted stared at the Prophecy that glowed slightly on the wood it had been carved into so long ago. He knew that the Knights were doing the same. Freddie was right. They had been too quick to rest on their laurels after their victory over St John Golden and his renegade Knights.

'It would appear that this Initiation couldn't come too soon,' Jones said. 'I think we're going to be in need of these new Knights very quickly.'

'Then let's get to St Paul's and make them welcome,' Blake's voice was strong. 'We're not in a battle yet. But if we must be' – he pulled his double-edged sword free from its gleaming scabbard at his side and held it aloft – 'then let us be ready!'

Metal sang against metal as the rest of the gathered men reached beneath their black capes and drew their own swords, holding them up, some more shakily than others, and letting the tips touch.

'Let us be ready!' All the voices, no matter how weak the arms, were strong and full of determination.

Let us be ready. Ted echoed the words in his own head as he watched the Knights around him. He hoped to God they would be.

FIVE

Standing at the bottom of the vast staircase in the atrium of the Old Bailey House of Real Truths, Finmere found that he was grinning. His nagging despondency had lifted as soon as Christopher had walked into the kitchen of Orrery House, and after the first few stilted moments, he'd seen the same thing happen with his best friend from St Martin's.

Fin was worried that Christopher had got himself in a whole heap of trouble since they'd last gone to The Nowhere, but hearing him recounting all his escapades was enough to have them both nearly crying with laughter. That was the thing about trouble, Fin was discovering: it was always much funnier *after* the event. Still, they'd been cut loose from Jarvis' supervision to visit Joe, and he was just itching to have some fun with his friends.

'Can we go, then?' Joe asked. 'I'm so over being cooped up here. Bored doesn't cover it.'

'Could've been worse,' Fin said. 'You could have been stuck at school with me.'

'Or in constant detention with me.'

'Have you two ever *tried* meditation? Trust me, both of those options are a walk in the park. At least you got to *do* something.'

'If you boys could just be quiet for one second?' Andrew Fowkes cut in. Fin looked up at the Knight's new Commander. This man was a far cry from the drunk they'd found bootless in the Crookeries, but there was still something about Fowkes that stopped Fin feeling entirely relaxed around him. Maybe it was because he felt that Fowkes was never entirely relaxed around *him*, and he didn't know why.

'It's the Initiation ceremony tonight,' Fowkes continued, 'and you two are going to have to be back on time or Ted will kill me. You've got two hours, all right? Things will be hectic enough at Orrery House without people wondering where you boys are.'

'Um ...' Christopher looked down at his watch. Like Fin's, it had frozen on Somewhere time as soon as they'd stepped over into the other London. 'With the best will in the world, how are we going to know?'

'Use this.' Fowkes fiddled with a band on his wrist and held it out. It was a thick gold bracelet with two watch faces on it: one black and plain, the other sparkling with colour. Fin stared. It was Judge Harlequin Brown's watch – it had to be. How many two-faced watches could there be?

Fowkes' hand hovered between the two boys before eventually, and almost reluctantly, handing the watch to Fin. He took it, surprised by the solid weight. It might have looked like gold, but it felt like lead.

'The black face is The Somewhere watch. As you can see, it's stopped. That awful gaudy thing is Nowhere time. Be careful with it. There's not much call for clocks and watches here – the days aren't reliable enough to stay in time with them, so watches tend to give up. This one was designed by a master craftsman, as a gift to the Order a very long time ago. Lose it,' he said as Fin strapped it tightly to his wrist, 'and I'll wring your neck.'

Fin nodded but said nothing. He had no intention of losing it, even without threats, but he didn't see why he should have to point that out to Fowkes. After everything they'd been through to rescue the Storyholder from St John Golden and his bad Knights, he'd've thought Fowkes would have trusted him a bit more.

32

'What about me?' Joe asked. 'Do I get to go to this Initiation thing?'

'Sorry, mate,' Fowkes said, 'but it's best you stay here. With Tova. No one knows what the outcome would be if the stories were separated, let alone in two worlds at the same time.'

Fowkes saw the same look of hurt and frustration in Joe's face that Fin did, because he added, 'And I *need* you here, to keep an eye on Tova. Her fever's broken, but she's got to have someone trustworthy watching over her.'

'That's funny.' Joe's eyes hardened into something Fin didn't recognise. 'And there I was thinking you'd been *guarding* us rather than looking after us.'

'It amounts to the same thing, doesn't it?' Fowkes' tone was light, but Fin didn't like the tension that was oozing from his best mate.

'If you say so,' Joe said, coldly, 'but it kinda depends what side of the door you're on.'

'*Aaaaany*way,' Christopher had moved over to the start of the narrow corridor that would lead them out, 'if we've only got a couple of hours, then let's shift it.'

'Cool,' Joe said, the anger in his eyes easing into hurt and then vanishing completely. That was the Joe Fin knew – moods that never lasted, and someone who was always quick with a smile. Maybe he hadn't changed that much after all.

'Two hours,' Fowkes growled.

'Understood.' Christopher clicked his heels together and delivered a smart military-style salute before turning and marching down the corridor towards the door. Finmere was glad to be going. He didn't like the atrium. Baxter had died there, and even if that dead Knight hadn't turned out to be his father, he'd died bravely, and in the place of a friend. Fin glanced over his shoulder at the dark-haired knight who was watching them go. No wonder Fowkes had been drunk for so long. That was some secret to keep inside.

*

33

Free from adult eyes, the boys' step became bouncier. The air was fresh and clean, but warmer than the crisp December cold they'd left behind, and as Fin took in the sights and smells of the higgledy-piggledy streets and buildings of the strange city, Christopher and Joe thumped each other on the shoulders and fired some insults backwards and forwards, laughing loudly at each inane phrase. No, Fin thought, things hadn't changed that much. He was with his friends, and life couldn't be much better.

'What time is it anyway?' Christopher asked, looking up at the blue streaks cutting through the morning grey. 'I don't need that watch to tell me it's not the same time as at home.'

'It's morning,' Joe said. 'I can't be more precise than that. When you sit around meditating all bloody day, the hours don't really count.'

'At least the mornings are back. Must be nice.'

Joe shrugged. 'Guess so.'

'According to this,' Fin stared at the elaborate hands which had been fashioned into swords with tiny jewels in their hilts, 'it's seven a.m.'

'Is it too early to go to Savjani's?' Christopher asked. 'You know, catch up with Mona ... what do you reckon?' He sounded nonchalant. Fin thought he was almost too nonchalant as he watched the slight redness creeping up his friend's neck.

'Nah,' Joe said, 'since the mornings got back, everyone's up early. They want to make the most of them, just in case they go again.' As if to prove his point, a man appeared around the corner wheeling a heavily laden barrow of loaves of bread, in all manner of shapes, sizes and colours. The delicious scent teased Fin's nostrils as the baker trudged towards them, his head down as he tried to manage the unwieldy cart on the cobbles.

'So Mona'll probably be up then?' Fin and Joe grinned at each other behind their friend's back.

34

'You *fancy* her, don't you?' Joe said. 'You think she's *well fit*!'

'It's not like that!' Christopher's indignation made both Joe and Fin laugh.

'Yeah right,' Fin said, ''course it's not.' He wasn't quite sure how he felt about Christopher so obviously having a thing for their friend from The Nowhere. He wasn't quite sure how he felt about her himself.

'Mona'll be up,' Joe said. 'She's got a job now.'

'What, for that Jack Ditch in the Crookeries?' Christopher said. 'It wouldn't surprise me. Nothing she does surprises me.'

Fin wondered just how much time Christopher had spent thinking about Mona during all his detentions at St Martin's over the past few weeks. It wasn't as if there were any other girls there to distract him. Christopher didn't just fancy Mona a bit – he had a full-on crush.

'No, she's working for the Prince Regent, kinda managing information and organising the various Borough Guards. Something like that.' He sniffed. 'I haven't seen her much, to be honest. They all reckon it's safer for me to stay in and away from anything remotely interesting, like it's going to make the stories leap out of me or something. I could tell them that's not going to happen. They've got their hooks in me. If they haven't, then why haven't they gone back to—?'

A scream cut through the air and silenced Joe. The boys stopped in their tracks, and there was a breath's worth of silence, before a second shriek filled it.

'That way,' Fin said. From behind them came a clatter of wood against cobbles and then the pounding of more feet joining theirs as the baker and the boys all ran in the direction of the sound, the cart of bread forgotten.

The screams didn't stop and the sound guided them through the narrow alleyways. 'What the hell *is* that?' Fin panted as a second sound, a high-pitched yowl almost like an animal in distress, joined the wails. They'd never heard anything like it before, and the three boys' pace instinctively slowed. Fin figured his wasn't the only blood that curdled at that dreadful sound. He shook off his fear and pushed his feet forward, the cool air burning his lungs as he tore through the narrow streets.

There was a moment's hesitation at one untidy crossroad, but by then residents were tumbling out of their houses and garrets with wide eyes, looking mildly dazed at the prospect of excitement this early in the morning. Some of them had clearly just tumbled out of bed, and their hands were clutching at hurriedly donned clothing that was threatening to expose an abundance of flesh best left covered.

Further away from the Old Bailey House of Real Truths, the buildings lining the streets became tattier and more cramped, and although Finmere wasn't entirely sure which part of history this Borough had been born from, the huge potholes, the stink of rotten cabbage and the piles of rubbish made it pretty clear that this wasn't the posh bit.

'Oh shit.' Christopher came to a sudden halt and Fin almost collided with him. Mutterings ran through the small gathering, and as the rest of the crowd backed away, Fin pushed past and slowly walked forward. Christopher and Joe came up behind him. A basket of washing lay toppled on its side, the contents now spread over the filthy street. The screaming woman stood with her back pressed against the wall, her ample body shaking.

'What happened to Millie? What's done this to her? It ain't natural,' she sobbed, the words coming out in jolts. Christopher ran over and put his arms around her, and although he was so much younger than her, she fell into them gratefully, tears flowing freely as she cried into his chest.

Finmere stared at the other woman sitting against the wall on the ground. She wasn't howling any more. Instead, her head lolled back against the rough stone and she smiled, as if laughing at a private joke. His stomach contracted into a ball of ice as he looked into her face. Her eyes were completely red – not bloodshot, there was no hint of white, or an iris or a pupil – just a ball of deep crimson in each socket. She flicked her tongue out two or three times as she giggled, and he could see the tip of it was black. She appeared to be completely unaware of the people around her, as if she were lost in her own entertainment.

'No, it ain't natural. You're right.' A man who was holding up his breeches with two thick fists, sniffed hard. It made his large belly wobble. 'And it ain't the first time this has happened.'

'How would you know?' A derisive call came from someone further back.

The fat man didn't turn round. 'I've got a brother-in-law who lives on Borough's Edge. He tells me things. He hears things.'

Fin and Joe crouched down by the afflicted woman. She was in her twenties, Fin reckoned, and maybe last night her hair and dress had been smart and tidy. Now her brown curls hung loose in a tangle around her shoulders, and even as they watched her, one hand fluttered up and yanked a few strands free. In places, her dress was high above her knees, and given how her legs were splayed, it was luck rather than judgement that kept her modesty intact. Her skin was alabaster-pale, a sharp contrast with her awful crimson eyes.

'Look at her hair,' Joe said, quietly.

Fin did. It took a moment before he realised what his friend meant.

'Bloody hell!' he whispered.

The hair that was pinned up in the original bun – or whatever it was girls called that thing perched on top of her head – was still chestnut-brown. The hair she'd pulled free and was hanging loose, however – that was turning black, first at the ends, hanging around her shoulders, but as they watched the blackness crept up to the roots.

37

'We have to get Fowkes,' Joe said. 'She saw this – the Storyholder, Tova. She scribbled something down about red eyes and black tongues. That was only a few hours ago.' He frowned. 'Why would she have seen this?'

The crowd fell silent, and it was only when Finmere looked up that he realised their focus had shifted from the strange woman on the ground to Joe. He stood up. The eyes staring at them had nothing friendly in them – suspicion, maybe, and a touch of anger – but nothing friendly.

'That's him!' The speaker was a thin man who looked as mean as his body was lean. 'He's got our stories.'

'They're ours too,' Christopher said defensively. 'The stories belong to all the worlds.'

'Don't,' Joe spoke softly, 'don't wind them up.'

'They belong here, in *our* Storyholder. Always been that way.'

'Maybe this is his fault too?' The words floated from somewhere at the back and Fin pulled in close to Joe. The woman who had been so keen for Christopher's embrace only minutes before now wriggled free and joined the throng.

'That one's got one of those swords. Look.'

'What's a kid doing with a sword like that? Can't be good.'

'Maybe he nicked it.'

'They look like trouble.'

Fin's face burned and the sword felt heavy at his side. 'We're not here for any trouble,' he said. 'We just wanted to help.'

A snort of derision came from somewhere near the front. 'Always trying to help, and always causing trouble.'

The fat man holding his trousers up nodded in agreement. 'That's your lot. We don't want you here.' He took a step forwards and those around him followed his lead. The woman on the ground giggled. It wasn't a pleasant sound, but now the gathering ignored her. She wasn't the focus of their attention any more.

Finmere's skin prickled. This situation was not good, not good at all.

'Do you think that maybe you should draw that sword of yours about now?' Christopher stood alongside Fin and Joe.

'Like that'll help this atmosphere?'

'I was thinking more about getting away than fighting.'

'If you two leave me here, I'll kill you,' Joe spoke softly. 'That's if they haven't killed me first.'

'Sod the stories,' Christopher said, 'I'd drag you through with us, don't you worry!'

The crowd took another group step forward and Fin swallowed hard. 'I'm not fancying our chances much.'

'Borough Guard!' A voice from the back cut through the increasingly unpleasant atmosphere. 'Coming this way!'

After a moment of held stares, the muttering crowd fractured, and people started slinking away down the side streets. Hooves clattered on the road and a tall, black horse appeared around the corner.

'Nobody move!' the rider barked at what was left of the gathering. 'The Guard will want statements from all of you.' Her eyes widened with surprise and then she smiled. 'Fin! Christopher!'

'Mona?' The open grin was the same, but the figure sitting high on the horse's back didn't bear much resemblance to the quirkily dressed teenage girl who had led them through the Crookeries. Her outfit was made of silver, and with the purple sash across her chest she looked like some kind of imperial army commander. Woven into her hair was a piece of silver, somewhere between a tiara and a headband, so heavily decorated with tiny gems that even in the dull morning light it twinkled like mother-of-pearl.

'You look great,' Christopher said.

'Thanks.' Mona swung one leg over the side and leapt to the ground with the grace of a gymnast. She looked down at

39

her fitted trouser suit and polished purple boots. 'I mean, it's a little dressy for me, but you know the Prince Regent.'

Fin smiled. She hadn't changed that much then – he saw the flash of pride in her face at sharing the fact that she was now so close to the Prince.

'My dad made it,' she finished.

'No, I mean *you* look great,' Christopher said with a smile.

Mona flushed ever so slightly. 'Thanks.'

Behind her, four men in black uniforms pushed what was left of the grumbling crowd backwards, but Mona ignored them and looked down at the red-eyed woman. She grimaced. 'Sylvester. Organise a cart and orderlies. Send a message down the line; we need one fast.'

'Yes, ma'am,' a gruff voice answered and its owner swiftly disappeared.

Fin was impressed with the command Mona had over these grown men, but it made him feel decidedly awkward and childish. How did girls get that grown-up thing so fast?

'Christopher's right,' Fin said, 'you do look great. But I have to say – you don't look surprised.'

'That's because I'm not.' Mona crouched beside the woman and carefully touched her bare forearm. There was no reaction. 'She's really cold. She must have been here a while – attacked in the night at some time, I'd think, just like the others.'

'"The others"?' Joe asked.

The original crowd had mostly disappeared, but more people were filling the gaps, drawn by the presence of the Guard. Finmere spotted a couple glancing at his sword and then over at Joe, then muttering to their neighbours behind cupped hands. They might not have been as openly aggressive as their predecessors, but obviously they weren't exactly friendly either.

'Tova said something about this,' Joe said again. 'Fowkes needs to know.'

Mona looked back at the Guard. 'Where's that cart?' she muttered.

'Is there anything we can do to help?' Christopher asked. 'You know, help take her somewhere, away from all these people?'

Up on her feet and with her hands planted firmly on her hips, Mona was back to being the girl they knew again: all defiant and stubborn, and full of brave, big ideas. It was all there in the way she stood, the slight arch of her spine, the crook of her head. She looked back at the growing crowd and her overworked colleagues.

'I think the best thing you can do for me right now is actually to just leave.' She looked down at the woman. 'This is bad enough, but you lot being here just draws more attention. This might not be the Crookeries, but it's not exactly the most peaceful Borough in London. Joe, I'll send someone back with you to tell Fowkes and the Storyholder.' She looked at Fin. 'You and Christopher had better go back to The Somewhere for now.'

Fin could see what she said made sense, but it didn't stop him feeling disappointed.

'Just when it's all getting exciting.' Christopher's words echoed Fin's thoughts.

'Don't worry, boys.' Mona grinned. 'This excitement will still be here when you get back. Now go and find a quiet corner and do that sword thing you do and I'll see you later.'

Fin and Christopher waved their goodbyes and crept away. It wasn't only Christopher who glanced back to get one last look at the petite silver figure.

SIX

It was 11.45 p.m. when the procession of black cabs – all displaying the tiny stickers in their windows, Finmere noticed, now he knew what to look for – wove their way through the various Road Closed and Danger – Gas Mains Leak signs to deliver their cargo to the steps of St Paul's Cathedral. Fin didn't believe for one moment that any pipes had burst; he wondered who had been in charge of that ruse to make the area so quietly private for them. How many people worked for the Order every day without realising it? Did they know something, or would they have really thought they were simply putting the signs up in the public interest? Either way, they were doing a civic duty. The Knights had the best interests of all the worlds at heart.

Finmere and Christopher's cab had been one of the last to leave, and as the boys stepped out into the freezing night air, Freddie Wise was waiting for them on the steps, his face hidden behind the pale mist of his breath.

'It never looks quite this big from a distance.' Christopher was peering upwards at the white pillars and vast arches that preceded the famous dome. Fin knew what he meant. Bathed in moonlight, the church almost glowed – a solid representation of all that was good and worthy, of what could be achieved if men worked together hard enough. It made Fin feel strange inside, emotional and overawed.

'Come along.' Freddie tapped his walking stick against the flagstone beneath his feet. 'They'll be starting soon, and we can't be just hanging around out here all night.' Despite the man's age and physical infirmity, Freddie Wise looked austere and impressive in his white shirt and black trousers underneath a thick red cape done up with a gold clasp. A sword glinted by his side.

Just looking at it, Fin felt his own blade grow warmer against the side of his leg.

'Maybe we should have dressed up more.' He was acutely aware of his jeans and trainers, and he was sure Christopher felt the same slight embarrassment.

'What would be the point?' Freddie said, bemused. 'Only active Knights wear the black cloaks, and retired Knights, the red. Anything else you choose to wear is incidental.' He peered at Fin as the boys climbed the stairs. 'And you might have Baxter's ring, young man, but you're not quite ready for a cloak yet.'

He pushed the doors open and they followed him in.

Justin Arnold-Mather listened to the old grandfather clock, standing like a sentry beside the door of the quiet reading room, as it ticked steadily round towards midnight. The sound was soft, though it came from such a sturdy piece of workmanship. Like all things at Grey's, the clock was clearly designed not to be too intrusive. Grey's was the finest gentlemen's club in London – which of course made it the finest such club in the world – and everything about it served to give a man some freedom from the stresses of the outside world.

Although friendships were made, and business done, the members of Grey's respected each other's space and privacy, and while within these walls at least, they behaved like gentlemen of old. It was all far better than the behaviour on display in the House of Commons, Arnold-Mather had often found himself noting with a small sense of despair during Prime Minister's Question Time. But then, most of those sitting in the House of Commons didn't even know Grey's existed, let alone had any chance of becoming a member. Grey's was an *honourable* club. That was the feature that had always appealed most to Harlequin Brown – the club's tradition of great honour. For his own part, Arnold-Mather thought honour was somewhat overrated in the modern age. Power, that was what counted.

The leather armchair creaked slightly as he stood up and walked over to the window. Outside, the London street was quiet. The peace suited his mood. It had been a quiet evening all round. The club had been emptier than normal – the members perhaps torn away by unavoidable familial festive events – and he'd eaten a solitary dinner of steak Diane with potatoes Dauphinoise, and then retired here to one of the reading rooms. He wasn't in the mood for company, other than that which he was expecting. He swilled the expensive golden liquid in the crystal glass for a moment before sipping it. Of all places here, he'd miss Grey's the most. He was sure of it.

'Would you care for a coffee, sir?'

Mr Arnold-Mather hadn't even heard the door open behind him.

'No, thank you, Carter.' He smiled at the elderly gentleman who hadn't quite stepped in. 'I'm waiting for a colleague.'

'Not going home tonight, sir?'

'Sadly not. My wife is rather unhappy that I've let our son stay away for the holidays. The temperature at home is somewhat chilly.'

'Sorry to hear that, sir. Women, eh?'

'Precisely.'

'Press the bell if you need anything. I'll leave you to it.'

Arnold-Mather nodded and the door closed as silently as it had opened. He wondered if he should perhaps call home, make a pretence of caring – but no, there was really no point. He'd married to aid his political career, but it was becoming clear that he was never going to achieve any higher office in the government than he'd already reached. In fact, if the rumours he'd heard in the tea rooms of Westminster were accurate, he was unlikely to stay in his current post for much longer. He had become *too distracted*, they said, and that was probably true. It would be quite fair to say that he had his eye on something rather grander for his future.

He didn't have St John Golden's fear of Travelling, and that had been his lost partner's downfall. How on earth had Golden ever thought he could keep his eyes on all the pieces of the game if he refused to move from one world to the next? Arnold-Mather's role might have been one of silent partner, but he'd been less silent than he'd let Golden know. He'd done his research, and – wisely, as it had turned out – kept a few cards close to his chest. In the fall-out after Golden's capture, the Knights hadn't found all the traitors; in fact, they'd missed one right in their midst.

He felt his heart race slightly with excitement beneath his ever-cool exterior. Things were nearly in position. He knew as much as he could possibly know about The Nowhere without yet having visited that world himself – and as soon as he was in power, Christopher would come round, he was certain of it. His son might have his moments of foolishness, but in the end he'd stand by his father's side. Or be damned.

He'd never been keen on having children, but Christopher had, all unwittingly, done his father a major service, by becoming Finmere Tingewick Smith's best friend after Harlequin Brown had been persuaded to send the boy to St Martin's. The boys' closeness had made the old man far more willing to share information – he'd *trusted* Justin Arnold-Mather, and it was that that had caused his own death. It was just a shame he'd never known it. And now Christopher had discovered a way that the Ageing could be reversed – a secret he was apparently keeping to himself. Well, Arnold-Mather thought, looking back at the clock hands that were nearly meeting at midnight, secrets could always be dragged out from people, one way or another, and that was one that would definitely be worth having. Perhaps his recalcitrant son would prove to be a valuable heir after all.

A heavy hand knocked on the door before it opened.

Justin Arnold-Mather smiled.

'Exactly on time, Mr Dodge. I like that in a man.'

Levi Dodge didn't smile but tilted his head forward slightly above his thickset besuited torso. His Bowler hat stayed on. He should, of course, have removed it on entry to Grey's, but Dodge wasn't the kind of man who truly understood about hats, despite his partiality to a Bowler. Justin Arnold-Mather had never seen fit to correct him, and neither had the staff at Grey's – with a man like Levi Dodge, the etiquette of one's dress was really of little importance.

'Wouldn't want to be late,' Levi Dodge said. 'They'll be waiting.' As soon as the words were out his thin lips pressed themselves back together. Dodge never smiled, and he rarely spoke purely for the sake of it.

'True.' Arnold-Mather looked down thoughtfully into his glass. 'They will. When they've completed this job of work, I feel it might not be in our best interests for them to be able to talk about it, as it were.' He looked over into Levi Dodge's impassive eyes. 'Do you think that will be a problem?'

'I chose these three with precisely that outcome in mind. Any accidental demise that might befall them will barely go noticed, and if it is, then the method will be in keeping with—'

Arnold-Mather raised his hand. 'I don't need the details of any necessary unpleasantness, Mr Dodge.' He sighed. 'If only the Cabinet were so efficient – this government might actually get things done.' He pulled out a set of keys from his pocket. Given the shake-ups in Westminster and the rumours about his own position, he'd taken the precaution of having his own set made – not that the old House of Detention was exactly high on anyone's list of priorities right now, but it was always better to be safe than sorry.

He gestured towards the door. 'After you, Mr Dodge. I take it our car is waiting?'

'It is.' The Bowler hat tilted once more and the two men headed out into the night.

The huge floor space of St Paul's was lit by hundreds of candles. Finmere looked around him for any kind of electric lights, but couldn't see any; the golden glow surrounding them was created entirely by the wax that burned in the heavy chandeliers overhead and in the various tall metal candlesticks that lined the walls and surrounded the arches. The sheer grandeur of the church, with its high ceilings and ornate decorations both painted on and carved into the stone, took Fin's breath away.

The old men – the Aged men, Fin corrected himself – were all shaved and dressed, and those who could still function had taken their places in the pews. Those who were lost somewhere between this world and the next sat comatose in their wheelchairs on the vast chequered floor behind the seats.

Christopher stopped beside him. 'I wonder if West Minster was this impressive before they wrecked it?' His soft voice was sad.

Fin knew his friend didn't mean the Westminster Abbey of their London, but the wrecked home of the Magi in The Nowhere, now merely a ghost of a past race left to haunt the riverbank. Christopher had told him about it. How much hate did there have to be to do so much damage to something so beautiful? He couldn't understand it.

'Chop, chop.' A sharp poke in his back from Freddie Wise's walking stick broke the moment, and the old man ushered the two boys into a pew near the back. Both Fin and Christopher sat with their backs straight, craning to see what was happening at the front. Over to their right somewhere an old man starting snoring and was nudged quickly awake, which resulted in a snort and a small exclamation breaking the silence.

Even with the entire Order present, the church felt empty, and Fin couldn't decide whether that was because their numbers were so few, or that the building was so large, but it made him feel small and humble, as did the presence of the comatose men behind him. He'd shaved most of them at some point, he was sure of it, back in the days when he'd taken them for exactly what they looked like: old men full of years, who'd lived out their days. He wondered for a second how old they really were, and then decided that there were some things that you really didn't need to know.

At the front he could see the three new Knights he'd met that morning, as well as three more faces he didn't know. The twins, Henry and Benjamin, stood tall and proud – although Fin noticed that Henry's white shirt wasn't tucked into his black trousers with quite the same military precision that Benjamin's was – but beside them Alex Currie-Clark shuffled nervously from boot to boot and as one hand came up to adjust his glasses for the fourth time, Finmere started to wonder if maybe the red-headed man wasn't quite cut out for the Order. Or maybe he'd just forgotten to go to the loo. Fin liked him, though. There was something normal about him, and there wasn't a lot of normal about at Orrery House.

Freddie Wise joined the boys in their pew and what little chatter there was fell to a hush. A door creaked as it opened and booted footsteps echoed as Andrew Fowkes, Simeon Soames and Lucas Blake made their way forward and turned to face the congregation. They looked serious, and very impressive dressed in full uniform, with their swords shining at their sides. Fowkes held a small box and the other two carried between them a larger, silver-coloured chest with swords etched into the side. Ted came last, his arms full of black cloaks. He stood a little way behind the Knights, slightly in the shadows.

'Benjamin Wakley,' Fowkes said. 'Stand before us.'

Simeon Soames took a cloak from Ted's pile and clasped it round Benjamin's shoulders. From within the box came the singing of metal against metal as Lucas Blake pulled out a double-edged sword. The golden blade shone brightly in the candlelight. Even from as far away as Fin was sitting, he could clearly see the stone in its hilt; it was an amber colour.

Fowkes held the sword high, and for a moment Finmere thought he might be about to tap it on each of Benjamin's shoulders, like he'd seen the Queen do on some telly programme somewhere, but then Fowkes brought it down suddenly and the blade sliced not only through the air, but through the very fabric of existence. A window opened up beside the Commander of the Knights of Nowhere, and through it, in grainy black and white, Finmere could see the Storyholder seated on the other side, looking elegant and cool. Fin felt Christopher's arm jolt slightly, matching his own fizz of excitement. He didn't think he'd ever tire of seeing The Nowhere open up in front of him, and the Storyholder fascinated him. Aside from her beauty and grace, and the bravery she'd shown when held captive by St John Golden, she was the only person who knew anything about his own origins. He only wished she'd tell him who he was.

Benjamin Wakley acknowledged the serene figure, then he started to speak. 'To defend the worlds, I freely commit my life to secrecy. I will place the Order above all others. I will protect all life, whether Somewhere- or Nowhere-born. I vow to protect the Five Eternal Stories, which hold the universe. And should the Prophecy come to pass, I will stand with my brothers and fight against the darkness. I shall be honourable and just. I will never wield my sword for my own gain. I shall never bring disrepute upon the Order. I will Travel with respect, and face the Ageing in peace, should it come to pass. All these things I vow in the name of the Order of the Knights of Nowhere.'

There was no hesitation, nor any sign of nerves in his delivery, and Finmere felt slightly awed. He might kid himself that he was nearly grown-up, but watching Fowkes and Ben Wakley going through the ancient service, he didn't feel anywhere near it.

'Are you ready to Travel?' Fowkes asked.

'I am ready.'

Fowkes opened the small box and from it handed Benjamin a ring. Fin didn't have to see it to know that it would be amber, just like the stone in the sword. He was the only one who had a ring and sword that were different – but then, he had Baxter's ring and Judge Brown's sword, and both were gifts from dead men. It was a weird thought, and one he tried not to think about too much.

'Are you ready to take up your sword?'

'I am ready.'

Benjamin Wakley took the handle of the sword from Fowkes and the window into The Nowhere didn't blink out, even for a second. The young man stepped through, the colour draining from him as he did. On the other side he kneeled and Tova smiled at him before touching him gently on the shoulder. If she could speak, Fin was sure she'd be thanking him for his sacrifice – because that was one thing Fin *had* learned over the past couple of months: there were a lot of sacrifices made by those who shared in the magical secret knowledge of other worlds.

A moment later, the young man reappeared and stood to one side. His face was impassive. Fin didn't think he could ever be that cool.

Alex Currie-Clark was next up, and he delivered his lines with only one stumble. He made it through the doorway and back, the edges shrinking only slightly when he took his sword from Fowkes. He might not have had the natural grace of the Wakley twins, and Fin was pretty sure the hilt of the sword would be sweaty, but he did fine, and Fin thought it was probably sensible to be just a little bit nervous.

As the other four new Knights went through their Initiations Fin's mind drifted. The Order was full of secrets and surprises, and Fin couldn't help mulling over questions which would probably never get answered. Where had they found these six men, and how had they picked them? How would you even go about advertising for a job like this? And how would you know they wouldn't run around telling everyone about the Order, saying that it was all crazy? And who'd been training them – they obviously knew about the swords and The Nowhere and stuff – so where had all that been going on? He missed Harlequin Brown with a sudden pang. Not that he'd have got much in the way of answers other than in the form of riddles from the old man, but at least he could have asked him the questions, talked to him about this stuff ...

By the time the sixth Knight was finished, Fowkes was looking tired. He'd been holding a gateway open mainly by himself for the best part of half an hour. Finally, with all the new Knights fully robed, and with Soames and Blake standing in line behind him, Fowkes pulled his own sword free and held it aloft.

'Let us be ready!' he called out.

Swords rose aloft all around the church, and those who could pulled themselves to their feet. Metal clinked against metal as the tips touched.

'Let us be ready!'

All the Knights, young and old, had answered his cry, and pride surged in Fin's heart to be part of it all. One day he'd stand at the front and take his vows, with Christopher and Joe alongside him – and they'd be the best Knights the Order had ever had.

A small crackle of light sparked from the tops of the swords and danced in the air for a moment before fading and as one, all the men in the pews turned to look at those in the wheel-chairs at the back, and then the elderly who had managed to stand looked down at themselves and each other.

'What's going on?' Christopher whispered.

'Sometimes,' Wise whispered, without stopping looking at the men around him, 'when we are all gathered for an Initiation or a meeting of great importance, the mixture of emotion and the sheer number of swords in one place can cause a reversal of the Ageing – well, we presume that's what does it, anyway. One can never really tell, can one? It's a very rare occurrence, but we always hope.'

Mutterings echoed around the vast hall: 'My hip still hurts to buggery.' 'My cataracts aren't going away.' 'Well, it's always a nice thought, isn't it?' 'Like the bloody lottery.'

'Tonight, it appears,' Wise stood tall, and if he felt any personal disappointment, he wasn't showing it, 'isn't our lucky night. Still, we have six strong new Knights, and that's not to be sniffed at.'

Fowkes had still been talking and when Finmere looked back at him, all the young Knights were filing out.

'Where are they going? Is it all done?'

'No, just our bit,' Wise said. 'The Initiates have to go up to the Whispering Gallery and say their vows again, but this time it's more personally, to each other – well, one of each other, really. A special bond forms between Knights who hear each other's vows in the Whispering Gallery.'

'Why is it called the Whispering Gallery?' Fin asked.

'Well, because ...' He paused and frowned. 'Actually, I don't see why it would hurt for you to see. Follow them up. If you're fast you'll catch up behind Lucas Blake. Then you'll see – but *behave* up there. The Whispering Gallery is one of our most revered places.'

Fin's eyes shone and Christopher was doing his best to suppress a grin – at least until they were out of the old man's sight. Interesting though the Initiation had been, all that

52

sitting and listening could never match up to actually *doing*, and aside from that, his arse was going slightly numb.

The two boys moved as quickly as they could in the direction the men had gone and then took the stairs two at a time until they caught sight of Lucas Blake's cloak turning into the gallery. Over the wrought-iron railings Fin could see the old men below; looking up, he gazed in awe at the majestic decorated ceiling. Finally, he looked at the young men, who had spread themselves round the circle, leaving huge gaps between each of them. At Fowkes' signal they turned and faced the benches and walls, three on one side of the circle and three on the other, with Fowkes between them.

'And now you will repeat your vows privately, to one another,' he said. 'Whisper the words, and listen to those of another of your number, and then hold them in your heart for ever.'

Fin grinned at Christopher, who smiled in understanding before walking in the other direction. When they stood opposite each other, separated by round empty space, they did as the Knights had done and turned away. He glanced sideways. Several feet away, Alex Currie-Clark was whispering silently, and Fin saw a moment of surprise on his face. He stared back at the wall. They might not be Knights yet, but they could make their own pact to defend all the worlds. He didn't remember all the words from the Initiation ceremony, but as a whisper by his ear almost made him jump, neither did Christopher. It didn't matter though, he thought as he whispered his own words to the wall, they meant it from the heart.

The quieter ritual completed, both boys ducked under the benches until Fowkes had left, and then, with the gallery to themselves, they peered over the edge.

'Does it ever occur to you just how weird all this stuff is?' Christopher said.

53

'Every day,' Fin answered, 'no, scratch that: every *minute* of every day. But it's *good* weird, isn't it?'

'I guess. In the main.'

Below, the oldest residents of Orrery House were being wheeled out, ready for the return journey. Each was being pushed by one of the newly initiated Knights. Fin figured that must be part of the ceremony too.

'Looks like this could take a while,' said Christopher, watching as Benjamin Wakley, who wasn't looking too handy with a wheelchair, ran over somebody's foot. 'Let's take a look around,' he suggested as a mild exclamation carried up to them.

They meandered downstairs and peered into various alcoves and side rooms, whispering between each other, even though they were the only people around. It was that kind of place – the kind where even if you didn't believe in God, you felt like someone far more powerful was watching.

It was Fin who found the floating staircase, and he went first, following the spiral up and round, pausing from time to time to look down at the star embedded in the floor below. Did that have some mystical meaning for the Knights? Or was it just decoration, or maybe something religious? Fin was no longer sure of anything having a place in his real world.

They came out on a landing, and Fin was about to speak when voices drifted towards them. He raised one finger to his lips and then followed the sound, Christopher a step behind him. Light peered out from under an almost closed door, and the two boys crept forward until they could see through the gap.

The room, high up in the church, was an old-fashioned library. Rows and rows of books filled the dark wooden shelves that in turn lined the walls even beyond the small balcony level. In the gaps, portraits of men probably long dead stared down sombrely from within their gilt frames. Old books, some so big it would take two people to get them down from the shelf, were lying open on the wooden desks, and table lamps added to the soft light thrown out by the crackling fire in the hearth.

Fowkes stood staring into the fire, his tired and thoughtful face half-visible to the boys. Lucas Blake sat on one of the desks, and Ted appeared from somewhere out of view and handed each of them a glass of red wine.

'It must mean something for Tova to have written about it,' Fowkes said. 'She doesn't get involved with ordinary crimes – and whatever happened to that woman, it wasn't normal.'

'There's more.' Ted reappeared in view with a glass for himself.

'What do you mean?' Fowkes turned.

'There's a crack in the table. It's tiny – you wouldn't notice it unless you were really looking for it – but it's definitely there. Goes right through to the map.'

'Even when the black storm was coming it didn't affect the table, just the map,' Blake said.

Fin was finding it hard enough to hear over the thumping of his heart and Christopher's breathing, and for a moment, as Fowkes turned his back to the doorway, the quiet conversation was lost to the boys and all they could make out was the up-and-down murmur of muttered words, but not their meaning.

Then Ted started pacing up and down a little, which made Fowkes turn.

'—but Golden is gone,' Fowkes was saying, 'so this can't be him.'

'What about the Knights who didn't hang?'

'Still locked up,' Ted said, 'in the secure unit at Broadmoor. All present and accounted for.'

'So let me get this straight.' Blake stood up from his perch on the desk. 'You think whatever happened to this poor woman in The Nowhere is linked to the crack in the table?'

'I don't know.' Fowkes took a swig of his wine. 'But the crack might be because of someone else.'

'Who?'

'The boy. Joe Manning.'

Fin felt his blood rise, and then Christopher squeezed his arm and frowned. He was right, of course; there was no point in rushing in – they wouldn't learn any more that way – but he hated hearing Fowkes speaking his suspicions of Joe out loud. He didn't even *know* him, not like Fin did.

As it was, within the room Ted was declaring his own indignation at the suggestion and Fin felt a surge of warmth for the old nightwatchman.

Fowkes raised a hand in the face of the outcry. 'I like the kid,' he said, 'I really do. But there's no denying he's changed.'

'It's the stories,' Ted said. 'But once they're gone—'

'That's the problem. I don't think he wants to let them go.'

There was a moment's hush.

'That's a terrible thing to say,' Ted said quietly. 'Truly terrible.'

'But I think it's true.' Fowkes was grim. 'I don't trust him any more.'

'He's a good lad,' Lucas Blake said. 'They all are. If something's going wrong with him, then it's our fault.'

'It's a rum business for kids, this.' Ted shook his head.

'But they won't be children much longer,' Fowkes said, 'and right now I don't know what to do for the best with them. Send the other two away? Keep them here? And every time I think I've made a decision, something comes along to change it. And until Tova tells us where the hell Finmere came from, we're playing all this blind.'

Fin's face flushed at the mention of his name. Sometimes he didn't even care where he came from any more – he was tired of everyone thinking he was something special when he clearly wasn't. And what if his *special* was *bad* special? What if Fowkes started to look sideways at him in the way he was with Joe?

'You've got to trust 'em, Andrew Fowkes,' Ted said. 'It's what we're all about, trust. Them kids have all done good – they've done the Order proud. Without them … Well, it don't bear thinking about.'

'I know.' Fowkes' broad shoulders sagged slightly. 'I just wish I understood their part in all this.'

'Just got to roll with it, brother,' Blake smiled. 'That's half the fun.'

Their voices dropped, and though Fin made out Christopher's name, and then mention of the Regent before the men turned and moved beyond his view, their words were mostly lost.

'Come on,' Christopher whispered and pulled him away. Both boys were silent as they crept down the stairs and out into the inky darkness to one of the last waiting cabs. Finmere's blood was still boiling. How *could* Fowkes say that about Joe? *How could he?*

'It doesn't take much to lose his trust, does it?' Christopher said quietly, halfway back to the house. He was looking out of the window, his face set in a frown.

'I suppose we only heard half the conversation.' Fin felt his loyalties conflicting. Part of him agreed with Christopher, and he *was* angry at what Fowkes had said – but things were different for him. The Order had looked after him forever, and he couldn't bring himself to slag any of them off out loud. Not even Fowkes. 'They were only talking.'

Christopher shrugged, unconvinced. 'Let's see what tomorrow brings. Maybe they'll send us packing.'

Somehow, Fin didn't think so.

SEVEN

He didn't like the days. They were long and hot and loud, and he had to find places to cower and hide. People looked at him funny when he passed them. Perhaps it was the way the sunlight made him squint. Or maybe it was his filthy, often wet, appearance that caused them to shy away. In his saner moments he knew it was neither of these. He knew it was because on some level those strangers who happened to pass his way sensed that there was something very wrong about him – something other – and they had been lucky not to have come across him when it was darker and the streets were friendless.

His days were empty. He didn't need to eat, not in any normal way. Instead, he stayed close to the walls and found places where people were too busy minding their own business to pay attention to a tramp curled up in an empty doorway, as he was now.

The day was fading to dusk and he felt his mind beginning to fade. He tried to cling on to some sense of himself, but it was hard. It had been so long, and even though sometimes his name would come back to him, he heard it as if it was a dream, just sounds – not him at all. He fought the urge to sleep, even though he was exhausted. Sleep just brought back the nightmares of that place, the deathly cold of it, the things he'd had to eat … the things that lived there. He didn't want to remember … He didn't …

He pushed his hand deep into his pocket and clasped the small item there. It touched his skin with comforting warmth and made him smile. He remembered finding it – the only brightness in that other place. He thought – he couldn't be sure – but he thought it had helped him leave, and had led him back. His palm itched with the increasing heat, and it spread out through his fist and through the fabric of his trousers until his thin thigh burned. It grew hotter every day, and even in the vagueness that filled his existence, he knew that to be true. It was pushing him somewhere. He wasn't sure where, not yet, but something was calling it. And slowly, as it his strength returned, he would find his way there.

He watched the sun fade. Soon it would be time to get wet. And feed.

EIGHT

Christopher woke Fin at five o'clock the next morning and dragged him blearily out of bed. 'I've been thinking,' he said.

'Always a first time,' Fin yawned.

'Ha bloody ha. We need to go and see Joe. Just in case Fowkes really is thinking of sending us away.'

'Why would he?' Fin squinted against the sudden light and raised one arm against the barrage of clothes Christopher was throwing at him from where he'd abandoned them on the floor the night before. 'We only just got here.'

'Yeah, but they didn't know about this crack in the map business then. I figure if we go now, we can be back before anyone else is up.'

'You don't know how this house works. Someone's always awake.' Fin sat on the side of the bed and tugged a T-shirt over his head. Sleep was clearly over for the night whatever they decided to do.

'Not today. They must all be knackered after last night.'

'They're not the only ones.'

When Fin was dressed, they snuck downstairs into the kitchen and grabbed some *pains au chocolat* and croissants from the large pantry. Fin stuffed a couple of each into a bag for Joe. However much Fowkes might think Joe had changed, Fin doubted his friend's appetite had shrunk.

'A little late for a midnight feast, isn't it?'

Both boys jumped at Jarvis' disapproving words.

'Told you,' Fin muttered. Jarvis was dressed as always in his spotless butler's uniform. Did the man ever sleep?

'Something like that,' Christopher said.

Jarvis didn't look impressed. Fin could have told Christopher that his upper class over-confidence wouldn't work here. Jarvis might look like a servant, but Fin got the distinct impression that he was a part of the fabric of Orrery House, rather than merely supporting it.

'Don't wake anyone.' Jarvis stepped aside to let the boys pass. 'And don't make a mess.'

Fin gave him an apologetic smile that wasn't returned and then slunk back upstairs as if he could make himself invisible. Christopher might have lost all sense of the rules since their last adventure, but try as he might, Fin couldn't shake his respect for his elders. Especially those in this particular house.

An hour and a half later and they were sitting on the steps of the Old Bailey House of Real Truths and the pastries were gone. Joe had managed all four of them. As he'd eaten, they'd told him all about the Initiation ceremony and the strange Whispering Gallery – leaving out the conversation they'd heard in the library – and when Fowkes appeared, Joe was in the process of telling them about how Mona might have changed a bit, but not that much. She still disappeared into the Crookeries when she was off-duty, and came back with tall tales of Traders and villains, though how much of it was true, Joe wasn't sure. Still, the stories were always worth a listen, especially the ones about the Traders, the only people in The Nowhere's London who could cross the River Times safely.

'I've been looking for you two,' Fowkes growled. 'You might think you're all grown-up, but you're not, and that means you still have to play by the rules. You must let people know where you're going. There's a pile of washing-up back at the house with your names on it for this little stunt. I don't know why Jarvis let you leave without telling anyone.'

'We were up early and came to see our friend. What's the big deal? It's the holidays, after all.' Christopher's animosity was barely hidden, but Fowkes didn't seem to notice.

'From now on, you *tell* someone before you disappear. You shouldn't need reminding that Travelling isn't as straight-forward as jumping on a bus.'

Somewhere under the rough tone, Fin was sure he heard the slightest hint of relief. Fowkes was glad to have found them. What the hell did he think had happened – something to do with that crack in the table? He wondered how funny it would be if that turned out to have been caused by Jarvis dropping something heavy on it ... but the light-hearted thought didn't ring true. The dark, unsettled feeling that had been haunting him for weeks said otherwise. And anyway, there was never a dull, *ordinary* explanation for anything to do with the Order. He didn't want to think about that crack. If there was something wrong with the Prophecy table, then it meant trouble was coming – perhaps even more than they'd faced with St John Golden.

Tova came out through the heavy wooden doors of the main entrance and stood a couple of paces behind Fowkes. Fin saw his back straighten slightly, even though he didn't turn, or acknowledge that she was there. Finmere didn't understand the tension between them – whenever they were together they moved carefully around each other as if they were scared they might touch. What was it – hate, or love? Why did it look like those two emotions were always so close together? *Why couldn't anything just be simple?*

'I need you to come with me,' Fowkes said, keeping his eyes firmly on the boys.

'Where? Back already?'

'No, not yet, to see the Prince Regent, to talk about that woman you found yesterday.'

'And you want us to come?' Fin was surprised. That didn't tie in with what they'd heard the previous night.

'It wasn't my idea,' he growled. 'The Regent insisted. He likes you kids – probably Mona's influence.'

'All right!' Joe grinned. 'Let's go.'

'Not you.' Fowkes' eyes darkened. 'He didn't say *you*.'

Joe recoiled as if he'd been slapped in the face, and after flashing Fowkes' back an angry glare the Storyholder went inside the building, closing the door hard behind her.

'Why?' Joe was on his feet, hurt and indignant, 'what's wrong with me? I've done *nothing wrong*!'

Fin's face burned seeing his friend so upset. Joe was right. He *hadn't* done anything wrong.

'It's not you, Joe.' Fowkes' tone was softer. 'It's the stories—'

'The stories, the stories, the bloody stories!' Joe shouted the words into the growing dusk. 'That's *all* anyone cares about! What about *me*, though? Who cares about *me*? Not you lot, that's for damn sure!'

He spat the last sentence out, and in the stunned silence that followed, angrily shook off Fin's hand, turned away and ran down the steps, shouting, 'Leave me alone! All of you!'

'We need to get him back.' Fowkes moved to start after the disappearing boy, but Finmere grabbed his arm and this time he didn't let himself be shaken free.

'Just let him go! He didn't ask for any of this – it's *not* his fault and you can't blame him for it. Those two stories chose between us, and they chose *him*. He didn't choose *them*. So just bloody trust him, all right?'

The words came out in a thoughtless rant, but Fin meant every one of them. They needed to trust each other – if they didn't, then what was the point of it all? Why didn't adults always see that?

'He's a footballer.' The anger had gone out of his words. 'I don't care how much you might think he's changed, but Joe's a team player. He doesn't understand any different. So just let him breathe a bit.'

Fowkes stared down at Fin's hand on his arm, his eyes

lingering on the ring and the deep jade stone at the centre of its black and gold base.

When he eventually looked up, he held Fin's gaze for several long seconds before speaking. 'Then I'll trust *you* on this one.' His voice was cool. 'But I still don't think he should be wandering the streets alone.' He raised one finger and held it close to Fin's face. 'And you note that: if anything happens, then you're grown-up enough to know you'll have had a part in it. You understand?'

Fin swallowed. Face-to-face with Fowkes he didn't feel very grown-up at all.

'Then let's go. The Prince Regent is waiting.'

'Where are we going?' Christopher asked. 'The palace?'

'No.' Fowkes was already striding ahead and the boys had to jog to catch up. 'The White Tower – the home of the mad.'

The White Tower stood where the Tower of London was in his own London, Fin realised as he looked up at the Keep. Unlike the one in his own world, this central Keep didn't have any secondary buildings surrounding it, other than some dingy hovels. It was surrounded by small, unkempt fields with plants of some sort growing in raggedy patches. They could make out figures, dressed in dirty woollen clothes, working with oxen, or digging the land itself.

Rather than coming at the White Tower along the river's bank, Fowkes had led the boys through the city, and looking up from where they now stood, Finmere could see where the borders grew into Whitechapel. The smog that hovered above that borough owed more to Dickens' nineteenth century than the almost medieval feudal lands spread out in front of them.

'Why don't they try moving away?' he asked as one of the field-workers straightened up and gripped their back for a second. 'I know most people stay in their own Boroughs in The Nowhere, but a bit of exhaustion from Travelling has got to be better than living like this.'

64

'They *want* to be here,' Fowkes answered. 'They belong to the White Tower.'

Fin thought the name itself was something of a misnomer. The building was entirely black, another difference from its counterpart back in his London. Even the cement, or whatever held the vast stones together, was black, and if it weren't for the lights burning in the small windows, Fin was sure it would be completely invisible by midnight. The figures of the waiting Prince Regent and his small entourage – one slight and purple-haired – stood out bright against the surface as the boys approached with Fowkes. The air stank, filled with the foul sweetness of the river's mist, and they were now so close that in the lull in conversation he could hear the lapping of that hidden water.

'What do you mean, they *belong* to the White Tower?' Christopher asked.

'They're the mad – or at least the semi-mad, or the recovering mad … the *safe* mad, at any rate. They like to keep near the Tower in case of relapse, but working the land keeps their bodies tired while allowing them time to think, and maybe lay their demons to rest. Everything grown here is used to feed the Tower. Every little helps.'

Fin looked at the coating of mist, which was receding slightly. The tide must be going out; that at least was a small mercy. Beside him, Christopher was staring at the water too, and Fin didn't like either the desolate look on his friend's face, or the way the dark locked-up place inside Fin himself threatened to open up whenever he glanced at the Times. The river was a bad thing, he knew that for sure.

'Don't know how they can live this close to the river,' Christopher muttered. 'That stench would drive me mad.'

'Strangely, the mad are calmer here. They find it soothing.'

'They *must* be mad then,' Fin said.

'Exactly.' The Prince Regent stepped forward. He looked hot under his heavy wig and a slight sheen of sweat glistened on his painted white face, despite the relative coolness of the day – looked like the river took its toll on royalty too.

'It's a pleasure to see you again, Finmere Tingewick Smith. You recovered our Storyholder, and for this I will always be grateful to you.'

'It wasn't just me,' Fin mumbled. 'I had help.'

'Indeed you did.' The tall wig nodded slightly in Christopher's direction, and Christopher gave the tiny dandy a quick hand-to-head salute.

'Commander Fowkes.'

'Your Majesty.'

As the two men made their formal greetings, Fin grinned at Mona, who winked back, before smiling at Christopher. Somehow, as they climbed the stairs up the external side of the midnight building, she fell behind, and Fin found himself beside the Prince.

'If you don't mind me asking,' he said, 'why is it called the White Tower when it clearly isn't … um … white?'

'It *was* white.' The Regent took two tiny, delicate steps to each one of Fin's own. 'A long time ago.'

The vast door that might have been made of wood or iron, for all Fin could tell, was pulled open from the other side and the small group stepped in. The Prince made no further comment, as if he'd given a full and comprehensive answer. On reflection, perhaps he had. The darkness of the external building was echoed inside. Although there were candles and lit lamps all along the walls, their light faded after a few feet, leaving the large atrium in a creepy gloom. Doorways and corridors branched off and were swallowed up within a few feet. It wasn't particularly chilly, but Finmere shivered anyway.

'Not very cheerful, is it?'

'Of course it's not cheerful,' Mona said, somewhere just behind his right ear. 'There's nothing *cheerful* about madness. And a lot of the people here have *bad* madness.'

'Bad madness?'

'You know – the sort that involves hurting other people. Often with knives.'

'Oh yeah. That *is* cheery.' Fin hoped the prisoners' rooms were securely locked. This place didn't look like it had the most up-to-date security. 'But surely they'd all do better in brighter surroundings. A lick of white paint wouldn't go amiss.'

'God, you really don't know anything, do you?' Fin didn't need to see her to know she was giving him her exasperated look. A thin, white-coated man emerged from one of the doorways on their left and scurried towards them, bowing his head repeatedly as he came out of the gloom.

'Your Majesty, it's such an honour—'

The Prince Regent flicked a white handkerchief at the man to silence him. 'Yes, yes, yes. But if we could just get to the matter at hand, Dr Strange?'

'Of course, of course.' The doctor was still bowing his head and revealing a very unfortunate and ill-advised comb-over – barely more than three or four strands of dark brown hair, draped across a liver-spotted scalp. 'We've put them on the lowest level.' He wrung his hands slightly and fidgeted as he led the way along a corridor. 'We try to avoid those rooms, but it couldn't be helped. They were – how can I put it? – *upsetting* the other patients.'

Dr Strange gestured towards some dark stone steps, and the small party followed him down. The air grew thicker and damper, and Fin wasn't sure if the drips of water he heard were just in his imagination, but the stench of the river was certainly growing stronger with each flight they descended. Soon they'd be below water level. He pushed the thought away, along with the wave of nausea that accompanied it. No one spoke, each of them no doubt battling the effects of the river in their own heads, and Fin wondered how it was affecting each of his friends. The chains on the box inside

67

him rattled impatiently, demanding to be opened, and he was chilled with fear at the thought. Not here, and not now – maybe not ever. He envied Mona and her immunity to the mist and the call of the water.

The steps petered out and they gathered under a lantern while one of the Prince's men lit several torches and passed them round. They would need them: it was much darker down here, and colder, too.

'Wait for us upstairs with my men, Dr Strange.' The Prince's voice retained its command, though it sounded hollow. 'The things we must discuss are private.'

'Well, if you're sure ...' The doctor was already climbing back up, followed by the Prince's Palace Guard, all moving much more quickly than they had on the way down.

'Don't stay too long,' Dr Strange called back. 'The water, you know: it's close.'

They watched the figures disappear.

'He's not quite what I expected,' Fin whispered. 'You know, with the white coat and everything ... a bit modern for this place.'

'Dr Strange was the Regent's grandfather's personal physician. He's older than he looks.' Mona stood between the two boys. 'After that king was claimed by the curse, Dr Strange made it his life's work to study the mad and try and find a cure. Some say it's his proximity to them and the water that has extended his life. Others say it's just sheer bloody-mindedness.'

'I can see why he'd make the Regent uncomfortable,' Christopher said quietly. 'For now, one is the subject of the other, but when the Regent turns forty, their roles will reverse. Life can be a funny bastard, can't it?'

'So the woman the boys found wasn't the first?' Fowkes was walking slightly ahead with the Regent, and at his words the three teenagers quickly caught them up. This wasn't a place they'd want to get separated.

'No, the fifth: a new victim has been found at dawn every day for the past five days.' He held the delicate handkerchief in front of his nose, as if somehow the soft fabric could overcome the stench that crawled over all their skin. 'Mona Savjani has kept me informed of all the details. It's clear there is something unnatural at work here.'

Fin peered through the black bars of a passing cell door. On the other side he could make out a tatty straw pallet in a cell that didn't look as if it had been cleaned in years. It was the only furniture. If there were toilet facilities in there, then he couldn't see them.

'It's horrible down here,' Christopher said. 'Inhuman.'

'It's their madness.' Mona paused beside him.

'What do you mean?'

'The Tower reflects it – or absorbs it; no one's entirely sure which. Even Dr Strange's office has shadowy corners now. I suppose working with the mad for so long has made a touch of it rub off on him.'

'So all this darkness comes from the people in here?' Fin asked.

'Yes, that's why the Tower isn't white any more.'

'It must be horrible inside their heads.' Fin looked back into the cell. Who would want to treat themselves like this? A trickle of horror ran down his spine. They must all be in torment.

'We're all a little bit mad anyway,' Christopher said softly. His words were like ice cracking. 'At least that's how it feels to me. There're bits of my head that probably look like this.'

Mona probably meant to be subtle, but the gloom made her pale skin shine brighter and Fin saw clearly as her tiny hand slipped into Christopher's. If he hadn't been looking down then, the brief flash of shock on Christopher's face would have made him anyway. He watched as his friend's fingers laced into the girl's, and as they squeezed together so did his heart, with something close to jealousy. Christopher

69

had never even *been* around girls – he didn't even know how to talk to them. So what made *him* so special? What did Mona see in him that was so much better than Fin? The stinking air flooded his lungs and darkness reached into his soul. Right then he could have punched Christopher, and kept on punching until his best friend's face was caved in and bleeding and he was a battered mess on the floor. Why did everything come so easily for Christopher?

The chains inside him rattled again, the secrets there impatient to be free. *He was tired of making sacrifices for friends – why was nothing about* him*? Why did he have to pay for other people's pleasures?* The thoughts stopped his anger in its tracks. Those weren't *his* thoughts – he was sure of it. What did any of that stuff have to do with him or Christopher? *He* hadn't made any sacrifices for his friends – if anything, it was the other way round. He shivered, Mona's hand in Christopher's forgotten. If this was the kind of thing being in the White Tower did to you, then he was surprised Dr Strange wasn't, well, *stranger*.

'This is the woman found this morning.' The distaste in the Regent's voice was undisguised, and as Fin stepped closer to the cell, he heard something hissing inside. 'She had finished her shift at the bakery five hours before she was discovered.'

'She didn't go anywhere after work,' Mona added. 'She was headed home when this happened.'

The woman was barely recognisable. Her pale skin was alabaster-white, and a sheen of sweat, as thick as Vaseline, made her almost glow in the darkness. Her hair hung entirely loose now, and had begun to matt together. There were no chestnut locks visible now; from skull to tip was all an unhealthy black. She was crouched in the corner, and as the group peered in, she scrabbled towards them on her feet and hands, moving like a crab. She hissed again, and stuck her black tongue out before tilting her head and grinning. That would have been almost bearable, if it hadn't been for the red eyes glowing madly out from between strands of that awful hair.

Fin took an involuntary step back and found he was not alone; Fowkes, Mona and Christopher had all done the same. The only one to stay close to the cell was the Prince. He touched the bars softly before turning and moving further along the passageway. Once again Fin felt slightly in awe of the tiny Royal. For all his effeminacy and ridiculous sense of fashion, he had always proved himself strong. How much of that surface was for show? Who was the real Prince Regent, and why did he hide behind so much?

No one spoke as they moved along the row. Of the five caged people, only one was a man, but he had exactly the same physical changes as the rest – black hair, black tongue, and those burning red orbs for eyes.

'This woman was found first. She was a barmaid.'

The creature scuttled forward, her movements more precise than the others they'd seen. She stared at them and hissed, and then her hands clawed up at the bars, pulling her thin body upright. Her nails were black and broken.

'You,' she hissed, tilting her head, 'boys. Running boys.'

'They never speak.' The Prince turned and looked at Fin and Christopher as if they had somehow made her do it. 'How does she know you?'

Fin's eyes suddenly widened. 'A barmaid?'

'Yes. A woman called Tilda Forshawe. She worked at a public house called The Red Lion.'

'The Harveys' pub.' Fin's stomach made a sickening slide. 'She was the barmaid – the one who warned us that the bad Knights were coming.' He stared at the creature tapping one finger erratically against the bars and found it hard to find anything to recognise in her.

'That is interesting,' the Regent said, watching him thoughtfully. 'You know the first victim, and the Storyholder

71

had visions of these eyes and black tongues. That is too much to be a coincidence, would you not say?'

He spoke as if it were 'interesting' in the kind of way that made Kings cut off people's heads, and Fin felt a wave of guilt, as if he'd somehow caused these terrible things to happen. It was like being stared at in class by Boggy Marsh at Eastfields, but with much graver consequences.

'It's nothing to do with us,' Christopher said.

'Unfortunately,' the Regent sniffed, 'one very rarely knows when something is anything to do with anything. Just because you do not directly cause something, it does not mean it is nothing to do with you. The evidence would suggest that this is very much Knight business, and perhaps the business of all of us.'

No one argued. The Prince had a point, much as Fin was loath to admit it.

'The people, however, have other thoughts, if my spies and Mona Savjani's connections are to be believed. Only the first two of these five were found in the same Borough, and they were at different ends of it. Whatever is causing this can apparently move around London quite easily. After the recent troubles, some are blaming the Knights.' He flashed a dark look at Fowkes. 'I cannot entirely blame them for that. But most are whispering about the Traders.'

'But how could the *Traders* do this to people?' Christopher asked. 'This isn't normal.'

'How can one know what constitutes normal South of the river? Perhaps they brought something back in one of their cargoes that has caused this illness?'

'No,' Mona said, 'this isn't any sort of sickness. All the victims were alone, and each one was affected at night. These are *attacks*, not infections.'

'There's more,' Fowkes said. 'It might not be relevant, but it's serious.' He hesitated, and then said bluntly, 'There is a crack in the table that runs through to the map – it's only tiny, but it's there. Something is going on, and it's bigger than a sickness.'

The Prince Regent stood perfectly still for a long moment. 'Perhaps the table should be brought back here,' he said, eventually. There was more than a hint of a command in his tone.

'No.' Fowkes met his gaze with equal determination. 'You have the stories, we have the table. That's how it's always been.'

'Perhaps one day we will learn to co-exist without all these checks and balances.'

'Everything needs balance.'

Fin watched the two men parry with words and wished he understood more of what they were fighting over.

'*Everything will be unbalanced!*' The mad thing that had been Tilda Forshawe pressed her face between the dark bars until her cheeks were squeezed almost behind her ears. 'We'll all fall through the cracks! All of us!' She laughed and hissed and dropped to the floor, scuttling back into a dark corner.

'Bloody hell,' Christopher said, shaken.

'It's just madness,' Mona said. 'She doesn't know what she's saying, she's just repeating things.'

It was a comforting thought, but Fin didn't entirely believe it.

'We need to organise a meeting with the Traders and the Knights,' the Regent continued, moving back towards the stairs. 'Somewhere neutral. We have not always had the best of relations. I prefer my subjects where I can see them. The Traders spend too much time where I cannot see them. Mona Savjani can liaise with them.'

'Can't you just command them to come wherever you want them?' Christopher asked.

'I could do that, but such actions are not always productive.'

'Where then?' Fowkes asked.

'I know where.' Fin looked back sadly at the cells. 'The Red

73

Lion. The Traders drink in there, and the Harveys are good people. They'll want to be doing something to help.'

'The Red Lion? Yes, that is appropriate. A good, quiet location, and one where such a meeting wouldn't be expected. Arrange it, Mona Savjani.'

'Your Majesty!' Feet clattered heavily on stone as two guards appeared on the bend of the stairs. 'Come quickly, all of you!'

The first guard remembered to give a quick deferential nod, just as the second guard slammed into his back, crying, *'Fire! It's a fire – there was an explosion – come quickly! You can see from the roof—'*

The group ran to the stairs, the poor changed creatures in the cells forgotten. The Prince Regent was surprisingly nimble on his feet and he took the thick stone steps two at a time, the silver buckles on his polished shoes flashing in the dark like reflectors.

Fin wasn't the only one moving fast to keep up; they were all breathless by the time they reached the top of the Keep. Fin's legs burned and he sucked in great mouthfuls of the sickly river air.

'Oh no,' Mona said, quietly. 'Look.'

For a moment no one spoke. Beyond the ruined dome of St Paul's balls of fire blossomed into the night sky.

'Where is it?' Christopher asked. 'I can't figure it out.'

'It's not the Old Bailey House of Real Truths, is it?' Joe was at the Old Bailey. With the Storyholder.

'No, it's not,' Fowkes said. 'It's—'

'—the Storyholder Academy,' the Regent finished his sentence. 'Convent Garden.'

NINE

Mona had gone ahead on her horse, but the boys didn't need a map to show them the way. The blaze was like a beacon in the night, not just for them, but for everyone in London, for the fire was visible to all Boroughs. The city came alive in crisis, and a network of buckets and water was already being ferried through the narrow streets. Strangers were trusting each other with their carriages and horses, using them to fetch and deliver water, then returning them to be refilled, over and over again. The Storyholder Academy belonged to the city, and the city had come out to fight for its salvation.

Fin's arms ached as he dragged two more buckets of water towards the fire, knowing the contents would be turned into steam as soon as the water touched the blaze. He had been working without rest for more than two hours, and they still hadn't even broken the back of the conflagration. His skin burned, his nose, throat and lungs were sore from breathing in the smoke, and he was squinting against the heat, but he ignored all the pain and discomfort and yet again moved in as close as he dared before launching the water, one pail at a time. Then he jogged back and swapped the empties for two new full pails and did it all over again. Against the roar of the fire the air was filled with the cries of men, women and children, needing water here, or blankets there ...

Somewhere behind him, past the now-opened gates of the walled convent, Mitesh Savjani, the Regent's personal cloth-crafter – Mona's father – was co-ordinating the water supplies at The Circus, where four Boroughs met. Finmere had seen him only briefly; there had been no time for real hellos in the chaos. Savjani had men keeping the water tanks full, and he himself was working the contraption that pumped the water through the long leather hose that ran down to the fire.

Fin ran back towards the heat. Around him Borough Guardsmen and Knights were working side by side, all covered in sweat and dust, and all with identical looks of gritty determination on their blackened faces. Finmere caught a flash of Alex Currie-Clark's mop of red hair; he was helping another survivor into a blanket and lifting her into the comforting arms of a buxom woman. Then he turned and headed back into the fray. This was – quite literally – a baptism of fire for the new Knights of Nowhere, and Fin couldn't help feeling a small wave of pride. This was what the Knights stood for, not the corruption and shame brought on them by the likes of St John Golden and his rotten crew.

Mona was somewhere around the other side of the burning building, lost from sight, no doubt shouting commands to her Borough Guard and ferrying information to the different teams working against the blaze. He'd seen Christopher, though – his friend had run almost into the flames to help Lucas Blake pull one woman free. The Knight had shouted at him, and Fin didn't know if his friend's actions had been recklessness or bravery, but it still made him feel small. *He* hadn't run into the burning building to save anyone, and he wasn't sure he would be strong enough to, even if he saw someone needing help like that woman.

He found himself beside Fowkes, who was looking equally grim as he threw water and ducked to avoid the burning debris. There were no other buildings too close to the Academy, but the wind was changing, and Fin thought it wouldn't take much more than a spark drifting from the fire to set the rest of the Borough alight.

Over on his left, a pillar of flame shrank. He looked around, trying to see what had caused that small success. For a second he couldn't figure it out, and then a blonde girl appeared out of nowhere with a hose that seemed to come straight out of the dark ground. Her long hair was pulled back in a ponytail. She fastened the hose around her waist, then pulled herself gracefully up into one of the garden trees. She found a sturdy branch and braced herself against the trunk before unwinding the hose. No one apart from Finmere appeared to have noticed her, but she whistled down to someone out of sight and a second later, water started pumping from the hose. It was flowing much faster than Savjani's. *Who was she?* There were Traders amongst those fighting the fire – he'd recognised their heavy overcoats and thick jumpers, and the aggressive way they moved – but she didn't seem to be attached to their group.

Her face, intent and serious, lit up in the reflection of the flames and Fin couldn't help but stare at her. She was beautiful. She didn't look his way.

'Oi.' An elbow nudged into his back, and he turned to quickly take the buckets that were waiting for him.

'Commander!' One of the new Knights had stopped beside Fin to call to Fowkes.

'What?' Soot had settled in the lines on Fowkes' face, and Fin had a flash of what he would look like in twenty years' time.

'It doesn't look like a natural fire – there was no reason for it to start. A few of the locals are saying they saw a black kid running away seconds before it started. Thought you should know.'

A black kid. Fin's stomach tightened as Fowkes' face grew dark and, without saying a word, he turned away from the young Knight and the fire and stormed out of the gates. Fin dropped his bucket, ignoring the shouts from the man behind him, and ran after him.

'It wouldn't be Joe!' he shouted, pushing his way through the crowds of people to catch up.

'Go back, Fin.' Fowkes didn't slow his stride.

'No,' he said, 'no, I won't! Joe wouldn't have done this. He *wouldn't*. What's your problem with him, anyway?'

Further away from the fire, the dark night closed in around them. 'I don't have a problem with him,' Fowkes snarled, 'I have a problem with all three of you. You're too young for this.' He paused. 'Ted sees it all as adventures, but Ted's never Travelled. And I don't know how you fit in. And if I do have a problem with Joe, it's not with him, it's because of these events. But sometimes the two become the same, and that just can't be helped.'

'None of it is Joe's fault.'

'That doesn't change anything, though, does it?' Fowkes walked faster, pulling away from Fin. 'And if you're not going to do what you're told and go back, then you can just shut up.'

The aggression in the words stung. Why was Fowkes always so angry – because of what happened between him and Baxter, so long ago? But why was he taking it out on *them*? Fin gritted his teeth and ran to keep up with the Knights' Commander. If Fowkes didn't want to hear him speak, that was fine, but he could make his own anger felt in other ways.

Listening to Fowkes accusing Joe made Fin feel sick. He hated confrontation at the best of times, but this was much worse. Fowkes had dragged Joe out of the apartments where the sick Storyholder was sleeping and down into the atrium.

'Don't tell me you came straight back here after I left because I'll go and wake Tova up and ask her!'

'I never said I did come back here!' Joe was indignant. 'I was just walking – wandering about. Calming down. I'm sick and tired of being cooped up in here!'

'Why didn't you come and help with the fire, then?'

'Because I was back here by then, and I was doing what I'm *supposed* to be doing: *staying here*! I don't know what you want from me!'

Fin stood between them, his own tongue tied in knots. Why couldn't they see they were all on the same side?

'Did you start the fire?' Fowkes spat the question out.

'No. But thanks for asking.'

Fin recognised Joe's surly comeback from school, but this was a different kind of accusation than those generally levied at the boys at Eastfields Comp: this was proper, grown-up and serious. This was the kind of accusation you couldn't come back from, and Fin wished Fowkes could see that.

'They saw a black boy running away,' Fowkes continued. 'I have to ask.'

'What? Do we all look the same in the dark?' Joe leaned forward, his jaw clenched.

Fin had never seen him so angry, not like this anyway – quiet and intense. It wasn't Joe at all.

'That's not what I meant.'

'So what did you mean? One black kid seen and it has to be me?'

'We can clear this up right now. We just have to go in there' – Fowkes pointed towards the heavy wooden doors separating them from the Archivers and the truth vials – 'and then we'll hear the truth.'

'Or you can just *trust* me! Is that so hard? You'd trust Fin, wouldn't you? Is everything that's going wrong in all these worlds my fault?' He stepped back and sneered, '*I'm* not the one who started this – *I'm* not the one who fucked the Storyholder, Fowkes. That was *you*!'

Fin's eyes widened. Not because of *that* word – the word itself was not a shock, even if its context was. His eyes had widened because the water in the fountain behind Joe had turned deep red as his friend shouted, and the colour spread up through the walls until the whole atrium looked as if it were bathed in blood.

The anger faded from Joe as quickly as it had come, and he looked shocked at what he had done. He looked helplessly at Fin.

'Don't worry, mate,' Fin said, and hoped he sounded like he meant it. 'Just let it go. I don't think for one second you started that fire.' He looked over at Fowkes. 'And I don't think he does either.' The colour around them faded back to its normal bleached white, but Fin couldn't help feeling that the atrium had been tainted by something awful.

Fin wasn't sure whether it was the power Joe had just displayed, or the impact of his words, but whatever fire had been driving Fowkes had left him.

The Knight watched Joe warily. 'Maybe I don't believe you had anything to do with it – but I had to ask.' He wasn't growling any more and Fin wondered if there was just a touch of fear in the man's voice. What had Joe done, anyway? Was it just that he couldn't control the stories inside him? Were they bleeding out of him a little? For the first time he could see why Fowkes was suspicious, even if he didn't agree with him.

'And you don't need to tell me my part in this.' Fowkes walked over to the door, not looking at Joe as he spoke. 'I live with it every single day. So, stay or go. Do what you want. I won't keep you prisoner.' As if proving his point, he left the door open as he stepped out into the night.

'I'd better go after him,' Fin said after a moment. 'I'll come back in a bit.'

Joe nodded. Fin wasn't sure if he'd even really heard him.

The night air stank of fire and filthy water, and bits of ash and burned material floated past on the breeze. Fowkes had slowed to a stroll, though Fin wasn't sure exactly where they were headed as they meandered through the streets. Fin walked beside him silently and let the minutes tick round as he mulled over their fight.

'Maybe we are too young for all this, who knows?' Fin said eventually. 'Sometimes I wish I could put it all back to how it was before – when life was just confusing.' He pushed his hands deep in his pockets and scuffed his feet along the ground, kicking up the dirt and loose stones. 'But I can't, even when I see that it's messing up my friends. Sometimes I think this story was started long before we came into it' – he felt the man beside him stiffen slightly at his words – 'and by that I mean before even you and Baxter and the Storyholder. I wish I understood it all more. But the one thing I do understand,' and he looked up at Fowkes, 'is that we can't just go back. You *have* to believe the best in people.' He kicked more dirt. 'Otherwise, what's the point?'

Fowkes stopped. His dark expression was impenetrable in the shadows of the night as he looked down at Fin. 'Do you do that a lot?' he asked.

'What?'

'Kick dirt when you're thinking aloud.'

Fin looked down at his shoes and the street. He hadn't really been aware he'd been doing it. Did he do it often? He didn't know. 'Does it matter?' he asked.

'I wish we knew more about where the hell you came from,' Fowkes said, abruptly. 'I wish Tova would just tell us.'

The words felt like a slap in the face. 'You're not the only one, trust me,' Fin said sadly.

'Let's get back to the fire.'

Once the blaze was finally extinguished, the exhausted Knights headed back to Old Town and the House of Charter's Lane, the Knights' headquarters in The Nowhere. Fin and Christopher went with them. It felt strange to be back there, and weird not thinking of it as the enemy's camp, after all that had happened with St John Golden, but Fin decided a house was just a house – it was only the people in it who had been wicked.

Neither he nor Christopher bothered even washing the black soot from their faces before collapsing into two single beds on the second floor. The heavy drapes hanging over the glass-free windows did little to keep out the stench of the fire; it smelled and felt like it had coated everything and everyone in the city.

'What time is it?' Christopher asked after a moment.

'No idea. Fowkes took his watch back. Got to be only a couple of hours from dawn, I reckon.'

'What time are the Knights gathering?'

'Dawn.'

'Oh, good,' Christopher drawled.

Their breathing slowed until both boys were on the cusp of sleep, and as he drifted, blonde hair flashed behind Fin's eyes.

'Christopher,' he said.

'What?' The word was more of a grunt.

'Did you see a blonde girl there tonight?'

'What, one of the novices?'

'No,' Fin said, 'a different girl. She was fighting the fire. Had a hose from somewhere.'

'No, sorry ...' Christopher yawned. There was a pause. 'Why? Was she fit?'

'Yeah,' Fin admitted to the gloom, 'kind of.'

Christopher snorted out a half-laugh, but neither of them had any energy for joking, and within moments both boys had drifted into a deep sleep, lost in their own worlds of dreams and nightmares.

TEN

Selfridges was crowded, and as he manoeuvred himself into a corner in order to take the phone call, Mr Arnold-Mather resisted the urge to dig his fellow shoppers hard in the ribs. It wasn't politeness that stopped him but self-awareness: he was a public figure, and behaving like that just would not do.

He had come out to buy a final few gifts, as had the rest of London, or so it appeared. Personally, he couldn't see what all this Christmas fuss and nonsense was about: people with no money getting into further debt buying tacky trinkets for each other, and those who *had* money buying superfluous goods that weren't wanted and whose only importance to the recipient was the price tag or the label. Finally leaning back against the wall, he pressed the answer button.

'Did it all go well?' he asked. The answer made him smile. 'Good. And our hired help? All dealt with?' He watched a fat woman almost tumble over as a passing stranger unbalanced her and her crammed shopping bags. If looks could kill, the disappearing stranger would have been a dead man. Christmas really did bring out the best in people.

'Then we should move to phase two while they're all busy. I'll be waiting for your call. Good work, Mr Dodge.'

He returned to one of the jewellery counters where he picked out a necklace for his wife. It was gaudy but expensive, and she would somehow see that price as an indication of the amount he loved her. She had never been too bright. He gave no thought to the three young black men who Levi Dodge had so efficiently used and then dispatched to the next world, which was neither in The Somewhere or The Nowhere but laid eventual claim to the residents of both. Loss of life was always mildly regrettable, but in this case, it simply couldn't be helped. They would never have been entirely controllable – those types never were – and they weren't the calibre of man he wanted around him for any length of time.

Still, the government was always going on about knife crime and gang wars on the estates of London; he'd got rid of three young men who would no doubt have added to those ever-increasing crime figures. At least they'd had the opportunity to see something quite remarkable before they'd died, even if he had broken the promises of wealth and power he'd made to them. Not that broken promises unduly bothered him – he was a politician, after all, so breaking promises came naturally.

He accepted the small gift-wrapped box and his receipt, giving the tired shop assistant a small smile before turning away and forgetting her completely. He should choose something for Christopher, perhaps – something to sit under the tree. It would keep the boy's mother happy. He had other things to give his son this Christmas, as long as the boy had got over his hot-headed naïveté by then. His son hadn't talked about his suspicions, as far as he could make out, so perhaps Christopher would be at his right hand by the end after all.

Joe's bum was numb from sitting on the steps of the Old Bailey House of Real Truths. He wondered if this was how Fin felt every year, waiting for Ted to show up on his birthday, back at the other Old Bailey in the other London. Sitting where he was he didn't feel special, not like it did to Fin. There was something different about his best friend – even if Fin himself didn't see it, other people reacted to it. It made it hard to stay annoyed at him, even though Joe was finding he got annoyed way more often than he used to. It was all this being cooped up inside with the sick Storyteller. He'd rather sit out here with a numb bum for another hour than go back inside. He needed some fresh air. He needed to think.

Where had all that colour come from, and what had made it fill the atrium like that – was it him? How? He hadn't felt anything change, other than he'd been totally pissed off and mad. One of the stories that had gone into him back in Postman's Park was red. He might not be the brightest boy in Eastfields, but he'd have to be a total dumbass not to suspect that the red that'd swept over the place earlier wasn't related to that. How much power did the stories have over him?

And how much power do you have over the stories? The dark voice was small, but every day it was growing louder. It was that voice that had made him taunt Fowkes about his past. It was him but *not* him; it hadn't existed before the stories chose him. He had a horrible feeling that it was the voice of the red and black stories, and it was weaving itself so tightly into his brain that soon he wouldn't know where his thoughts ended and that voice began. He wasn't cut out for this kind of thinking. He wasn't smart like that – street smart, maybe, but not clever smart.

He thought about going for a walk, but he knew better. Even though Fowkes had told him he could go where he wanted, he wasn't thick enough to believe that. What if something else happened and he couldn't prove his whereabouts? The blame would be slamming right at *his* door, that was for sure. He ran one hand over his curly hair. He was tired of being the one in trouble. Even at school Finmere was the golden boy and he was the dunce, the comedy sidekick. Now Fin and Christopher – who was a real golden boy with a silver spoon in his mouth – were off with the Knights and he was stuck here, with everyone suspicious of him when he hadn't done *a thing*.

He *wasn't* stupid, anyway: if it hadn't been for him, Fin

would never have got the Storyholder out of that crazy prison. They'd all been so quick to forget that ...

Joe sighed and stared down at his shoes. He wished he didn't feel so angry all the time. Part of him – the *real* him, if there was one – thought that maybe Fowkes was right to be wary. He wasn't entirely himself any more, or at least, different parts of him felt more in control than they used to be.

A familiar sound of leather against dirt cut through the quiet darkness, and it struck a chord in Joe's heart. *A football?* He looked up to see a thickset man wearing a dark suit with an old-fashioned Bowler hat on his head, standing about twenty feet away in the square, bouncing the ball between his knees and his head. The hat appeared to be absolutely no impediment. He ignored Joe, concentrating instead on the movements of the ball, and Joe watched the strange sight from the steps, fascinated. For a large man, he was nimble on his feet, and as he turned and hopped from foot to foot, the ball remained aloft.

The ball was white, and Joe could clearly make out the Nike tick. So if the ball was from The Somewhere, then the man probably was too – especially with those skills. In the weeks Joe had spent cooped up in The Nowhere, there'd been many afternoons when he'd have given anything for a kick-about, but the mention of football just registered a blank with everyone he asked. The people of The Nowhere had been quite bemused by the concept of getting pleasure from kicking a ball into a net. Joe had considered trying to explain the offside rule, just to really confuse them, but that idea had just made him miss the simple pleasure of the game even more.

But now here was a football, and a man who clearly knew how to use it. Joe stood up.

For the first time, the stranger looked at directly at Joe. It was a hard gaze, the kind that settled permanently in the eyes of the boys on the Brickman Estate when they reached about nineteen. The man kept the ball in the air as he studied Joe, and then let it drop to the ground, sending it towards the boy with a deft left foot. Joe trotted a couple of paces to one side to meet it and kick it back. It felt good. He'd missed the feeling of the ball connecting with his trainers, and although they weren't having a proper game and he couldn't feel that sweet spot moment you got when kicking the ball into the goal or halfway down the pitch, it was a real release just to trot around the square at the command of that pumped-up leather ball.

Eventually, just as Joe's breath was becoming slightly irregular from the exercise, the man in the Bowler hat stopped and put one foot on the stilled ball. 'Someone wants to see you,' he said. They were the first words he'd spoken. Joe wasn't surprised. A man in a Bowler hat playing with a football in the middle of the night in The Nowhere was never going to turn out to be a simple passing stranger.

'Who?' he asked.

'Just someone. You'll know when you know, and that's if you decide you want to know.' The man's voice was rough: gravel dragged under the wheels of a truck.

'Back there?'

The Bowler hat tipped slightly in a nod. Joe took a few steps forward. They were talking quietly, but the night around them was silent and although none of the buildings close by were residential, Joe didn't want to take the risk of their conversation being overheard. The twist in his gut told him this wasn't the kind of quiet chat that Fowkes would approve of.

'But I can't go back to The Somewhere,' he said. 'Not with the stories in me.'

'How do you know? You tried it?' The man flicked the ball up and caught it, tucking it under his arm.

'No, but— That's what they tell me.' A kernel of doubt grew inside him. How *did* they know he couldn't go back? The ache to see his home, that he'd lived with for weeks, became a sharp stab into his heart.

'They don't know. No one knows.' The man dropped one eyelid in a wink, but there was no humour in it. If anything, it made him look more intimidating. 'That's just what they tell you. They want you contained. You'll be back in an hour or so. You've got my word on that.'

The man spoke as if that should mean something, but as Joe knew nothing about him at all – not even his name – he didn't see how he could take his word for anything.

'I don't think I should,' Joe said eventually. 'But thanks all the same.'

'Suit yourself,' the man said, turning his back on Joe and strolling away. 'You stay here and sit on the steps feeling sorry for yourself while everyone else has an adventure. You do that, Joe Manning.'

Joe watched him leaving and felt a flush tingle through his skin. *They want you contained.* That bit wasn't a lie: the Knights *had* kept Joe in the Storyholder's apartments, and although they'd said it was for his own good until Tova took the stories back, it felt pretty much like they'd locked him up. Everyone else was out there doing stuff and he was left behind. Finally, here was someone who was interested in *him* – just him. He hadn't mentioned Finmere, even once. This was his chance at some excitement and he was letting it walk away. Was he going to be a second-place loser forever? And what harm could one meeting really do?

He wasn't sure which of his voices asked the last question, but the knot in his stomach that answered it was all the real him. He chose to ignore it. This was a chance to go back home. To breathe proper London air, even if just for an hour. And no one need ever *know*.

'Wait!' he called as he jogged to catch up. 'I'm coming.'

The man in the Bowler hat didn't slow his pace, nor smile.

'Don't we need a sword?' Joe asked.

'Just come with me. It's all under control.'

Joe wondered why the idea of this man having everything

under control gave him a vague niggle of unease. He didn't even know his name. Still, he thought as they walked through the night, wherever they were going it was better than staying here and having more accusations lobbed at him by Fowkes, or keeping the silent Storyholder company while she waited for him to give her stories back, like he was keeping them on purpose or something. At least here was someone who was interested in *him* as himself, Joe Manning – it had been a long time since he'd met anyone like that. If ever ...

The Knights were gathering in St John Golden's old office and as Fin shuffled in across the reed-covered floor and around the large table that hadn't been there before, he realised there was no sign of the Incarcerator Mirror. Where was it now? In the palace, or hidden somewhere else in the house? Sometimes, deep in the marrow of his bones, he could still feel the unnatural cold of its air. He shivered automatically.

A cup of steaming coffee was thrust into his hands and he crept over to the other side of the room where a fire crackled gently in the grate. Christopher sidled in next to him, stifling a yawn. Within five minutes the small room was filled to capacity. Three middle-aged men with powdered and painted faces were the last to enter. They all wore shiny knee-length pink coats over black shirts and breeches, and each had a black wig standing high on his head and a silver cane held in one hand. They were so close to identical, Fin found it hard to tell one from the others. They sat carefully in three old wooden chairs along one side of the table. Their perfect tailoring and precise appearance was in contrast with the young Knights. None wore their black cloaks, and their shirts and faces were smeared with soot and grime from fighting the fire. Exhaustion filled the room with every breath they exhaled. Fin felt embarrassed at his own tiredness – at least he'd had *some* sleep. He sipped his coffee; it was strong and earthy and burned the roof of his mouth. There was no sign of Mona – maybe she'd been allowed home to get to bed.

Fowkes stood at the head of the table and the soft hubbub in the room quietened down as he raised one hand. 'I know it's been a long night and you're all tired. If there were more of us, I'd let at least half of you go and get some sleep, but as things are ... Well.' He looked around the room. 'First, I'd like to welcome three of the Prince Regent's Chancellors, who will be reporting back on our findings. They are, from right to left, Chancellor A, Chancellor B and Chancellor D. Thank you for coming.'

The three men tilted their heads slightly in unison, but their painted lips remained grimly pursed.

'Don't they have names?' Christopher whispered.

'Guess not,' Fin answered.

'They do have names,' Soames whispered beside Fin, 'but they don't ever use them, not while they are serving in public office. All of that make-up and wig malarkey comes off when they go home. If they pass an unpopular tax, the odds of someone trying to attack them for it are greatly reduced if no one knows their real names or what they look like. In a lot of ways, it makes perfect sense.'

Fin looked at the strange dandies again. It was true; he couldn't really tell what they looked like without all that stuff on, and he was standing only a few feet away from them It still felt a little deceptive, though: if they didn't have to personally account for anything, then surely they could do some bad things? He didn't understand politics back in his own world; he'd never manage it here.

At the head of the table Fowkes made way for Benjamin Wakley. The young man looked around the room for a moment before starting speaking. 'It's early days, and much of the area is still too hot to examine thoroughly, but this fire was definitely arson.'

A sharp mutter rippled through the room and even the three Chancellors turned to each other.

'How can you be sure?' Chancellor D asked, each word clipped and exact.

'Before he became a Knight, this man was with our Army in The Somewhere. He was an expert on explosive devices.'

The Chancellors did not look impressed, but nodded for Wakley to continue anyway.

'There were three start-points to the fire, all within the exterior wall, and each one at a wooden section of the building. They were clearly chosen to maximise the damage. At the moment I'd say it was crudely started, with something like petrol used to douse the surfaces and then petrol bombs thrown to really get it going. I don't think there was any particular intention to kill. Although the blaze would become fierce quite quickly, the novices and their instructors were all sleeping in the central stone tower, giving them plenty of time to get out of there and run through the gardens to escape. It looked almost as if the fire was designed to leave them an escape tunnel. Unfortunately, the sickbay was in a separate part of the Convent, and we were unable to get there. Two novices and a nurse died.'

'I might be being thick here ...' Lucas Blake frowned, then continued, 'but what's the point of burning the academy down if not to kill the novices? Awful as that idea is.'

'They can't hold the stories now. They're supposed to live without stress or extreme emotion.' Fowkes' face coloured slightly under the grime. Fin wasn't surprised. Fowkes had fallen in love with Tova, and she'd fallen in love with him. They'd broken that rule. 'The stories are too strong to be held in someone who's too conflicted. That's why these girls have had such sheltered existences, ever since they were infants: to keep them empty of any emotions that might affect the safety of the stories.'

91

'And fear,' added Chancellor A dryly, 'is the strongest of the emotions. These girls have indeed been rendered useless.'

Fin tried to get his tired head around what the Chancellor and Fowkes were saying. 'So that means ... ?'

'If Tova doesn't recover enough to take the stories back from Joe, then there is no one else ready for the job.' Fowkes finished Fin's thought. 'And given the current situation, who knows what ramifications that might have, not just for The Nowhere and The Somewhere, but for all the worlds?'

'And what of this black boy seen running away?' Chancellor B asked. His voice had an unpleasant nasal quality.

Fin felt his face tingle with anger. Were they all going to accuse Joe now?

'I know what you're thinking, Chancellor,' Wakley said, 'but these fires could not have been started by one person alone. There were three distinct start-points, and in my considered opinion, they were all lit simultaneously.' He paused. 'Plus, I've looked at that boy's file. He has no history of this kind of behaviour – and whatever damage the stories he holds might be doing to him, I doubt he would be capable of planning and executing something like this. It would have taken a certain amount of expert knowledge.'

'But he is the only one to gain from such an action,' the Chancellor added.

'Not necessarily.' It was Benjamin's twin, Henry, who cut in from the back of the room. 'Anyone with an interest in the stories having nowhere else to go but staying split between the Storyholder and Joe would want the Academy destroyed. It'll cause some civil unease, if nothing else.'

'Only a madman would want such a thing!' Chancellor A exclaimed.

'Sadly, the world is full of them. Don't tell me yours is any different to ours.'

'I'll have a fuller report in a couple of days,' Benjamin Wakley said, 'but for now, I'd say we were looking for three suspects, black or otherwise. That's the best I can do in the short term.'

The men continued talking, weighing up who might want to burn down the Academy and why, and whether it might have something to do with the strange attacks that were taking place throughout the city, but now Finmere was barely listening. His tiredness had vanished and his feet itched to race over to the Storyholder's apartments and tell Joe that he was in the clear. Maybe now Fowkes would stop coming down so hard on all of them. Perhaps now he'd start to think a little bit more like Ted. He sipped his coffee. As much as he wanted to leave, it looked like he wasn't going anywhere for the next twenty minutes at least.

Joe had to give the man in the Bowler hat credit, he didn't flinch when they stepped through the Doorway into the lower levels of the House of Detention. Two things didn't happen. The man didn't age suddenly, and as far as Joe could tell, there were no tremors in the universe or an impending apocalypse because he had split the stories between two worlds. So much for Fowkes' panic. Maybe the great Knights of Nowhere didn't know everything, after all.

'How did you get in here, anyway?' he asked, following the man up the dimly lit stairs. 'And where was that old gatekeeper? Doesn't he have your coin?'

The man said nothing.

'What's your name then?' Joe pushed. 'Or won't you tell me that either?'

'Levi Dodge. You can call me Mr Dodge.'

'Nice to meet you, Mr Dodge. Good footie skills.'

'Thank you.'

It was colder in the The Somewhere, and Joe was already shivering even before the icy December air hit him. Once on the pavement he hugged himself, shuffling from foot to foot.

'So what now?' It was dark, but the city was still throbbing with life, the streets full of impatient traffic and hurrying pedestrians. From what he could tell it was much earlier than it was in The Nowhere. His stomach tightened for a second. What would everyone back there say if they knew what he'd done? Where he'd gone? Fin would probably be disappointed. Fin believed wholeheartedly in everything the Knights did, but he had also defended Joe to Fowkes. He felt vaguely sick at the thought that he'd somehow let his best mate down, but swallowed it. After all, they were all too busy having their own adventures to think about him.

However much Fin pretended otherwise, it was obvious that Joe was on the outside now. Fowkes didn't trust him and he was the Commander – aside from Finmere, and maybe Christopher, Joe didn't really have anyone on *his* side, and it wasn't a good feeling. He wasn't even sure the Storyholder liked him ... although it was hard to tell, given that she was still weak from everything that had happened, and with no tongue she could no longer speak. Getting a bit of banter going with a notebook was hard work – and he didn't really think Tova was the kind of woman you could have a banter with anyway. He often found her watching him, and he didn't like it; he was sure there was a lot of pity in those looks. He didn't *want* people to feel sorry for him; he just wanted them to go back to *liking* him.

Well, he'd show them all, he thought looking out into the lively London evening. He was on his own adventure, wherever it led. And it wasn't as if he was doing anything terrible. *Not yet.*

'Shit, it's cold,' he muttered, the expletive more for bravado than necessity. Levi Dodge stood unmoving beside him, as if he didn't feel the cold at all. Joe wondered if he'd be the same in the heat of summer. Probably. He figured Levi Dodge was that kind of bloke.

A sleek black car pulled up to the kerb and a blacked-out rear window slid down a couple of inches. The face inside was just a shadow. 'Wait here until we're done, Mr Dodge,' the disembodied voice said. 'And once you've returned our friend, please remember to make sure this door is damaged appropriately.'

'Yes, sir.' Mr Dodge went round to the other side and held open the rear door. He nodded at Joe. 'Get in.'

It was a command rather than an invitation. With his stomach halfway to his mouth, Joe got in. The door had only just clicked shut when the car pulled away, purring quietly.

As his chilled body adjusted to the heat pumping round the limousine, Joe stared at the smart middle-aged man beside him.

'Mr Arnold-Mather,' he said, an exclamation of surprise rather than a greeting. He didn't know why he was so shocked, really. He should have known as soon as he got to the Doorway. Ted probably had a set of keys, but there was only one person they'd been able to go to when they needed to get in before.

'How nice. You remember me.' Mr Arnold-Mather smiled. 'I certainly remember you.'

'But what—?' Joe couldn't finish the sentence as his brain turned over this revelation and tried to make sense of it. He wasn't succeeding. 'Why would you be interested in me?' was the best he could come up with. 'You're *Christopher*'s dad.'

Mr Arnold-Mather pressed a button on the armrest and a glass divide slid up between the driver and his passengers. 'Why wouldn't I be interested in you, Joe? What a ridiculous question,' he said. '*You* are the special one. They all think it is young Finmere, but they are wrong of course; you are the one who holds all the power of all the worlds. You could, at any rate, if you really wanted to.' He paused. 'And that is why they are afraid of you – you must know that, it is why they accuse you of things. If they had their way, they would probably try to get rid of you altogether.'

Something mean and ugly fizzed inside Joe. They were

scared of him, that was it. And maybe jealous, too, because the stories chose him. The anger that lived in a ball in his stomach began to unfurl and stretch out. Somewhere deep down, a small voice tried to tell him that Fin would never be jealous or scared of him – they were *best friends* – but the anger drowned it out in a haze of red and black. Fear, that was it. They were *all* afraid of him.

But why did Christopher's dad even care?

'How do you know about the other worlds? You didn't let on when we came to get the keys off you that night.'

'Oh, I know far more than you could imagine. I have been keeping my eye on things for as long as you have been alive, give or take a few months.'

'Does Christopher know that you know?' Joe was having a hard time taking it in. All the secrets and pretence: did *everyone* keep things from everything else? Were all friendships fake?

'Oh, I think he suspects,' Mr Arnold-Mather said, casually. 'He will come to me when he is good and ready.' He looked over, any expression in his eyes hidden in the shadows. 'But he can wait. He is not as important as you.'

Joe looked out of the window at the passing city. Even through the tinted glass the bright Christmas lights teased him with their vibrant colours. *Home.* He wanted to go back to the dirty estate and its grubby familiarity and hang out with friends who only knew one world, and barely knew anything of that beyond the capital's boundaries. He wanted to stuff himself with Quality Street and drink crap mulled wine at his Auntie May's. It was Christmas, and he should be having fun. He ran his hand over his hair, but the old habit brought him no comfort. There was too much to think about, and he hadn't been built for this kind of thinking. He was football, not chess.

'So, Ted and the Knights don't know that you know any of this?'

'No.' Mr Arnold-Mather's eyes glinted in the passing lights. 'They are all really rather self-absorbed, self-satisfied – I could almost go so far as to say *smug*. That is why they do not see your potential. They lack vision.'

'Are you against them?' Joe asked. He wasn't sure that it mattered. *They're afraid of you. They'd try to get rid of you.* The words filled the angry pit in his gut. But still, the sickly twist in his heart knew that he didn't want to be against Fin. Why did life have to be so complicated?

'The world isn't so black and white, Joe. Let us just say I am *apart* from them.'

Apart from them. That didn't sound so terrible. It wasn't *against*, at any rate. 'What is it you want with me?' Joe asked.

'It is not what I want *with* you, Joe Manning, it is what I want *for* you.'

'And that is?' The car crossed Oxford Street and Joe had the idea that the driver was just meandering aimlessly until Mr Arnold-Mather told him to take them back.

'The stories – *all* of them. They are your destiny. You must feel it.'

Joe did: at just the mention of them, his skin tingled, and the two he already held roared into life, sending splitting pains of need right through his head. He focused and shut them down. All that meditation hadn't entirely gone to waste, but he was still left with the sense of two strong snakes twisting and writhing beneath his skin.

'How?' he said, his throat tightening. He could feel every tick in the engine and bump in the road and his skin burned. Whatever his fate was, it was starting now. It hummed in his bones like black magic.

'There are two things you need to do, that is all.'

'If I do them, can I go and see my mum? Say hello on Christmas?' The wave of homesickness and the need for an easier, less complicated life was almost overwhelming, even as the stories pushed him forward to something far more complex.

Mr Arnold-Mather let out a sudden laugh, in the way that adults do when children say something unintentionally amusing. 'If you do them, dear boy, then we can do anything we want. *Anything*.'

Joe turned away from the window and started to listen. There was no going back now, and a tiny part of him inside wanted to cry at that. He still wanted to cry, even as he stepped back into The Nowhere barely half an hour later, his soul heavy with choices and temptation.

Dawn had blossomed into morning by the time Fin finally got to leave the Knights' house and get back to the Storyholder's apartments. He followed the straight narrow pathways, designed to ensure every resident could reach the Old Bailey without too much discomfort from Travelling out of their home Boroughs. Even without the paths, Fin was slowly figuring his way round The Nowhere's London. It might look very different to his home, but the basic layout was the same, and Fin knew The Somewhere London's streets pretty well.

Despite the fire, the city was resilient, and people were already out and about, impatient to start the new day. Streets opened up at intervals on both sides of the pathway, and each new crossroads was marked by a lamp, some more modern than others. They ranged from an oiled rag tied to a stick embedded in the earth to an old-fashioned gas lamp that could have come from a Dickens novel. Fin thought that must be how anyone who visited the Old Bailey House of Real Truths could find their way home – by the appropriate lamp. He peered down one alleyway and in the street beyond he could see a horse and carriage, standing on the cobbles. A man in a top hat stepped down from the carriage, checked his pocket watch and looked up at the building in front of him. Fin couldn't see what that was – a shop? An office? He fought the urge to go and explore and left the small scene behind. Joe was more important.

'So, what I'm saying is that they *know* you didn't do it,' Fin repeated himself. Joe still looked glum. 'That new Knight, the really serious one, he used to be in the Army, or something. Anyway, he's an expert, and he says there's no way one person could have started all this, and whoever it was knew what they were doing.' He looked at his friend's blank expression. 'Don't you *get* it? You're off the hook – and Fowkes owes you one big fat apology.'

'I get it,' Joe said. They were sitting on his small bed in a side room away from Tova's. Joe kept glancing at the door, and Fin thought he was worried that the Storyholder might be listening on the other side – although why it would bother him, Fin didn't know. He hadn't *done* anything – that was the point.

Fin looked over at the white wood wall dividing them from the silent, ethereal woman. He didn't think she was the eavesdropping kind.

'I get it,' Joe repeated, 'but I knew I hadn't done it anyway. Would have been nice to have been trusted.'

Fin said nothing. He hadn't thought of it like that.

'Sometimes I feel like they want to get rid of me. I can't believe Fowkes thought I'd started that fire. He's a right bastard.'

'He's just got a lot to think about,' Fin said. 'And I know it's not perfect that they believe you because of evidence rather than what you said, but you've got to admit, it's better than nothing. At least now they'll feel like they messed up, and they'll have to trust you more.'

'Easy for you to say.' There wasn't even a twitch of a grin on Joe's face.

Fin had never seen him so serious. 'Look, mate,' Fin said, softly, 'you know that if I could swap places with you I would.

I know this is all my fault. I shouldn't have dragged you into this.'

'You didn't *drag* me. I came because I wanted to. Shit, this is one big adventure!' Joe's lips cracked into the tiniest smile, and Fin's heart thumped with relief.

'It'll get better, you know.'

'You sound like my mum.' The grin spread slightly and then he frowned. 'Where's Christopher, anyway?'

'With Mona.' Fin rolled his eyes. Mitesh Savjani's daughter hadn't gone home to sleep, as he'd originally thought, but instead had been organising a meeting with the Traders about the attacks. Fin wondered where she got her energy from. 'He said he'd "walk her home" when we left the Knights' house.'

'You think he's going to go in for the snog?'

'I hope not. Don't think either of them have cleaned their teeth since yesterday.'

Joe snorted out a laugh, and Fin joined in. 'Can't believe he's really going to make a play for Mona,' Joe said, shaking his head. 'But still, he's a good-looking rich kid. Bet he gets all the girls.'

'He goes to a boys' school. He doesn't *know* any girls.'

'I bet he gets all the *boys*, then.'

'That is sick, man.' Fin punched his friend's arm, enjoying the banter.

'Yeah, well. We all know what goes on at those all boys' schools. What were you, the toast rack?'

They carried on knocking each other for a few minutes and then settled into a comfortable silence.

'It's good to just have a laugh, isn't it?' Joe said, letting out a long sigh. 'Stops you thinking about things.'

'Yeah,' Fin agreed. 'Yeah, it does.' He got to his feet. 'Look, Mona's organised this meeting with the Traders. You want to come? We could go and grab some breakfast from somewhere first.'

'Cool,' Joe nodded. 'But Fin – go and brush your teeth

first. Your breath stinks.' Fin turned to thump his friend, who ducked out of the way, and when they left the building minutes later, they were both laughing. Fin wasn't even all that bothered by Christopher and Mona any more. Maybe his stomach got a little bit twisted if he thought about them actually *kissing*, but no more than that. It was the blonde girl he kept thinking about. Not that there was a hope in hell of ever running into her again.

Ted's footsteps creaked up the spiral staircase to the office at the top of the Rookhaven Suite and he felt the strain in his joints. He was getting too old for this. Soon it would be time to hand the nightwatchman's uniform over to someone else, along with all the more secret duties that went with it. That would be a strange day, but he'd begun to think recently that it would also be something of a relief. As Fowkes so clearly missed Adam Baxter, he missed Harlequin Brown. Now that his old friend was gone, Ted had become unsure of his own judgement. Perhaps that's what it was like for Fowkes too. He and Baxter had been very different personalities, despite their great friendship, just as he and Harlequin had been. Maybe that was what a great friendship was based on: differences, rather than similarities.

Fowkes wasn't sitting behind the wide leather-topped writing desk as Harlequin would have been, but instead stood staring out of the window of the hexagonal room. He didn't turn as Ted arrived, so the old man poured himself a drink from the decanter on the low side table before joining the new Commander. Fowkes' cloak was slung over the back of an antique chair, and at some point he'd managed to shower and change his shirt. Ted was pleased about that. Harlequin used to drum that into his Knights: half of *being* strong was looking the part. No one respected a man whose shirt wasn't tucked in properly. It was indicative of other things. He wished they would teach that in schools the way Harlequin had, rather than just screaming at kids about smart uniforms. Maybe then all those teenagers – including Finmere and his friends – would understand.

The only light in the room came from two unobtrusive lamps that glowed yellow. Outside, icy rain slapped silently against the glass, smearing the view of the city's skyline and creating an abstract artist's vision where colour and shade blended into manic confusion. Ted looked at Fowkes' reflection in the glass. The man had aged since Fin had found him and brought him back into the fold, for all his current clean living.

'You get any sleep yet, son?' he asked, breaking the silence.

'An hour or so. I wish my body could figure out what time it was supposed to be. I don't know whether I'm supposed to be going to bed or getting up. Not that I can sleep much anyway. Not with all this going on.'

'It'll get better. That's the nature of things.'

'I have a bad feeling that the nature of things is changing,' Fowkes said softly. 'And I'm not sure I'm the man to lead us into that. I'm out of my depth. I'm not good enough.'

'It's thinking like that that makes you the right man.' Ted sniffed. 'And it's not what *you* think about you that counts; it's what the rest of us think. We're more objective, see?'

Fowkes half-smiled, then said, 'I keep thinking about that crack in the table. What happened with St John Golden? I don't think it was us putting an end to the Prophecy – I think it was just the beginning.'

Ted sipped his drink. 'I think you might be right, son.'

'Can we stop it, Ted?'

The old man felt every year of his age sink into his bones. This was a conversation he and Harlequin had had privately, many times, over the years. The very nature of a prophecy, if you chose to believe it, was that it *would* come to pass, and that meant trying to stop it was an impossible task. All a man could do was to look for the signs and prepare for it.

Be strong and ready. The question had always been whether they were believers or not, and neither he nor Harlequin Brown had ever been able to decide that, certainly not back in the days when they were both young men. In recent years, and after the events with Fowkes and Baxter, they'd become more circumspect. And now – well, Ted thought that if it was true, then the Prophecy was running at them like an out-of-control juggernaut.

'Maybe it's not about stopping it, son. It ain't a failure not to prevent something that was always going to 'appen. It's about 'ow you face things when they come at you. In 'ere' – he slapped his chest – 'where it counts.'

'That's the place that worries me.' For the first time, the Knight looked away from the window and directly at Ted. 'My heart's not as good as yours – it's not as good as anyone's. That's what scares me.'

'It don't 'urt to be suspicious of the world, and it don't 'urt to 'ave some deeds done that you ain't proud of. Trust me, we've all got 'em. Most people's are just more secret than yours.'

'I accused Joe of starting the fire at the Storyholder Academy. He didn't do it. I should have waited until there was some kind of evidence.'

'It was a fair assumption, things being as they are.'

'But not an assumption you'd have made.'

Ted said nothing. He felt for the boys. He'd looked after Fin in his own way since the lad had been found as a baby on that step. That alone made him want to trust the other two as much. Maybe Fowkes' way was wiser, but he was too old for mistrust.

'Whoever started that fire came from this London,' Fowkes said. 'The gatekeeper, Jacob Megram, he was found with his throat slit down an alley near a pub. It was probably supposed to look like a bungled mugging, but there was a patch of blood by the Doorway. He must have been attacked when

103

whoever it was came through. He wouldn't have been expecting trouble. He'd have been an easy target. I should have had someone with him.'

'What for? You didn't know trouble was coming, and we ain't exactly so flush with active Knights that we can spare one to guard a Doorway no one ever uses. What you've got to learn, Fowkes,' Ted's voice softened, 'is that you can't save everyone. We all take our own risks. Megram, God rest 'is soul, included.'

'But who is it, Ted? And how did they get to the Doorway?'

'I can't answer the first part, but I can the second.' Ted pulled a folded newspaper from his pocket. 'Tomorrow's first edition. Cardrew Cutler always goes out for it. Never sleeps, that man.' He turned four pages and pointed at a small article. 'See that? "Vandalism at London's 'eritage prison". The 'ouse of Detention was broken into.'

Fowkes scanned it and frowned. 'I should have had all the information before I accused Joe. He thinks I hate him, but I really don't. Tova's given him help in managing them, but he can't help but be changed by the stories. Without the other three, the two he's got, well, he's unbalanced, and they can't be good for him.'

'Surely then, that must go for the Storyholder as well?' They'd all been so worried about Joe, no one had given much thought to the effects on Tova with two of the stories missing. She'd been carrying all five for most of her life, so to suddenly be without two of them must be doing her some harm too.

'She *is* different,' Fowkes said, sadly. 'She's sleeping too much. She's not got any fire. Everyone needs some hate and pride to push themselves forward. Whatever she has naturally must seem like nothing, compared to when she was carrying those two stories. She needs them back. That's where they belong.'

'Yes, it is.' Ted drained his glass. 'But it ain't the kid's fault that they picked 'im and won't go back.'

'That's pretty much what Fin said.' Fowkes took his cloak from the back of the chair and clipped it round his neck. 'He's another one who bothers me.'

''e's a conundrum, that's for sure.' Ted smiled. He couldn't help it when he thought of Finmere. 'But he's a good 'un. You've just got to learn to let the cards be dealt and then figure out 'ow to play 'em. Not the other way round.'

Fowkes looked at him. 'Thanks, Ted.'

'You're welcome.' Ted gave the younger man a wink. He had faith in Fowkes. He was going to be a strong Commander.

'You go and get some sleep. I've got this meeting with the Traders.'

'I'll see what I can find out about this break-in. I'll wait till it's a respectable hour and call one of our police contacts. Should be able to find out something.'

Fowkes drew his sword, ready to cut through to The Nowhere, and then hesitated. 'Does Fin remind you of anyone?'

'No.' Ted frowned. 'Not that I can think. Why?'

'It's just some of the things he says ... and some of his mannerisms.' He looked for a moment as if he was going to say more, then shrugged. 'It's probably nothing. Like you said, sometimes I've got to let things play out.' He smiled at the old man and raised his sword. 'Let us be ready, Ted Merryweather.'

The nightwatchman tapped his hand to his forehead in a small salute. 'Let us be ready, Andrew Fowkes.'

ELEVEN

This time he stayed and watched. It had been a busy night, and he had fed from it well. For a while he had been fascinated by the glow of fire brightening the darkness, and he had cried at its comforting glory, but then the hunger had got too much and he had set about feeding. There were rich pickings to be had and now that his head was slowly growing clearer, he chose more carefully. Men and women rushed to and fro with buckets of water and food and talk. No one paid him any attention. He took one fat woman in the short stretch of alley between her house and an inn on the corner. Another he dragged into a shady doorway. The third had a screaming baby in her arms, but in all the noise one crying infant didn't raise any alarms. He didn't feed from it, though more from practicality than sentiment. How much energy could a tiny thing like that provide?

They had taken the child away, and the woman had not resisted. She had barely noticed, and as soon as her hands were free she began to fiddle with her hair as she giggled to herself. The person who took the baby wore thick gloves of crudely sewn leather, some sort of protection, maybe, as if perhaps she could catch some awful infection from the woman.

No one noticed him in the crowd. He no longer wore the clothes that had marked him for who he had been for so long. Instead, he'd scavenged some well-worn trousers and a rough tunic from a drying line, and he'd even found some shoes just inside an open doorway. He covered his head with a cowl. It kept out the bright daylight that irritated his eyes, and prevented anyone looking too closely at him. Not that anyone did. Perhaps there was something about him that made them look away. Maybe it was the stench of the water that must have seeped into his bones by now.

Whispers of bad magic rippled through the small crowd that the Borough Guardsman, armed with a pitchfork, was trying in vain to keep at a distance from the giggling woman. It wasn't surprising. As they watched, the woman's hair was turning from blonde to black, as if her hair had been dipped in a pot of ink and was sucking it up each strand like litmus paper. Her plait unravelled itself until it was hanging lank and limp around her shoulders. Her eyes were red orbs and her tongue flicked black against her lips.

'They'll be here to take her soon,' the Borough Guardsman shouted. 'Please stand back so the cart doesn't get held up. I don't want to have to arrest anyone for obstructing the course of justice. Literally.'

The crowd muttered some more and then took a few obliging steps back. He could feel their heat as they nudged by him, and for a moment a wave of hunger hit him and his tongue itched as if it might grow, but then it passed. No feeding in daylight. It wasn't right.

He was hungrier now than he had been when he first clawed his way back. At first he thought it was just that his strength was returning and demanding more energy, but now he wasn't so sure. He touched the stone that burned against his leg. He let his fingers caress it. That was what was making him hungrier: the little white piece of rock that had come all this way with him. It wanted something, and that made him need to feed. He could live with that. Feeding made him stronger, and the stronger he was, the more he could feel where the stone wanted him to go.

A cart with a wooden cage strapped to the back negotiated a way down the narrow, potholed track that served as a road for this part of London. The driver jumped down and stared impassively at the woman. 'Another one, then?' he said to the nearest Borough Guardsman. 'That's the fourth this morning.'

The guard shushed him, but it was too late, and the crowd

began to disperse, eager to carry that piece of gossip back to friends and relatives. He moved to slink away, to find somewhere to hide for the day, but paused as they lifted the woman from where she sat on the ground. It was her fingernails that caught his eye. They were as black as her hair and tongue. He glanced down at his own. Underneath the grime, black crescents bloomed on each nail, perfect half-moons growing out from the quick.

He stared at them, and then at her, and then turned away. The stone was making his leg itch and he wanted to sleep with it in his hand somewhere. The blackness could wait.

TWELVE

The door of The Red Lion was locked when they got there at ten, and after Fin gave a couple of polite but ineffective knocks, Joe took over and hammered hard on the thick wood. After a few seconds bolts slid back on the other side and Fin had barely stepped across the threshold before Ida Harvey had embraced him in a tight hug. She smelled of talcum powder and baking – the kind of scent that should be bottled and kept for times when you needed to feel that everything was okay when it very obviously wasn't.

'Look at you two,' she said, letting Fin go and pulling Joe in for his turn. Joe hugged her back, hard. Fin got the feeling that his friend needed it even more than he did. Ida Harvey looked the same as she had last time they'd met; her hair was set in curls that looked moulded rather than teased, and beneath her knee-length skirt she wore thickish brown tights that crinkled at the knees. This time she wasn't wearing bright red lipstick, and there were dark circles underneath her eyes.

'I'm sorry about Tilda,' Fin said, awkwardly. 'We saw her – you know, in the White Tower. It's terrible.'

'Thank you, lad.' Her eyes crinkled at the edges and she smiled sadly. 'It's her poor ma and pa and her young man my heart goes out to. She was a good girl, Tilda. She deserved a better life.'

It was good to be in the relative modernity of this part of town. Even the air smelled different – and Fin hadn't realised quite how draughty the Knights' headquarters were until he was back within the solid brick walls of the 1940s-style pub.

'I've got a surprise for you,' Mrs Harvey said, and dropped Fin a wink.

Fin tried to look pleased, but he wasn't sure how many surprises he could cope with. He was learning from experience that they weren't always good ones.

'Finmere!' A thickset woman with a ruddy, cheerful face bustled through from behind the bar and nudged her way past the other woman. 'Let me look at you properly then,' she said. She was pinching Fin's cheek before his brain put a name to the familiar face.

'Mrs Baker!' She looked different with her hair done like Mrs Harvey's.

'Oh, you can call me Maggie now – you're sixteen; you're nearly all grown-up.' She looked across to Joe. 'And young Joe Manning: you're looking well, lad.' She sighed, happily. 'It's good to see you both.'

Fin felt a surge of affection for the woman who'd been his landlady back in the Pardoner Street bed and breakfast.

'Your face looks a lot better,' Joe said. 'I'm glad.'

'Got two new teeth as well.' Maggie grinned. 'Look.' She pointed into the dark cavern of her mouth. 'Better than the originals.'

'Are you living here now? In the pub?' Fin asked.

'I'm in our old mam's place, just round the corner. I always knew I'd come back here at some point, most likely when you were done with school – it's probably a good job it was sooner rather than later. The poor old dear died two years ago and the place has been empty since. Took nearly a month to clear the smell of damp.' She leaned towards the boys. 'I couldn't live here with my big sister, could I? She'd drive me mad,' she whispered with a grin. 'No, I just come in and help her out with the pub lunches. I always was the better cook.'

Mrs Harvey made a harrumphing sound and the two sisters smiled affectionately at each other.

'Mrs Baker,' Fin started awkwardly.

'Call me Maggie, dear.'

'Maggie ... Well, thanks for everything you did for me. Looking after me.' He faltered, not sure exactly what to say next. Why was saying what you actually meant on the inside always so difficult?

'It was very kind,' he finished. It didn't really sum up the guilt he felt when he realised he'd never taken the time to get to know Mrs Baker – especially after Golden's men had hurt her so badly when they were trying to find him. Just thinking about it made him feel a little bit sick.

'Don't be daft, Fin. It was a pleasure.' She ruffled his hair. 'Never had any little ones of my own, so you're as close as I got.'

'Are you coming up or what?' Mona appeared at the bottom of the stairs at the side of the main bar. Her hands were on her hips and one small foot tapped. 'This wasn't the easiest of meetings to organise. Promptness would be appreciated.' She raised one eyebrow and stared at each of them, including Mrs Harvey. Fin almost laughed at the melodramatic gesture. Who ever really raised an eyebrow? It was just something people did in books. When people did try they mostly looked like they were trying to push out a somewhat unwilling fart – but it actually suited Mona. Of course, she was all about the melodramatic!

He watched as she turned and flounced back upwards and out of sight. Flounced wasn't quite the right word, stomped would be more accurate, if the sound of her feet thumping on the wooden stairs was anything to go by.

Fin looked at Joe and grinned as he rolled his eyes. 'Good luck to Christopher with that one,' Joe said. 'He's going to be *whipped*.'

'He'll be her be-atch,' Fin joined in.

That made Joe laugh out loud, and as they climbed the stairs side by side and giggling, for the first time in what felt like a very long time, Fin thought that maybe everything would work out okay for his friends.

Upstairs in The Red Lion was a function room, available to hire. There was a smell of beer and tobacco in the air, and it was filled with men. They were dressed in two very different kinds of uniforms: the knights wore their usual spotless white shirts, black trousers and polished boots, and each had a gleaming sword at his side, contrasting with the Traders, with their unshaven faces, rough wool sweaters and heavy leather jackets. The two groups eyed each other warily. Mona, standing between them, looked even smaller than normal. She was talking to one of the Traders, and the man had to bend quite a way to hear her. She was clearly not quite as shouty with them as she was with Fin and his friends.

They spotted Christopher, sitting at a round table in the corner, and hurried over to join him. Albert Harvey was delivering pints of grey-frothing ale to the gathered crowd, but Fin thought it might take more than a couple of drinks to ease the tension. The Knights sipped politely, while the Traders took long draughts from their glasses. Fin looked around at the fearsome men who held most of The Nowhere's population in their thrall. No wonder the Prince Regent didn't like them much; they had a dangerous glamour that even he couldn't match. The Traders could go South, across the River Times, a journey through the mist that for all normal folk would end in madness.

'They're looking at me funny,' Joe said.

'No, they're not, I think they're looking at *me* funny. Or maybe that's just what they do. It's not all about you, you know.' Fin tried to keep his tone light, but he couldn't deny that the low hubbub of voices had fallen silent when they'd come in, and more than one pair of eyes had settled warily on Joe. He'd seen the occasional glance fall to his own sword, but it wasn't the same kind of looks Joe was getting. Those really weren't friendly.

'Can we sit here?' Fin asked Christopher, 'or do you want to be alone with your *girlfriend*?'

'Oh, you're funny.' Christopher blushed slightly though, and Joe's sharp eyes didn't miss it.

'Has she got you a coke and a packet of crisps to keep you busy while she does all the important stuff?' Joe tugged a stool out and sat down. 'Got a comic to read?'

'Ha bloody ha. She's not my girlfriend, anyway.'

'Not yet, but you're definitely trying.'

'Unless of course she's knocked you back.' Joe winked at Fin.

'You two leave the poor boy alone,' Mrs Harvey chuckled as she put three glasses down in front of them. It wasn't beer, unfortunately, but juice of some kind. Fin figured Mrs Harvey was going to make them wait the full year before they got to taste that warm, grey froth.

'Nothing wrong with a bit of romance, eh?' She ruffled Christopher's hair and he looked as if he were ready for the ground to open up and swallow him whole. 'Don't you let these two bother you. They're just jealous.'

'Yeah, right,' Joe said, slightly too sharply, 'like either of us would want to go out with her. She'd be a nightmare!'

'Whatever you say.' Ida Harvey was still smiling as she walked away, but Fin glanced over at Joe. Looked like he *was* a bit jealous. Fin hadn't even realised that Joe fancied Mona – there definitely hadn't been any clues like with Christopher. Joe was looking down at his shoes and biting his bottom lip. Maybe he wasn't jealous of Christopher with Mona as such, Fin concluded; it was more that Christopher had something that he didn't. That just wasn't like Joe, though. He wasn't the jealous type, and he didn't harbour grudges, not like some people did.

Fowkes clapped his hands together and called the

gathering to quiet. 'I'd like to thank Mona Savjani for her part in persuading the Traders to come here today, and Albert and Ida Baker, for letting us use their room.' He nodded over at the couple, who were standing in the far corner by the stairs. 'We've all had a long night dealing with the fire at the Academy, and I know the Traders worked as hard as we did against the blaze. That in itself is a crime that needs investigating, but we have another pressing issue: these attacks on the citizens of this city. I think most of you now know that the Storyholder foresaw them in a fevered vision, and this makes both us of the Order and the Prince Regent convinced that they must harbour some danger for all of the worlds.' He took a sip of his beer. 'Four more have been found this morning, all in the same state as the previous victims.'

A mutter ran round the group of swarthy men sitting together on the left side of the room. It built into an aggressive growl.

'Enough.'

That single gruff word stilled the Traders.

It came from a man who was leaning against the side wall, his arms folded across his chest. His dark hair was combed straight back from his head and his eyes were sharp green. A thick white scar cut through the tan of his leathery face, starting at his hairline and carving across his nose and down through the stubble on his cheek before disappearing beneath his polo neck.

The whole room watched him as he reclined against the wall and looked at Fowkes. 'And you think this is something to do with us Traders?' he said.

'If I thought it was something to do with you, then we wouldn't be having this meeting.' Fowkes took another swallow. Of all the Knights present, he was the only one drinking with any enthusiasm. Old habits obviously died hard. 'You must be Curran Tugg, leader of the Traders. I've heard a lot about you. Not all of it good.'

114

'Funny thing that, Andrew Fowkes. I could say exactly the same about you.'

The air crackled with tension as the two groups waited to see how the interchange played out. The meeting suddenly felt as if it could quickly descend into one hell of a pub brawl. Fin didn't fancy the Knights' chances – Harper Jones was at the Storyholder's apartments, watching over her, and Lucas Blake and Benjamin Wakley had gone back to The Somewhere to continue investigations into the arson attack. As much as Henry Wakley's eyes were twinkling at the prospect of a fight, the Knights were down in numbers compared to the Traders.

'But in my case, all of it's true,' Fowkes said.

Curran Tugg burst into a sudden laugh, and a gold tooth flashed in the side of his mouth. 'At least you're an honest man – with yourself, at any rate.'

The Trader's accent was strange – not quite London, but a sort of Cockney with an occasional Manchester twang. Did they all speak like that? Was it something they picked up in the mysterious South?

'There are only two groups of people who can move round this city without feeling any effects,' Fowkes continued, 'you and us. If it's not you and it's not us, then there's now a third party with that ability – maybe a one-off, like young Mona here. If we work together, we will have a better chance of catching whoever – or *what*ever – is responsible for these attacks before too many more people are hurt.'

Curran Tugg sniffed, and his eyes narrowed. 'You Knights are always so keen to be involved in Nowhere business. Us Traders, we like to mind our own. We don't do what the Regent commands, nor do we follow your Order. We're river people.' Barks of support came from his men, who thumped their beer glasses down on the tables.

'Well, this is your business, whether you like it or not.' Fowkes ignored the crowing. 'The people are scared – you've heard the rumours out there as much as we have – in fact, I'll

115

bet you hear them first most of the time. Don't tell me that Trading isn't down at the moment, for that would make a liar of you. Those of the population who don't think these attacks are down to us are convinced you've brought something bad back with you from the South.'

A derisive laugh came from one of the Traders.

'I'm just telling it like it is,' Fowkes said. 'It won't hurt you to be seen to be helping to get to the bottom of this nastiness. And the people respect you – right now they have more faith in you than in us, I fear. You're their own, or as close as makes no difference.'

'We haven't brought nothing back other than our normal orders. No livestock – they never make it across the water alive anyway. And none of us is sick, so if it *is* an illness, then it's not us spreading it. But you *are* right: this *is* harming us.' Tugg lit a long brown cigarette and the sweet scent of warm liquorice filled the air. 'These victims are giving me a bad feeling in my bones. Even the water seems to be flowing wrong. Between the attacks and the fire last night, it's a rum business, sure enough.'

He pushed himself away from the wall and moved to stand alongside the Knights' Commander. 'All right, Andrew Fowkes, we'll work with you – for now, at least. Any man who can survive in the Crookeries for as long as you did must have something to him.' He nodded at two of his men. 'Tables.'

The Traders leapt to their feet and pushed four of the small square tables together.

'Now, I don't know about you,' Tugg said, looking at Fowkes, 'but the way I reckon it, the first thing we need to do is see where these attacks happened. All at night, is that right?'

'All found at dawn.'

Tugg sniffed again. 'When the mist is highest. Bad business. No wonder the dandy's worried.'

Fin saw Mona bristle slightly at the dig to her boss, but she wisely kept her mouth shut.

'Elbows?' Tugg said. 'Give it over.'

A stocky man whose elbows weren't on show so Fin couldn't see whatever had prompted the nickname opened a leather case and pulled out a small folded sheet. As one, Fin, Christopher and Joe got out of their seats and crept forward to join those now gathered around the tables. The item had looked quite small at first, but as the Traders' leader opened it up, each square layer revealed more folds beneath. By the time he had finished, the leathery paper was stretched across all four of the tables. Fin couldn't believe how something that big could have come from so small a package, but he didn't see any surprise on anyone else's faces, so he let his own slip away. This was The Nowhere after all, and nothing was ever quite ordinary, however it might look at first.

The sheet was grubby, greasy fingerprints covering its surface, and for a moment Fin wondered what the point of it was – if they wanted to write things down, then surely an ordinary notebook would have done the job better. He glanced over at Christopher, who shook his head; he didn't get it either. Then Joe nudged his attention back.

'Look,' he whispered.

As Curran Tugg smoothed the crinkles out, lines and words were slowly appearing, almost as if ink was seeping through from the other side, and streets took shape and were named in careful calligraphy. The process started speeding up as it progressed, as if the map had taken a minute or two to wake up. Finally, two large words were clear on the surface: The North.

Fin stared at the completed picture. At the bottom, the curve of the river signalled the end of the map, and above it all the Boroughs of London were spread out. Along with each name, the streets contained a variety of different symbols – squares and stars and odder shapes that Fin had no names for. There hadn't been any of those on the map the Harveys had given them when they were looking for Mitesh Savjani's shop on their first visit to The Nowhere. This was a much bigger map, and unlike the Harveys', it didn't have a 'You are here' sign suspended over their current location. Maybe the Traders would be a little insulted at having such basic information pointed out to them.

The tables shook for a moment, and then the ink on the vast page stretched upwards into the smoky air of the pub, until the buildings running along the edges of the streets were visible in tiny 3D. Fin stared. He could see the very black White Tower down towards the right-hand corner, and the deserted Borough of West Minster with its ruined cathedral at the other end. At various points spread through the city there were small patches of smog hanging, marking the nineteenth century Boroughs. With a flick of his wrist Tugg brushed them aside and they crumpled into nothing at his touch.

'Have you got a map like this of the South?' The question was out before Fin had realised it wasn't just a thought, and he shrank back slightly as all the rugged men turned to look at him.

'Maps of the South don't read here. And vice versa.' Elbows stared at Fin as if he were stupid.

'Did the Magi make them?' Christopher asked. He wasn't blushing like Fin, and he didn't even look up from examining the city laid out in sepia before them. Once again Fin envied his friend's confidence. Christopher had always been able to hold his own with adults, while Fin just came away feeling like a stupid kid every time he tried opening his mouth in a room full of blokes.

'The mapcrafters make them,' Elbows snapped. 'Do you know nothing?'

'He sounds like Mona,' Joe whispered, and Fin grinned, though the smile fell when he realised that Curran Tugg was

118

staring directly at him. An uncomfortable hush settled across room.

'You,' the Trader said. Fin could see his eyes were seaweed-green with flecks of gold at the centre. 'You're the one they talk about.'

Fin squirmed where he stood.

'The Nowhere boy from The Somewhere. Even the Magi don't understand you. They've heard of you everywhere.'

'Yeah,' Joe said, 'Fin's the special one. Everyone wants to be around Finmere Tingewick Smith.' He finished it with a small laugh, but Fin could feel the barb in the remark. What was the *matter* with Joe? He wasn't like this ...

'Oh, they talk about you too,' Tugg said, turning his attention to Joe. He raised one heavily jewelled finger. 'They talk in whispers, here, and in the South. They think you are trouble.'

'If we could just get on with the business at hand and leave the boys alone, that would be good.' Fowkes glowered at the Trader. 'They've done nothing wrong.'

'No.' The Trader straightened up. 'No, but doing wrong or not has no hold over trouble. Trouble's its own master.'

'Oh please, just stop.' Mona hadn't spoken yet, and her voice sounded young compared with the gruff barks of the two men. 'No one is in any position to make judgements here – especially not against those three. They did all they could to help in the recent troubles. So let's just do what we're supposed to be doing, shall we?' She stepped forward between the two men. 'Right. The first victim was found here ...' A slim finger stabbed at a side street not far from where they currently were. Tugg pulled a pencil from the inside of his jacket and marked an X where Mona indicated. Although Fin saw him press the lead to the paper, the mark appeared a little above the actual street, hovering rather like the smog had done. It was black, rather than the sepia brown of the map.

'And the second was found here,' Mona continued, pointing at a completely different part of the city.

Forty minutes later, they were all staring at the nine Xs spread across the map. Many of the Traders were smoking, and a pall of sweet-smelling smoke clung to the low ceiling of the room, drifting downwards in curious wisps that formed a new smog across the strange parchment.

'These are definitely the deeds of a Travelling man,' Tugg said, ominously. 'Even the four attacks last night are in different Boroughs.'

'It can't be a Knight,' Fowkes said. 'Taking the trust issues out of the picture, we're just too thin in numbers these days and I can account for every one of my men at the times of the attacks. But ...' He took a long drink of his second pint while he thought for a moment. 'But it could be a Somewhere man. Or woman.'

'They'd need a sword.' Tugg's eyes narrowed. 'Everyone knows that.'

'No, not always,' Fowkes said. His face had darkened. 'The original doorway between our two worlds is below ground, in the basement of an old building in our world. It's kept locked up, to keep the doorway safe. It has come to my attention that there has been a break-in there.'

A ripple of dismay ran through the small group of Knights, and Finmere felt both Joe and Christopher stiffen slightly.

'And there's more,' Fowkes continued. 'The Gatekeeper, Joseph Megram, has been found murdered. His throat was cut.'

Fin gasped. He couldn't help himself. Poor Joseph Megram – he was just a friendly butcher who'd inherited the post from his dad; he wasn't a Knight or anything, he wasn't even involved in anything that had happened over the past few months, except to check the coin that opened the Gate and let them pass.

Fin wasn't the only one to feel shocked. Christopher had paled, and Joe's eyes were so wide Fin thought his eyeballs might fall out.

'I hate to say it, but whoever burned down the Storyholder Academy probably came from our world, and that raises a lot of fresh questions that I would really prefer not to have to think about, but must. If they could be responsible for that, then maybe they're something to do with this.' He gestured at the map. Fin really felt for him. Fowkes might have been damaged by what happened in his youth, but he was a proud man, and if Fin was feeling a slow burn of shame that once again The Somewhere was causing damage in The Nowhere, then for Fowkes it must be a hundred times worse.

'When they're found, Smithfield's too good for them,' Tugg muttered. 'I'll pin them out at Traitor's Gate, like in the old days. Justice the Traders' way.'

'Trust me, we'll help you.'

'But this can't be anything to do with us,' Christopher blurted. 'We don't have anything like this back home – you've seen those people in the White Tower. Something *else* did that to them.'

'Maybe – and you're right, we don't have anything like this in The Somewhere,' Fowkes agreed. 'But the problem is that it doesn't sound like they have anything like it here, either.'

Something in that sentence jarred in Finmere's head. He wanted a second of silence, just to let it take shape. All he could manage, before the conversation moved on, were two words: *Sherlock Holmes*. And that didn't really answer any questions, however much he thought they should.

'If only we could figure out why the attacks happened in *these* places,' Mona said, sweeping her hand across the map, 'then at least we could beef up the presence of the Borough Guard where we think new attacks might happen.'

'I can't see any sort of pattern, though.' Fowkes ran a hand through his untidy hair. 'Apart from the attacks all taking place in side streets rather than main thoroughfares – which hardly comes as a surprise – I can't see anything special about any of these sites.'

'I don't know all of these places very well.' Simeon Soames stepped forward, frowning. Fin still found it odd to see him so young after shaving his aged face every year. There was nothing watery about his sharp eyes now.

'But the streets don't look so pleasant,' the Knight continued. 'They're like little pockets of slums in the middle of nice areas. It's strange.'

'The river—' Tugg and Elbows spoke in unison.

'But it can't be that,' Mona said. 'Most of these places aren't anywhere near the river.'

'Not the Times.' Tugg was shaking his head and Elbows was nodding as excited murmurs started amongst the Traders.

'Not the Times,' Tugg repeated, 'but the Lost Rivers – the forgotten waterways. They run underground. They all lead into the Times, but their power isn't as strong as that primary river.'

Mona looked just as confused as the boys felt, and Fowkes voiced their thoughts when he asked, 'What are you talking about?'

'There used to be – well, there still are – several smaller rivers, all across London, tributaries of the Times. The Magi and the Early People built over them, but they still flow, and where they run, their strangeness seeps upwards. The streets never stay clean or in good repair, and the buildings are always shabbier. Generally people softer in the mind end up living in those places.'

'But if they're all built over, how can they be any sort of influence over where these attacks are happening?'

'There are manholes,' Elbows cut in, obviously impatient for the non-Traders to catch up. 'They're mostly forgotten, but they were put in to allow access down to the water. What the boss is saying: whoever's doing this might be using the water to move around the city and come up through the manholes.' He paused and then squinted slightly at his boss. 'I got that right, didn't I?'

'Yes, you did.' The Trader leader lit another thin cigarette. 'But I don't know how they're managing it; those rivers are like a maze down there, and they ain't all that safe. Things live in those waters, or so the stories go.' He stopped short and then looked up. 'Only one group of people know those rivers well. Should have thought of them straight away.'

'Who's that?' Fowkes asked.

'The Gypsy Traders.'

'Never heard of them.'

'They keep themselves to themselves. They don't hold with the Regent, or the way of life up here. They try and keep to the old ways – they still trade, but they don't pay no taxes and they don't care what they bring to and from if the money's right. Maybe *they* brought something bad back from the South?'

That Sherlock Holmes thought itched again in Fin's brain. He wished it would just work itself out. He had a feeling it was important.

'Sounds like the kind of people I might have come across in the Crookeries,' Fowkes said. 'How come I didn't?'

'They use their own networks of people. They know the Regent will come after them if they start showing themselves up top. They're like ghosts. Even us ordinary Traders don't think about them much – no one does. It's kind of like they don't exist. They like it that way.'

'We do need to talk to them, though. Can you organise a meeting?'

He shook his head. 'It ain't that simple. We'll have to go down there and find them.'

Fin couldn't help the shiver of excitement that ran through him at the thought of underground rivers and Gypsy Traders.

'But not him.' Curran Tugg pointed a heavily ringed finger

at Joe. 'They'll slit his throat to set the stories free rather than have them somewhere they don't belong. We take him and they won't trust us; we'll be lucky to ever see the surface again.'

Fin's mouth dropped open, but Joe laughed before he could speak. It wasn't a nice laugh. There was too much hurt in it. 'It's all right,' Joe said, as the whole room looked at him. 'Hanging out on the stinking river isn't my idea of fun anyway. I've got other stuff to do.'

'It ain't personal, boy.'

'Nothing ever is, is it?'

The Trader didn't answer that but looked down again at the map. 'Me and Elbows will lead. We'll take two of your Knights, the Regent's girl and the two boys. No more. If we've got that Finmere with us then maybe they'll be curious. The Gypsies love people with talk of Destiny about them, and they trust the young more than the old, so perhaps they'll let us parlay.'

'If we can find them,' Elbows added.

'If we can find them.'

'We'd best send someone for the compactables,' Tugg said. 'And someone flask up these Somewhere folk a beer each. The boys too. We'll stay away from the Times, but they'll still need something for their nerves down there.'

THIRTEEN

Joe didn't wait around to see them all get excited about their stupid journey underground. Fin and Fowkes had followed him down the stairs, but he'd slapped a sickly grin on his face and shrugged them off. Fowkes had even tried to apologise for his accusations, and although Joe had told him it was all okay, he couldn't get out of The Red Lion fast enough. The last time he'd been there it had been him, Finmere and Christopher against the world, but now he just felt like a leper wherever he went. They all just wanted him to sit quietly twiddling his thumbs in the Storyholder's apartments, where they could be sure that he wouldn't cause any trouble.

He gritted his teeth and stormed through the streets, his head down, barely noticing where he was going as his brain raged. He left his feet to find their own way as he pushed through people unfortunate enough to be coming in the other direction while going about their business.

Well, if that's what they all wanted then he *would* go back to the Storyholder's apartments, but if they thought they could contain him, they were *wrong*. Let them go off on their stupid hunt for secret tribes on hidden rivers – he had his own destiny to fulfil, and Mr Arnold-Mather was waiting for him to start putting it into practice. They all thought that *Finmere* was so special – but it wasn't Fin who had the stories, was it? They were backing the wrong horse, and it was only Mr Arnold-Mather who was clever enough to see it. He was even putting Joe ahead of his own son. Maybe one day Mr

Arnold-Mather could be a kind of dad, Joe thought, replace the one who ran out so many years ago.

But even in his anger, he couldn't quite get his head round that thought. The cold politician was a far cry from his own mum, with her ready smile and loud sense of humour. What would she make of what he was about to do? Deceiving his friends? Going against the wishes of the Knights? She wouldn't be happy. He felt a trickle of shame that almost turned into a tear, but he bit it back. His mum also said that you had to decide on the side of right and stick to it – so maybe his side *was* the right side? And it wasn't as if anyone was actually going to get hurt, was it? Would she mind that much? The voice in his head that wasn't tinged with red or black knew the answer to that: of course she would. That voice – the real Joe – wasn't getting much airplay, though. The stories were far too strong for it.

He missed his mum. He wanted to be back in the cold, crisp air of the London he loved, where even the gangs on the estate would be mellowing for Christmas. Still, if he did what Mr Arnold-Mather asked then he'd be able to see his mum. That's what he'd promised. Christmas was only days away, he was pretty sure of that, and he was also sure that Mr Arnold-Mather wasn't the sort of man to wait forever for Joe to do what he asked.

Harper Jones and the Borough Guard had set up a strong security barrier around the Old Bailey House of Real Truths, and there was a sign on a big A-board outside the main entrance doors stating that the building was closed for the day due to 'unforeseen circumstances'. As he headed round to the side door he wondered why they'd bothered. It wasn't as if the sign was needed. Firstly, no one in The Nowhere ever visited the House, because Real Truths could be too hard to take, and secondly, everyone in the city must have heard about the fire at the Storyholder Academy by now, and they'd have to be really stupid not to see that all of this was just about protecting the one Storyholder that the worlds had left. Or the only one they acknowledged anyway, even if she was damaged goods.

He paused for a few minutes to answer Jones' questions about the meeting with the Traders, trying to appear enthusiastic, and then as soon as he could, he claimed to have a sudden headache. At Jones' expression of sympathy he said he just wanted to go to bed, but Joe had seen the shutters come down suddenly in the Knight's eyes. For a few moments they'd been just two blokes, chatting, and he'd forgotten that Joe had two of the Five Eternal Stories in him, but with the mention of the headache, all that concern and mistrust was back.

Still, Joe thought, taking the stairs two at a time and nodding at the new Knight outside the door to the Storyholder's rooms, he had the headaches under control these days. He was ready for what he had to do, he was sure of it. How hard could it be?

Inside it was so quiet that even the air had been drifting in a doze until he closed the door behind him and sent a ripple of disturbance through it. He peered through the gap of the Storyholder's bedroom door. She looked like a porcelain doll, propped up against the pillows, with her hair spread out against the white material.

She didn't open her eyes, even to acknowledge him. As far as Joe could see – and he was around Tova far more than anyone else – she was getting worse since they'd brought her back from The Somewhere with two of the stories now in him. The stump where her tongue had been had healed weeks ago and although her time in the Incarcerator mirror had been tough, it hadn't caused any physical damage. But she spent most of her days in bed and it was clear she was getting weaker, suffering from some mysterious ailment that was draining her strength.

In the kitchen he made them both a hot chocolate, using

the small sweet chocolate bombs that were so popular in this London, and when the drinks were ready he took the two capsules Christopher's dad had given him out of his pocket and emptied the powder from them into one of the cups. His hands were shaking, and one of the small plastic halves rolled away and got lost at the edge of the cupboard by the white waste bin. His palms sweated as he stirred the frothy liquid carefully. Why was he so scared? Anyway, maybe doing this would actually help her? And more than that, said the voice inside his head that he didn't quite recognise as his own, no one will ever know you had anything to do with it. The words wrapped around his nerves like a coiled snake and his pounding heart slowed as he picked up the mugs. His hands no longer trembled and the liquid stayed steady as he walked back to the Storyholder's room.

'Tova?' he said, softly.

Her eyes fluttered open and she smiled and raised one hand in a weak wave.

'I thought you'd like a hot chocolate.'

Joe took a sip of his own and waited for her to pull herself into a more upright position before handing hers over. She took the first sip and Joe began to tell her all about the meeting with the Traders. He talked slowly, wanting to make sure that she finished the whole mug, rather than just sipping it politely and then leaving half of it. She listened carefully, smiling and laughing here and there as he embellished the story with quips from Fowkes or Fin. From inside his head it was like listening to someone else – or maybe the new person was on the inside, and the real one was the enthusiastic teenager telling the story. He didn't want to think about that too long.

By the time he took the empty mug from her hands her eyes were drifting shut. The sleeping pills worked fast, dragging her all the way down into unconsciousness, rather than just the light doze that was how she spent most of the day now.

Joe watched her sadly for a few moments. There was no going back now. He took a deep breath and then started to concentrate. He had a feeling it would be easier than anyone was expecting.

FOURTEEN

Christopher hung back, not wanting to catch up with Finmere, who was talking to Fowkes, no doubt getting instructions to behave themselves and do whatever Lucas Blake and the geeky new ginger Knight told them to. He was glad the Commander of the Order wasn't coming with them; he was going to go back and take over the investigation in The Somewhere. Lucas Blake wasn't as suspicious of everyone as Fowkes was, and Christopher felt sick enough about the House of Detention break-in without having to worry about Fowkes noticing something was wrong with him.

He tried to wipe the mud of the street off one shoe with the heel of the other, but just succeeded in making the first dirtier – the story of his life. He knew he should have said something about his dad ages ago, when he'd first realised, but if he spoke up now, what would they think of him for not saying anything earlier? It wouldn't be good – just look at how differently they were all treating poor Joe, and he hadn't even done anything wrong. If Christopher told them he was pretty sure that his dad had been St John Golden's secret partner, and was probably behind the break-in at the doorway then they'd kick him out for sure. He just couldn't do it, even though the thought that his own father had been involved in killing Jacob Megram made his blood curdle. If he did tell, it would mean no more adventures, no more Fin, and no more—

'Can I come in a compactable with you?'

—Mona. His stomach did a small flip. He couldn't help it. It wasn't like he'd never kissed a girl before or anything; he'd had his fair share of snogs and fumbles at various posh school dances, but he'd never had this weird feeling about someone before. He'd never wanted to actually *talk* to a girl before. As well as kiss her. And he *really* wanted to kiss her. After everything with the Magus and his dad, Christopher hadn't thought anything would make him feel better, and then, all of a sudden, there was Mona again, and she was different too. More grown-up. Maybe they both were.

'So? Can I?' Her foot tapped impatiently and she frowned. 'Hello?'

''course you can.'

'Good.' She smiled, and Christopher's face moved to mimic the gesture. He wasn't sure he managed it.

'I mean, it's not that I'm scared or anything, because I Travel fine – I bet I've got Trader blood in me – but I've never actually been on the river. And I know they say these Lost Rivers aren't the same' – she looked over at Curran Tugg, who'd joined Fin and Fowkes further up the road – 'but if I'm going to go a little crazy and embarrass myself, then I'd rather it was with you.'

Christopher followed her gaze. The Trader gave Fowkes a hefty slap on the shoulder, as if they were suddenly brothers or best friends, and then Fowkes cut himself a way through to The Somewhere and disappeared. Tugg was still smiling approvingly as the black and white hole closed up. Trust was funny like that in The Nowhere. They were all ready to believe the best in each other, right from the start. It didn't take a lot to gain some trust – just a single honest word or deed. Back at home, it was all the other way round. He looked back at Mona. She looked so unafraid that he could tell she was more than a little scared under her bravado.

'Same as,' he said, 'although you mustn't go laughing at me if I go nuts.' He hadn't even thought about it until the

131

words were out, but the idea of totally humiliating himself in front of the outspoken girl made him feel like throwing up.

'I'd never laugh at you.' Mona frowned. 'You should know that. I don't know what happened at West Minster, but I know it wasn't an easy thing that you did. My dad says that nothing to do with the Magi is ever easy. And whatever you did, that Magus died doing it. It can't have left you with no scars, even if you won't ever talk about it.'

Christopher's skin prickled as she spoke, and for an awful moment he thought he might cry. He kicked the dirt, messing up his shoes some more.

'And whatever it is,' she continued, her voice soft and wise, a hint of the woman she might one day become, long after Christopher's foreshortened lifespan was up. 'I get a feeling you're not done with it yet, not in your head, anyway.' It was her turn to blush, red blotches spreading up under the collar of her fitted suit and clashing with her hair. 'I like you. I want to help make whatever it is better.' As the words came out she looked as if falling head first into the Times would be preferable to having said them. 'Anyway, we'd better get to the others. Lucas Blake will be here soon.' She turned to stride away.

'Mona ...' Christopher grabbed her arm. His face was burning and his heart threatened to explode out of his chest, but he couldn't stop now. Sometimes you just had to go with the moment. He'd gone with the moment at West Minster, and he'd made a snap decision when he'd seen that cigarette holder all those weeks ago – now he wanted to follow a snap decision that might just have some good consequences for him for a chance.

Behind them, Tugg let out a sharp whistle, but Christopher ignored it, pulling Mona round so that she was facing him.

'I like you too,' he blurted out. 'A lot.' Before he could talk himself out of it he leaned forward and kissed her. He almost missed her mouth, and there weren't tongues or anything,

132

but her lips were soft and warm and pretty much perfect, and as her blush matched his and she didn't immediately pull away, he grabbed her hand. 'Now we can go,' he said, his whole face tingling.

For once, Mona said nothing. Hand in hand, they made their way over to the Trader. A grin was splitting Christopher's face and he knew he probably looked as if the rivers had already worked their madness on him, but he didn't care. He felt better than he had in ages.

They found the entrance to the Lost Rivers around the corner from where Tilda had been attacked, no more than a couple of hundred metres from the pub's front door: a perfect square manhole, a few inches away from the gutter. The building in front of it was boarded up, and moss filled the gaps between the bricks.

'Here,' Elbows said as he crouched down and peered at it, 'you can see where the dirt's been disturbed. This has been opened recently.'

'Well, it's as good a place as any to start,' Curran Tugg said. 'We'll go in this way. You got chalk at your gaff?' He looked up at Albert Harvey, who nodded deferentially and scurried back to the pub to fetch it. 'We can mark the tunnels; that way we'll know if we're going round in circles.'

Fin was standing behind the Traders, looking up at the building when Christopher and Mona joined him. Their hands slipped apart.

'It's weird to think it's the rivers that have made this place so gross,' Fin said.

'Let's hope it doesn't have the same physical effect on us.' Christopher smiled. 'I don't want my good looks messed with.'

'Yeah, right, Frankenstein.' Fin snorted. He stopped and looked at Mona, who'd hung back around the Traders. 'Are you two, like, seeing each other now?'

Christopher shrugged. For a moment he almost thought he was looking cool about it, and then that cheesy grin spread itself right across his face again. 'I think so. I really like her.'

Fin looked like he might say something sarcastic, and then he stopped himself. 'I think she likes you, too.'

Christopher kicked the dirt again. They never really talked about girls – not properly, not beyond the usual 'how far did you get' stuff that went on after some inter-school dance or whatever.

'You going to stop being such a dick at school now? If you get expelled then it's going to be really dull when I have to go back for sixth form.'

'You reckon we will go back?' Christopher looked over to where Lucas Blake had appeared with the returning Albert. 'I just can't see myself going through A Levels after all this, can you? Just doesn't seem real.'

'It's all real, mate.' Fin said, 'here *and* there. And it's all important, that's the point. Sometimes I wish I'd never dragged you and Joe into all this. I wish I'd just left you both alone to get on with your lives. It's not exactly been fun all the way, has it?'

Christopher looked up from his shoes to find Fin was now staring down at his. 'You didn't *drag* us anywhere – we came because we wanted to. And it's been a whole lot more fun than school, even Joe must think that.'

'Yeah, but—'

'Anyway,' Christopher cut Fin off, 'you didn't get me involved. I think I already was. Now come on,' he grinned, before Fin could question him further, 'let's go and get on with this adventure. If you start wearing your pants on your head down there I'm going to so wish I had a camera.'

'No one will notice if *you* go mental,' Fin said. 'How would they? No change.'

'Very funny.'

Laughing, the boys stood either side of Mona as everyone

gathered around the manhole cover. Christopher felt his hair being ruffled, and looked up to see Lucas Blake winking at him. Elbows heaved himself to his knees, found the catch and lifted the hatch. Warm, damp air drifted up towards them, and even with the threat of madness that it carried, Christopher felt the excitement shimmer through him. He looked at the friends beside him: Knights and Traders alike, they were a team, and he couldn't give this up, not until he *really* had to. If it looked like his dad was planning something terrible, then he'd say something, but until then he was going to leave the Knights to find out about Justin Arnold-Mather themselves.

The air had settled into stillness once more – or perhaps it was something beyond still, the kind of quiet that happened only at moments like this, when something significant was going to change from one thing into another. It was like four o'clock in the morning, when the whole world had settled and was waiting, the moments between night and day were when the old were most likely to die, when things just let go and drifted away.

Joe's eyes were shut. He couldn't remember closing them, but neither could he remember when they were last open. The world was black behind them, not a single shadow darted across the filmy surface to remind him that his eyelids were there. He stared into a void, and darkness was all around him. After a while, he was sure he was floating.

Somewhere beyond, he could hear Tova's breathing. It was slow and steady, like the beat of an ominous drum. *Inhale*, *exhale*: he found that his breathing was matching hers, locking into her rhythm. Time passed, minutes or hours, and his limbs floated away. For a while he forgot it all, and just drifted in the darkness. There had been no sleeping drugs. There was no guilt, no greed, no envy. There was just a calm emptiness with nothing to dwell on, no sense of self, no Christmas, no football, no Somewhere or Nowhere, and no stories. For a long time there was only the void ... and then small stars flashed bright in the distance, three of them, winking at him from very far away. He drifted closer. At first he thought they were nothing more than sparks of light, but as they grew larger, he could make out colours: green, blue and white.

Tova gasped, and he knew that he did too. Their minds were locked in unison, just as everyone had wanted. How had he struggled, he would have wondered, if his brain were capable of that conscious thought. It had come so easily, so naturally. The colours were nearly filling his vision now, and the gasps had become stereo sobs. Although he cried with her, Joe's heart raced ahead of Tova's, the black and the red inside him twisting in anticipation. The remaining darkness trembled. *It was so nearly time ...*

Very few people ever saw inside the Prince Regent's private chambers, especially when the Prince himself was in residence. His valets were carefully chosen for their discretion and serious-mindedness; they tended to be of an unusually studious nature for men working in service, and when they were done bathing and dressing the Regent, they were allowed to scurry away to Alexander Palace's vast library, allowing their curiosity free reign in the examination of history and science, rather than gossip from the Regent's chambers. Not that there was much in the way of gossip for them to get excited about, but one day there might be, if – *when* – the first signs of madness came. Then he would need people around him who could be relied upon.

The bedroom was thirty feet long, and the ceilings were so high that dusting the chandeliers required the kind of ladder it took two men to carry, and was not a job to be undertaken by anyone with the slightest fear of heights. In fact, there had been talk in the servants' hall that the job should be allocated danger pay. No one had taken the suggestion to the head butler yet, but every time the ladders came out, the mutterings got louder.

This morning, however, the crystals glittered like stars overhead, shining perfectly after the previous day's polishing. The heavy midnight-blue velvet drapes that at night blocked out any hint of light from the city were pulled wide and bound back with silver cord. Sunlight streamed through the spotless glass windows that stretched from the floor almost to the ceiling. The window cleaners didn't think the chandelier polishers really had a great deal to complain about.

At the far end of the room, next to the double doors that led to an equally oversized bathroom, the huge four-poster bed was perfectly made, and under the selection of frockcoats and breeches laid out for his attention, there wasn't a crease to be seen on the expensive sheets that had been imported from the exotic South. The Prince Regent didn't like that some of his subjects could travel to areas that he himself couldn't, but he wasn't going to let that interfere with his love of a fine fabric. Some things were important, and appearances had to be maintained.

Mitesh Savjani, one of the few people allowed to see the Prince in a state of undress, twisted one corner of his precisely elaborate moustache. The jewels on his fingers flashed, and the purple stone in the centre of his beard twinkled merrily. His eyes, however, did not.

'If you don't mind me saying,' he said as he took a step closer to the small figure standing in front of the mirror, 'I do believe your Majesty has lost a little weight.' He pinched at the edges of the red satin knee-breeches. 'My measurements two weeks ago were exact. But now,' he said, 'they are a little too big.'

'I presume they can be adjusted?' With his chest bare and no high wig covering his short dark curls, the Prince looked nearer eighteen than thirty-eight. 'The ball is not until next week.' Unlike his forebears, who grew more insular with each birthday and refused any sort of celebration, the Regent insisted on gaiety to mark the passing of time. If madness was going to claim him when he reached forty, then that was his Fate – but he refused to go quietly. For his guests, with each year that went by the awkwardness grew, and it could be only partly masked by loud laughter and over-enthusiastic dancing to the awful Harpsichordian. Mitesh Savjani was busy creating extravagant gowns and plush frockcoats for most of the guests, and he knew how much these events were dreaded. He would not tell the Regent, though; instead, he told of the excitement and sleepless nights the guests had shared with him in the run-up to the glorious Birthday Ball. One night of discomfort for them was nothing compared to the burden the slight man before him had to carry.

'The trouser can always be adjusted,' he said, softly. 'But what of the cause?'

The Prince Regent looked away from the mirror and into the concerned eyes of his clothcrafter. 'You are a fine man with a needle, Mitesh Savjani.' The high-pitched words came out clipped. 'But you are a finer friend.' He let out a long sigh. 'I have been having dreams,' he admitted, 'and they wake me every hour. I dream of Black Storms – not the kind we have seen before, but far worse, even than when the Knight Adam Baxter died. A true Black Storm.'

He slumped onto a velvet chaise longue, but rather than adopting the effeminate pose expected of him by his courtiers, he leaned forward, his arms resting on his knees and his hands clasped. The more masculine stance was a rare glimpse of the man who truly lived behind the pale make-up and dandified clothes. 'Sometimes I dream that I am the only sane man in a castle full of madness.'

'Dreams often mean nothing, other than an expression of our own inner fears.' Mitesh Savjani knew his words had little comfort for a man who was most likely only a year away from losing his own sanity.

'I understand that,' the Prince said, 'and I have thought the same, especially as we both know that it is far more probable that I shall be the only madman in a palace of the sane but ...' He hesitated, then continued softly, 'I cannot shake off this presentiment, that something wicked this way comes.'

'Do you fear the Prophecy, Your Majesty?' Savjani sat down alongside the much smaller man. As his weight made him sink into the upholstery he saw the Prince Regent shifting to remain upright – a major breach in Royal protocol punishable by imprisonment, at the very least. Both men ignored it.

'Yes, Mitesh Savjani,' the Prince whispered, almost to himself, 'yes, I do believe I do.'

As he spoke, thunder rumbled across the clear sky outside and they looked up, frowning, confused by the unexpected sound. They got up in unison and moved to the window, and gazed out, first down at the city beyond the gates to check that it hadn't been hit by a new explosion, and then up to the sky. The sun was still shining brightly, but in the midst of it, the clothcrafter thought he saw a flash of white jag across the blue sky. Moments later there was another unmistakable growl of thunder.

A storm in a clear sky.

Neither the Regent nor his clothcrafter spoke. They didn't need to. Something very bad indeed was happening out there.

Joe didn't hear the thunder that crashed across the sky the instant his eyes snapped open. He didn't hear anything, other than the torrent of sound that rushed inside his head, a cacophony of noise – voices, music, the sounds of nature, and so many other things, all wound into an unholy orchestra. Colour flooded through every inch of his body in a lightning bolt of electricity that he was sure had stopped his heart. He had been thrown from his place on the bed and thudded against the wall by the sheer force of the Five Eternal Stories reconnecting inside him. For a long moment he was sure his head would explode from the pain and the pressure and the storm within.

Tova sat bolt upright on the bed, her eyes wide in alarm, whatever effect the sleeping pills should have been having on her now lost in the shock to her system. Joe, pinned to the ground, watched her mouth drop open, but the view was distorted, as if he was seeing through a bubble, a film of something *other* between him and the world.

Beneath him the building trembled, and as he finally gasped air into his desperate lungs, his head flicked suddenly towards the door. People were coming – Knights, and Borough Guardsmen, rushing up the white stairs below. He wasn't sure how he knew this when the noises ripping through his brain were far too loud for him to have heard anything, but he knew it anyway.

They musn't come in, not yet. That other voice, his new voice, was stronger now, and as soon as the words were thought, all the doors in the Old Bailey slammed shut. A breeze touched his face, and it felt like cool water. He ignored the shouts of frustration and alarm. They could all stay outside. He knew without a doubt that even were they to attack the doors with a battering ram, the wood would hold until he decided otherwise. He almost laughed. He almost cried. There was so much power in his fingertips that he wanted to tear his own face off and scream until the end of eternity.

For a long time he sat against the wall with his heavy, overburdened head in his hands. After a while, the cacophony settled enough to allow the calmer music of the outside world in. Tova was sobbing. That was the first thing he really heard. It wasn't loud and hysterical, but soft, and low, and almost devoid of energy: it was the sound of true grief, of someone scraped empty. He looked up. The whiteness around him was flecked with all the colours of the rainbow. When he'd had only two of the stories inside him he'd thought he'd understood the need for the whiteness everywhere in her apartments. He hadn't. Now he had all five, even the white was full of teasing flashes of colour, and whenever his eyes lingered too long on one place, words and emotions rose unbidden in his head. He would go mad; he knew it.

From somewhere in the apartments he heard a low howl, the sound of a fatally wounded wild animal, like an injured wolf on a frozen winter's night. There were more pictures in his head, all stories ... It was only when Tova scrambled from the bed and joined him on the floor, wrapping her arms around his head and crying with him, did he realise that the terrible sound was coming from him.

Her hands were hot on his head and for a moment he felt overwhelmingly jealous of her emptiness, even though it was he who had brought it about. His pulse throbbed through his veins and in its beat were the stories, and everything they carried in them. He wondered what he had done. He wondered how he would cope, and if he would ever manage to control the stories before they completely overran him. He knew where to find the second thing that Mr Arnold-Mather had wanted from him, but wasn't sure he cared any longer. He let his own tears flow.

The Storyholder – no, *he* was the Storyholder now – *Tova's* hands fell away from him, and for the first time he was aware of the rumbling storm outside. He looked up at the window. The sky was blue, and yellow lightning was streaking across it. He thought it was beautiful. It calmed him. He smiled and turned to Tova, expecting to see the same expression on her face, but her mouth had fallen open in horror. He could see the awful scarred stump of her tongue inside. He realised then that she was a fool.

Change was coming, and it would be beautiful, and terrible, and *his*. His fingers tingled. Eventually the doors opened and the Knights and the guards came rushing in, but Joe just kept staring out at the miraculous sky.

PART TWO

PART TWO

FIFTEEN

It was hard to believe that just a few feet above their heads were the bustling streets of The Nowhere's London – at least Fin thought they were a few feet overhead. It had felt that way when they'd climbed down into the compactables – which had turned out to be The Nowhere equivalent of inflatable dinghies, except that they were made out of wood and didn't inflate, so quite how they'd sprung out of (or would fold back into) the small rucksacks they'd come in left Fin baffled. But now the damp walls stretched much higher above them, curving into dark arches overhead. It was hard to tell whether they were getting deeper underground as they paddled, but it felt likely – if not, then there'd be far more slums in weird places where the rivers ran too close to the surface, he supposed. But it felt strange to be sinking further away from the city on river water. At least it wasn't the mist-covered foulness of the Times.

It was a small group who had climbed down the rungs and into the musty air of the tunnels below. Curran Tugg stood, perfectly balanced, at the front end of Fin's boat – the bow, he'd called it – while Alex Currie-Clarke and another Trader shared the rowing between them. On their right Elbows mirrored Tugg's position in the second compactable, with Lucas Blake and Christopher at the oars and Mona watching from the stern. They moved at a gentle pace, with no real exertion required from the rowers, and every so often Tugg would mark the wall with Mr Harvey's chalk to note their route. Elbows did the same on the other side of the channel. There were other signs and symbols etched into the stone here and there, but they didn't mean anything to any of them. If the swirls and shapes and numbers were a code, then it belonged only to the Gypsy Traders themselves.

Time passed quietly. Fin peered over the side, fascinated by the water, which wasn't what he'd expected. It flowed in swirls of bright blue and green, and glittered as if bright sunlight was shining on it. Was this what the water of the Times was like under that stinking mist? Where the tides had risen and fallen, a crystal residue had been left behind on the stone walls around them and that sparkled too. Occasionally the gentle sound of creaking oars and running water was broken by a louder splash, and they would catch a glimpse of brightly coloured fins or tails, or bits of creatures Fin didn't recognise as they dipped in and out of the water, briefly breaking the surface.

On the other side, the second boat wobbled and Fin saw Mona pulling Christopher back as something weighty slapped against the wood and sent water splashing upwards. Thanks to Mona's swift response it didn't touch his friend. Fin wondered what effect it would have if it did.

'Lots of river eel here,' Tugg said, quietly. 'Must be a nesting ground.'

The Lost River was beautiful, with its glitter and brightly-coloured water and life, and yet Fin felt the darkness creeping in like the damp around him. Locks rattled on the box inside him where he kept all that stuff he didn't want to think about. He looked down at the jade ring on his finger – Baxter's ring – and felt a wave of nausea that exploded in his head and made its way back down to the chilled pit of his stomach. The river curved ahead of them and as Tugg steered them through the twists and turns, past forks and choices, the feeling of dread gradually got worse. Fin wondered if they'd ever get back to the surface; would they be lost down here for ever? He hadn't seen another ladder leading upwards to a hatch – not that he'd been looking closely, he had to admit, he had been far too busy staring at the water and trying to ignore the idea that somewhere in his head bad things were trying to free themselves.

He looked at Alex Currie-Clarke. His eyes blinked too often and his jaw was clenched hard. He grimaced with each pull at the oar. So Fin wasn't the only one finding it hard to concentrate.

'What did you do before this?' he asked the red-headed Knight. It was a stupid question, and it made Fin feel like he was fifty years old. What people *did*, that was the kind of thing that boring grown-ups who had jobs and thought they were important always wanted to know. But it was the first question that came into his head. Maybe he should have asked what football team Currie-Clarke supported or something, but he hadn't.

'Freelance IT stuff.' The Knight looked up at Fin briefly and then his eyes slipped away. 'For the military. And the intelligence services. Hacking. That kind of thing.'

'Did you hack yourself, or trace hackers? I've seen that stuff in films.' Fin really just wanted to keep him talking – anything was better than that constant trickle of water and the chains rattling on the box in his head. He didn't want to know what was inside the box, not ever.

'Well, both, but it's not as exciting as it is in the films. It's a desk job, really.' His words came out quickly, as if he was out of breath, when he clearly wasn't. They were rowing too gently for that.

'Not quite like this then,' Fin said.

'No.' The new Knight actually managed a small, tight smile at that. 'Not quite like this.'

Fin couldn't think of anything else to say. The damp air filled with the rhythm of the paddles cutting through the water and the ragged sound of his own breath. There were

147

hints of noises elsewhere, but he thought they might perhaps be in his own head. The walls were growing further apart again.

He looked up to see Curran Tugg's dark eyes on him.

'Just make sure you don't touch the water.'

Fin almost laughed aloud. He could think of nothing he'd rather do less right at that moment. He looked down at the surface that glinted and winked at him so prettily.

'Water, water everywhere, and all the boards did shrink,' Currie-Clarke muttered. 'Water, water everywhere, nor any drop to drink.'

'*The Rime of the Ancient Mariner,*' Fin said, absently, staring into the water that popped and crackled with glitter around them. 'Samuel Taylor Coleridge.'

'You know it?' The Knight sounded surprised, and Fin looked up, for the first time aware of what he'd said. The words were unfamiliar; neither the poem nor the name of the poet meant anything to him.

'No,' he said, 'I don't think I do.'

'I think you'd better have some of that beer.' Curran Tugg was watching them closely. 'It don't do to think too much on the rivers; not for you lot, anyway.' He whistled to Elbows, who understood the quick gesture and turned to say something to those in his boat. They seemed a long way away to Fin, and he wished they were closer. Even with the Knight and the two Traders beside him, he felt very alone. Whatever was bothering him was inside his head, and it wasn't just the river playing tricks on him – there really was something wrong, he was pretty sure of that. The water was just making him think about it.

The silent Trader Tugg had brought with them fished out two small leather flasks from his bag and tossed them carefully to the Knight and Fin. The boat slowed as the rowing stopped. Fin twisted the cap off and the familiar aroma of citrus and hops cut through the cool dirty damp that surrounded them.

He'd wanted to try this beer ever since he'd first smelled it at The Red Lion on his first visit, but now he found his hand trembled, distracted by the rattling chains and the locked box in his mind. Where had the poem come from? Maybe he'd heard the lines somewhere before, but to know the title, and the poet as well? Surely he'd know if he knew that?

Not even taking time to savour the taste of the ale, he lifted the flask to his lips. As long as it stopped these dark thoughts, he didn't care if he was drinking forbidden beer or orange juice or plain water. The foam hit his mouth first, and it was thicker than the cappuccino-style he'd been expecting, and entirely flavourless, but it did make the edges of his lips tingle. The liquid itself was warm, a mixture of honey with the heady bitterness of a strong lager, and it made him flinch inside. He wondered who on earth would drink this just for fun. He took another long sip – he thought that there were bits of something smooth in there too, but his teeth couldn't catch them – and watched as Currie-Clarke did the same. Fin wondered what demons the Knight was quietly fighting. Did he have a locked box in his head too?

After a moment, Fin's skin warmed and tingled and the small knot in the back of his neck that had been gradually tightening loosened slightly. It felt like the sparkles had crept inside him, but in a good way. Fin smiled at the Knight, and he smiled back. He drank some more, and saw that his hand had stopped trembling. He'd snuck the odd beer before in his own London, and although the buzz that tickled his system was similar, he didn't feel like it was going to make his brain blurry like alcohol back home did. This was just relaxing him, lifting his mood.

Curran Tugg marked the wall and gestured over to Elbows, who did the same, and the two boats started their slow progress again, the oars dipping back in and out of the crystal-blue surface. They turned another bend and into a tunnel that was gloomier and narrower than any they'd passed through already. Fin was glad of the beer. He thought this place might bring out the madness in him even if it wasn't the River Times. Rather than looking down, he started staring at the walls as they passed by. He'd meant it simply as a distraction from the fascinating water, but he found his eyes narrowing. Something was wrong. He frowned.

'You okay, boy?' Tugg asked.

Fin nodded; he was okay, well, sort of. His head wasn't quite right, but it was a lot better than it had been. It was the walls that were the problem. They looked odd: the thick cement between the slabs of stone was almost too neat. He looked at the other side, but it was too dark to make it out clearly.

'It's just that—' he started, but two things happened at once, stopping his sentence in mid-flow. The first was that for the briefest moment the river turned black, and a frost that hungrily reached for the boats crackled across it. The second was that heavy nets dropped behind and ahead of them, falling from the darkness above and trapping them. Knights and Traders alike were up and calling to each other in an instant, the Knights drawing their golden swords and the Traders their own rougher but, Fin was quite sure, equally as effective blades.

As soon as the nets were down a thick section of wall dropped like a drawbridge, held in place by heavy rusting chains and stopping just short of the water's surface.

'—I think there's something wrong with the walls,' Fin finished lamely. He got to his feet. 'Did anyone see the water? Just then?'

No one was paying him any attention; all eyes were focused on the drawbridge. Three men stood there, dressed in black leather, with colourful scarves on their heads or around their necks. Each had a crossbow raised and pointed at their captives, and they all had several more weapons harnessed into the carriers on their backs.

'Drop your swords,' the man at the centre growled. Bright torches burned in the walls beyond where they stood, making it hard to see more than their basic shapes. Fin's heart was racing. They'd found them – these had to be the Gypsy Traders.

For a moment, nobody moved.

Then, beside him, Tugg flinched. A tip of steel was pressed against the swarthy man's neck.

'My dad said to drop your weapons, Curran Tugg.'

Fin looked up, and his heart raced again. Hanging backwards from the netting, with a small dagger now pressed against the fierce Trader's throat, was the blonde girl from the fire. The one he'd been afraid he'd never see again. And here she was: a Gypsy Trader.

Mitesh Savjani had persuaded the Prince Regent that he needed to stay in the palace. He hoped it was the right decision – logically, it was. Alexander Palace was heavily guarded with the best that London had to offer, and until they could find out what was causing this strange storm in the clear sky, then it was surely best for the Regent to stay put. His heart was heavy with the decision though, for the Prince had looked very small, and very alone, when he'd left him. Savjani wondered how someone with so much wealth and power could be so friendless that he would want the company of his clothcrafter in a time of crisis. Perhaps it was all that wealth and power that was the problem – and, of course, the promise of future madness to come. As he scurried through the streets, Mitesh Savjani knew he would not change place with the Prince Regent for all the secrets of the South.

Another bolt of yellow lightning flashed across the clear sky, making him flinch slightly. People were gathered in small groups on the streets, whispering and muttering, and pointing upwards with dread awe. Nothing like this had ever been seen in The Nowhere before, and he'd never read anything like this in all the history books he'd studied, or read to Mona when she had been small. This wasn't like the start of the Black Storms they had seen and fought before.

His head ached and his feet stumbled slightly as his breath came more heavily. He Travelled better than some, but he was not a Trader, and no Mona, and moving through the Boroughs was taking its toll. But he had a duty to fulfil: he had to find his old friend Fowkes and get to the bottom of this. Something had shaken the worlds' order and the feeling in his portly gut told him that something was terrible.

Unlike most London cabbies, this one knew better than to chat inanely to his fares. The small sticker in the front of his windscreen made sure of that. It came as a relief to the two old men who sat in the back. One was leaning forward with his walking stick firmly planted between his feet, and the other held a long, narrow holdall on his knees. Cabbies were like hairdressers; if they couldn't engage you in conversation about the interminable frustrations of trying to drive in London traffic, they invariably talked about the weather, and as far as Ted was concerned, the last thing he wanted to be talking about right now was the weather.

'What did the news call it?' Freddie Wise peered out of the window and up at the sky that was just turning to twilight. 'A solar flare? Where on earth do they come up with these things? Since when did it hurt anyone to just say "I don't know"? I mean, really.'

'Would you rather have people running around panicking their head off, Freddie? That's what "I don't know" tends to bring about.'

'That's not the point. It's the principle.'

Barely an hour before white lightning had flashed across the clear December afternoon sky, followed swiftly by a rumble of angry thunder, and each time it did so, the words

152

etched into the Prophecy table in Orrery House had glowed – and worse even than that, the tiny crack in the table had also shone brightly. In was painfully obvious that whatever was going on in the sky was nothing natural. Something happening in The Nowhere was affecting The Somewhere again, just like it had with the dirty rain a few weeks before, but if that ancient piece of furniture was affected, that meant there had to be something truly terrible coming. The map of the worlds was held within it, but what did the exterior represent? The universe itself?

The Knights were already stretched thin, searching for the arsonists and the Gypsy Traders and guarding the Storyholder, so Orrery House was virtually empty. They left Cardrew Cutler and Jarvis there to keep an eye on the Aged while they came out to find Fowkes and the Wakley boys. The Aged were of no interest to anyone this time. It wasn't like when St John Golden came at them; Ted could feel in his gut that whatever was happening now wasn't just about the Knights. It was bigger than that, so Orrery House wouldn't be a prime target, especially when there weren't any active Knights there.

'It's at times like this that I think we should perhaps review our policy of no mobile phones.' Freddie looked over at Ted, and the nightwatchman smiled.

'Wouldn't make no difference though, would it? They'd still 'ave to come back for their swords.' He tapped the holdall on his knee. 'Can't 'ave grown men running around London with swords on now, can we? Not around estates like these.' He looked out the window at the grey tower blocks. 'And anyway, all that technology makes people lazy, that's what Harlequin always says. You can lie easier on it than face to face, and people can use it to lie to you. That's what 'e said, and I still trust 'is judgement on these things. You've got to admit, all this communication ain't exactly made the world a nicer place, 'as it?'

'Fair point, well made,' Freddie said as the taxi pulled over next to a bus shelter covered in bad graffiti and swear words that would leave the reader in no doubt as to exactly what the anonymous writer thought of Kourtney and Jade S and their sexual habits.

'Is this where they are?'

'Three men 'ave gone missing from 'ere, according to the police – well, not even men, more like boys. One of 'em was bragging 'e had some big job on. They all went out and never came back ... and all around the same time as the fire.'

'Do you think they're still in The Nowhere?' Freddie reached for the door handle.

'Could be. Doubt it though.' The swords clanged in his bag as Ted climbed out of the black cab. 'Them boys was just puppets, if you ask me. If they're still in The Nowhere then they're dead. Mind you, I'm pretty sure that wherever they are, they're dead.'

Freddie Wise tutted. 'Such a waste of life. And such stupidity.' He stretched slightly and grimaced as his back cracked. 'That's better.'

A group of teenagers sitting on a wall smoking stared at them with a strange mix of open aggression and curiosity. They didn't move, though: two old men weren't any threat to them.

'You should be wearing gloves, Freddie. It's bloody freezing out.'

'Who made you my mother?' The old man with the ebony cane broke into a rare smile.

'Yeah, well, even if you 'adn't Aged, you'd still be no spring chicken.'

'But I'd still be younger than you.'

They laughed together and were about to stroll towards the first of the bleak tower blocks when the cabbie's window unwound and he whistled them back. Ted turned immediately. The cabbies were well-trusted, but for as long as their agreement had been running neither side had ever spoken more than was necessary to the other. It was just the way it was.

'Just had something through on the radio.' The driver looked at Ted, slightly nervously. His full face was covered in a network of fine red veins that might have had more to do with a love of strong liquor than the cold. 'One of ours. Usual codes and on the special frequency.'

'What is it?' Freddie Wise leaned in towards the window.

'Someone's just been picked up at the Cab Shelter in St John's wood. Right scruffy bastard, if you'll excuse my language. Says he needs to see you – well, he said he needed to see the Judge, but you're close enough, right?'

Ted felt a small stab in his heart. Harlequin Brown was gone and on days like this Ted Merryweather didn't feel close enough at all. He felt decidedly inadequate. He nodded anyway. 'Did 'e give you a name, this feller?'

'He just said he was the Seer.'

For a moment, neither of the old men spoke, then hey simultaneously let out their breath in a stream of mist.

'Did he now?' Freddie Wise muttered before looking across at Ted. 'The Seer, he says. After all this time.'

'Tell your mate to take 'im to Charterhouse Square, but keep the cab doors locked until we get back there. 'e's not to get out unless me or 'im is there, you understand?'

'Loud and clear.'

Ted wasn't sure Harlequin would have dealt with it this way, but he knew his old friend would have approved of his wariness. The Seer was the joker in the pack, and Ted was in no mood for fools.

'Best get these men their swords and send them back to find out what the hell is going on with the weather,' Freddie said, 'and then it's time for an interesting meeting of our own, wouldn't you say, Ted?'

'Something like that, Freddie.' Ted slung the bag over his shoulder and they picked up the pace. 'Something like that.'

After the initial burst of activity, when the Knights and Borough Guard had come flying into the Storyholder's apartments, there was now a subdued quiet. Harper Jones' face had fallen instantly as he'd stared at the two figures huddled together on the floor, and Joe had seen his disappointment. And his fear. Joe didn't care. He hated Harper Jones in that instant, for all his goodness, and for his blond hair that matched Tova's, and his renewed youthfulness, and the respect that he was accorded for having been through the Ageing and back again.

Fin had told him the story, how all the Aged Knights had wanted to give the Magus' elixir to each other, rather than take it themselves. It had sounded noble at the time, but now, with all the world in his head, Joe thought it just sound very stupid indeed. How would Harper Jones and the cheerful Lucas Blake feel today if someone else had taken the restoration liquid? Bitter and twisted, that was how, because really, everyone was selfish. Joe knew that – he could *see* it. He could see so many things now.

Harper Jones crouched beside Tova and checked her first, while Joe scurried to the bathroom and threw up. He didn't feel better for it. When he came back out, there were just the three Knights – Harper Jones and two new ones who were doing a really crap impression of not looking lost and out of their depth. They'd sent the Borough Guard back downstairs. Gossip was going to be rife, and with the strange storms outside, the people of The Nowhere might suddenly remember that they did know where the Old Bailey House of Real Truths was, even if it was answers rather than truths they'd start coming to find out.

The noise of them was too much, and eventually Tova had shut the men in the sitting room. Fowkes would be coming soon – Jones had checked on that – and until then there was little they could do apart from sit tight. Harper Jones had thought to go to the Regent, but within moments, two of the Regent's Chancellors had arrived in overblown gilt coaches and wafted up the stairs. They were now shut into the living room too – much to their disgust – and they and the Knights were left to ask each other questions none of them knew the answers to.

She had gone to the kitchen to fetch him a glass of water, even though he could tell that just the effort of moving was exhausting her. Joe felt a small twinge of regret. She didn't think this was his fault; she was protecting him from the nosy interest of the Knights and the Chancellors as if they were still joined together in this mess. They weren't, of course – he'd cut her loose and set her adrift, an empty void – simply a person again. He wondered how long it had been since she'd lived like that. Twenty years? More? For a moment the searing heat of guilt stabbed at his gut, but he clenched his teeth and wished it away. This would have happened anyway, he told himself. This was his destiny, that's what Mr Arnold-Mather had said, and so far he wasn't looking wrong. It didn't matter, as long as Tova didn't know what he'd done.

Glass smashed in the kitchen, and the sound of the splintering shards pierced his brain. Joe dragged himself to his feet and walked carefully to the door. His head was heavy, and he found it difficult to balance. Was this how his mum felt with one of her migraines? Tova was crouched on the floor, picking up pieces of glass, gathering them in one shaky hand.

'I'll do that,' he said, and was surprised at how normal his voice sounded. He'd cleaned up this flat a bit not so long ago, and the wreckage of Mrs Baker's kitchen after St John Golden's men had beaten her up. The memories were clear, but they felt like someone else's.

Tova froze, examining something in her small palm. She frowned and stood up slowly, her blonde hair hanging in sweaty strands over her face. In the midst of the pieces of glass he could make out something tiny, something that sent that shudder of guilt running through him again. Half of one of the plastic capsules. He must have dropped it earlier. His heart thudded, and he was sure it was making the whole door frame shake.

'Tova, I—' His words drained away. He *what*? He could explain? Their eyes met, and all the knowledge in the world sat between them. Her mouth dropped open, but Joe couldn't take his eyes from hers, and all the desolate betrayal he read there. She knew what he'd done, and he knew she knew. Joe felt his old world crumble to dust. The truth of it finally hit him. No more happy-go-lucky Joe, always in a scrape, bit of trouble here, bit of trouble there, but no harm done. This trouble was *permanent*. This trouble was *bad*. *He* was bad. No more Finmere, no more Christopher, and no more Knights, who would now no doubt congratulate themselves on not having trusted him in the first place. He had *nothing*—

No, he corrected himself, that wasn't true. He had the stories, and he had Mr Arnold-Mather. His blood cooled, taking his guilt and fear with it, at least for now. He had something to do, and there was no time to lose. Bits of her story were his story now, and the last piece of his task had fallen into place when he'd stolen her treasure from her. He knew where she had hidden the last thing he needed. For what?, he wondered, and found he didn't have the answer to that. Sentimentality? A reminder of her own guilt?

He fought the urge to find a new story in that and instead turned and ran for the bedroom. His feet were steady now and his mind focused, and the thud of his heart ran like a well-oiled engine. But Tova was fast behind him, grunting through her ruined mouth as if she was trying to yell for help from those she herself had shut out so they could have some peace. She grabbed at his T-shirt and he turned, shoving her hard. In her newly weakened state she was no match for him, let alone the power sizzling through him, and she fell hard against the wall they had so recently curled up against.

He looked in the large mirror hanging beside the bed and had a moment's pause. It was just him looking back: Joe Manning from Eastfields Comp, ordinary Joe from the estate, who would probably end up working in a dead-end job, but he'd find a nice girl and settle down. Joe who once dreamed of playing football in the Premiership, but who always kind of knew it wouldn't come true, not for the likes of him.

Behind him, Tova was sobbing and gurgling, sounding as if she was choking on her own tears. He looked at his reflection again. It *wasn't* the same. The eyes and mouth were different – harder. The sense of humour was gone. This face belonged to the voice that had taken up residence in his head along with the first of the two stories. This was the face of someone who had a destiny to fulfil, wherever it took him. He lifted the mirror carefully from the wall, thinking that a second smash, and such a big one, would draw the attention of those men only a few feet away (this Joe was smarter too, it appeared). Behind the mirror, an oblong had been cut into the wall behind it, a dark hidden grave for something that belonged to a man long gone. Joe grinned. Fin might have Baxter's ring, but it would be Joe Manning who wielded the sword.

He pulled the belt that housed it free and even before he'd tugged the sword out, the hilt was burning in his hand, the metal too long unused. The jade stone in the hilt glittered brightly as he raised the weapon high. The Joe of old would never have managed to master its magic, but the Storyholder Joe had no fear that it would not work.

Two figures appeared in the bedroom doorway as he sliced his own, more special, gateway open. One was sweating and out of breath, and a purple jewel twinkled in his beard. Alongside him was Andrew Fowkes, glowering and angry, returned from The Somewhere just as Joe was leaving. His eyes fell to the sword in Joe's hand.

Joe thought they might both have called out at once. He

didn't know, and he didn't care. He stepped through to the icy December of his own town and left them both behind. They weren't part of his world any more. His story was taking him somewhere far greater. He was sure of it.

SIXTEEN

Curran Tugg had carefully re-holstered his own blade, not moving his neck an inch, and the girl hanging backwards from the net hadn't taken her dagger from the soft part of his throat until all the Knights had done the same. Then she'd righted herself and clambered across the nets with ease, landing on the drawbridge before their two boats had even pulled up.

As they climbed out onto the rough stone, Fin looked over at Christopher and Mona and saw his own excitement reflected there. They'd found them, the mysterious Gypsy Traders, and for a while, now that they were on relatively dry land – even if it was deep underground – the madness of the water could be forgotten. He thought of the river again and frowned as the blonde girl came alongside him. That weird blackness had been wrong, he knew that, and he was going to have to make sure that all these men knew about it, in case they hadn't noticed it … but perhaps this wasn't quite the time. Plus, he was finding it hard to concentrate on anything with the girl from the fire standing so close. She smelled of something wonderful, a bit like that oil that some of the emo girls at Eastfields wore. This scent was just as wild, but warmer – like flowers would smell if they grew on an ocean.

Fin's throat tightened and his face burned a little. 'I've seen you before,' he blurted out quietly.

'What?' Her voice was like water. She pulled her hair free from the loose knot and it ran like iced silk down her back.

She was almost as tall as him, and willowy, and her skin was porcelain-white, no doubt as a result of rarely going out on the surface. She didn't look unhealthy though – if anything, Finmere thought she glowed with life. She was the most beautiful thing he had ever seen in his sixteen years alive.

'At the fire.' He was quite surprised he could even get the words out. 'You were helping put the fire out. You had a hose.'

'No, I wasn't.' Her eyes were the palest blue and looked crystal-flecked at the edges, as if she'd got some of the strange Lost Rivers' water in them. 'You must have me confused with someone else.'

'No, it was definitely you.' Fin barely felt the nudge in his back, pushing him forwards. 'I'd recognise you anywhere.' The words were out before he could stop them, and as his face caught flame he thought about just turning round and throwing himself into the water. What kind of muppet was he? So much for playing it cool. She must think he was a right spanner.

Her eyes widened slightly and then, with a half-glance over her shoulder, she went and stood next to the man she'd called her dad. Fin's heart thumped slightly. At least she'd looked back at him. In the movies that was always a good sign.

Now that he was in the light – the torches burning in the wall-sconces produced a bright white light that was almost as good as an incandescent bulb – he could see the Gypsy Trader clearly. He was pale, like his daughter and the other two men with him, and all three men were just as blond, although his hair was shaved close to his head. Unidentifiable coloured tattoos ran like sleeves up his arms and disappeared under his leather waistcoat, but there was no disguising the strong muscles in his arms and chest. His eyes were pale, like his daughter's, but hard as diamonds.

'Look,' Lucas Blake came stumbling past Finmere as a

Gypsy Trader pushed him forward, 'we're really not here to cause any trouble. We just want to talk to you, all right?' He righted himself and stood tall with his hands on his hips.

'We don't talk to Nowhere people, let alone Somewhere strangers.' The Gypsy Trader peered suspiciously at him. 'We don't care for surface business.' His voice was soft, but just as full of menace as any of the normal Traders. He looked away from the Knight. 'And shame on *you*, Curran Tugg – doing the dandy Regent's bidding, are we now?'

Fin watched as the Trader leader visibly bristled. 'You know better than that, Francois Manot,' he growled. 'I don't do *anyone's* bidding. But sometimes only a fool chooses to ignore the problems of others that might affect himself.'

'Are you calling me a fool?' Fin couldn't hear any trace of French in the man's accent, despite his name, but he could almost see the tension crackling between the two Traders and their men – two sides of dark and blond who pulled in alongside their leaders.

'Ooookey dokey.' Lucas Blake took up a position between the two, smiling from one to the other. 'Perhaps we got off on the wrong foot here. We really just want to talk to you – to see if you can help us – and then we'll bugger off back to the surface.' Beneath his dark hair his eyes were twinkling, but Finmere wasn't fooled. Blake could fight with the best of them if it came to it; he'd seen that for himself. But he also knew when to use his natural good humour to lighten a mood. Fin liked Lucas Blake. He liked to imagine that maybe Fowkes had been like him once, before all the stuff with Tova and Baxter had happened and darkened his soul. Christopher liked him too, Fin could tell. There was a magic about someone who could shrug away the worries and cares of the world and just live in the moment of adventure like Blake could. It was hard to believe that he'd spent five long years Aged – that must have been terrible for a man with such a zest for life – but if it had damaged him, then there was no outward sign of it. Lucas Blake was like Ted: he believed the best of people, always.

'Really,' Blake reiterated, 'trust me, I don't want to be around this water any longer than I have to. And I don't want the kids down here for long either – this might not be the Times, but it still affects us.'

As he said that, Fin started to wonder what demons had been stirring behind his cheerful demeanour – a return to the Ageing, perhaps? Whatever his fears were, he hid them well. At least now he was off the water, the box in his own head had settled back down in its dusty corner. He didn't want to open it, not ever.

Francois Manot stared from Lucas Blake to Curran Tugg before both Trader leaders sniffed hard.

'You might have heard of this boy,' Tugg said, looking at Fin. 'He's the one they talk about, neither Somewhere or Nowhere born.'

Fin squirmed again, not only because the icy blue eyes were staring into him, but because he could also feel the man's daughter, suddenly looking over at him. *I'm not special at all*, he wanted to say. *I'm just me*. But as usual, the words got tied up on his tongue and he stayed silent.

Manot spat. 'He's not a Lost River boy, that's for sure.'

'Nor a surface one,' Tugg laughed, and for the first time the tension eased a fraction between them. 'A little green around the gills on the water, he was. He needed a drink.'

Francois Manot and his men let out a small barrage of derisive snorts, and Fin was pretty sure that from the corner of his eye he could see the girl smiling too. Great. This was just getting better and better.

'But at least we came down to your rivers,' Christopher said, coldly. His words stopped the laughter; the grown men looked surprised that the tall boy had cut in. Christopher wasn't in the slightest bit intimidated – not on the outside anyway. 'Lots of adults wouldn't have done that. And you can laugh at how the water affects us, but it's easy to laugh at things you can't possibly understand, isn't it? The fact that the water doesn't harm you doesn't make you brave.' He moved alongside Fin. 'The fact that the water *does* harm us and we know that, yet we still came down here looking for you – that makes *us* brave.' The edges of Christopher's mouth sneered slightly. It wasn't an expression Fin had ever seen on him before, and once again he wondered what had actually happened with that Magus to change his friend so deeply. 'So laugh all you want,' Christopher finished, 'but if you don't help us, we'll be the ones laughing at you, for being fools.'

There was a sharp gasp as the whole gathering sucked in their breath, and as much as Fin admired Christopher's directness, he couldn't help but think he'd gone too far.

'The boy has a point,' Tugg grumbled.

'I don't like him.' Manot stared through narrowed eyes at Christopher. 'I don't like him at all. He needs to learn some manners.'

'We just need your help,' Fin said, speaking up at last. 'We don't mean to be rude, honest, we just want to find out what's hurting these people and why the Storyholder had visions of it. You might not care about what happens on the surface, but the surface still affects you, whether you want it to or not.'

'They may be young and a touch on the arrogant side' – Lucas Blake glared at Christopher – 'but they're speaking the truth.'

There was a moment's silence and then Manot nodded at his men. 'Go out and check the water. See if anyone followed them down.'

Within seconds the two blond men were at the drawbridge, turning heavy wooden handles Fin could now see embedded in the walls. Something creaked overhead and Fin looked up. It was a boat, and as his eyes adjusted to the gloom in the spaces above where the bright lights stopped, he saw that the ceiling was filled with a long line of wooden hulls, all pointing downwards. The boat reached the floor and settled precisely on the runners waiting for it on the ground and the two men leapt in. Fin's mouth opened slightly. The Gypsy Traders' vessel made their compactables look like something bought from a cheap toy shop.

The boat wasn't huge, but its varnished wood shone like richly varnished floorboards, and across the sides were vividly coloured paintings as detailed at the tattoos on Manot's arms, of creatures so real they were almost bursting free of their confines. The sails were of thick red and green fabric, ridged like the fins of an eel. They looked stiff to Fin, rather than soft and billowy as he'd have expected. Maybe they didn't need them down here – perhaps it was only when they ventured out across the Times to do business with the South that they used the wind to help propel the boat.

Christopher and Alex Currie-Clark looked equally in awe as the boat slipped down the drawbridge and splashed into the water, and Mona was doing her best to look nonchalant, which was always a clue that she was a bit astounded by something. Only Tugg and Elbows didn't see anything extraordinary about the beautiful boat, which made Fin wish he could see what the ordinary Traders' boats were like. Would they be just as glorious to look at, or plain and rough but strong, just like their owners? There was definitely something more ethereal about the Gypsy Traders than the normal ones. Fin glanced sideways as the drawbridge pulled up and sealed them in. There definitely was about the girl, anyway.

'Anaïs,' Manot said, 'go and tell your grandmother we're coming.'

The blonde girl nodded and darted off ahead. Fin watched her go. He couldn't imagine how anyone could be so graceful and beautiful and clearly brave all rolled into one. Just as she was about to disappear around a bend in the pathway, she flashed a quick smile back and Fin's heart leapt. Maybe she didn't think he was such a muppet after all.

'Just ask her to marry you and be done with it,' Christopher whispered. Beside him, Mona laughed, but it was a cheerful sound with no malice in it.

'What?' Fin mumbled. 'Don't know what you're talking about. She just looks interesting, that's all.'

'Yeah, right. *Interesting*.' Christopher grinned.

'Leave him alone!' Mona nudged him and then linked arms with him.

'Yeah, you two can hardly talk,' Fin smiled, and started to chant softly, 'Christopher and Mona sitting in a tree—'

Christopher punched him, stopping him from finishing the sentence. 'You're such a twat sometimes.'

'But you like me,' Fin said. 'Probably not as much as you *luurve* Mona, but—'

This time it was the purple-haired girl who thumped him, and he laughed. As they approached the heart of the Gypsy Trader enclave, the darkness of earlier dissipated completely. Fin grinned with excitement. If only Joe were here with them, it would be perfect.

An hour later and they were sitting cross-legged on large, brightly coloured cushions that looked as if they were made of the same material as the Gypsy Traders' scarves. They'd finally arrived at their destination – Francois Manot had called it the 'Parlay Room' – after weaving their way through a maze of narrow tunnels carved through the earth. Fin guessed not even Curran Tugg would be able to find his way back to their compactables without a guide.

The Parlay Room – well, some of it, at least – must once have been part of a building, before the Lost Rivers had been built over. It was a large round chamber that had been hewn out of the ground, the dark walls a stark contrast to the huge pillar of pale marble that rose from the floor to the ceiling far above. The entrance was odd, too. When they were just a few feet away from the pillar, Manot led them down a small flight of stairs and along a tunnel so low that even Mona had to crouch a bit, and then up another flight of stairs that came out in the middle of the Parlay Room itself. There were plenty of those same strange bright torches that lit the tunnels, so it was almost like sitting in virtual daylight.

As he'd followed Blake through the underground, Fin had caught a glimpse of two small children, peering at them around the edge of a wall, their eyes bright with wonder before a voice yanked them away. The Parlay Room must be near where the Gypsy Traders lived, but not close enough for Fin and the others to actually see any of them. He could understand why that was, but he still felt vaguely disappoint-ed. He started to imagine the riotous colours and paintings that these strange people might have decorated their living spaces with – if they were anything like the boats, it would be a dazzling sight. And what kind of houses would they live in – tents? Or maybe bits of old buildings hidden behind the walls? Perhaps one day Anaïs would show him. His stomach tingled a bit, just thinking of her name.

They all sat down on the cushions in the circle, the teen-agers sticking together, and the adults doing the same, the two Knights sitting side by side, next to the Traders. As soon as they were settled, Francois Manot banged a bronze gong that was hanging against the wall. The sound vibrated up the marble, a single note remaining in the air for almost a minute after the initial crash had faded. Within moments, the re-maining cushions were filled by arriving Gypsy Traders, ten men and women, all blond, and all dressed in black leather, sporting scarves of various colours, on their heads or around their necks. Fin stared: even the women, all athletically slim, regardless of their age, had tattoos on their pale arms. One woman even had a dragon or lizard of some variety, curling its way up from her neck and onto one delicate cheek. Of all the wonders he'd seen in his time in The Nowhere, Fin decided the Gypsy Traders were the best – but judging by the suspicious looks he and the rest of the visitors were getting, he presumed that the awe wasn't mutual.

Manot opened a wooden box in front of his cushion and banged on the bottom of it three times. Something out of sight clicked, the wood shifted and a tray appeared in its place holding a steaming jug and several wooden beakers. As the box returned to where it had been, Manot poured what turned out to be sweet black tea and passed the cups round. Fin sipped his and decided he liked it – it was better than the beer, and tasted like it had honeycomb in it, to sweeten the bitter bite of the dark leaves.

Two cushions remained empty; one large golden one had an albatross woven into it and the other a smaller version, in red. Just as he was wondering who they were waiting for, Anaïs appeared up the central stairs and gracefully lowered herself to the small cushion. Behind her came another slim figure, this one dressed in white breeches and shirt. Fine blonde hair hung all the way to the backs of her thighs. She strode the few steps to the final empty space and when she turned, Fin couldn't hold in a shocked gasp. He heard it echoed from Christopher beside him. Despite her agile gait and beautiful hair, this wasn't a young woman. In fact, she was the absolute opposite of young; Fin thought that in all his years of shaving the old men of Orrery House, he had never seen a face that looked older than this woman's. Her skin was just as pale as every Gypsy Trader Fin could see, but it hung in loose wrinkles around her neck and jaw line, and huge bags sagged below her milky eyes. She smiled at Francois Manot as she took a cup of tea from him, exposing several dark gaps where teeth were missing. This must be Anaïs' grandmother – but how old was she? Her face and skin suggested she was a hundred years old!

'So these are our visitors.' Her words whistled slightly

through the gaps, but her voice was soft as goose down. Her eyes lingered on Fin. 'And you're the boy.' She sucked in some air and leaned back. 'You're a good boy, but bad things happen to people around you. You are a paradox.' She glanced at Christopher and smiled. It wasn't a pleasant expression. 'Just ask him,' she said.

Fin's guts turned to water and he looked at his friend. Christopher didn't look back, but kept his stony gaze straight forward. It wasn't a comfort. Fin had wanted to see Christopher shrug as if to say *what's the crazy old bat on about?* but he didn't. What did this old woman know? What had happened to Christopher? His good feeling of earlier evaporated.

'The boys haven't caused any trouble,' Lucas Blake said. 'They're trying to stop some, same as the rest of us.'

'Surface trouble?' she asked.

'Surface trouble that's using your rivers and street-level manholes to move around.'

A dissatisfied murmur rippled around the room.

'And you come here to accuse us?' the old woman asked.

'No, not at all.' Lucas Blake met her milky gaze. 'But the same questions apply that we asked Curran Tugg and his Traders – has anything strange been brought back from the South? Something that could maybe infect people?'

'We might not live by the laws of the land, but neither are we stupid.' Francois Manot leaned forward. 'We know why many of those laws are in place. The South is the South and the North is the North. Curran Tugg must have told you already that livestock doesn't travel well. Most things don't.'

'I know that,' Blake said, 'but *something* is attacking the people of London, and the Storyholder saw one of the attacks in a vision. And that means that terrible as the attacks are, there is some greater portent to them than just the damage to the poor individuals.'

'We're not interested in surface troubles.' The old lady

170

smiled, revealing gums that were almost white below the dark gaps where many of her teeth should have been.

'But that's not true,' Fin cut in. He knew he should keep his mouth shut, but sometimes adults just took so long, going round the houses, and right now he had a feeling time wasn't on their side. The way the water had turned black was still bothering him, and he couldn't deal with that until they'd sorted out the Gypsy Traders.

He squared his shoulders and looked at the old woman. 'If it was true,' he continued, 'then you wouldn't have helped put out the fire at the Storyholder Academy, would you?'

'We didn't help.' The whole group's attention was on Fin as the old woman turned to him.

'But you *did*. I saw Anaïs there, with a hose, so there must have been more of you, using a hatch to feed the hose through.'

It was only as the words left his mouth and the old woman and her son turned to stare at the blonde girl did the realisation dawn on Fin: he'd just *totally* dropped her in it. They hadn't known.

'Is this true?' Francois Manot didn't shout, but if the Gypsy Trader normally sounded like water, now his voice was ice.

Anaïs stared at the floor for long seconds, then she sat up tall and lifted her head high. If she was scared, she didn't look it. 'Yes,' she said, 'I helped them. They needed more water, and we have plenty of it.' She looked past her grandmother and glared at her father. 'I *like* the surface. It's *interesting*.'

'If they catch you up there, the Regent's men will arrest you.'

'Not if she hasn't done anything,' Mona cut in, indignant. 'There is due legal process, you know; you can't just haul people into jail.'

Francois Manot ignored her. 'I can't believe you bring this shame on me. Who was with you?'

'It doesn't matter.' Anaïs tossed her blonde hair over one

shoulder. 'We didn't do anything wrong. It isn't wrong to help people – and these visitors are right. Whatever's attacking these people and turning them mad *is* using our rivers to get around. The manhole covers and hatches where they've been found have definitely been opened, and not by me – I only ever use the same two or three.'

'How did you know about the madness?' Lucas Blake was looking at Anaïs as if he'd not even noticed her before, which Fin just couldn't imagine. How could anyone *not* notice her? Although he doubted she'd ever speak to him again after that clanger … not that she'd exactly spoken to him before, but she had smiled at him, and he'd hoped there was going to be some talking at some point.

'I saw it: I was exploring when I saw a woman find one of the victims. I saw what happened.' Her voice softened. 'It was *horrible*.'

'There's something else,' Fin said. The meeting was hardly staying on track anyway, and he needed to get it out. 'Just when you caught us in your nets, did anyone else notice that the water went completely black for a moment?' He looked around the circle. 'Is that normal? Does that happen sometimes?'

There was complete silence from both the Traders and the Gypsy Traders. Tugg and Elbows stared at him, their eyes widening.

'The water went black?' Lucas Blake frowned. 'When?'

'We would have noticed such a thing.' Manot looked over at Tugg, and for the first time there was almost an alliance between them.

'True,' Curran Tugg said, 'although I did have your daughter's blade at my throat at the time.'

'I'd have seen,' Elbows grunted.

'I definitely saw it,' Fin insisted. 'The water went black.'

'Just because you didn't see it,' the old woman purred, 'it doesn't mean that the boy is lying. I believe him. Some people see things that others don't.' She steepled her gnarled fingers under her chin. 'But a black river? This is very bad. A portent. Something has happened – something that will perhaps affect us all.' She bent to one side and spat on the ground.

'If Anaïs is determined to scurry around the surface, we shall let her help their dwellers, until we understand these events better. Then we will decide whether the Gypsy Traders should play any further part.' She turned to Lucas Blake. 'We shall provide you with a map of the flow of the Lost Rivers and where the surface hatches are, so you do not have to rely on my granddaughter's memory alone. We will want the map back, though – and should a copy be made and ever presented to the dandy Regent' – her eyes darted to Mona – 'then we shall take our vengeance, and it will not be pleasant.'

'Understood,' Lucas Blake said.

Mona nodded.

Footsteps clattered up the stairs and a small boy of no more than eight or nine appeared through the hole in the ground. He ran straight over to the old woman and handed her a scrap of paper. She grinned at him and he scampered back down to the tunnel below.

The ancient woman unfolded the scrap of parchment and then looked long and hard at Fin. 'We have news of the surface,' she said. She spoke quietly, but with such seriousness that every word made the air around it tremble. 'There is white lightning in a clear sky.'

'There is *what*? What does that mean?' Manot looked as confused as the surface-dwellers.

'It means that something terrible has happened. The boy was right when he saw the river turn black. A storm is coming, one like never before.' She looked at Lucas Blake. 'I think perhaps you have bigger things to do now. Leave this hunt to the young. *You* must stop this storm.' In a swift, graceful movement that belied her age she was on her feet. 'Get them back to where they came in, Francois.' She turned to her granddaughter. 'And as for you, Anaïs, go and have your adventure, but remember: you're a *water* girl. You may find the surface fascinating, but it will never bring you joy. Guard yourself.'

The girl nodded seriously, but as soon as the old woman had turned around, she grinned at Finmere. He didn't think he'd ever seen anything as beautiful as her eyes sparkling with excitement. He smiled back, but his cheeks felt like they were stuck in some kind of glue and he dreaded to think how he looked. If only she didn't make him feel so awkward and nervous – still, she was coming with them, and that was the *best* thing.

Thunder heralded their arrival back at the street not far from The Red Lion, and for a moment the whole group paused and gazed upwards. There was not so much as a whisper of cloud in the clear blue sky, but within seconds a bolt of yellow lightning had cut a scar across it and this time, when the thunder followed a few moments later, a red hue coated the horizon. It made Fin think of blood.

'This isn't like the last time,' Curran Tugg muttered, 'the storm that came after the Knight died.' More streaks darted bright across the blue, making the Trader squint. 'This is something far more powerful.'

'It's the stories,' a Borough Guardsman told Mona. He'd just arrived and was standing at attention, but he was trembling all over. 'I've come from the Old Bailey House of Real Truths to tell you.'

'What about them?' Lucas Blake's normal good humour had faded, and Fin saw the muscles in his jaw twitch.

'They've gone into the boy – he's got them all now.' The Borough Guardsman's Adam's apple visibly bobbed up and down in his thin neck as he said the words aloud. 'And then the storm started.'

Fin turned, all thoughts of adventures with Anaïs forgotten, and was about to start running when Blake grabbed his arm, spinning him round.

'Where the hell do you think you're going?' he asked.

'To Joe – I have to see Joe!'

'No.' Lucas Blake's grip was firm on Fin's wriggling arm. 'No, you can't.'

'But I *have* to.'

'He's got people with him. Fowkes will take care of him.' Blake refused to let go. 'Listen to me, Finmere, this isn't some stupid game. Look at the sky – there's *something* coming, something *bad*, and right now we all have stuff we need to do to fight it. And that means you too.'

The fight went out of Fin. Lucas Blake was right, there was nothing he could do by running back to the Old Bailey except try and make Joe feel better. His stomach churned. The problem was, he *wanted* to make Joe feel better. If it wasn't for Fin, Joe wouldn't even be in this mess. He'd never have even heard of The Nowhere if it hadn't been for him.

'But he needs me,' he said, quietly. He wasn't pulling away now, and Lucas Black let go of his arm.

'Yes, he probably does,' the Knight said, 'but so do we, and right now our need is more urgent. Tova saw these attacks, didn't she?'

Fin nodded.

'Storyholders don't normally get visions. They can sense stuff, but they don't see things like that, so whatever is happening here is important for everyone – maybe just as important as Joe becoming the Storyholder.' Lucas Blake slapped Fin gently on the arm. 'And there aren't enough of us to spare you for your friend right at the moment.'

'What are we going to do?' Christopher asked.

'We need to know how serious this coming storm is. Knowing how far it's spread will give us some idea.'

'I'll take my men across the river to the South,' Curran

Tugg said. 'The Times doesn't lie. If there's something bad coming, the water will know. If she's hard to manage, that will be a tell in itself. The South will need to know what's happened to the Five Eternal Stories too.' He paused. 'They'll talk of the Prophecy. They're superstitious in the South.'

'Maybe they're right to be.' Lucas Blake's expression was grim. 'Alex and I will head north to the edge of the city and see if it's just as bad out beyond the walls.' He looked back at Curran Tugg. 'Let's aim to get back here by dawn. Mona, you can send one of your men to tell Fowkes what we're doing.'

Fin stared. He hadn't even known there were city walls around London – it hadn't occurred to him before now. In fact, it hadn't occurred to him that there was more to The Nowhere than just London. If he thought about it, he wasn't overly convinced there was much of any worth outside of London in his *own* world – after all, who would live anywhere else if they had any choice?

'We'll get you horses,' Mona said. 'You can have mine for one. Her name's Domino. She's fast, and she's got a sixth sense when it comes to finding the quickest ways to places.' She flashed a look at the guardsman. 'You can take them there.'

'So it's down to you four to find this attacker, and stop him if you can,' Lucas Blake said. 'It's not going to be easy – I don't even know where you should start looking – but you're bright kids and I trust you to do as good a job as any of us could.' He grinned, and the sparkle was back in his eyes. 'Probably better.'

Fin grinned, and when he looked at Christopher he saw his best friend was doing the same. Lucas Blake's good humour was catching.

Mona reached into her jacket and pulled out a small notebook, handing it to Fin. 'This has got all the names and addresses of the key witnesses – you know, the people who found the victims and stuff. Go and talk to them again, see if they've remembered anything else. They're more likely to talk to you than they ever were to me or my men.'

'But you're in charge of the Borough Guard.' Fin frowned.

'Exactly.' Mona raised an eyebrow. 'They always want us gone quickly. Everyone's got secrets here. I used to run around in the Crookeries, remember?' She smiled at Anaïs. 'Plus, she's a Gypsy Trader. *Everyone* will want to talk to her – no one ever sees Gypsy Traders above ground.'

'How will I find my way to all these places?' Fin asked, taking the notebook.

'Don't worry,' Anaïs said, 'I know my way around.'

In return, she handed Mona the map her grandmother had given her. The two girls smiled at each other with a healthy respect. On the outside, they were completely different, Mona petite and dusky, the opposite of Anaïs' willowy, cool paleness, but Fin thought that on the inside there wasn't so much between them. They were both determined and rebellious and more than a little wilful. He had a feeling it was likely to be less of he and Christopher looking after the girls, more the girls keeping an eye out for the boys.

'So you take the Rivers and we'll take the surface,' Fin said. He looked at Christopher. 'You all right with that?' He couldn't help feel a huge sense of relief. If he could avoid going back out on the water, he would. He liked to forget about the box in his head, not hear it rattling about so angrily.

'Yep,' Christopher answered, 'not a problem.' He didn't grin though.

'Take my beer.' Fin handed over what was left in his flask. 'Just in case.'

'We should arrange to meet up,' Mona said. 'If one pair finds something out, the others are going to need to know.'

'Where?'

'Why not my dad's shop? At The Circus? That's as good a place as any, and it's easy to find. How about midnight? That gives us a few hours.' She grinned. 'We'll have it all figured out by then, I'm sure of it.'

'Yeah, course we will.' Fin smiled. 'Piece of piss.'

'Yuk.' Anaïs screwed her face up. 'That's disgusting.'

Fin smiled at Christopher. 'Take care, mate.'

'You too.' Christopher raised a hand and high-fived him. 'See you at midnight, Fin.' He winked. 'And don't do anything I wouldn't do.'

'Well then,' said Lucas Blake, clapping his hands together, 'let's get going. Good luck to you all. And whatever happens: *let us be ready*.'

He pulled out his sword and Fin and Alex did the same, tapping the end of their blades against one another's.

'Let us be ready!'

SEVENTEEN

'We thought you were dead,' Cardrew Cutler said cheerfully as he reached for his teacup with an arthritic hand. Jarvis slid closer from his position against the wall to help, but the old man waved him away.

'I bet you did,' the Seer smiled back. His eyes were like dark raisins against the leather of his face, but his teeth were clean, and gleamed white. From the pocket of his battered denim jacket he took a small bottle of whisky and added a shot to his china cup. He offered the bottle around the room, but there were no other takers. 'Suit yourselves.'

'I take it from your accent that you've spent quite a lot of time in America.' The distaste was clear in Freddie Wise's voice.

'Seemed like a place with a lot to offer.' The Seer leaned back in the wing-back armchair. 'And the West Coast is a long way from London and that suited me fine.' He sipped his drink and smacked his lips together. 'Jarvis, you are a man of many talents. You always did make a damned fine cup of tea.' His eyes lingered on the butler for a moment, and then moved around the room. 'Sorry to see you've Aged while I've been away.'

'I doubt you've given us a thought,' Freddie Wise snapped.

'Oh come on, Freddie, that's not entirely fair.' Cardrew pointed a finger at his old friend. 'You can't decide someone's path for them – we all know that.'

'But a Seer who refuses to *see*? It's ridiculous.'

'Harlequin used to talk about you a lot, you know,' Ted said. 'I'm sad 'e didn't get to see you again before 'e died.'

The Seer's face softened. 'Me too, old man. Me too.'

They were in the downstairs sitting room in Orrery House, Freddie Wise having suggested that keeping the Seer and the Table apart might be for the best, given that the man insisted on not *seeing*, and the Table could behave oddly around those that were a little bit *other*. The large grandfather clock in the corner ticked away the minutes as the men sipped their tea until the quiet was broken by Simeon Soames' arrival.

'Ah – a new face,' the Seer said, his face crinkling into a grin.

'I might be after your time,' Soames said, taking a cup of tea from Jarvis, 'but I've been here a long old while now.'

'Been through the Ageing and back again, 'as young Simeon,' Ted added.

'Well, you're looking good on it,' the Seer smiled. 'Last time I was here my hair was golden-blond, just like yours.' He wiped away a silvery-grey strand that was hanging loose over his face. 'But my ageing is purely natural.'

'And high time a man of your age cut off that ridiculous ponytail,' Wise added, dryly.

The Seer laughed out loud; a sound like a warm breeze on the Arizona desert at dusk. 'Maybe I should at that.' He stood up and walked over to the large French windows that looked out over the small like cotton, walled-in garden at the back of Orrery House. Under his denim jacket he wore a loose cream shirt made of cotton, and scuffed tan cowboy boots peeped from under his faded jeans. His hands were tanned deep brown from the sun, and around his neck he wore a circle of beads with a silver pendant hanging just over his Adam's apple.

'Interesting weather we're having,' he said softly. Outside, night had fallen and the air was black, except that out at the edges it was tinted with crimson, a colour that had no right

180

being there. Every now and then thunder rolled overhead, defying the clear sky and the twinkling stars.

'Is that why you came back, Arthur Mulligan?' Cardrew said. 'Have you seen something to do with this coming storm?'

'No one's called me Arthur Mulligan for a long time.' The old cowboy didn't turn from looking out at the night. 'But I guess it feels right to use it back here.'

'Well, I can't very well call you the Seer, can I?' Cutler laughed slightly. 'In your case it'd be an honorary title or something.'

'They called me Billy in America,' he said reflectively. 'I always liked that name. But I was born Arthur Mulligan, and I'm the Seer, whether I like it or not.'

'So you *have* seen something,' Wise said thoughtfully.

'Is it to do with the storm?' Soames asked, 'or the fire at the Storyholder Academy? Or the people being made mad?'

'Or the crack in the table?' Cutler added.

The Seer turned at the flurry of questions and his eyes widened slightly. 'Sounds like things are busy around here – no wonder you were all so pleased to see me.' He raised a sardonic eyebrow at Freddie Wise. 'Well, nearly all of you.'

'Anything you've got that can 'elp us,' Ted started.

'There's one thing I keep seeing – just one thing. It's easier not to see here than it is over there, but this just keeps coming through. I couldn't block it.'

'What?' Soames asked.

'My own death, son.' The sky darkened a little more outside. 'And it's coming up fast.' He looked at Ted. 'That's why I've come back. I don't die here, you see, I die in The Nowhere, and I ain't got no method of getting there myself other than a wish and a prayer that a hole will open up for me, and I've never held much with wishes.'

'You want us to take you back?' Cardrew Cutler's teacup paused an inch away from his lips. 'To die?'

'That's what I've seen.'

'But what about all this?' Freddie Wise cut impatiently through the stunned quiet. 'What help can you give us for this?'

'I can't help you, man.'

'You *won't* help us.'

'Nothing is as it seems, but everything is as it should be.' The Seer smiled.

'And what the hell is *that* supposed to mean?' Cardrew Cutler asked. 'I was never great at riddles. Never saw the point. Like the *Times*' bloody Crossword.'

The door opened and Henry Wakley strode in, sliding his sword back into its scabbard.

'What on earth—?' Freddie Wise started.

'Sorry, should have knocked.' The young blond man grinned slightly, but the smile didn't last more than a second. 'Fowkes sent me.'

'What is it?' Ted asked, getting to his feet.

'It's the stories,' Wakley said, 'they're in the boy – all five of them. Fowkes thinks that's what's causing the weather.'

There was a long moment of silence as the men looked at each other, then outside. They might not have been sitting in the Oval Room, but the Prophecy still hung between them, two lines clear in all their thoughts.

Eternal stories held unready shall bring
Black tempest, madness, and a battle for King.

'Well—' It was Arthur Mulligan, the long-missing Seer, who broke the silence. 'I've been feeling quite maudlin about my imminent demise, but hearing that? You've really cheered me up. I think perhaps I'm getting out just in time.'

As Joe closed up the hole behind him he found himself in exactly the place he'd been thinking of as he fled the Storyholder's apartments, the only place he'd wanted to be for ages: home. The Brickman Estate. It was mid-evening, and freezing cold, but the swings were full of teenagers about ten years too old for the seats, and they rocked backwards and forwards and scuffed their shoes along the tarmac as they smoked cigarettes or something stronger.

Joe emerged from the gloom by the bushes. Perhaps they'd seen him, but he didn't think so, and he found he didn't much care. What would they say? 'We saw Joe Manning appear out of nowhere beside a bush?' Who'd believe them? *Out of nowhere*. The phrase made him smile a little, despite his aching head. He was surprised he even got the joke. Had the stories made him cleverer? It was so hard to tell. His mind was racing over what felt like the enormity of space and time, and everywhere it hovered there were voices and people and stories. There was darkness too, an underlying creeping dread, and when he stopped trying to control the roar of life in his brain he found his thoughts full of the mad – those red-eyed, black-tongued creatures locked up in the White Tower.

He started walking with the sword hanging at his side, holding the belt and scabbard in one hand. The play area – it had been designed for kids, but was rarely used by anyone under fourteen these days – was part of a square of greenery enclosed by the grey blocks of flats. Lights shone from the windows, and fairy-lights and Santas were twinkling away in many, the bright colours dispelling some of the dingy grime that coated the 1960s buildings. Joe was pretty sure that other people might find the Brickman Estate ugly, even scary, but there was beauty to be found in familiarity, and this was his home. He'd never lived anywhere else. He'd never even been abroad, not until he'd followed Fin into The Nowhere and towards his own destiny.

His head hurt so much it made his teeth sing. As he passed the small gathering hanging out in the gloom he felt their eyes turn on him and his sword that glittered in the moonlight. Overhead thunder rumbled, and for a moment the pain loosened its grip. The teenagers – all older than him, a gang he'd always sought to avoid – dropped their eyes as he passed. No one called out or heckled him, and he didn't look their way. They were nothing to him.

He paused at the edge of the rough grass and looked up at the third floor and the familiar blue door there. His mum had repainted it only a few weeks before and now it shone out between the battered and chipped doors on either side. Shadows moved on the other side of the decorated window and Joe thought that if he listened very carefully he could hear the strains of her gospel choir Christmas songs CD. There was happiness behind that window, and it made his heart ache to be on the wrong side of it.

He was spotlit under the yellow outside lights, a lonely figure staring up at the window, the sword forgotten in his hand. He'd wanted to see this – he still did, but it was like a bottomless well of wanting draining his soul. He'd thought that if he could just get home, then she'd make everything all right, just as she always had, but now that he was back, he knew that he'd been wrong. His mum couldn't make things better for him, and if he went upstairs and knocked on that freshly painted blue door, then he'd most likely make things worse for her – much worse. He couldn't pretend that everything was normal, he couldn't be his old light-hearted self, not now that the other voice was in charge. She'd see through that in an instant. And anyway, how would he ever begin to explain what he was doing there?

A tear trickled down his cheek, feeling hot against the freezing mist of the night. Expensive shoes clicked on the concrete and he turned to see Levi Dodge walking towards him. The man stopped a few feet away from the boy.

'I was going to see my mum,' Joe said.

Levi Dodge remained impassive.

Around them, figures crept out of the gloom.

'I think my head is full of the mad.' The two sentences were unrelated, and yet they went together perfectly to Joe.

'The car is waiting.' Levi Dodge didn't look at the people who were drawing closer, coming out of the shadows that housed the bin areas and lifts and stairwells, but Joe did. He recognised some of them – junkies from the estate, their battles with the needle lost so long ago that they probably didn't even remember any other way of life. An old Jamaican woman approached and rattled bones at him, but she didn't come too close before stopping. In the flats that surrounded them a few doors opened, and more people came out and stared down at him, their expressions unreadable in the night, but their bodies completely still.

Joe turned. The gang on the swings were on their feet, and all eyes were on him.

'What do they want?' Joe asked.

'They want to follow you,' Levi Dodge said. 'They're your people.'

Joe looked around him again. These were the mad and the diseased – these weren't his people at all, they couldn't be. The darkness in his mind yawned wide and he wanted to cry.

'Get me out of here,' he muttered.

Levi Dodge did what he was told.

Mitesh Savjani and Andrew Fowkes had sent the Chancellors back to the palace as soon as Joe had disappeared into The Somewhere. Having them gone was a relief – Fowkes could feel the disdain oozing from beneath their disguised faces, as if this was something they could somehow have prevented, if only the situation had been left in the hands of The Nowhere. What bothered Fowkes most was that they might have been right.

'It seems that whenever we get involved in Nowhere business, we cause trouble,' he said. 'Trouble is trouble.' Mitesh Savjani joined him midway down the white curving staircase between the Storyholder's apartments and the large hall of Truth Vials. 'And the worlds have always been linked, especially yours and ours, my friend. Your trouble is our trouble.' He handed Fowkes a glass of red wine and sipped his own.

'It doesn't feel that way from here.'

'Not to you,' Savjani sighed, 'because you have always felt responsible.'

Both pairs of dark eyes lingered on the step below them. That was where Baxter had lost his life, so many years before.

'I was responsible for that,' Fowkes said.

'No, no, no.' Savjani wiggled one chubby jewelled finger back and forth like a teacher. 'We each make our own decisions. Adam Baxter, he was a good friend and a fine Knight, and he *chose* not to let the mob up to you. And remember, I knew him too, Andrew Fowkes, and he would have done this with a light heart, because he loved you. This was his choice.'

'Do you think Tova will be okay?'

'I do not know. This will depend on how much she wants to be okay.' Savjani swallowed more wine. 'She knows she is well-loved. And perhaps when we find young Joe, all will be restored.'

Fowkes looked at the clothcrafter. 'You do a fine line in optimism.'

'It is easy for me,' Mitesh Savjani's eyes twinkled, 'for no one is looking to me for answers. But for you, Fowkes, the answer lies in finding who is pulling the strings of this boy as if he is a puppet.' Savjani stroked his perfectly pointed beard with the purple stone at the centre. The colour almost matched the stone in Fowkes' ring and sword, and Fowkes wondered if that choice was a throwback to when they had all been barely that much older than Finmere and his friends, when Savjani had yearned to be a Knight. He bet there were moments now when the clothcrafter was happy that hadn't been a possibility.

'This boy is a good boy, yes?' he continued. 'I remember

him when they came to my shop. He had an open face, a happy smile. He is not a natural deceiver, I think.'

'I think you're right,' Fowkes agreed. Shame itched at him for his earlier suspicions of Joe. 'I don't believe he chose this.'

'No, this chose him.' Savjani gave Fowkes a sideways glance. 'This you must remember, whatever happens. He was chosen, and someone has manipulated that – someone, I think, unseen.'

'I know,' Fowkes agreed. 'I believe that someone had the Gatekeeper killed, and sent some men over here to start that fire. I think they're probably dead too. I suspect whoever did that is behind Joe taking the stories and Baxter's sword.'

'This person knows things – things they shouldn't,' Savjani mused. His forehead wrinkled slightly as he concentrated, and Fowkes was reminded of all the years that had passed since they'd been young and devil-may-care.

'That thought has crossed my mind.'

'It is with a heavy heart that I say this,' Mitesh Savjani squeezed his friend's shoulder, 'but someone is betraying you, I think.'

'I think so too.'

Benjamin Wakley appeared at the top of the steps. 'Henry's back. And he's got someone with him.'

'No need for introductions.' The American drawl came from behind the tall blond man. 'I'm not stopping, just passing through.'

Fowkes was sure he heard a hint of Leeds in the North American accent. He climbed to his feet as the denim-clad cowboy started to stroll down the stairs. He grinned at both Fowkes and Mitesh Savjani. 'Don't mind me, just carry on.'

Henry Wakley appeared behind his brother and they both came down the stairs and joined Fowkes and Savjani.

'They said he was the—'

'—the Seer.' Mitesh Savjani finished the sentence, his eyes

focused on the pendant hanging from the weatherbeaten neck.

'It's just a title,' the man with the grey ponytail said, 'I don't do a lot of *seeing* – not that kind, at any rate, and not for forty years or so.'

'I've heard about you,' Fowkes said.

'And I've heard about you, so that makes us even.'

The Seer headed towards the side door with the ease of someone totally familiar with his surroundings. For a moment, Fowkes was too stunned to speak. This was the Seer, Arthur Mulligan: a character from the old days, when Ted and Harlequin Brown were as young as the Wakley twins, someone who'd been gone so long he was almost fictional.

'Where are you going?' he said eventually, running to catch up. 'We need you!'

'No, you don't. And even if you do, the timing's all wrong.' The Seer pulled open the door. 'Time can be funny like that. Speaking of which, it looks like time is misbehaving right now.'

'That's strange.' Mitesh Savjani looked past the Seer and out into the quiet street. 'It's getting dark. Surely it's only three o'clock?'

'Cold too,' the Seer added.

'Henry,' Fowkes started as he stepped past Arthur Mulligan and into the fresh air. It was definitely crisper than it had been early, and the sky was midnight-blue, hesitating on the edge of night, 'what time was it back home?'

'About eight?'

'Feels like about six here,' the Seer said, drawing in a deep breath. 'Damn, that tastes good.'

'How can it be six o'clock?' Benjamin Wakley muttered.

'The worlds are aligning.' The Seer grinned. 'You've got some stuff coming to you – I don't have to be a Seer to know that.'

As if to back up his words, the sky rumbled and then a crack of barely visible black lightning shot across the sky.

'That's not good,' Fowkes muttered.

'White lightning in a clear sky, and black at night?' The Seer shook his head. 'It's the storm they all talk about. It's coming.' He pulled a cigarette from his top pocket and lit it with a match from a battered box. 'I saw it once,' he said softly, 'a long time ago. I closed my mind after that. There's some things no one should know.'

'You could have helped us,' Fowkes growled.

'Maybe I did, son, in my own way.' He blew out a long breath of smoke. 'Maybe I did.'

'You should quit. Those things will kill you.'

'No, they won't. You can trust me on that.' The Seer gave Fowkes a soft smile. 'And now I'm heading out to wander round. It's been a long time and I want to see how much this crazy place has changed.' He stepped past Fowkes and turned to face the group gathered in the doorway. 'I won't see you all again, but I wish you the best of luck. Stay true to your hearts and you can't go wrong.'

He turned before he'd finished his sentence, the last words drifting back to them as he ambled round to the front of the building.

'The Seer,' Mitesh Savjani breathed, and in his voice Fowkes heard an awe that took him back to the first time he and Baxter ever cut a doorway open in front of their young Nowhere friend. 'The Seer is back.'

'For all the good he'll do us.'

'He will.' The clothcrafter twirled his moustache. 'In this we must trust.'

Thunder rolled, and lightning cut shadows in the sky.

'It's the wrong way round,' Henry Wakley said.

'What?'

'The thunder and lightning,' Benjamin answered for his twin. 'The thunder's coming first.'

'This is not good,' Savjani repeated, 'not good at all.'

'The Rage is coming, isn't it?' Fowkes looked at his friend and then back up to the sky. No one answered. They didn't need to.

EIGHTEEN

Anaïs hadn't lied: she did know her way around the city, almost as well as Mona, and within an hour or so she and Fin had seen three of the witnesses on Mona's list. Not that it had done them much good.

'I thought I had a vivid imagination,' Anaïs said quietly as they left the bakery, 'but these people!' She leaned in closer to Fin, so as not to be heard. 'A two-headed dog bit her? I mean, really!'

Finmere wasn't really aware of what she was saying, but he smiled anyway. She dazzled him slightly, and as they moved through the indoor market there was nothing on the stalls or the hot food stands that could distract him from looking at her for long. He'd almost tripped twice, but she hadn't noticed his clumsiness because she was so absorbed in the sights and sounds of the city around them. He'd hoped she'd be a little keener on looking at him, but the upside was if she wasn't looking at him too much, then she might not notice what a gormless prat he was around her.

'My father is so out of touch,' she said, leaning in to smell a pot of soup bubbling on a wooden counter. The portly stall-holder had shooed away someone away just before them, for doing the same thing, but he just smiled at Anaïs. So it wasn't only Fin she had that effect on.

She tossed her fine blonde hair over one shoulder. 'The surface and the water *are* linked – they always have been, and they always will be. Dad thinks that by accepting the surface and its ways, he has to give up our traditions.'

'Sounds like the Prince Regent isn't so fond of the Gypsy Traders, though,' Fin said.

'I think he'd like us just fine if we came above ground and acknowledged his rules. And I don't really see why that would be such a problem.' She frowned slightly, the sudden creases on her forehead like ripples on a lake. 'I can't understand who couldn't love the land as much as the water. Can you?'

Fin had never really thought about it all that much. It wasn't something that really applied in The Somewhere.

'What's the river like in your world?' she asked. Her bare arm brushed against Fin's and his mouth dried.

It took him a minute or two before he could speak again. 'Pretty boring really,' he muttered, looking at the ground. 'It's just *water* – we can swim in it and everything, but nobody does that in the centre of town because it's so dirty.' She was watching him intently, and although he couldn't quite bring himself to meet her gaze her felt his skin prickle under it. 'Well, it's cleaner than it was, but all the same ... Oh, and we have loads of bridges, so anyone can get from one side to the other. One of my schools is in South London actually. And there are tubes – trains that run underground – that take you from one side to the other, and all over the city.'

He looked up and saw her eyes were wide and her lips slightly parted. She really was beautiful – and she wasn't wearing even the slightest scrap of make-up, as far as he could tell. You'd never catch a girl at Eastfields without at least an inch of that stuff they pancaked on their faces. He didn't really know why they did it either. What was wrong with just looking pretty naturally?

'That doesn't sound ordinary to me. That sounds amazing.' She smiled at him, and for the first time he saw a slight nervousness.

'Well, your rivers and boats and stuff look pretty amazing to me, so I guess we're quits.'

'Perhaps one day you can take me to your world.' She

flashed a grin over her shoulder at him as she leaned in to look at some brightly coloured caged birds, and for a crazy moment Fin thought she might just be flirting with him.

'I've heard stories about you,' she said as she slipped a slim finger through the cage. 'How you went into the Magi's mirror and saved the Storyholder? How you stopped the black tempest?'

'How did you hear about that?' Fin was surprised. It was weird to think about people he didn't know talking about him.

'Our worlds are built on stories, Fin.' Anaïs paused to whistle back at the bird, mimicking its merry tune perfectly. 'People tell them all the time – you can call it gossip or rumour, but in the end it's all just stories. And when people do things like you and your friends did with the Knights – well, those stories spread, so now there're loads of stories about you. Even my grandmother likes you. She says you're a wild card, whatever that means.'

'I didn't do much really.' He was beginning to feel horribly embarrassed. Looking back on the events of the last two months, it was difficult to remember exactly what he had done, apart from going into the Incarcerator prison. It had all happened so quickly, and lots of other people did as much – or more – and were definitely braver than him. 'There's nothing special about me,' he said firmly.

'There's something special about everyone,' she said, softly. 'None of us can be replaced, and none of us can ever be here again. No matter how much time slips and slides around, we only ever get one line in it. My grandmother taught me that.'

Although he smiled back at her, he felt suddenly sad at that thought, though he wasn't sure why. The gold-and-red bird hopped onto Anaïs' finger. There was definitely something special about her; even the birds noticed it. She gently shook the bird back to its perch and stood up.

'Let's get on to the next one, shall we? The market will be

here another day.' She looked down at the list in Fin's hand and tapped a fingernail on the page. 'The washerwoman. We can get to her easily from here.'

They hurried to the entrance of the covered market, ignoring the various attractions on offer, until they reached the fresh air. The stalls were quieter there, customers and vendors huddled together and muttering. Fin frowned, but it wasn't until they stepped outside themselves that he realised what was bothering them.

They both slowed to a halt. It had been bright sunlight when they'd gone into the market, not so long before, but now it was almost dark. Evening had fallen in the space of an hour. How had that happened? The white lightning that had split the air earlier had been odd enough, but this was something else.

'I know time can be funny in The Nowhere,' Fin muttered, 'but surely this is too much of a coincidence ...'

'What do you think is happening?' Anaïs was breathless as she looked up. Around them, the street had stilled, all its occupants gazing skywards, like them. Some had even come out of their front doors to see. No one was smiling. Anaïs didn't sound scared, though; there was a brightness about her that hinted at excitement.

Fin wished he could share it.

'I think all those stories are wrong,' he said slowly, working it out in his head. 'I don't think we stopped that storm at all – not the one that everyone talks about, the one in the Prophecy.' Cold dread unfurled in his stomach. 'I think that's what's coming now.'

'But how?' Anaïs looked at him, her face flushing slightly.

'The stories – they're in Joe now, and I don't think that's a good thing.'

'What shall we do?' The tempest brewing in the sky was clearly exciting her more than chasing down witnesses, but Fin was determined not to be distracted, however much he wanted to head straight back to the Old Bailey and check on Joe.

'We go and see the washerwoman, like you said.' He looked up at the darkening sky again. 'We've got less time until midnight than we originally thought.'

When the car pulled up outside Grey's, Joe found he wasn't surprised, though it might have been that he just didn't care. His head hurt, and the voices of the mad were crowding in. What did they want from him? Listening to them on top of containing a universe in his mind was like having strips torn from his brain. The street people had disturbed him, the homeless and the drunks and the mentally damaged – they'd all stopped and turned to stare at the car as Levi Dodge cruised slowly through the city. None of the normal people looked, those laughing and joking outside pubs, shops and restaurants with faces glowing with the happiness, they didn't glance in his direction once. It was just the others – the forgotten and unnoticed. Joe didn't like it; it made him shiver, even in the warmth of the car.

The plaque outside Grey's – Established 1682. 'Semper fidelis, Semper paratus' – *Always faithful, Always ready* – was as highly polished as it had been when Joe had come here with Ted, Fin and Christopher, when he first met Mr Arnold-Mather. He'd pretended to be on a scholarship, and Mr Arnold-Mather had pretended to go along with their story about a school project. It looked like Christopher's dad had always been one step ahead of them. The memory was a bit of a joke now, he thought as he stepped through the door and into the softly lit hallway. He waited by the red and green chesterfield sofas. The room was imprinted in his memory – boys from the Brickman Estate didn't venture into gentlemen's clubs all that often – but now he was seeing the room through different eyes; now he had knowledge. Not that he was sure he had ever wanted knowledge – it was full of deceit, and he had never been a liar or a cheat. But now he was bound to betrayal – he had been ever since he'd slipped the sleeping drugs into Tova's hot chocolate. Part of him wanted to cry, and part of him – the new voice, the new Joe – wanted to rejoice. That part of him would happily take the pain in his head for the power it promised, the ability to be *special*, something more than Fin or Christopher or Mona, to *show them all*.

'Come this way please.' The door on their left opened silently and an elderly man in a maroon jacket and dark tie waved them into a corridor. He didn't smile, and neither did Joe. 'Mr Arnold-Mather is upstairs.' The man's eyes moved to the bundled-up jacket and jumper that contained the poorly disguised sword as a flash of gold glinted from one of the folds. Joe looked up and held the man's impassive gaze with one of his own. After a moment the old man sniffed slightly, and then led them up a wooden staircase. He knocked softly on the first door to the left, and opened it.

'Now that is interesting,' Mr Arnold-Mather was speaking into the old-fashioned receiver of the green dial-up phone that sat on a large desk against one wall. 'Stay in touch. I want to know everything.' He gestured for them to come in as he carefully replaced the handset, and Levi Dodge clicked the door shut behind them, leaving the man in the red jacket still standing on the other side.

'Welcome, Storyholder.' Justin Arnold-Mather leaned back on the desk and smiled.

The word fizzed in Joe's head. It was the first time anyone had acknowledged his new role. He *was* the Storyholder, whether the Knights and The Nowhere liked it or not, and he was beginning to realise the Storyholder had far more power than Tova had ever allowed herself.

'My head hurts,' he said, flopping into a large armchair. Even though the fire in the grate hadn't yet been lit, the room was warm, and he allowed the bundle he carried to fall to the floor as he stretched out his legs. On top of the headache, he was completely exhausted – the kind of tired that makes you feel nauseous, like when you've done too much circuit training at football practice.

The sword tumbled free from its precarious wrapping and Arnold-Mather's smile stretched. His face shone in the reflected gold. 'Excellent,' he said. 'I knew everything would go according to plan. And you found using the sword easy enough?' He sipped his own brandy before pouring a small tumbler of iced water from the jug on the desk and handing it to Joe with a packet of Nurofen.

Joe took them, but what did Mr Arnold-Mather think they were going to do? It almost made him laugh. The man might be clever, and have great plans for them both, but he had no real understanding of what was raging inside Joe, leaving feeling like his skin might tear apart with the awful pressure of it. Two Nurofens really weren't going to touch the sides of that.

'Yes, it was easy,' he said. 'I didn't even have to think about it.' A large portrait of a man in judge's robes hung above the fireplace. It wasn't old, not like most paintings of people he'd seen, where the colours had faded to somewhere between green and brown and none of the faces actually looked real. This portrait was bright, and fresh. The thin, middle-aged man in judge's robes had kind eyes, and even though it wasn't possible, Joe thought that the judge in the painting was looking pityingly at him.

'So what now?' He looked away, his eyes falling on the small Christmas tree by the window that was elegantly dressed in silver and gold beads and very little else. There was no garish tinsel, or baubles and too many fairy-lights, like there would be on his mum's tree. This tree looked like it was almost sneering at the idea of Christmas. Eventually he looked up at the man who had led him here.

'It is time we took our places in the order of things.' Mr Arnold-Mather spoke softly. 'And that is in The Nowhere. I don't know about you,' he tipped his glass at Joe, 'but I like to go straight to the seat of power. No point in messing around with the lower echelons when you don't have to.'

'Are we going to the Knights' house? Over there?'

'Oh, I was thinking somewhat higher than that.'

A bottle smashed in the street outside, and Levi Dodge pulled the heavy curtain slightly aside and peered out, frowning. Joe could hear what should have been the strains of 'God rest ye Merry Gentlemen' floating up from the pavement, but it sounded wrong. There were at least six voices, but they weren't singing in unison, and they weren't quite in tune. His heart thumped as he got up and joined Levi Dodge at the glass. The singers weren't Salvation Army, or respectable middle-aged churchgoers. They were a disparate bunch of misfits, swaying on the pavement. A broken bottle was lying at the feet of a man in too-short trousers and a Disney sweatshirt. His hair was unkempt, and he was scrawnily thin. Joe's skin crawled with revulsion. The singers looked up and met his eyes as one, and he saw the adulation there. He let the curtain drop and stepped backwards.

'What on earth is that racket?' Mr Arnold-Mather said.

'It's me,' Joe answered. 'They're wanting to be near me.'

'How fascinating.' Justin Arnold-Mather ignored the fear that was clear on Joe's face. 'I think it's time we were leaving.' He smiled. 'Time for you to show me The Nowhere, young man.'

Joe picked up the sword, and the warm metal worked better on soothing his aching head than the painkillers ever could. 'So, if you don't want to go to the Knights' house, where do you want me to take you? The Old Bailey House of Real Truths?''

'No,' Mr Arnold-Mather said, shaking his head. He smiled and drained his brandy before telling Joe. And suddenly it all became clear.

*

After clearing the discordant carol singers away from the quiet street outside, Carter brushed down his red jacket – because one drunk had *insisted* on coming inside because *he* was there, whoever *he* was – and went back upstairs with a small plate of freshly baked mince pies. The Club was busier than normal this close to Christmas, but it lacked the usual joviality of previous years; he'd actually heard two or three of the members snapping angrily at each other. He frowned. It just wasn't the way members at Grey's behaved. But then, neither was bringing teenage boys into the building. There were clear age restrictions, and Mr Arnold-Mather knew that as well as any member did. It was bad form to expect a blind eye to be turned. Not that he had, entirely: he'd seen the flash of metal, and he was quite sure whatever the item was, it was not a normal gift for a government minister.

He knocked once, and then opened the door to the small private study. 'I've brought you some—' But the rest of the sentence drifted away. The room was empty. Carter peered into the hall and at the stairs behind him. Surely they couldn't have left without him seeing them? He put the plate down on the table and looked up at the newly hung portrait of Judge Harlequin Brown, one of the finest members Grey's had ever had the privilege to admit.

Perhaps this was something, and perhaps it was nothing. But the Judge would have erred on the side of caution. Carter picked up the telephone and very carefully began to dial the number he'd memorised years ago. He had never before had occasion to use it.

The number rang several times before someone answered.

'Hello? Oh good afternoon. I'd like to speak to Mr Ted Merryweather, please. Yes, it's important.'

He glanced back up at the Judge's painting and he was sure the eyes looked at him approvingly.

NINETEEN

Night had fallen completely by the time Finmere and Anaïs got to the washerwoman's house, which was only half a mile from the Old Bailey. The sculpted truth vial at the building's peak shone palely against the dark sky. The thunder had eased off, and for that Fin was grateful, but it had been replaced with a cold December chill.

'I remember you,' the washerwoman said as she opened the thick wooden door to them. 'You were there when I found poor Millie.'

'Yes, I was,' Fin said. 'I'm sorry about your friend. It must have been a terrible shock.'

The woman was in her fifties, dressed in a plain dress with an off-white apron over the top. Her sleeves were rolled up, revealing reddened arms and chapped hands. 'She was a good girl, Millie. She weren't afraid of hard work.' Her eyes reddened slightly but she didn't cry. Neither did she invite them in. Her eyes moved from Finmere to Anaïs and sudden curiosity replaced the sadness. 'You're a Trader girl, aren't you? Gypsy stock, if I'm not mistaken.' She smiled. 'No drawings on you yet – and on the surface, too. Unusual.'

It was Anaïs' turn to look surprised. 'You know a lot about us.'

'It's been a long life, girl.' The washerwoman smiled, an open, friendly gesture that revealed several blackening teeth. 'I had a romance with a Gypsy Trader once, a long time ago, when I was a wild young thing like you. Never came to

nothing, mind; couldn't really, could it? But oh, it was fun.'
She folded her broad arms across her ample chest. 'So what
are you two doing visiting me?'

'It's about Millie,' Fin said. 'We're trying to help find who's
attacking all these people. It's not just happening in this
Borough, you see ...'

'Oh, I know that, boy,' she snorted. 'I've got ears and gossip moves faster than wind in London.'

'So you know that whoever's doing this can Travel,' Anaïs
added.

'It did cross my mind – and probably quicker than it did
the Borough Guard. Always interfering, that lot, and never
doing much good, it seems to me.'

'The Knights and the Traders have joined forces,' Fin said,
'trying to find a pattern. I know the guards will have asked
you if you saw anything unusual when you found Millie, but
we thought we'd ask again.'

The washerwoman stared from one to the other for a long
moment.

'There was something,' she said eventually, glancing over
her shoulder and then leaning in to them. 'I was going to go
and find the guard and tell them, but my old man, well, he
weren't so keen, and it weren't such a big thing ...' He voice
wavered off towards the end of her sentence.

'What was it?' Fin asked.

'Well, there was a fella there when I got there, just sitting
against the wall, like he was drunk, or asleep or something.
But when I came along he got up and disappeared round the
corner, so I didn't get a good look, and then I was too distracted by Millie. I called after him, but he was gone. Didn't
see much of him at all.'

'What *did* you see?' Fin's heart thumped. This was the
closest they'd come to something real all day.

'I think he was wearing black trousers. And a really muddy
black coat. Or cape.' She frowned. 'And he didn't have

any boots on – I do remember that. I thought it was odd to be wandering around barefoot when shoes ain't exactly expensive.' She looked back over her shoulder. 'I'd better get back in. He'll be wanting his dinner soon and I haven't even peeled the potatoes.'

'Thanks,' Fin breathed as she closed the door abruptly on them, 'you've been very helpful.'

'Well, that's not much to go on,' Anaïs said, her grin falling.

Fin stared at the door, his mind elsewhere. Sherlock Holmes was back in his head. *Once you eliminate the impossible, whatever remains, no matter how improbable, must be the truth*. He'd never understood it before, but now he did.

'What?' Anaïs asked him.

'If it's not someone from The Somewhere, and it's not someone from The Nowhere, then whoever it is has to have come from somewhere else.' Pieces slowly clicked into place in his head. Could it *really* be him?

'You mean someone from another world?' She stared at him. 'But how is that possible?'

'He wasn't wearing any boots,' Fin muttered.

'You're not making any sense.'

What was it Fowkes had said about the bottomless well? *It'll come out somewhere. Everything always does*. What if it came out in a different world, and that had somehow changed him? What if he'd managed to get back? He turned to Anaïs and grabbed her arm. 'I think I know who's doing this. I need to tell Fowkes!'

'Who?'

'A man – he was one of the bad Knights, and we threw him down Clerke's Well.'

'You did what?' Her eyes widened.

'It's a long story.' Fin didn't really know where to begin. 'But it's going to have to wait.'

'Shall I come with you?'

'No, if time keeps moving at this pace it's going to be

midnight before we know it. You go and see if any of the other witnesses remember anything similar, and then meet Mona and Christopher at The Circus. Just tell them I think George Porter is back, and something's happened to him.'

'George Porter,' Anaïs repeated. 'Okay.'

'I'll try and meet you there – with any luck they'll have found some pattern to his movements and have worked out where he's going to go next.' It was a long shot, but if anyone could figure it out, then Christopher and Mona could.

'Go then.' Anaïs smiled at him.

'Will you be okay?' Fin asked. He wanted her to come with him, more than anything, but he knew that Lucas Blake would be disappointed if he took her. He was right, there weren't enough of them to go round, and someone needed to liaise with the others as they'd arranged.

'Of course,' she said.

Fin squeezed her hand and turned away, but she pulled him back.

'What?'

'This.'

She stretched up on tiptoe and kissed him.

Fin, taken by surprise, almost pulled back, but he found that his lips had a mind of their own and were determined to stay put. She felt warm, and as their tongues met briefly the electricity sparked through his whole body. Whatever chill was settling in the air wasn't touching him any more.

When they parted he was breathless. 'Wow,' was all he could manage. 'I've forgotten what I was supposed to be doing now.'

Anaïs laughed, water on crystal, and pushed him in the direction of the House of Real Truths. 'Saving the day, re-member, Finmere Tingewick Smith?'

'Oh yeah.' He almost tripped over his feet. 'I'll see you at The Circus.'

'Yes, you will.' She grinned at him again, and headed in the opposite direction. It was probably a good thing that she left first. With the taste of her lips still on his, Finmere couldn't imagine trying to go anywhere without her. He watched her disappear, still in a slight daze until the thunder rolled angrily overhead and a cold wind sliced into him. He shivered. It was time to find Fowkes.

He wished he had his sword. This thought came to him more and more often as the days and nights rolled by. If he'd had his sword he might have remembered quicker – about this place, and the other place, and the cutting in-between. The stiff manhole cover squealed slightly as he pushed it up an inch. If he'd had the sword, though, he wouldn't have had the small stone in his pocket. Those two things had been the only things that had shone in that place of endless cold and black emptiness. He'd used the sword to dig the stone free – that had come back to him in a dream that stayed when he awakened – and when one was released from the greedy grip of the hard earth, the other had shattered, each piece solidified in charcoal. He'd got the stone, though, and it was the stone that had led him back, that was leading him still. But there was something about the memory of that sword and what it had once meant that made his heart bleed a little. Blood. *His heartbeat quickened.*

The stone shifted as he climbed out into the quiet street. He didn't need to touch it for warmth any more, for as he'd grown stronger, so it had too, and now the heat coursed through his skin, drying his clothes as soon as he emerged from the water. He didn't need the water any more either, but he liked it. There was comfort there.

Cold air slid over his face. The black half-moons at the base of his fingers were a match to the sky outside – no wonder he was hungry; it was dark again. He frowned. He was spending less time in the haze that had gripped him when he'd first returned, when he'd climbed that long, long way with only madness and the glimmering hope of the stone for company; since feeding more frequently, the days were clearer. He had expected daylight when he peered out, not this cold evening. Had he slept too long? He didn't think so, not now he was more lucid. The world was clear to him again. As the chill freshened his face he evaluated his judgement and stood by it: it should be no later than three or four in the afternoon, and yet here the day was plunged into darkness. Time could be funny in The Nowhere, he remembered that, but this was definitely not just a shift of hours into a different space. Night had its own flavour, and he could feel his tongue itching to grow.

In the distance, maybe half a mile away, there were lights and noise: a busy, familiar place, filled with stalls selling things from different Boroughs – the place where four Boroughs met ... He knew the stone wanted him to move on, to ride the currents of the Lost Rivers to their destination. He could sense its impatience with his feeding, with his need for the streets, the busy lives that wandered through them. Perhaps, as he gained his strength from the people, the stone gained its strength from the water. The stone might be more powerful than he was, but they needed each other, and he needed to feed, or become that terrible, mindless creature from the other place, and that would be worse than death. The stone would have to wait. As if sensing his decision, the heat eased slightly.

George Porter pulled his cowl over his head and headed cautiously towards The Circus.

TWENTY

Tova's legs were heavy as she climbed. She wondered if she should stay, just for a while longer, just long enough to tell Andrew Fowkes all the things she wished she could. They were not words to be written down, though, because she couldn't bear the shame of them, and any chance of forgiveness from the man she loved would have come only from hearing her spoken words, in her own voice that he loved in his heart but hadn't heard for so many years. Those things could not be put down coldly on paper, to be judged without the emotion that went with the deed. She needed to *tell* him what she'd done, what she'd done *after*— But that chance was lost in the Incarcerator prison. She wondered as she quietly opened the hidden door in the wall of her bedroom whether perhaps that was justice, that it was so. Everything had suddenly become clear in recent hours, and the overwhelming realisation what the outcome of her deeds had been was too much to bear. There *should* be no forgiveness. She was a foolish woman who had thought herself wise, a woman trusted by thousands, who had abused the power placed in her by them. She was damned for what she'd done.

Even after the guilt of Baxter's death, the love between her and Fowkes had not died, though their hope had. They knew there would never be any future for them in all that guilt and grief. For the first time her eyes welled up. She was leaving him behind; she would never see his face again. He was downstairs, trying to hold everything together, keep everyone safe, and she knew that deep inside himself he wasn't sure he could. He probably thought he needed her ...

The narrow spiral staircase blurred, but she forced herself to continue to climb. He *could* manage, with or without her. He was a born leader, and always had been, for why else had Baxter, who loved him as much as she did, sacrificed himself as he did? *Baxter*. More tears fell, but she also felt the tiniest glimmer of hope. After this was done, once he knew *everything*, Fowkes would be forced to face the truth, and perhaps as she broke his heart she would mend part of it too. She wondered, as she climbed, whether he would still love her memory afterwards. Her insides ached as she felt the first real emotion since the stories were taken from her: she was more afraid of him hating her than she was of facing death. *That* would be a release. She'd spent most of a lifetime carrying the care of the worlds inside her, and now that she was free of that, the weight of the worlds had settled on her shoulders. But she had done this to herself – if she hadn't been so arrogant, would she have acted differently?

The memories were all too clear: Adam Baxter's broken body, bleeding onto the white marble, a stain she would see for every minute of all the years that followed, no matter how much the stairs were scrubbed. Baxter's empty grey eyes, staring at some spot in the distance, forever out of sight, as Fowkes, lost in grief, shook the dead man, trying to force life back into his shattered body. And the memory of that sudden emptiness in her heart, the knowledge that in the moment when Baxter had taken Fowkes' blame from the mob, everything had changed. *She*'d killed Baxter, with her *wanting*, and her selfishness, and her need for love – all the things she had vowed never to have. Then she'd done the secret thing, the *terrible* thing, and not repaired, as she'd thought, but broken—

And now the consequences of her actions were damning them all.

She climbed with more purpose after that. Nothingness would be a release.

Fin's heart raced as he ran, and the cold air burned his lungs like when he was out on the pitch at Eastfields, chasing Joe for the ball. He felt the same kind of excitement, too, that sense of something being achieved – the goal was in sight. Without a map, and with only the tip of the building to guide him, he'd taken two wrong turnings, and finally he'd done what boys never do, and stopped and asked for directions. Although the old man had looked slightly perplexed at the sight of the panting, red-faced running boy, he'd pointed out the way, and then gone back to looking at the sky and muttering, as most of The Nowhere's residents were doing.

George Porter. The name echoed in his head with every slap of his feet on the road. It was almost unbelievable, but he knew in his gut that it was true. No one in The Nowhere or The Somewhere had ever seen attacks that turned people mad like this, and even changed their physical appearance. *A man with no shoes and a scruffy cloak.* And the first attack was on a barmaid from The Red Lion, the very pub Porter had been in, hassling the Harveys about Fin and his friends, the night they threw him down the well—

Sudden guilt washed over Fin: if they hadn't pushed George Porter down the well, then none of this would be happening. What terrible thing had happened to Porter in – well, wherever the well came out – to make him able to do these things? Was it their fault, too? He ran faster, trying to shake his insecurity away. If they hadn't pushed George Porter down the well, then he would more than likely have killed Fowkes, and then they'd never have got the Storyholder back. Plus, he'd been one of the *bad* Knights – he'd been willing for them *all* to die – including Judge Harlequin Brown. No, Fin *wouldn't* feel any guilt about what happened to him. No way.

The Old Bailey House of Real Truths loomed into sight

and the path opened out onto the large square, of which the building was the centrepiece. Paths like the one he'd just travelled led off at all angles, in between the more normal thoroughfares. The arrangement looked a little strange, but somehow it worked – it more than worked, Fin concluded, as he slowed to a walk and allowed his breath to steady. It gave the square a quiet dignity. The whole of The Nowhere was filled with places of brilliance and weirdness, but if Fin had to pick a place that was the heart of the city, this would be it. *Truth* lived here, and you couldn't ask for a more important place than that – no palace, however rich, or any ancient abandoned church could compete.

He frowned slightly. Something was moving on the roof of the building, though it was hard to make out details in the gloom. There was a chill in his heart that wasn't all from the cold wind. Peering up, he thought it looked like a door was opening on the side of the huge carved truth vial that stood out against the city's skyline. Why would someone be going out onto the roof in the dark? Why would someone be going out there at all?

Blonde hair fluttered like silk ribbons as a figure stepped out, feet unsteady on the uneven surface. Fin's heart almost stopped completely.

'Tova?' he called, as loudly as he could. What *was* she doing? And where was Fowkes? Fin ran forward, his feet moving almost before he'd asked them to, until he was barely a few feet away from the steps and he could see her properly. She took a step closer to the edge.

'Tova!' Fin shouted, his heart leaping sickeningly to his mouth as the awfulness of what she was about to do became clear. 'Tova, *don't*! Please don't!' Two Borough Guardsmen emerged from the gloom, drawn by the noise, and looked up before running back into the building, calling out for help as they pounded through the hall, but Fin barely registered their presence. On the roof Tova looked down.

The tiles of the roof were made of slippery slate, and her feet skidded slightly as she stepped out from the door hidden in the truth vial. No one came to hear real truths that often these days, and most had forgotten the stairway to the roof. In the old days it had been used more; those wishing to keep their dignity, or have some peace after the revelations from the hall below, would come up to the Storyholder's apartments and set their affairs in order before taking the secret spiral stairs to the roof.

Some would change their minds as they stepped into the fresh air, as imminent death focused their minds on whatever truths had been revealed and the realisation that if it really was a matter of life or death, well, they could live with it. Then they'd slink back down, collect and burn their last letters and then head back out into the city. There were always a few whose route back down to the hard streets was more direct; this was the route Tova intended to take. She didn't need the House to tell her the Real Truths – she'd kept them hidden inside her long enough, and now they were unravelling in ways she could never have predicted. And she could not cope with that.

'Don't! Please don't!'

She'd been so lost in her own thoughts she hadn't noticed the boy so far below. It was fully night now, another symptom of the malaise she'd so thoughtlessly brought on them, and although the sky was currently quiet above them, the air crackled in expectation of the coming storm. She'd caused a storm once; and she'd almost caused a second, when St John Golden put her in the Incarcerator mirror, so far from the Five Eternal Stories, and she knew how it felt. But this one, this storm that was coming, this was like none any of the worlds had seen. She wanted to cry again, for it was all her fault. The stories were gone, and in their place were guilt and shame, filling the empty spaces inside her. Even when they had been in Fin's blanket, she had left a part of herself with them, and contained them from a distance. A piece of her mind had always been there, woven into that fabric. But now they were gone, no longer her responsibility.

The blanket.

She looked down at the blond-haired boy who was staring up at her with such dread. He was getting taller, a child who was so nearly a man, and so full of innocence, and things that he couldn't understand. She loved him and dreaded him and hated the reflection of her own deeds that she saw in him. She'd thought he would be special, and he was. He was *good*; he was everything she'd intended – but she had never thought that he would have a role to play, he and his friends, a fate of his own. He was her guilt, wrapped up in a breathing, living package.

Their eyes met and she shivered. The wind cut through her thin dress. She liked the cold air – it made her feel alive, and to feel alive in one's final moments was more than anyone could ask. Had she had a moment's doubt about her intended actions, then seeing the boy Finmere dispelled them. Doors clattered open below her and she knew that Fowkes would be coming out to see what had upset the Borough Guard and the boy so much. This was right, she knew that. She knew Fowkes, better than he knew himself, and his grief would make him demand answers. He would seek the truth, and that was a good thing: the truth must come out, for all their sakes.

She looked down again at the boy, and the pain etched into his young face. He would want the truth too, and for better or for worse, it was time, if they were to face this future with any chance at all. She took a long deep breath, savouring the all the flavours of the city. Fowkes would be coming, and if she saw his face she wouldn't have the strength to finish this. Holding the life in her lungs, she closed her eyes, made her silent apologies, and let herself fall.

TWENTY-ONE

Despite the constant temperature in Orrery House, Ted Merryweather's hand was cold as he replaced the receiver. He stared out of the window, and saw his own ghostly image reflected in the glass. He looked old and tired. It shouldn't have come as any surprise. He *was* old and tired. Behind him, Simeon Soames and Cardrew Cutler were still talking about the Seer. There was so much focus on those whose times were past that they'd all missed the point. He struggled to get his head round what he'd just heard. It made his blood curdle with what almost felt like a young man's anger.

'He was his *friend*,' he muttered, more to himself than anyone else than the rest of the room. 'That bastard was his *friend*.'

'Ted?' Freddie Wise said softly, and the conversation between the other two dribbled down to nothing as they realised that the old nightwatchman had spoken.

'What is it, Ted?'

'Maybe Fowkes 'as been right all along.' Ted didn't turn round. 'Looks like them kids have more parts to play in this than we first thought.'

He realised his shock must be showing on his face as soon as he looked at Freddie Wise. His mind turned back to that other old friend: poor Harlequin, betrayed by his own sense of trust and honour. He always believed others to be as noble as he was. Slowly the pieces were falling into place. They'd always thought St John Golden had not been acting alone. Now they knew it for a fact.

'He's played a long game, I'll give 'im that,' he said, surprised at his own bitterness.

The room was silent for a long moment, then, 'We're not following you, Ted,' Cardrew Cutler said gently, with none of his normal boisterous good humour in his voice. 'Who was on the phone?'

'That was Alan Carter, from Grey's. Always been a good man, Carter. 'e loved Harlequin Brown, really looked up to 'im.' Somewhere deep inside, Ted's heart broke slightly for his dead friend: the judge had been deceived, but Ted knew he would be rolling in his grave in shame for not having seen this.

'What did he say?'

'It's the boy, Joe. I suppose we should call 'im the Storyholder, now, for better for worse – and I think per'aps it's for worse. Carter says 'e was at the club.'

'He was *what*?' Soames exclaimed. 'But what on earth would *he* be doing there?'

Freddie Wise raised a hand to silence him and nodded at Ted. 'Go on, Ted. What did Alan Carter say?'

''e came in with a dodgy-looking bloke, Carter's seen 'im once or twice before. 'e was carrying a sword.'

'Baxter's sword,' Cutler breathed.

'They was all in the study, that's what Mr Carter said, and then when 'e took 'em up some mince pies, they was gone.'

'Who are *they*, Ted?' Wise prompted softly. 'Who invited the boy to Grey's?'

'Justin Arnold-Mather,' Ted said.

'Christopher's dad?' Simeon Soames frowned.

'And a good friend of Harlequin Brown's – they'd been friends for years. Mr Carter said it was Arnold-Mather who commissioned the portrait they've got there now. Bloody snake in the grass.'

'Sorry,' Cutler cut in, 'I am being a bit slow here. Justin Arnold-Mather? Young Christopher's father? The Minister?'

'Takes some getting your 'ead round, doesn't it?' Ted said almost venomously.

'Oh, I see,' Wise said, gazing off into the distance. 'We were far too quick to think it was all over.'

'Well, I'm glad *you're* seeing, Freddie,' Cutler huffed. 'If you could just make it clear to the rest of us, I'd be grateful.'

'We thought St John Golden was working alone when he turned the Knights – he was certainly arrogant enough. I thought he had too much ego to have a partner, but it looks like I was wrong: he did. A silent partner.'

'You're saying Justin Arnold-Mather was pulling Golden's strings?' Soames leaned forward in his chair. 'And since Golden's been in the Incarcerator, and we're all thinking the danger was over, he's busy plotting his own move for power?'

'It would make sense,' Freddie Wise said. 'Golden bit his own tongue off – why would he have done that if he wasn't afraid that we'd realise he had someone working with him and want to know who it was? Arnold-Mather was his only hope for rescue – guess he thought that as young Finmere had saved the Storyholder from within the prison, perhaps his benefactor would send someone for him.'

Cardrew Cutler snorted derisively.

'Desperate people will cling to hope,' Wise tapped his fingers on the end of his cane as his mind ticked and whirred, 'foolishly in his case. I should imagine that he did this Arnold-Mather chap a big favour by taking himself out of the game.'

'Harper said something.' Simeon Soames was on his feet, one hand running through his blond hair. 'Might be relevant. Something that happened just before Golden bit his tongue off.' He turned to Freddie. 'He said that Christopher said something to Golden – went up and whispered something through the mirror. He said the boy had a really weird look on his face.'

There was a moment's pause as the words settled in.

'Are you saying you think young Christopher knew that

his father was in it with Golden?' Cardrew Cutler shook his head and his jowls shook with the vehemence in the action. 'I can't believe it. I saw that boy when he came here with that potion. We all know *that* didn't come without a price, and he was the one who paid it. My eyes may be old, but even I could see that.'

'I'm with Cardrew,' Ted said. ''e's a good lad – they all are, even young Joe Manning, no matter whatever's 'appening now. It don't sound right.'

'I agree that he seems like a decent kid. And I saw that look on his face too, Cardrew – something went on with the Magus that he won't tell us, we all know that.' Soames was pacing, and watching him, Ted wished he had that much energy to spare. He couldn't begrudge it though – it wasn't that long ago that young Simeon had been barely able to get out of his wheelchair by himself.

'But,' Soames continued, 'something happened between him and Golden that day – Harper was sure of it – and when you hear a story like that, and then add this to it, it's hard not to think the worst. I can't help it.'

'Perhaps both sides to this are right,' Wise ruminated.

'What do you mean?'

'I do believe – like you, Ted – that Christopher is on the right side here. He's given us no evidence to the contrary – in fact, all the evidence points to his bravery, right?'

The men nodded and muttered agreements.

'All that we know for a fact is that his father is working against us; as far as the boy is concerned, we have absolutely no indication that he's turned. But—' He stopped, and looked around at the group. 'But what we do have evidence of is a young man who is clearly having some issues with authority, yes? Lucas Blake said Christopher's been in trouble with the police, and he's on the verge of expulsion from St Martin's. All of this is very unlike the boy who first joined Fin on his journey barely two months ago.' His fingers gripped the head of his cane. 'Christopher was also eager to come and join us here for Christmas.'

'Who wouldn't be?' Cardrew Cutler sounded indignant. 'We do a great Christmas. As well as all the other stuff.'

'Yes, yes – we have The Nowhere, and adventures on tap, that much is true – but most young people would want to spend at least Christmas Day with their families, wouldn't they? It's certainly something Fowkes said young Joe had been struggling with recently – being separated from his mother over the holidays.'

'What are you driving at, Freddie?' Ted asked.

'Perhaps Christopher knows – or suspects – his father's role in this, but wants no part of it. It could be the reason behind all the trouble he's been in recently: he hates his father for what he's doing, but doesn't know what to do about it – hence the flagrant disregard for authority, which is very uncharacteristic.'

'I presumed it was whatever deal he'd done with the Magus that was causing him problems,' Simeon Soames said.

'It could be all of it,' Cardrew Cutler suggested. 'He might have suspected his dad, and that made him braver when facing the Magus and whatever price he required for that potion – which I know still bothers all three of you who took it' – his watery eyes peered at the young blond man – 'but it shouldn't. What's done is done, and one day Christopher will tell us what the Magus wanted in return, and maybe we can go some way to putting it right, but until then—'

'This is all very valid, Cardrew, but you're veering off the point a bit.'

'Sorry, Freddie. My point is: I see what you're driving at. His shame, his dad, all of that.'

'But why didn't he *tell* us, if he had suspicions that the Minister was involved with Golden?' Soames asked. 'I just don't get it.'

'*I* do,' Ted said, his heart heavy. 'If 'e told us 'e thought 'is dad 'ad gone to the bad, 'e'd risk us not trusting 'im, and 'e'd risk losing Fin and Joe too. If Christopher found out 'is dad was a wrong 'un, and that maybe all along 'e'd been used, 'ow would he know we wouldn't tar 'im with the same brush? Must 'ave shaken 'is world. if 'e'd found that out. And if his life outside of 'ere was crumbling, this is all 'e'd have left, so of course 'e wouldn't want to risk losing it all.'

'So many secrets,' Freddie tutted, 'even amongst the young.'

'Poor young sod,' Cardrew Cutler said. 'Imagine carrying that lot around with you.'

'We can put that part of this mess right.' Freddie Wise used his cane as leverage and got to his feet. 'Unfortunately, though, that's not the most pressing matter. If Arnold-Mather has somehow seduced Joe to his side, and has gone with the boy to The Somewhere, then he's planning something big. The man is a British government minister – if he's willing to turn his back on *that* and disappear, then he'll be looking for something far greater.'

'If anyone mentions the Prophecy,' Simeon Soames muttered, 'I swear to God I'll punch them.'

'No one's going to mention it, Simeon, because it would be too bloody obvious.' Cardrew Cutler harrumphed. 'It's all anyone's been thinking about since the weather went all loopy, the stories went into Joe and the flipping Seer showed up!'

'But how would Arnold-Mather know so much about all this? The stories, the Prophecy, Finmere?'

'Harlequin,' Ted said softly. ''im and Harlequin was mates, I told you. 'e's played the long game 'ere, watching and waiting, probably right since young Fin turned up, if not before. I bet 'e almost lured 'im in. Harlequin would have trusted him – 'e was a member of Grey's, and they'd known each other a long time.' Slow anger burned in the pit of his stomach. He hadn't been sure he had that sort of emotion left in him these days; even through everything that happened with St

John Golden, he'd kept his cool, and although he'd been disgusted, maddened, even, by Golden's treachery, it had been a calmer sensation, tempered by the years under his belt. This was different. Right now he was ready to tear Arnold-Mather apart with his bare hands for the trust he'd abused.

'When we find 'im,' he said through gritted teeth, 'I'm going to make 'im regret ever 'earing about any Knights of Nowhere.'

'Let's hope you get that chance, Ted,' Freddie sighed. 'And you'll have my blessing, whatever you do. But our immediate problem is with the first half of your sentence. We need to *find* him – and fast.'

'The Nowhere's a big place,' Cutler said. 'He could have gone anywhere.'

'Not true.' Soames was on his feet. 'He can only go to places that Joe can *see*. And Joe may have been in The Nowhere more than the other two, but he's been pretty much stuck in the House of Real Truths since Golden was captured. Arnold-Mather isn't going to want to waste any time now that he's out in the open. He's going to want to go somewhere important, where he can be secure and establish himself. It won't be The Red Lion or even the House of Real Truths – that's one place Joe is not going to want to go back to right now.'

'And he's burned the Storyholder Academy down,' Cutler added, 'so he won't be going there.'

'There's only one place I'd go if I wanted power in The Nowhere,' Freddie Wise said. He looked from one man to the next.

'Alexander Palace,' Ted finished his thought.

'Where else would a dark man start a battle for King?'

The clear reference to the Prophecy in the old man's words hung like shards of splintered hopes between them as rain began to hammer against the window. Ted could still see the stars outside, winking merrily against the blanket of the night. Rain on a clear night.

'God help us all,' Cardrew Cutler whispered. 'The time is upon us.'

TWENTY-TWO

The Prince Regent had escaped from the bickering Chancellors' meeting in the austere Cabinet Room upstairs and was alone in the Throne Room when the doorway opened up in the empty air at the other end. There was no time for security measures, and even if there had been, how could anyone defend against those who could arrive anywhere they wished, whenever they wished?

He should have gone with Savjani; that was the first thing he thought when he felt the brush of a cold, unfamiliar breeze. He should have fled the palace as soon as the sky had changed. Too late now. Twenty yards away three figures from another world stepped onto the mosaic floor. He shouldn't have stayed – but what kind of Regent would run? A coward? Or perhaps a wiser man ...

The Chancellors would still be in conference on the floor above, unaware that the subject of their intense bickering was now amongst them. Their arguing had plagued him with memories of his dreams, but it wasn't just them: every conversation he'd overheard this afternoon had been edged with aggression, fraught with accusation. He'd tried to blame it on natural fear of the strange weather, but the Chancellors were creatures of protocol; it took years to master the set patterns and precise delivery of their speech. For them to lose their hard-won reserve was a true sign that something dark was going on in The Nowhere.

It was the Rage coming, he was sure of it. The Nowhere

thought it had fought Black Storms in the past, but none before had started this way, born in light skies. His ancestors might have banished the Magi to the South, but their words were still stored in the Library Halls and etched into his mind. There were scraps of half-burned parchment, and long-forgotten poems, and they talked of one storm: a Black Storm like no other, and it would mark the beginning of the unfolding of the Magi's Prophecy. That storm would start in light skies and before the battles of good and evil started, the Rage would have its day, and sides would be established. Everyone knew about the Prophecy, but few had ever heard of the Rage – the Knights, perhaps, they might have heard a whisper of it, shared with them in times past by Kings long-dead, but none of The Nowhere's residents ... other than him. As he stared at the uninvited visitors in the heart of his home, the Prince Regent wondered if perhaps keeping that from them had been a mistake. If they knew, they might at least try to defend against it.

He stood up, slowly and carefully, as if he wasn't in the least surprised by their arrival, until he was standing still in front of his golden throne. With all the *maybes* and *what-ifs* running through his mind, he could reach only one conclusion: this must be Fate, and Fate had a way of playing out her own way. He'd just have to see what that was.

'So this is The Nowhere.' The middle-aged man was wearing a smart three-piece suit of superfine wool, and as he walked there was a flash of a dark checked sock between the hem of his trousers and his perfectly polished shoes. He clapped his hands together in a gesture that might have been seen as gleeful in someone else. This man, however, did not look to be someone pre-disposed towards spontaneous joy or outbursts of emotion. The gleam in the eyes shadowed by his heavy eyebrows was closer to victory than excitement. He smiled; a cool expression. 'And you must be the Prince Regent. How fortunate we find you alone.' He turned to one of his companions. 'It appears we have no need of the gun, Mr Dodge. And if you could take the sword?'

For the first time, the Prince Regent felt a knot of fear curl in his gut. People always presumed that evil was obvious, but it was a naïve assumption. The worst evil appeared perfectly ordinary, couching itself in respectability and normalcy – how else could it go about its business? This man had that air about him. This man made St John Golden look like a schoolboy fool.

'I fear you have me at a disadvantage.' The Prince Regent was well aware of the irony in his words. 'I have no idea who you are.'

'My name is Justin Arnold-Mather – although I feel we are not really in need of polite introductions.'

The thickset man he'd called Mr Dodge was wearing a Bowler hat, which he failed to doff. He took the sword from the third traveller and placed it in a scabbard that looked out of place around his waist. He tucked a small firearm back into his suit pocket. The Regent wondered if they knew how unlikely it was that such a weapon would work here. He'd seen guns before – a long time ago – and it was always a bit of a lottery as to whether they fired at all. A musket might work, but not this tiny tool he carried. Perhaps this man was not as prepared as he thought.

'I recognise your young friend, of course,' the Prince Regent said, pleased at how calm his voice was. 'I hear you are the Storyholder now, Joe Manning. That is quite a burden.' He looked at the boy, who avoided meeting his gaze. 'I hope no one persuaded you to push Fate in that direction.'

A muscle twitched in the teenager's face and his head dropped further. The answer was clear: they had violated Tova. This was worse than anything that had happened before, but where he had expected to feel anger, an urge to allow the Rage in the air to take hold of him, he found himself instead overwhelmed by pity.

'We cannot stay here for ever, but as a starting place it certainly makes Westminster look pretty old and tired.' The man called Arnold-Mather chuckled and looked around him, admiring the opulence.

The Prince Regent kept his focus on Joe. 'This man is not your friend,' he said, 'to burden you with such shame. You will find that much harder to bear than the weight of the stories. It will drive you to madness, and taint the power you carry inside.' He paused. 'He will use you.'

'Shut up,' the boy snarled, for the first time looking up. His eyes were filled with hate and hurt.

'I see he already is,' the Regent continued, ignoring him, 'if he will not let you carry the sword. That must tell you something. He will make you his servant.'

'I am all the boy has,' Arnold-Mather said, smoothly. 'The rest have turned their backs on him. I am the only person who understands.'

'It is not too late to go back, Joe Manning. You can still put this right. This has not been your fault, however you might see it.'

'I said shut up.' His growl sounded like a cornered animal in pain.

Perhaps there was a chance, the Regent thought, catching the quick look of concern that flashed between the two grown men. This was a good boy trapped in a bad situation, and it might not take that much to turn him back, to make him see that he could be forgiven. Maybe all that was coming could be averted now, right now, in this moment. 'Think of your friends.' He took a step forward. 'Think of—'

At the far end of the Throne Room the heavy gilt doors were flung open and a baker-boy, still dusty from the kitchens, tumbled across the intricately patterned marble and slid on his knees until he came to a stop. Behind him stood two guardsmen, their faces dark and angry with Rage, bickering

223

between themselves. Their eyes fell on the interlopers and their voices dropped.

The Regent's head sank slightly as he saw, in that instant, his own guards switch sides. On the floor, the baker-boy looked up.

'Sorry Your Majesty,' the boy blurted, 'but they wouldn't tell you! I wanted to tell you what people are saying they seen. A terrible thing.'

The Prince Regent frowned. The boy, not so much younger than the one torn apart with conflict in front of him, was crying. His heart chilled. 'What have people seen?' The question barely carried the length of the room. At the edge of his focus, beyond the tunnel vision in which he could see only the terrified, weeping baker-boy, Levi Dodge had reached the entrance and ushered the guards inside before quietly closing and locking the doors.

'What have they seen?' the Prince whispered. Tears sprang to his own eyes, as if he knew something was coming that would break his heart.

'They're saying it's the Storyholder.' The boy licked his lips, and then wiped his eyes with the back of his dirty hand. 'They say they looked up and she was standing at the top of the Old Bailey House of Real Truths. They say they seen her, just standing there for a moment. And then ... and then ...' His breath hitched, and in that pause the Regent felt the first crack in his heart. 'And then she leaned forward and let herself fall,' he finished simply. 'She's dead, Your Majesty. The Storyholder's dead.'

For a moment the world stopped completely and everything was lost from the Regent's head. Somewhere outside of the numbness that gripped his being, he heard Joe choke on a sob. Hope crumbled to dust. There was no going back. There never had been.

*

224

The baker-boy was still crying twenty minutes later, sitting up against the wall, his head in his hands. He was a good lad, and he had chosen his side in the coming fight, if he lived that long. The two guards sat at the back, joking as they played cards. They, the Regent concluded, were not so good. Or perhaps they were just not as pure, or as strong. The Rage could take the good too, if they let it in.

His head felt lighter without the heavy wig, and the tears that quietly made tracks down his cheeks helped Levi Dodge as he wiped the Prince Regent's face clear of his powder and paint using cotton pads and cold cream.

'Stand up,' Arnold-Mather said when his henchman had finished, and the Regent did as he was told. With dead eyes, he watched as the boy, the Storyholder who would bring them all to ruin, approached him. The fear and pain in the boy's eyes had now been replaced with wonder. Joe stopped inches from him, their dark brown eyes staring into each other.

'He looks just like me,' Joe breathed.

'And more importantly,' Arnold-Mather smiled, 'you look just like him. Apart from a few inches' height difference, and who will notice that if the rest matches so well? I think it's time you tried the wig on. I should imagine it fits.' He looked over his shoulder. 'And you two, would you be so kind as to locate any books or documents relating to the Storyholder's powers? I think our young friend has a lot to learn.'

The Prince Regent watched as the boy placed the heavy purple and silver wig over his short afro. Still his heart ached. How much could those young shoulders carry? He could see where this was leading: soon this Somewhere teenager would be dressed in his finery, and he would be in the baggy garb. What would happen to him then? In the midst of his grief and his failure, one thing still niggled at him, and he mustered the courage to ask, 'How do you know so much? St John Golden didn't have your knowledge.' Golden was lost and even Harlequin Brown was dead. Not all of what this man knew could have come from them, he was sure of it.

'People are so quick to trust, don't you find?' Arnold-Mather said. 'I'm a politician. I know that trust is for fools. Even amongst the closest of friends and devoted servants there will be a snake in the grass.' He gave the Prince a tight smile. 'And I have always been very good at charming snakes.' He turned to Joe. 'Now I think it is time we completed our transformations. We have much to do, and little time.'

The Prince Regent stared out of the vast wall of windows. Night had completely fallen outside. He wondered if the darkness would ever lift.

TWENTY-THREE

Eventually, Fowkes picked up Tova's broken body from the hard ground and carried her inside. The three Knights – Harper Jones and the Wakley twins – stood silently to the side, their heads bowed. Fin followed behind the Commander, unaware of the icy chill of the sudden wind that beat at his face. His heart felt like a cracked stone, and he flinched against the memory of the sound of her soft body hitting the steps; the smashing of her skull. He'd stood dumbfounded as the others ran out to join him, just staring. He felt sick. He thought that his mind would play that scene over and over for ever: her silent fall, followed by that awful crack.

Fowkes hadn't even looked at him as he fell to his knees, howling like a wounded animal. For a long time the man had cried, cradling her head in his hands and talking to her quietly, refusing to acknowledge the blood that streaked her blonde hair and her lifeless eyes staring up at the midnight sky. He'd knelt there for a long time.

Finmere had wanted to cry, but his body had forgotten how. He was barely aware of his feet as Fowkes led them into a small room at the side of the central Chamber and laid the tiny pale body out on the desk. She didn't lie quite right, as if her back was no longer properly aligned, but she still looked beautiful in the glow of the large candles that illuminated the small room. Fin swallowed hard. Maybe he hadn't forgotten how to cry at all. Chains rattled loudly in his head, too loudly for the silence. He needed to fill it – he needed to stop the box's desperate need to be opened.

'It's George Porter,' he mumbled, somewhere just outside of a whisper. 'That's what I came back to say.'

'What?' Harper Jones looked over at him. His voice was soft. Fin didn't think it would matter how loudly they shouted; nothing was going to break through to Fowkes, who was leaning over the dead Storyholder, wiping the blood from the side of her face.

'Why would she do this?' His gravelly voice held none of the strength Fin had always heard there. It was as if someone had sucked all the resonance from it.

'George Porter?' Harper Jones repeated.

'He's come back from wherever the well went,' Fin said. All the excitement and enthusiasm he'd felt in his rush to the Old Bailey was gone. The pride he'd had in being the one to figure it out tasted bitter in his mouth. 'He's the one attacking the people. Someone saw a man in a tatty cloak running away from the first victim. He didn't have any boots on.' His tongue felt thick in his mouth, as if the words had to squeeze past it, rather than be formed by it. 'We took Porter's boots. And this thing isn't of either world. Must be Porter.'

'Good work,' Harper Jones said, with a small nod. The Wakley brothers had stayed outside, instinctively knowing that they shouldn't invade the grief of those who had known Tova so much better than they had. Fin wished he was with them. She'd seen him before she'd jumped and she'd still done it. She'd looked right at him on the way down. What had he done? His stomach churned. He *wasn't* special; he hadn't deserved everyone thinking he was. It was all just a terrible mistake. She must have hated him, to do that.

'It's not your fault.' Fin jumped as Harper Jones broke through his thoughts and rested one hand on his shoulder. 'You didn't do anything.'

'She was looking at me,' Fin said. 'She was looking right

at me when she jumped.' He started to shake, the trembling starting in his legs, but soon racing up to the chained-up box in his head. He heard the crack of Tova's skull, and one of the links snapped.

'It's not your fault,' Harper Jones repeated more aggressively, gripping Fin's shoulders tightly.

'Whose fault is it, though?' Fowkes finally looked up, his dark eyes moving from the man to the teenager. 'She did this for a reason. I need to know why.' In the shadowy light the muscles of his jaw clenched under his dark stubble. 'I need to know *why*.'

'You can't know why.' Jones was impassive, but his eyes had softened. No one had gone near Fowkes with any words of comfort. Even at the age of sixteen Finmere could see that there were some kinds of pain that words were no use against.

'Yes, I can.' Fowkes straightened up, fire in his black eyes, and scooped the body into his arms. 'Get out of my way.'

For a moment Jones looked as if he might challenge his leader, but after a pause he stepped aside. Fowkes didn't even look down at Finmere as he strode past them, kicking the door open.

'What's he doing?' Fin asked. The chains rattled some more in his head, and a black space as vast as eternity threatened to open up in his memory. He flinched against it. *Everything's unravelling,* he thought. *What's done will be undone.*

'The Oval Room,' Jones muttered. 'He's going to the Chamber of Real Truths.'

Fin turned. 'No!' he called after Fowkes, his heart thumping too loudly in his chest. 'No, don't!' The words were out, coming from somewhere in that dark space beyond and within the box. He wanted to cry, he wanted to throw up. He wanted to run back to Eastfields Comp, or St Martin's, or Mrs Baker's boarding house, or somewhere normal where he didn't know anything about the Knights and there was no Nowhere.

'Open the doors.'

Finmere watched as Henry and Benjamin Wakley did as Fowkes commanded, pushing the heavy ornate doors open and revealing for a moment the vast room, filled from floor to ceiling with glowing vials. The colours were dazzling. Pale men in black robes – some up ladders, others moving silently between the shelves – all paused as the doors opened. As one, they turned their blind eyes to stare as Fowkes strode across the marble floor.

'I want to know why,' he growled, holding the broken body up as if it were some kind of sacrifice. 'I want to know *why*.'

The doors closed behind him.

They waited in silence. Harper Jones' face grew darker as the storm built outside, and occasionally he would mutter something to one or other of the twins. Finmere figured they were talking about George Porter – what to do about him, and how important it was, compared with Joe's disappearance with the Five Eternal Stories. Fin was too tired to join in. It was all connected, he knew that: everything was part of everything else, and now it was unravelling. He shivered, and his bones ached as he sat on the step where Baxter had died so many years ago. That event had brought on a Black Storm, but he doubted it was anything like the one brewing outside. Even through the thick walls of the Old Bailey House of Real Truths he could hear the wind howling as it chased around the square. Tova was dead. Joe was gone. Everything was changing.

And then his heart slowed with sudden acceptance: *what would be would be*. There was nothing he could do to turn the clock back; he could only try and make the future better. The kiss from Anaïs seemed like a million years gone.

Finally, the doors opened. Fowkes stood empty-handed, his face pale. Tova's body was lying abandoned on the marble beyond. Trembling, he stared at Finmere.

230

'You,' he whispered.

Fin looked up, dread crawling from the space in his head to every extremity, chilling his blood. It wasn't the word; it was the way Fowkes said it. The Commander was looking at him as if he were every impossibility that had ever been dreamed.

'It *can't* be you,' the Knight continued, and now the shiver in his skin had reached his voice.

Fin listened for a second to the wind howling outside. He remembered the crack of Tova's skull against the ground and another chain in his head snapped.

All eyes were on him as he pulled himself to his feet. Maybe the truth *was* always better out – and how bad could it be, anyway? He hadn't actually done anything wrong. So what was the box in his head trying to tell him? The only thing he knew for certain was that the chains were weakening, and he couldn't fight the box any longer. Maybe everything had been leading here, from the very moment he'd been abandoned on that other second step.

He walked slowly towards the open doorway, and Fowkes took a big step away, as if something terrible would happen if his arm so much as brushed against Fin's.

What will be, will be, he thought, and stepped inside the chamber.

'I want to know who I am,' he said softly, looking down at Tova's body. 'Where I came from.'

The doors closed quietly behind him. And then, as the Archivers began to keen, Fin's world crumbled.

TWENTY-FOUR

Neither Mona nor Christopher had dressed for the cold weather that was starting to grip the city, and as they wove their way through the dark alleys, trying to get their bearings, they huddled close together; Christopher's arm was around Mona's shoulder, and Mona was too cold to complain about chauvinism. She was leaning in towards him, and that made Christopher's heart warm, even if his hands and ears were freezing.

There was no denying the strangeness in the sudden chill, and the lightning and thunder that raced across a clear, dark sky but brought no rain. It was affecting people too – everywhere they went they could feel a sort of palpable anger in the air – especially near the hatches, where the Lost Rivers were close to the surface and the madness in the water escaped into the upper world.

Mona led them into a wider road. It wasn't cobbled or paved, and the stalls that lined one side were made of rough wood, with tanned hides or rags thrown across their tops as shelter. The vendors selling hunks of bread and various other foodstuff were standing bored behind their wares, virtually ignored by the passers-by, while further down, a fat man in bright clothing had a large crowd around him. He was standing on a box, and as they got nearer they realised he was hawking amulets and potions that he claimed could protect against a Black Storm, the Prophecy, and all that came with them.

'That's not good,' Mona muttered. She pulled in closer to Christopher. 'It's too soon since the last brush with a Black Storm,' she continued, 'and everyone's superstitious.'

'I don't think this is superstition,' Christopher said, enjoying the feel of her tiny body, warm in the crook of his arm. A few feet away a woman in a long brown dress and pointed hat with a veil was arguing with a man dressed in tunic and breeches. They looked like they hated each other enough to be married. He recognised the look in the man's eyes – it was the same disgust that he caught his dad looking at his mum with sometimes, as if wanting to be loved and cared for was somehow too much to ask. His own loathing for his dad roared into life as he watched the couple argue, the woman pulling off her hat and throwing it to the ground before storming away, her waist-length hair flying out like a wedding train behind her.

Christopher was unaware that he had gripped Mona's shoulder tightly, and he clenched his teeth, anger at his treacherous father burning the cold out of his veins.

She pulled away and looked up at him. 'Christopher, don't let it get to you – if you let your anger take hold, then the Rage will get you.'

'The what?' Christopher had never seen her look so afraid before.

'It's something my dad talked about once – it's kind of a legend ... at least, I thought it was, but now ... The Magi foretold that The Nowhere would suffer one terrible storm, and it would start the unfolding of the Prophecy. But before the storm would come something they called the Rage. Dad used to tell me about it when I was a kid – you know, as a kind of scary story.' She huddled under the awning of a stall where the owner, apparently having given up trying to make any money, was now packing away his crude pots and bowls.

'I didn't really like it then, and I definitely don't like it now.'

'Maybe it'll pass ... maybe it's just nervousness,' Christopher said, but he knew he didn't sound very convincing. He could almost feel the undercurrent of tension on the streets; even if they weren't actually arguing, every face looked drawn, and there was not a single smile to be seen. That wasn't like The Nowhere at all. He shivered.

'Let's concentrate on the one thing we can help with, shall we?' It might not sound as important as the growing storm, but people were still being attacked, and they still needed to find out why.

'Good plan.' Mona stretched up and kissed him for a moment before smiling. Her smile must have had an effect on the tired stallholder because he slid a candle over to them to help them see the map more clearly. He gave them a friendly nod before continuing to pack up his wares into a cart.

Christopher pulled out the street map of London given to them by Curran Tugg which had all the attacks marked on it and laid it side by side with the Gypsy Traders' map of the Lost Rivers which had the hatches marked on it. They leaned over them, studying them in the yellow glow of the flickering candlelight, the strange weather and the angry population forgotten for a moment.

'I wish I could see a pattern,' Mona said after a while, 'but I just *can't*. There's no rhyme nor reason for attacks in these places. I thought perhaps they might be in a circle around the Old Bailey, or the palace, or even St Paul's, but there's nothing – no clear shape at all.' She frowned and chewed her lip. 'We're no further forward than when we started.'

Christopher wished he had something positive to say, but Mona was right. He couldn't see any kind of plan, location-wise, at all. They'd never be able to predict where the attacker might come up next, not without putting a Borough Guardsman over every hatch. Looking around him at the street full of angry people, he figured the Borough Guard would probably have their hands full right now. As if to prove him right, two men wearing roughly sewn tunics jostled each other as they passed, heading towards the conman peddling his wares at the far end of the street.

'Watch where you're going!' the larger man growled, and gave the other a hard shove, sending him stumbling into the pottery stall.

'Be careful!' Christopher said, grabbing Mona to keep her steady as the rickety structure lurched drunkenly to one side.

'And you can bloody well shut up too!' The man jabbed a finger at the teenager before continuing on his way. The smaller man followed a safe few steps behind him.

Christopher watched them go, his stomach in a knot. 'How bad does this Rage thing get?' he asked. 'Did your dad know?'

Mona didn't answer. Ahead, the two men were jostling again, and she reckoned it wouldn't be long before it turned into a fully blown fist-fight.

And if they started in the middle of the small crowd, Christopher thought they'd all be joining in, men *and* women. Those pointy hats could probably do some damage if aimed at the right part of the male anatomy.

'Mona? Did you—?'

'Look.' She nudged him, cutting his sentence off. 'Look!'

Christopher looked down at the maps. When the men had knocked the stall, the two maps had been shoved together; the waxed map of the rivers and its hatches sliding slightly under the street map.

'What?' He couldn't see what had grabbed her attention.

Mona unfolded the top map out completely, and the heavily inked outlines of the Lost Rivers below were just about visible through it.

'Look again.' She grinned. 'We were looking for a pattern on the *surface* – how stupid! We've been looking in completely the wrong place. Look at the rivers, and then look at the streets again.' She gave him barely a second to try and figure it out for himself before impatience got the better of her. 'The rivers don't follow the same layout as the roads, and the attacker is coming up from the rivers! Don't you get it? Look at how they all bend and twist and go back on themselves!'

Christopher stared harder at the two maps, and finally he saw it: what looked like random places on the street map weren't so haphazard when you looked at them in conjunction with the rivers. 'Holy shit,' he said finally, 'I can see it – they're all leading to—'

'West Minster,' they said in unison. The memory of what he'd done in that wrecked cathedral shivered down Christopher's spine.

'But why there?' he asked, staring at the maps, still a little nonplussed. 'The place is abandoned.'

'Doesn't mean there's nothing there,' Mona said, folding up the parchments. 'Places are left abandoned for a reason.' She shoved the street map at him. 'You need to get to The Circus and tell Fin what we know. I'll go to the palace and try and find some of my guardsmen to cover the hatches between where the last attacks took place and West Minster.' She smiled up at him. 'And make sure you take care without me around to look out for you!'

'Ha bloody ha,' Christopher said, before leaning down and kissing her. 'I'll do my best.'

Overhead, a huge crack of thunder exploded in the dark sky, and the whole street flinched. The teenagers didn't stop kissing, though. It would take more than that.

Simeon Soames stepped from the overheated warmth of Orrery House into the cool of the palace and closed the doorway behind him. His eyes searched the gloom for anyone who might be coming for him, but there was nothing but silence. He shivered slightly and gripped his sword. Double-edged swords weren't designed for fighting, but if he came

236

across Justin Arnold-Mather, then he'd be using it anyway. There were always times when needs must.

The quieter side corridor he'd chosen to emerge into was on the same floor as the Throne Room, but it wasn't the main gilded thoroughfare that Royal visitors and politicians used. If Arnold-Mather *was* here, then he'd have those doors guarded. He wasn't planning to attack anyone – this was just a quick reconnaissance trip, to see if the minister and boy were indeed in the palace, and if so, just how well-established they were. Perhaps they'd conned the Prince Regent into giving them shelter? He wasn't convinced by that thought, but it was better to be optimistic, even if it didn't always come naturally to him. His intention was to get the lie of the land, and then report back to Fowkes. With any luck he'd be in and out before anyone even noticed he was there.

This corridor led to a servants' entrance at the back of the Throne Room. It might have been less opulent than the main thoroughfares, but it still had floors and ceilings of perfectly white marble, and the external wall was filled with high windows. Simeon Soames had only been in this part of the palace once, when he was a young, inexperienced Knight – before he'd Aged – but it had lingered in his memory. There was a maudlin quality to the unadorned whiteness, an echo of madness.

Thunder cracked loud in the sky outside, filling the quiet air around him. Simeon trotted over to the large windows and peered out. There was no rain falling, unlike back at home, and the stars twinkled in the clear night sky. His eyes fell to the ground below and he stared. Normally, the streets around the palace were relatively clear. The Palace Guard marched up and down and put on a show of protecting their Royal master, but in the main the population weren't that interested in the goings-on of the Royals. Regents came, Regents went mad, and then the whole thing started again. As long as they got some pomp and ceremony and the odd holiday, people were happy. They had their own lives to be getting on with, and didn't much care about whatever was happening inside the high black gates.

But something was different: the gates were closed, as usual, and sentries stood on the inside, but a small crowd had gathered outside. Simeon peered through the glass, fighting his own reflection to see what was happening down there. Who were those people, and what were they doing? The answer to the second question soon became clear: they were doing absolutely nothing, other than staring up at the windows of the palace. No one appeared to be talking to anyone else, no food or drinks were being consumed. The crowd were simply standing, hands by their sides, and staring. As Simeon watched, more solitary figures drifted over from the surrounding streets and joined the throng. A few were holding torches and lamps, but Simeon wondered if that was just because they'd forgotten they were carrying them.

The guards on the other side were doing nothing, though the Prince Regent must have been made aware of the strange gathering. He shivered again, but this time it was nothing to do with the cold. It was something about the people gathering around the palace. Even from this distance, he thought he could see their eyes were empty – no, he corrected himself, empty wasn't right; they looked damaged, hurt – like his eyes had been after the Ageing, during that first year, when he'd raged against it. For a moment he felt the onset of the Ageing all over again: the sudden rush of aching in his bones, the terror of looking down and seeing his hands, but not his hands, his body, but not his body, and the awful realisation that it had happened to him – not someone else, but *him*. He'd adjusted, he'd had to, otherwise he would have gone mad, but in that first year he'd been so full of hate ...

His teeth clenched, remembering it. He was a little surprised he'd forgotten so much, been able to put it behind him, and he remembered the jealousy he'd felt at Lucas Blake's calm acceptance of his own fate. How Blake had talked to Simeon, and then Harper, when the Ageing got him too, about their oath and the importance of the Order, and how it was a risk they all took.

He'd never been like Lucas Blake, though, and for a long time he'd hated the Order. Sometimes he thought he still did ...

He stared out at the crowd as thunder roared above them. No one moved. Not a flinch among them. Their clothes were ragged, their faces tired. They were the forgotten people of The Nowhere, the destitute and the damaged. He knew how that felt. He'd felt forgotten in the Aged years.

For a second, the darkness threatened to overwhelm him, but he shook it away, if not completely, then at least to the corners of his heart and mind. He didn't hate the Order – how could he? It was all he'd been, for as long as he could remember. This wasn't like him – he hadn't felt that kind of anger in years. He gritted his teeth and turned away from the window to face the dark passageway, but that didn't help his mood much. As another rumble of thunder broke the silence again he walked quickly up the corridor, the soft soles of his boots barely heard against the shining floor.

Somewhere in the distance, glass smashed, and two people shouted at each other, their voices quickly ascending to screaming pitch. He listened for a moment to ensure they weren't heading in his direction, but the voices faded as their owners stormed off into a different part of the palace. It wasn't only him who was irritable today then.

He turned the corner and headed towards the small door that would lead to the back of the Throne Room. He could open it just an inch and peer through. If the Prince Regent was alone, then he'd take the opportunity to warn him about Arnold-Mather and Joe's likely presence somewhere in the building, and try and persuade him to get to safety. He slowed to a steady walk. Now the walls were hung with paintings, imaginative vistas of the South, all with one or other of The Nowhere's Kings on the back of a regal horse, as if they truly had taken control of the other side of the river in anything other than name. Who ever saw this priceless art? A valet? A cleaning girl? The diminutive Prince Regent has so much, and Simeon Soames suddenly felt rankled by it. The Knights should have this palace, and everything in it – the Knights should be running the business of *both* the worlds, as they were the only people who could travel between the two. And the Knights risked the Ageing ... his blood started to boil with bitterness at the years of his life he'd lost to the Ageing – and for what – honour? Good? What did those get you, really? Not a mansion, or millions in the bank; no holiday home in the Bahamas for him. Just a secret life that was lived entirely for the purpose of protecting others and fighting a Prophecy that might or might not come to pass. And there was absolutely no guarantee that the Ageing wouldn't take him again. Freddie Wise and Ted Merryweather might try and say otherwise, but what the hell did those two old men know?

Wind whipped around the building, making the windows rattle in their frame, and the air that wafted through the gaps stank of the mist. He paused and breathed it in. Somehow it didn't smell as bad as normal – the sweetness wasn't sickly at all; instead it made his mouth water.

He turned his attention to the small door in the curve of the wall and gripped the golden handle, turning it slowly. It made no sound as he pushed it open, letting a sliver of light escape, and he pressed one eye into the gap. It looked like he was too late to warn the Prince Regent about Arnold-Mather, for twenty feet away, on the other side of the gilt throne, he could see the government minister standing between Joe and the Prince. He was looking from one to the other, and a small twist of a satisfied smile tugged his face upward slightly.

'Who could tell?' Arnold-Mather clapped his hands

together. 'Not from a distance anyway, and that's all we need.'

Simeon Soames looked closer. Tears had made tracks down Joe's face and his dark eyes looked at the Prince with something close to pity. A thickset man in a Bowler hat was applying rouge to the Regent's pancake-pale face, stepping back to admire his handiwork. There was something just not quite right about the picture, and it took a moment before it struck him: the black kid in jeans and a scruffy top wasn't Joe at all; he was older and smaller than the boy from South London. His eyes darted between the two figures standing on either side of Arnold-Mather and suddenly he saw it: Joe had become the Prince Regent, and the Prince Regent was now Joe. The sleight of hand was helped enormously by the fashion for painted faces and big wigs, for no one knew what the Prince really looked like. It was very, very clever; he had to give the government minister that. From the window behind him another draught of angry wind sought him out, and this time he embraced it. Perhaps St John Golden had been right – why should they make all these sacrifices for no reward? The thought was almost subconscious, but it fed the bitter bile of rage towards the Order that had been building since he'd arrived in the middle of the brewing storm.

The grin had formed on his face before he even felt it, and as he pushed the door open his heart pounded strongly in his chest, a denial that the Ageing had ever had him. He was Simeon Soames, and he would not let those old men and fools decide his fate any more. He strode into the Throne Room.

'You should know that they know you've come here.' *They.* Somewhere in the past fifteen minutes all that he'd believed sacred had become *they.* A small voice deep inside him fought against the treachery, but the Rage choked it down. *They* weren't worth it, they didn't deserve him. Or maybe he just deserved better. 'My coming will hold them back for a while, because they think I'm on their side.' He smiled. It was a new

241

expression, colder than his normal, natural grin. 'But I hope you have a plan.'

Silence reigned for a few shocked seconds and then Arnold-Mather smiled. 'Good lord,' he said. 'Just look at your sword.'

Simeon Soames looked down, momentarily confused by the strange greeting. His eyes widened. Where the stones at the heart of his ring and embedded in the hilt of his sword had been a bright tangerine orange, they were now completely black, devoid of colour, with no shine. He stared at them for a long time as Arnold-Mather chuckled. 'Welcome aboard, whoever you are. Welcome aboard.'

TWENTY-FIVE

Though their milky eyes were blind, the Archivers were staring at Fin as he stood over Tova's body. He looked at the closest one, who was standing beside the first endless row of vials. His black robe was a harsh contrast against his albino skin. Like the others, his lips were drawn back over his teeth, and from never-used vocal chords came a high-pitched whine, like one long note being played on a violin. The room was filled with sound as each Archiver keened a different note, creating a symphony of loss and pain.

'I need to know,' Fin whispered. The sound the Archivers were making was so desolate that tears filled his eyes. What immense sadness were they going to share with him? What terrible truth? His heart pounded and in his head the chains fell away completely as the darkness began to open up. He sank to his knees as the world swam, and colour drained from the glowing vials that filled the room. As the Archivers fell silent, each and every truth vial shone bright gold until the whole chamber was as bright as the core of the sun and the men around him became black silhouettes against the brilliance. Fin's eyes burned as he squinted against it, then, just as he was sure he was about to scream, the terrible brightness was gone and he *saw* ...

Fists, knives, hate, noise, fear, pain, darkness. Nothing.
   There is a boat, and the stench of the river. It's night. A cart clatters against a deserted street – no, not a cart. Something

243

smaller, a sled maybe, but it's making more noise because of the weight it carries. The load is hidden under a hessian cloth. It's a dead weight, and Tova grunts slightly as she drags it across the abandoned streets. The noise doesn't matter. There is no one here – no one comes here any more, not in a long time. The people might be gone, but it's still a place of magic – that can't be taken out of its bones.

Her blonde hair is thick and her skin glows with youth, but tears run down her face and she pauses to wipe her nose with the back of her hand. She pulls herself together, biting back the tears and standing tall. This is no time for weakness. She is done with that; that's what brought them all to this pass.

She hasn't spoken to Andrew Fowkes since it happened. She let him cry over the broken body for a while, and then she threw him out. She saw the pain and guilt and his need for her in his face, and maybe that's what's making her cry now: he thinks she blames him too. She doesn't, of course; the blame lies entirely with her and her selfish desires for things that other women have. Perhaps the gossips at the Academy had been right all along: despite all her natural ability, she was too flawed to be the Storyholder.

She needed Fowkes gone – she needed them all gone, because she knew their shock wouldn't last long, and soon they would want answers. And the body. Plus, there was only so far she could bring him back from, if she could do it at all.

The river stinks and she sucks it in, defying it to stop her in her task. It doesn't try, of course; the River Times isn't like that. It just watches. A trail of mist creeps over and coils momentarily around her load, and she kicks at it as if it were real. There is never approval in the mist, but it feels almost sentient, and she would swear it was curious to see just how far she is prepared to go to shift the awful guilt.

No. *She grits her teeth and yanks her load away from the water and towards the broken building that had once been the heart of everything sacred. No, this isn't to make herself feel better; this is to try and put things right. It is.* Her heart thumps: is doing *wrong to do right really possible? Can there be no repercussions? She squashes the thoughts and lets the power that she is bound by oath to contain and control course through her veins to make herself feel better, if only for a while. When this is done, she will make amends. She will be the best and wisest Storyholder The Nowhere has ever had, and when she is gone, they will tell stories about her quiet grace and perfect control, and everyone will forget that a Knight bled to death on the stairs leading up to her apartments to save his friend.*

Her hair glows in the night. She is nearly past the point of no return, but she is too young to know the meaning of that. She is too young to understand that there is always a price. Things can not be undone; they must just be lived with.

The body lies on the cracked tiles, squashing the persistent weeds: a broken thing laid out on another broken thing, and both destroyed through no fault of their own. She thinks it is right to do the magic here, among the ghosts. His face is still smeared with blood, and she tries to wipe it away. One of his eyes is nearly gouged free of its socket, and his chest is more stab wounds than skin, so she's not sure why she's bothering to try and clean his cheeks, but she feels it's important. When she is done, she prepares herself. She has studied this – she's not alone; many of the initiates at the Academy learned some of the old ways from secret, illegal books. The temptation was always so great: to be told you have a power, a gift, and not to know how you could use it, should you be the one chosen to hold the worlds. She's had to dig deeper over the past two days to find this, though. This is not for a dabbler – this is real, dark magic.

The flickering candles are burning down, but she is lost in concentration and has no idea of time passing. Hours, minutes, seconds: they are all one. The candles shine in streaks of colours: red, blue, black, white and green, and every shade in between. She is on her knees beside the cold body – for weeks after she will bear the

245

bruises from those uneven slabs – but in the here and now she feels nothing except the power that sings in her veins and the dark magic in the building around her. Her mouth drops open, and as the sky rumbles, she quietly chants the words. The tip of the old cathedral's spire glows bright for a moment and sparks a crack of black lightning before returning to its ruinous state, almost invisible against the night.

Inside, she is so focused on the ripple of change she can feel buzzing in the air around her that she doesn't hear the rumble of the storm she is giving birth to. She keeps her eyes tightly closed and raises the double-edged sword, the dead Knight's sword. On the body, wounds knit themselves back together beneath Baxter's destroyed shirt. His damaged eye pulls back into the socket. Blood disappears.

Tova's chanting gets louder, although she is convinced she is barely whispering, until her words come screaming into the night. As she releases the last syllables she shrieks, and thrusts the sword into the dead man's chest.

Two things happen at once: the body convulses madly and she's thrown backwards, not strong enough to hold the jolt of power running through her and the sword and into Baxter. Her head slams against the hard ground, and after the stars and the bolt of pain the blackness takes her.

Too many images: flashes of life, running backwards ...
Nothing.
Fists, knives, hate, noise, fear, pain, darkness ...
Waiting on the stairs. Nervous, loyal. The sound of the mob: they know.
Faster now.
Laughter – Fowkes, much younger, no lines, no dark shadows behind his eyes. Drinking ... London ... Nowhere ... Somewhere ...
Younger ...
Too fast.

Bright light ...
Nothing.

Tova's eyes open and she stares. This wasn't what she expected at all. Baxter is gone, and the ring that is now too big for the infant finger has tumbled to the floor. The sword lies beside it. The baby gurgles.

The Somewhere. Cold streets. November.
She didn't know what else to do. Fowkes talked to her of this place; these people will know what to do. She looks at the child in the box and the blanket he's wrapped in. The Stories are safer there than they are in her. For two months she has held the storm she caused at bay. She knows now that things cannot be undone. She is so much older than she was, and she is afraid and alone.

She places the box on the second step of this Old Bailey. The nightwatchman Fowkes was so fond of would be here in a moment, if the stories he'd told her were true. She leans forward and kisses the child. Her fingers linger on the blanket.

She doesn't look back. In a dark alleyway she pulls the golden sword from within her coat and makes her way home.

Fin gasped and his eyes flew open as he struggled to breathe. The memories that had assailed him were fading, but Tova's story remained. His head spun. *What will be, will be.* That had been Baxter and Fowkes' saying – their show of unity, of friendship.

'I'm Baxter,' he muttered. His throat was dry sandpaper. 'I'm not *me* at all.'

The walls shook as the storm outside beat at them. Fin was going to be sick, he was sure of it.

'I *can't* be Baxter,' he whispered. 'I'm *me* – that makes me nothing.'

The vials had dimmed to a golden glow, still defying their natural multi-coloured brilliance. The Archivers stood still, staring at Finmere. As one, their mouths opened and they spoke.

'*When life and death are bound in one, the balance of all will come undone.*'

Their words were harp-song, and they filled every inch of the vast oval room. Fin staggered backwards, his ears aching with the sound. They would hear it beyond the double doors, for the sound of spoken truth was a sound that could not be contained. Fate and the Prophecy.

The Archivers lifted their right arms, and each pointed a slender finger in his direction. Pain shot through his head as he saw more flashing, nauseous images, here and gone in moments: Christopher and the Magus in West Minster, and Joe taking the stories from Tova. Tears coursed down his hot cheeks. It was too much.

'*When one plus one plus one is four, then all the worlds shall wait no more.*'

Fin got to his feet. One plus one plus one – him, Joe and Christopher. The fourth was Baxter, bound from death into Finmere's life.

He *was* going to be sick. He stumbled to the doors and pushed them open, his head swimming and his whole body coated in a cold sweat. He wasn't Baxter. He wasn't Fin. He hadn't even been properly fucking born. Not looking at the Knights, he fought his way to the side door and threw himself out into the stormy night, relishing the mad wind on his skin.

'Fin!' Harper Jones was the first outside. 'What happened? What Fowkes said ... it can't be true—'

Finmere almost laughed. Can't be true, from the House of Real Truths? Who was Harper trying to kid? The sarcasm was bitter – old and young wrapped up in one.

'What the fuck would you know?' he screamed against the wind. What the fuck did *anyone* know? He sat on the cold earth and let his anger and fear take hold, yelling at everyone who slowly emerged until his throat was hoarse and his heart had exploded with too many feelings he didn't understand.

And then, once his raging was done, like the child he still was, he cried.

TWENTY-SIX

The Rage took hold. Air formed into mist and the clear dark skies howled as impossible rain began to fall, pelting both Londons, The Somewhere and The Nowhere, with equal ferocity. In Leicester Square two Santas on their way home from feeding the magical belief of toddlers in grottos in expensive department stores were set upon by a group of teenagers coming out of the Odeon from a feel-good fantasy film. In Hammersmith, the Salvation Army choir swore and cursed at a primary school choir for daring to set up at the entrance of the shopping centre. Sirens wailed throughout the streets; ambulances, fire engines and police were constantly called out, the emergency services stretched to their limits in this evening which should have been filled with goodwill but which was instead bordering on anarchy. Behind closed doors in one of Kensington's finest streets a broken man stared at the beautifully decorated tree that filled one corner of the room, then down at the stack of bills and final demands that he'd spread out across his desk. Within an hour he would be suffocating his two small children as they slept and then strangling his wife before putting an end to the whole sorry mess by hanging himself.

In Orrery House Freddie Wise watched the local news on the rarely used television while Ted stared out at the night beyond.

'Do you think it's as bad there as it is 'ere?' Ted asked.

Freddie Wise sighed and leaned back in his chair, wincing slightly as his old bones creaked. 'Honestly?' He looked grim. 'I should imagine it's worse. For now anyway.'

'Are we going to do okay, Freddie, do you reckon?'

'We're going to do our best, and that's all we can do. We'll have help too. The good will come. The cabbies'll bring them.'

'I hope so, Freddie. I bloody hope so.'

The Crookeries were on fire.

The place had always been a metaphorical tinder box but about an hour before, during one of the many fights that had been breaking out all afternoon, someone must have tumbled into an oil lamp or torch, and everyone else was too busy finding a person to punch to try and put the ensuing fire out. The Crookeries weren't known for their community spirit at the best of times, but normally some sense of self-preservation kicked in and the thieves and junkies and hookers would pull together to save their dilapidated excuse for a home. After all, it was in their best interests – no one wanted to go and live outside, where the Borough Guard could come and pick them up at any time. This wasn't the first fire to have started in the cramped confines of the rundown tenements, but it was the first that had ever been allowed to get out of control.

When the man who'd been coming at Jack Ditch with the hammer felt his shirt light up after a piece of burning timber tumbled down on them, it had distracted him for just long enough to let Jack twist him round and slide the knife right across his throat. The fire was the least of that unfortunate man's worries now. Jack sniffed and tucked his knife back into the thick black belt that held his tatty woollen army jacket closed across his barrel chest. Jack Ditch had never been in the army in his life; he wasn't even sure that there was such a thing in The Nowhere's London, but he'd found the outfit years before, and it suited him. Gave him a sense of command over his motley crew.

Without a second glance down at the man he'd just killed, Jack stepped out of the way of the blazing building and over to the fences. The air was cold and the falling rain was stinging against the warmth of his bald head. He rubbed at it with thick fingers, enjoying the cool on his skin after the heat of the fight.

'Awright, Jack?'

His knife was free of its belt and almost in the man's liver by the time he realised who it was. The man squealing out his name helped.

'Bloody 'ell, it's me, Turpin!' The skinny man had skin with pothole scars like craters all over it. 'You nearly fucking killed me!'

'I don't do nearly killing,' Jack Ditch growled and looked at the dead body that was rapidly being consumed by flames. 'Ask him.'

'Look at that.' Turpin's eyes were wide as he watched another building spark alight like a childhood game of tag was being played by the fire. 'That'll be Mary's place gone then.'

'When the fire hits Mary's we don't want to be anywhere near here. She's got enough raw liquor stored there to blow the whole place up, mark my words.'

The rain splashed in the mud at their feet and Jack sniffed again before looking up. The stars winked back at him from a clear sky.

'This ain't right, Jack,' Turpin said, fearfully. 'This ain't right at all.'

Turpin had never been the brightest penny in the till but this time Jack couldn't argue with him. 'Get the boys. Gather 'em up where you can and meet by the entrance. Fifteen minutes. If you ain't found 'em all by then we'll just have to leave 'em to it. They'll 'ave to sort themselves out.'

'Where are we going, Jack?' Turpin sounded like a whiney child, but some of the fear had left his voice. Jack had a plan, and that was enough to calm most of the boys down when things got out of hand. Jack looked up at the rain and then back at the fire. There was the sound of glass smashing inside, and someone screamed. Things in the Crookeries had never got this out of hand before, and he'd be lying if he said he didn't have a fair amount of fear curled up inside his stomach too. Not that he'd show it – the day Jack Ditch showed fear was the day the worlds would end.

Looking at the rain, that thought felt somehow ominous. This was the kind of storm his old mum had told him about, before the gin got to her and her words became nothing but rambling nonsense. She'd had a lot of dark stories back then, though she wasn't all that imaginative, and he was beginning to wonder just how many of them were housed in truth. The old tales should never be underestimated. Stories *was* the worlds, after all …

'Time to take sides, Turpin,' he murmured. 'Time to take sides.' As the little thief scurried away to find the rest of the boys, Jack Ditch leaned against the gate and watched the rain and the fire. It was a new age trying to dawn, he was sure of that, just like his mum had said was coming.

Dr Strange tugged another hair free from his freckled pate. The sting was a slight distraction from the noise around him. It had been going on for hours, and he had a sneaking suspicion that even if they all stopped, he'd still hear the words; they were lodged in his mind now. He let the hair drop to the floor by his desk.

'Release us …'

He preferred it when they were screaming; this insidious, persuasive repetition made him nauseous. A sob escaped him, but he didn't hear it. A patch of blackness had appeared on the pristine white walls of his office, creeping from behind his filing cabinet like embarrassed mould. He wondered what the Prince Regent would think if he could see that. He didn't have to worry about the guards noticing it – he'd sent them all home when the chanting started, though he couldn't exactly remember why now. He giggled through his tears and reached up for another of the few straggles of hair that poorly covered his baldness. His fingers were shaking so much it took several goes before he could grip the next hair.

'Release us ...' His own whisper joined in with the throng of voices and the black patch became more confident and a fresh tendril crept up the wall. Dr Strange got up from behind his desk and reached for the heavy ring of keys in his drawer. Was this what madness felt like? He paused by the door and tried to compose himself, but the giggling and tears overwhelmed him. He'd begin in the basement, that's where the chanting had started. For the first time the thought of those red eyes and black tongues no longer scared him.

Francois Manot muttered under his breath in the old language while his mother rocked backwards and forwards on the red cushion. The two of them were alone in the Parlay Room. The light was dimmer than normal, and as he studied his arms the vivid colours of his tattoos faded, the edges growing darker, veering towards the ghost of black. He didn't notice. He was too lost in his own foul mood.

'What do you mean *a mistake*? *What* is a mistake?' he snapped like a starving river eel. 'Talk some sense. I'm tired of your riddles.' He had too much to think about and interference from others was just making him angry. An hour ago he'd sent the women and children to their dwellings and told them to stay there. He couldn't be doing with their noise and chatter and worry. There was too much talk, that was the problem. The boat had returned with men talking of the Lost Rivers turning black again, just like the boy said had happened earlier, but this time it had lasted for minutes, not the merest blink of an eye.

'We shouldn't have let her go up there. We should have kept her here.' Tears filled the wrinkles that covered the old woman's face. Francois tried to feel pity for her, but he couldn't. His nerves were jangling.

'*We* didn't,' he corrected her, '*you* did.'

She moved quickly, grabbing his arm, her dry fingers digging into his skin. 'Go and get her back,' she hissed. 'Get her back. This is *wrong*. This is all wrong. We need to make our people safe. I misjudged the situation: this is not something we can control.'

Francois pulled himself free, but said nothing. The men were restless and it wasn't only his own temper that had suddenly become frayed. All had been well until Curran Tugg and those fools from The Somewhere had come down to their waters. Now Anaïs was gone and there was trouble brewing – he could smell that in the cooling air. And it might well have left them alone, if only the strangers hadn't come down here looking for help. His crystal eyes hardened. Had they really come for help, or was that just a cover for their accusations? All the talk of the Lost Rivers being used by someone *other* – is that what they really thought? Or had the dandy Prince sent them? Had he offered Curran Tugg something to find a way to steal the Gypsy princess and hold the tribe to ransom? He cursed and spat at the ground. The more he thought about it, the more likely it was they'd been duped. And now there was trouble in the water and the old woman was crying – something he hadn't seen in too many years to remember. His tattoos darkened, the light and lively reds becoming deep as blood. A headache bloomed into life behind his eyes.

'I'll send men to each of the hatches in the centre of the city.' His words were like cracking glass. 'If they're truly searching for someone up there, then they won't be far. We'll find them and bring her home.'

His words didn't stop the old woman crying and he fought the urge to slap her hard. His sudden aggressiveness frightened him and for a second he took a step back from himself

255

and didn't like what he saw. This wasn't him, this anger, just like the tears weren't her. They were *better* than this.

'I'll go and ready the men,' he said. Snot hung from her nose and his irritation rose again. 'Clean yourself up. This is a disgrace.'

The familiar streets felt alien as Mona jogged through them. Everywhere she went, there were fights and arguments, on the corners, in the buildings, everywhere. Some people stood in a daze, as if confused by the anger that was taking hold of their friends. They should go home, she thought; this wasn't a night that someone trying to avoid confrontation was likely to have any say in the matter. Here and there she spotted Borough Guardsmen separating a brawl or trying to resolve a disagreement, but she didn't stop to help. They would do the best they could, and if she did try and join in, she'd be there all night. She didn't even pause when she saw two Guardsmen fighting each other. Anger was spreading through London like a tidal wave as the cold rain tumbled more heavily from the clear sky. She didn't look up. She was scared enough already.

As she drew closer to the centre, she could make out a glow on the horizon: it had to be coming from the Crookeries. Her heart ached slightly. The Storyholder Academy and the Crookeries were at different ends of the spectrum of the wonders of her home town, and she had loved them both. Now both had been hit by fire – but this time no one was pulling together to fight it. It looked like no one even cared. Maybe the cold rain would ensure something of the Crookeries survived, but it would never be the same again. Mona wasn't sure anything would.

'A hanging! His Royal Majesty has ordered a hanging at Smithfields!' The street urchin's voice carried over the whistling wind, and Mona stopped in her tracks and pushed her wet hair out of her eyes so she could take a better look.

The boy was only about ten – a good age for a Crier. Kids could always go that bit further before the side-effects of moving around the Boroughs set in. This one was standing on an upturned crate on the corner of two streets, a small flat cap on his head and a slightly-too-big jacket over his calf-length trousers. On his feet were thick boots. This was his part of town, judging by his clothes; no wonder he was shouting so enthusiastically. He had the confidence of a Crier, though. If it had been an adult shouting about a hanging, Mona might have put it down to whatever craziness was affecting the population, but as it was, her heart stilled for a moment.

She wasn't the only one to notice him. Even those who had been fighting paused and wandered over to hear what he had to say. Their eyes gleamed and they chattered excitedly; these people were eager to see someone dance at the end of a rope. Mona had watched when Conrad Eyre had been hanged at Smithfields for his part in St John Golden's attack on the Storyholder, and it had been horrible. There had been a big crowd, but it had been a silent, sombre affair. No one had been baying for blood, and the Knight had been allowed to die with dignity, without abuse. Looking at the excited faces of those who were now scurrying towards Smithfields, Mona thought it would be different for whoever was going to be hanged now.

She set off again, and saw, further up the street, a chubby figure squeezed into a guardsman's uniform that might once have fitted him before he started exercising less and eating far more, flailed wildly as a middle-aged woman shrieked at him. Mona whistled, loud and so high-pitched that somewhere in the distance a dog started barking. He looked over and saw her, relieved to escape the harridan attacking him. He lumbered over to her, panting as he joined Mona beside the Crier's box. Mona looked at his red face. If The Nowhere came out the other side of whatever *this* was, then it was time to introduce regular fitness checks for her guards – and maybe create more desk jobs, even though she didn't understand why anyone would want one.

'What's your name?' she asked.

'Trevor,' the man wheezed. 'Trevor Hedge. Been a Guard for twenty-five years, ma'am. Good to meet you.'

'Do you know anything about this hanging?' More people had gathered around the boy, who had jumped off his box, ready to pick it up and run to his next crying post.

'Not paid it much attention,' he said, 'what with having our hands full the past couple of hours. The littering alone—' He pointed at a pile of rubbish lying soggy in the street. 'And then there's all the fighting – I've got my missus holding three people in our house until tomorrow, when I can get them locked up and charged all proper.' He sighed, and now Mona recognised tiredness, not laziness. 'It's been a long day, I can tell you.'

'I know. Thank you.' The man might be old and overweight, but she regretted her initial impression that this automatically made him a bad Guard. He was obviously exhausted. Most men would probably have quit by now – for all she knew, a lot of them had, and might even be fighting each other in an alley somewhere. 'I might have another job for you, though.' She squeezed his arm. 'You think you can get to the palace? I need an important message delivered.'

Trevor Hedge's eyes widened and his chins wobbled as he nodded enthusiastically 'I can do that – for the Prince himself?'

'Yes.' Christopher would tell Fin and the Knights what they'd learned, but her first loyalty was to the Prince Regent. On the practical side, he knew The Nowhere better than the Knights did – maybe he'd know why George Porter was heading to West Minster. 'You need to say Mona Savjani sent you, and tell him we know who's creating the mad: it's a Knight called George Porter, who was pushed down Clerke's Well. We think he's heading to West Minster, but we don't know why. The Regent needs to send some men there to trap and arrest him. Can you remember all that?'

'Yes, yes, I've got it all right. You can trust me, ma'am.'

The man might be tired, but she could see his eyes were still sharp.

'Thank you, Trevor Hedge. I'll see you get promoted for this. Maybe a desk job?'

'That would be grand.' Relief flooded through the man's face. 'Make the missus happy too.'

Mona smiled. She couldn't ever imagine wanting to exchange the excitement of the city for filling in bits of paper all day! Beside them, the boy had picked up his box and was about to move off.

'Good luck, Mr Hedge.' Mona slapped the man's arm and he scurried off into the rain, then she turned and sprinted after the boy.

'Oi!' he cried as she grabbed him.

'What's this about a hanging?' She ignored his indignation and kept a firm grip. 'Who's ordered a hanging?'

'The Prince hisself!' He wriggled hard and Mona jumped back to avoid a kick from his muddy boot. 'He came out on the balcony of the palace and declared it.'

'When?' Mona spat out the rain that had fallen into her mouth. This all felt very wrong. The Prince *abhorred* violence – and who would he be hanging anyway? Maybe he was caught up in this anger that was sweeping the city …

'Who?' she asked. It was only when she'd voiced the question that she realised how much she was dreading the answer. 'Who is he hanging?'

'A Traveller,' the boy announced, proud of his knowledge. 'A Traveller what's brought all this on us.' He looked up at the stars through the pouring rain. 'That's what the Prince says.'

'What Traveller? Did the Prince give a name?'

259

'Who cares?' The boy finally wriggled free. 'They shouldn't be here anyway!'

'When's the hanging?' Mona shouted as he darted away, leaving his box behind.

'Now!' he called back, 'so you can't stop it!'

Mona stared after him, barely aware of the cold rain that was pelting her face, almost as if it were taunting her. *Hanging a Traveller?* Her breath was caught: both Fin and Christopher were out there somewhere. Could they have been captured? – but why would the Prince want to hang either of them? They were working for him. Fear washed over her. She'd seen how people were acting – she and Christopher should have stayed together … why had she been so dumb?

Her heart in her mouth, she ran towards Smithfields.

TWENTY-SEVEN

He went back to Orrery House – he needed to see Ted. It was the only thing he could think of to do. Just as the Archivers slammed the doors on them and locked them out, the first heavy drops of cold rain began to fall from the clear skies, as if the sky were crying with him. Of course it was, he thought as he drew his sword and sliced between the worlds: *he* was the cause of the tempest that was coming. He was unnatural, wrong, and all the worlds knew it.

As Ted led him down to the kitchen at the heart of the old house his tears stopped and a dark calm settled over him. He wondered if this was how people felt when they were told they had cancer or something terrible like that. A boy at St Martin's had got leukaemia, and he'd gone funny for a while – but he'd got better. Fin figured this was worse, because he was going to have to live like this, with the box unlocked, for ever. He *knew* what he'd seen was the truth, he could feel it resonating inside, but he didn't really understand where that left him. Who was he, if he was anyone at all?

Jarvis made a pot of tea but thankfully avoided making polite conversation as Fin slumped in the armchair in front of the vast Aga. Ted patted him on the shoulder and told him he'd be back in a tick. Fin assumed he'd gone to talk to Fowkes first. When Ted came back, he was alone. Finmere was glad of that. He wasn't ready for Fowkes yet.

'You all right, son?' He poured himself a cup of tea, then

pulled out a chair from behind the wooden table and sat close to Fin.

'All this is happening because of me, isn't it?' Fin sniffed hard, feeling himself beginning to tear up again. 'This storm and everything ... You should have just left me on the steps, Ted. We'd all have been better off.'

'That's not the way of things, mate.' The old man smiled and his eyes twinkled with kindness and good humour. 'And even if I could, I wouldn't turn back the clock, not for nothing. Fate is as Fate does – she would've found you, one way or another. But that don't make this your fault. Sometimes things just is. Storm or no storm, I wouldn't 'ave 'ad Tova, God rest 'er, 'ave done any different.' He leaned in closer. 'I love you like you're me own, Fin. And your story ain't told yet, so don't you go writing yourself off. You belong 'ere: you're one of us. You're special.'

'I'm *wrong*!' Fin said, feeling like his heart was breaking. 'I wasn't even *born*.' He couldn't get his head round that. He'd spent the best part of sixteen years wondering about his mum and dad – but he never once thought that he might not have parents at all. *Everyone* had parents—

'You *was* born,' Ted said firmly. 'It might 'ave been different to the way I was born, but you was born all the same. And I tell you this, son, you was born out've love, which can't be said for a lot of people.'

'"And love, the greatest damage cause, and forge the war to end all wars",' Fin muttered. He was glad they weren't upstairs in the same room as the Prophecy table, where it could glow and taunt him. 'That was my birth the Magi were talking about, wasn't it? I'm the walking bloody Prophecy.'

'No one's just one thing, Fin. You're you – Finmere Tingewick Smith. Remember that.'

'Funny—' Tears pricked the back of his eyes again and he swallowed them down angrily. 'From what I just heard,

Finmere Tingewick Smith doesn't exist. I'm just Baxter, back from the dead.'

'You ain't Baxter, son,' Ted said, softly. 'I knew 'im. 'e might be in there with you, but you ain't him. The worlds don't work like that. New life is new life, and that's what she made.'

'What was he like?' Fin asked, almost in spite of himself.

'Adam Baxter?' Ted thought for a moment. ''e was a good man, like you're a good boy – not in that way teachers and old women say it: I mean good in 'ere.' He tapped at his chest. ''e 'ad a sense of 'umour on 'im too: liked a laugh, did Baxter. But he was brave – quieter than Fowkes, but just as brave.'

'I think I had him in a box in my head all this time. I used to get these little flashes of stuff coming through – guess he's how I could use the sword so easily, not me being special at all, just him doing it,' Fin said, staring down at his shoes. 'Now the box is open, and I'm scared of what happens to me.' He looked up. 'What if *he* takes over – where do *I* go?'

'It ain't gonna 'appen, Fin,' Ted said. 'For a start, if 'e could and wanted to, then 'e would've done so already, don't you reckon? That'd make sense, especially when you was sorting out St John Golden. Second, we don't know what Tova actually *did*. You might 'ave Baxter's essence in you, just like I've got bits of me Mum and Dad – don't mean they're living in me 'ead, though, do it? One thing I do know, and that's that you're going to 'ave to make your peace with it. You ain't got no choice, and we ain't got the time at the moment for thinking. We ain't got the time to grieve for Tova even.' He sipped his tea. 'We've got a battle coming, Finmere, and we need you.'

Fin sniffed hard again and wiped his nose on his sleeve. Even if he could run, where would he go? He would be running from what was inside him ... And Ted was right, if anyone was locked into this battle between the worlds, it was be him. On top of that, he couldn't leave Joe, not like this.

'I think I come as a pair. You need both of us?' It was a weak joke, but Fin felt better for making it, even as he wondered if it was Baxter's humour or his own. It made Ted smile, though, and that was something.

'That's the spirit, son.'

Ted's face darkened, and for a moment Fin's worries came crashing back.

'What is it? What haven't you told me?'

Ted pulled his old tin out of his pocket, took out one of his pre-rolled cigarettes and lit it. Fin had never seen anyone smoking inside Orrery House before. He glanced over at Jarvis, who was placing some bone-china mugs and a large pot of tea onto a silver tray to take upstairs, but he didn't even turn their way, let alone raise that judgemental eyebrow of his. Jarvis not reacting was almost as weird as the weather outside: Jarvis hated anything dirty, and completely ignoring the smell of cigarette smoke in his kitchen was really unnerving. Things must be bad.

'It's about Christopher, Fin – well, about 'is dad. And Joe.'

By the time Ted had finished telling him, Fin had almost forgotten everything that had been revealed in the Old Bailey House of Real Truths. Christopher's dad in league with St John Golden? And *he'd* got Joe to steal the stories? And everyone thought maybe Christopher had known? Suddenly it all became clear.

'The cigarette case,' he muttered.

'What cigarette case?' Ted asked.

'Before – when Tova was in the Incarcerator prison and we'd just found Fowkes, Christopher picked up a cigarette case in her apartments. I guess it must've been his dad's. That's when he changed, at any rate.' His stomach sank. He wasn't the only one Fate was playing with. 'Whatever that Magus made him pay for the stuff to reverse the Ageing, I bet he did it to make up for his dad. That's the sort of thing he'd do.'

Fin understood why Christopher hadn't said anything when he'd begun to suspect his father: his life had been as much of a pretence as Fin's had turned out to be. Mr Arnold-Mather must have set him up to be Fin's friend – it was lucky for him they'd got on so well. How utterly terrible for Christopher to find out it was all just part of a plan to betray him.

'Where has Mr Arnold-Mather taken Joe?' he asked. *One plus One plus One*: him, Christopher and Joe, all with roles to play. He suddenly felt ashamed of his own self-pity. He wasn't the only one Fate was playing with, and he needed to remember that. He needed to be strong for the friends he'd dragged into this whole mess.

'The palace, we think. Simeon Soames's gone to check it out, and 'e'll 'ead over to the Knights' place in The Nowhere once 'e's got the lie of the land.'

'Poor Joe,' Fin said. 'This really isn't like him, Ted – he *always* puts his friends first. I don't understand what's happened to him.'

'He's got the stories inside 'im now, and they can do funny things, even to them that's trained to hold 'em. Lord only knows 'ow Joe'll cope. There's a lot of power in them stories, and power changes people, Fin.' Ted's face was grim. 'Let's 'ope when all this is over we can get 'im back and get them stories into someone who can cope with 'em better. What do you say, lad?'

'Yes! Let's make sure we do that, Ted.'

'We'll do our best, son.'

Fin drank his cooling tea and fought the urge to hug Ted tight – after all, he wasn't a kid any more. Being around Ted always made everything feel better, even when Fin knew it wasn't, not really. But the feeling was enough; it gave him hope, and there was something special in that.

The kitchen door opened and Fowkes strode in. 'More cabbies arriving: a pretty motley crew, but it's certainly better than nothing, especially this early in the storm.' He glanced at Jarvis. 'You'd better get that tea up there. You know what taxi drivers are like!'

As Jarvis picked up the tray and disappeared into the hallway, Fowkes focused on Ted. 'Freddie says that Grey's is set up. He's sent some people over there. The same with the British Library. It'll be better when we have a clearer idea of how bad things are going to get.'

'If the weather's anything to go by, then it ain't looking so good,' Ted said quietly.

'No.' Fowkes sighed. 'And time's gone funny over there – it's aligning with here, and that can't be a good thing either.'

Ted got to his feet. 'We can manage 'ere. You and the boy need to get back.'

'Yes, we do.' For the first time since he'd entered the kitchen, the Knights' Commander looked at Fin. For a long second he didn't say anything, and then he said, 'Look, I don't know what to make of any of this stuff any more than you do. If I'm honest, it totally freaks me out.'

'Me too,' Fin mumbled.

'Well, we've got a job to do, and I'm happy to ignore it for now if you are. We can deal with it all once we've sorted out the worlds – what do you say?'

'Fine by me.'

'Good.' Fowkes almost smiled. 'Let's go then. The Knights' house.'

'Okay.' Fin stood up and looked at Ted, who winked back. With one sweep of his sword he cut an opening up between the two worlds. He loved them both, despite everything they were throwing at him. 'What will be, will be,' he muttered. Fowkes eyes widened, and Fin realised that was Baxter's saying, not his.

'What will be, will be,' Fowkes answered and Fin saw tides of emotions swirl across his face. The effects of Tova's actions rippled outwards, touching them all, and now she'd left Fowkes to face their joint guilt alone. Fin guessed she hadn't thought of that. Fowkes moved up alongside him and together they stepped through the tear between Londons.

Lucas Blake slowed his horse and waited for Alex Currie-Clarke to catch him. The younger man clearly wasn't used to riding, but they'd been lucky: his mount was so well-trained that it managed to follow its rider's clumsy instructions. But both horses were getting jittery now, snorting and pawing at the ground each time the two men stopped as if they wanted to keep on running until they were somewhere other than here, in a place where rain and thunder didn't rule a clear sky. As the wind whipped his cloak into his face he bent over and stroked the horse's neck, trying to calm the fretting animal.

They were back early, but Lucas reckoned they'd seen enough. Once he'd realised the change in the city's mood, he was immensely glad they'd stopped at the London Wall, the crumbling waist-high stone boundary that encircled the city some fifteen miles from the centre. Beyond it was cropland, though most of those who farmed so close to London preferred to live within the protection of the city wall, heading out to tend their fields at dawn every day.

Blake had no idea what lay beyond that farmland; most Londoners didn't appear to know either. To them, the city was everything – well, perhaps it was. For all Lucas knew, it was nothing but desert. He'd always wanted to explore further out in The Nowhere, a way to make up for the life he lost during the five long years he spent Aged, but this wasn't the time.

When he and Alex had finally reached the city limits, the magnitude of what they were facing had become clear. The air was just as cool there as in the centre of town, and the darkening sky had rolled with thunder, even though there were no clouds, not even on the horizon.

Alex Currie-Clark had looked at that vast vista and, his voice shaking a little, suggested they go no further. Lucas Blake had been quick to agree. The Londoners of The Nowhere might forget that a world existed beyond the city boundary, but the storm that was fast approaching had no such compunction; it stretched out across the whole world. As he had looked up at the endless sky, Lucas had felt a twinge of darkness eating at his natural optimism. He'd heard tales of the last Black Storm, the one that had come after Baxter had been murdered. He'd always been told that it never went beyond the city. And it hadn't started like this, either; it had come hard and fast, brought on by the Storyholder's grief over the Knight's death. This was something quite different, he was sure of that.

They stared for a few moments longer, and then as a small orange glow in the distance lit up the gloom and the first drops of cold rain fell from the clear sky, they turned their tired, nervous horses and started to gallop back.

'Where are we going?' Alex Currie-Clarke came alongside. His reddened face, lashed by the wind and rain, clashed badly with his ginger hair.

They'd arrived at King's Cross, a four-way crossroads where tanners and butchers plied their associated trades from inside the run-down buildings. Passing punters could look in through the opened doors and windows to see exactly what they were getting for their money. It was a rough part of town, and many of the people who lived here were drunks and prostitutes and those with an allergy to working for a living, only one step away from the residents of the Crookeries. The whole area stank, a heady mixture of the slain animals and the tanneries, and some days the streets literally ran with blood as the animals were slaughtered by the dozen. Luckily, there was good drainage here, and as the rain fell, Lucas Blake watched it trickle away down a grated hole by the kerb. Where did the blood and water go, he wondered, straight into the underground rivers? There was a hint of madness in the air, and he suspected the rivers were close to the surface here. Anyone who wanted to work with death and blood all day, regardless of the enormous benefits for the rest of the city, must be a little touched by the insanity of the rivers, he thought.

The tanneries and slaughterhouses had been closed up or abandoned already, but half-skinned animals and hunks of meat were visible through the gaping doorways, the red-raw flesh gleaming in the dark. Lucas Blake shivered and wiped rain from his eyes. In one open entrance a table had been overturned and protruded into the street, and the Knights could hear a man and woman shouting at each other in the room above. Lucas couldn't make out the words, but the rage in them was clear. This was no place to stop: if things went bad here, they might well end up hacked to death.

'You need to go to the Knights' house, the House of Charter's Lane,' he told Alex, leading them further into the city. 'It's in the exact same spot as Orrery House, back in our London. Do you think you can find it?'

'Sure.' Alex Currie-Clarke looked like he wasn't very sure at all.

'It's that way.' He stuck his arm out at approximately eleven o'clock. 'It may all look different, but the layout is pretty much the same. If you get lost, ask for Charter's Square.'

The younger Knight nodded. 'Where are you going?'

'I'm not happy about those kids being out in this. Look at the sky.' He nodded upwards. 'Time's gone haywire. It's got to be nearly midnight already – I'm going to go to The Circus and find them. I'll bring them back to the house.' He grinned at Currie-Clarke's drawn face. 'Don't look so nervous! This is what it's all about: adventures, Alex Currie-Clarke! Isn't it great?'

Thunder cracked overhead so loudly that both men ducked into their saddles.

'Yeah, brilliant.' Currie-Clarke managed a smile, and Lucas Blake winked at him. His own fear was raw in the pit of his stomach, but it wouldn't do the new Knight any good to see that. Spirits up, that was the only way forward – anything else would let the darkness in.

'Good!' He turned his horse so that they were facing each other and drew his sword. When Alex had finally steadied his own mount and got his golden weapon free, Lucas touched the blades together, making them sing. 'Let us be ready!' he called above the howling wind.

'Let us be ready!' Alex Currie-Clarke sang out strongly.

TWENTY-EIGHT

Mona pushed her way through the growing crowd, desperate to see what was going on by the gallows. Her heart thumped as she yelled at people to get out of her way, but the crowd was too excited at the prospect of someone's imminent demise to pay any attention to her uniform – not that it was easy to recognise, now it was soaked through and filthy.

'Let me through!' she yelled again, elbowing her way past a fat woman carrying a crying baby. The woman swore in reply, but Mona was already gone, weaving her way towards the front. She wasn't too late, that was something. The curved glass ceiling over the vast space kept most of the rain out, but though the wide arches that made up the entrance at either end had created a wind tunnel, the constant blasts of cold wind could do nothing to dispel the foul odour of the hawkers' greasy food. Mona could see they were doing a roaring trade, and her stomach twisted: what had *happened* to these people? Why were they so keen to see someone die? That wasn't the way of The Nowhere.

On the wooden structure ahead of her she could see a line of Palace Guardsmen dressed in their red and gold dress uniforms, facing the crowd. Their faces were impassive. There were more behind the steps, no doubt guarding the unseen prisoner. The Crier hadn't been, lying then. Only the Prince Regent could have been responsible for the soldiers' presence here. Frustration gnawed at her as she reached the fourth row back. If they'd been members of the ordinary Borough Guard, she might have been able to make them listen to her, or at least to delay this terrible deed for long enough for her to appeal to the Prince himself. But she had no hold over these men; she'd seen how they looked at her, like she was just a mongrel Trader kid who'd got lucky. There was no chance she could reason with them. She could hear cruel laughter everywhere and the air was blue with cursing as people constantly shoved forward, all trying to get a better look. She thought there must be two or three hundred people here, all with the same aggressive gleam in their eyes, and she was pretty sure it was only the hanging that was stopping them fighting each other. This was the Rage, she was sure of it. For the first time in a long while she felt closer to a child than to an adult, and a wave of despair washed over her. How could she possibly fight this? How could any of them? A burly figure pushed her out of his way; only the crush of bodies kept her upright.

A low, steady beat started, and an expectant hush fell over the crowd as the young drummer boy appeared at the bottom of the steps at the back of the wooden gallows. Mona's heart leaped into her mouth and she tried in vain to break through the blockade of thickset men who'd beaten and bullied their way to the front. One of them elbowed her in the face, and didn't even turn round as she yelped. Pain spread across her cheek so swiftly that she knew she'd soon have a huge bruise. Tears pricked her eyes, and for the first time in her life she wished she were a boy, a big one, who could punch back. She gave up trying to get through and instead stood on her tiptoes, peering though a small gap between the heads and shoulders of the people in front of her.

She was just in time: the executioner was climbing the steps, her grey hair piled up on top of her head in a mockery of one of the Prince Regent's formal wigs. She was old, but even from where she was, Mona could see the steely glint in her dark eyes. Her job was to execute criminals on her Royal taskmaster's order, and so rarely had that happened in recent years that it would take more than one screaming teenager to stop her carrying out her duty, even if the girl was one of the Prince's favourites, plucked from obscurity to be the Borough Guard's chief spy. The torches that surrounded the gallows illuminated the blood-red tips of the old woman's gnarled fingers, the polish matching the red velvet dress that was her uniform.

The crowed bayed and booed and the executioner lifted her chin, revealing the scars of the rope around her own neck. She had been cut down while dangling from the gallows herself to take the place of the previous executioner – after all, why would you make a good man take the lives of others when there were plenty of bad people around to do the job? Mona had to admit the woman had a dignity that commanded a certain fearful respect. She didn't speak, or attempt to entertain the crowd, but there was something disturbing about her, and that was more compelling than any boorish joke could ever be.

Mona couldn't quite make out all the figures who followed one of the Regent's Chancellors onto the platform. The Chancellor's tall black wig shone in the light of the blazing torches, and with his perfectly powdered and rouged face, in his pristine pink jacket, he cut an impressive figure. The acrid burning oil was making Mona's eyes itch. Hangings were rare, but they *never* took place at night. Even with the presence of the Chancellor and the Palace Guard, this was feeling more and more like a lynching.

The Chancellor turned to face the crowd. He banged his silver cane on the wooden floor three times before starting, 'Joe Manning—'

Mona froze for a second, unable to breathe. *Joe?* They were going to hang *Joe*? She started to struggle forward, but got nowhere. The men in front of her were determined no one was going to shift them.

The Chancellor was still speaking. '—found guilty of treason against The Nowhere. You stole the Five Eternal Stories and perpetrated arson against the Storyholder Academy—'

'That's not true!' Mona's cry was lost in the catcalls and baying cries from the impatient throng around her. 'That's not true!' she shrieked, 'listen to me!'

'—brought this storm to us. Our glorious Prince Regent has now recovered the Five Eternal Stories, and the good people of The Nowhere can rest assured that they are safe.' Each clipped word felt like a dagger in Mona's heart.

'Stop! It's not true! Listen—!'

'Shut your fucking mouth or I'll fucking shut you up!' The burly man with a lot of missing teeth raised his hand and what looked to be a very sharp knife glinted in the torchlight.

'But it's—'

'I mean it, girlie!'

Up on the wooden stage, the Chancellor had finished delivering the Prince Regent's judgement and now stepped to one side, revealing the slight figure in jeans and trainers, looking dreadfully out of place, standing between the two soldiers. They pushed him to the front of the stage, next to the rope noose, and the crowd went wild.

Mona stared silently, and her mouth fell open. Joe's clothes – they were definitely Joe's clothes – but the person wearing them ... it wasn't ... he was too small to be Joe ...

An awful chill prickled over her skin, and she realised it was—

The Prince Regent looked out at the sea of angry faces as the cold wind lashed at the back of his neck. Tears welled in his eyes at the thought of the years he'd spent worrying about the onset of madness. All that time he'd wasted fearing an eventuality that would now never come to pass. At least he would die sane. And if the battle heralded by this storm was won by the good, then these poor people would have to live with the memory of what they had done, even if it had been influenced by the Rage.

And as he walked awkwardly in Joe Manning's clunky footwear towards the noose, he almost smiled: when this was done and he'd moved on elsewhere, this cursed line of kings would be finished, once and for all. He looked at his Chancellor, but the man wouldn't meet his eye – not really a surprise, the Prince Regent thought, for this man did not even have the excuse of the Rage on which to blame his decision. He had chosen to betray his royal master out of fear. Arnold-Mather had had his henchman stab two of the Chancellors through the heart, after which Chancellor C had very quickly agreed to this act of treason.

The Prince's heart was heavy as the screams of the crowd became a wall of hate in front of him. There was so much bloodshed ahead for his people; he had let them down by allowing himself to be removed from the game so easily. He wondered for a moment if they actually felt anything for him at all; would they have followed him, had the Rage not descended?

The executioner's gnarled hands slipped the coarse rope over his head and pulled it tight around his neck. He found that now the moment was here, he wasn't overly afraid of dying, and he was glad of that. He might not have been the most memorable of the Royal line, and he knew he did not deserve to die in the midst of such loathing, but he would die with dignity, with his sanity intact, and he discovered he was deeply grateful for those small mercies. And at least it would be quick. The rope was itching against the bare skin of his neck, but he ignored it as much as he could. Tova's death had destroyed his own joy of life. He had loved her all their lives, quietly but completely, ever since their childhood friendship, and that had never faltered, not even when she chose Fowkes.

The temperature was dropping fast; there would be a hard

frost coating the ground in the morning. Not that he would see it. In the crowd, faces burned red with excitement. He refused to look as if he was afraid, and he dug his fingernails into the palms of his tied hands and gritted his teeth so they wouldn't chatter. If his people did not feel the bite of winter, then neither would he. One day they would know it was their own Prince Regent whose blood they had bayed for, and they would remember that he died strong and proud. There would be no one who would be able to say that they saw him tremble on the scaffold.

Hands pushed him into place over the square of wood that would soon disappear under his feet, and the noise from the crowd hushed as the executioner stepped up to the heavy lever. The Prince Regent stared straight ahead. He would not look at the old hag who had been spared this fate herself. He didn't want the last thing he saw of this beautiful world to be something wicked. Perhaps, he thought on reflection, his best option was just to close his eyes.

'No! No, stop! You *have* to stop!'

The voice cut through the stilled hush and his dark eyes dropped to the crowd. He almost smiled: there she was, little Mona Savjani, tears streaming down her face, trying in vain to break through the burly bodies of those in front. She had no chance, he saw, as she was shoved backwards.

'But it's the Prince! It's the Prince Regent!' she shouted as loudly as she could. 'It's *not* Joe Manning!'

The Chancellor shuffled nervously from foot to foot, but the mob merely laughed at Mona's words and some started muttering, 'She's mad.' The Prince kept his eyes fixed firmly on the girl, and eventually she looked up. Behind her he could see a man in a purple turban, with a jewel in the centre of his shaped beard, wriggling through the masses. He reached her and wrapped his arms around her, pulling her back.

The man looked up at the Prince Regent, his face full of sadness and loss. Mitesh Savjani, The Nowhere's most exquisite clothcrafter; his good friend. The Regent heard a strange noise, the groaning clicks of metal grinding on wood, as the Chancellor told the executioner to begin. The Prince Regent kept his eyes firmly on the man standing still below, his arms wrapped round his sobbing daughter. He smiled, a little wistfully, and Savjani bowed his head slightly in a gesture of respect, never losing eye-contact, and smiled gently himself, though his heart was breaking.

The Prince Regent let out a breath as the ache in his heart eased. His last sight in this world would not be wickedness and hate after all. He was not dying alone.

'Get off me!' Mona fought the hands that grabbed at her. 'Get off me! I have to stop them! I *have* to—'

'There's nothing you can do for him now, sweetheart.'

It took a moment for the words and the familiarity of the voice to register, then she stopped struggling and turned in the strong arms. 'Dad?' she breathed, and the tears she'd been fighting to hold back flooded out. 'But it's not Joe, it's the Prince, it's—'

He pulled her into his arms and hugged her tight. 'I know,' he whispered. 'I know – but there is nothing we can do.' He held her head gently against his silk-clad shoulder and whispered, 'Don't look, my daughter, just don't look.'

She buried her face against him, inhaling his familiar smell and feeling like a child as she sobbed. Though she tried blocking out the world around her, she still heard the sharp *thud* as the trap opened, and the cheer that flew up seconds later reverberated through the bloodthirsty crowd.

'Look at his legs!' one woman called out, 'he looks like he's dancing!' As she burst into cruel laughter, many others joined in.

Mona didn't look back at the gallows as her father led her out through the mass of people. She clung on to his hand like she had when she was a little girl, when he could protect her against everything bad in the world. No one tried to stop them or get in their way this time; everyone else was struggling forward to stare at the body.

'What's happening to everyone?' Mona's teeth chattered in the cold, and her exhaled breath hung in a curious mist in front of her, almost as if it were unhappy at having to leave the warmth of her lungs. 'Why would they *do* this? Why? Is it the Rage?' She wiped her eyes and shook away the fresh tears that threatened to fall as her father led her into a tiny alley. He stopped and peered out to check they hadn't been followed, and only then did he relax slightly.

He gripped her hands. 'We must find the others,' he said. 'We need to be together for strength.' His normally sparkling eyes were dull and his mouth twitched nervously.

Mona had never seen him afraid before. 'What is it?' she whispered, 'what else has happened?' The words stuck in her throat – she wasn't sure she wanted to know.

'I do not know for certain,' her father said softly. 'When I left Fowkes, the boy had the stories and he had gone to The Somewhere. Now I hear rumours—'

'Rumours of what?' Mona's face flushed. She had not yet taken in the Prince Regent's death. What else could there be wrong with the world?

He gripped her hands. 'I will tell you as we walk, but right now we must find the others.'

'We were going to meet at The Circus at midnight,' Mona said, her voice shaking.

Mitesh Savjani looked up at the sky. 'Then we should hurry. Midnight is almost here.'

TWENTY-NINE

*T*he Circus was still humming with life, but the hawkers were subdued. Some shoppers were snapping and snarling at each other; others were huddled together talking quietly, or rushing to get out of the bitter cold. He watched from the shadows for a moment. There was something different in the air, more than just the strange shift in time from afternoon to night. It felt expectant; change was coming. His new strength was making a glutton of him, and it was making him careless too – his most recent victim had screamed loudly enough for the passers-by to hear. But society was definitely breaking down, for no one had come to help the man, who had shouted and cried for help all the while he had been feeding – and that wasn't normal. These people weren't like that – he remembered that. The more he fed, the more he was remembering . . .

Frost crystallised on the dark ground, glinting in the torchlight like shards of diamonds. The wind blasted round the buildings, but the small stone in his pocket warmed his skin. He wasn't de-pendent on the stone; they were co-dependent, that was a better way to think of it. They needed each other. He had tried leaving it once, taking it out of his pocket, placing it on the ground and walking away, but he had managed no more than three or four steps before his head began to get foggy, and all he could see was the stone and the darkness; a gateway to madness opened, filling his mind. By the time he'd picked up the small pebble again, he was trembling from head to foot and was coated in cold sweat. Its soothing warmth had flooded him and within seconds the awful blackness was gone.

He wrapped his fingers around the small shape in his pocket. The stone had brought him back from that place, and he would rather be its slave than ever return. And what the stone wanted was for him to transport it to its destination. The itch was getting worse: it needed him to get going – but he wouldn't take the underground rivers this time, he'd stand his ground against the stone on that one. He wanted to wander amongst the life in the streets. Now that his head was clearer, he was curious about this place. As he looked around at the illuminated windows and doorways of the buildings that encircled The Circus and the busy streets leading off into the different Boroughs he was hit by a sudden flashback of that dead world and its crumbling, derelict cities, consumed by endless black night and populated by the mad and the infected, the carriers. Had that place once been like this? He shook the thought away and took in a deep breath of air filled with the stench of life. That world didn't matter any more, for he was never going back to it.

He turned down an alley; the rundown dwellings were inhabited by those who begged at the crossroads. As he passed the almost invisible hatch to the Lost Rivers he found he was hungry again, and he wondered if perhaps the stone was drawing energy from him instead of the rivers. Well, the stone could wait long enough for him to feed once more.

A flash of blonde hair caught his eye as a slim figure came into the alley at the other end. He took a long, deep breath and the scent of her blood filled him. It was strong and vibrant, filled with life. Five more minutes wouldn't hurt. He slid into a doorway and waited.

Despite the growing unrest, Anaïs was happy. She'd found another witness who'd seen a man with no shoes, wearing a tatty cloak and once-white shirt, disappearing just as they discovered a poor victim. She thought it was funny that people would talk to an ordinary person, but they wouldn't talk to the Borough Guard, even if something might be important.

It'd be the Guard's fault if the man wasn't caught, though.

She didn't understand her dad's aversion to the surface completely. If you lived on the land, you had to obey the Prince Regent's laws and pay all his taxes – but over the past few months she'd begin to realise that most of London's residents were more than happy to exploit the system's grey areas – almost everyone had something they weren't quite honest with the law about up here. Her father should fit right in!

She spotted the alley with a hatch in it that she'd used several times when she was sneaking away. She was wondering if, once she'd helped Finmere and the Knights solve this case, her father might think about finding a way to co-exist with the surface people … or at least not get so angry about her wanting to live between the two. Maybe after a little while he'd get to like Fin. Her skin warmed slightly thinking about the strange teenager. He wasn't like any of the Gypsy Trader or Trader boys, that was for sure – they were always trying to impress her with stupid tricks on the water and high dives, and fighting each other and generally behaving like idiots. Finmere wasn't like that. Up ahead she caught a glimpse of the lights of The Circus and she picked up her pace a little. Maybe he would already be there. He might be waiting for her.

Something slick slapped at the ground beside her feet, and despite her natural grace, she almost stumbled. What was that? The end lifted slightly, as if smelling something in the air. She recoiled slightly and gasped. It was a tongue. But how—?

The question was answered as the tall figure stepped out from the doorway. His eyes glowed red and his smiling mouth was open, the long tongue curling back up.

'Who—?' was all she managed to say. She wasn't even sure there was any more of the question to ask. He wasn't like *any*one she'd ever seen before.

Just before he lunged at her the man's eyes glowed red, and for the first time, Anaïs thought that wandering the streets of London alone might not have been the best of ideas, not near the hatches. And then coldness flooded through her as his tongue reached out and touched her.

Christopher emerged at the top of The Circus and paused to get his bearings. He spotted Mitesh Savjani's elaborate shop sign on the far side and started to make his way around the edge, rather than try to force his way through the tightly packed stalls in the middle. He felt happier in the glow of the lights that hung from the awnings and brightened up the night like a swarm of fireflies. The Circus was always busy, even tonight, in the midst of the disquiet that filled the city. He was glad about that – there was enough bad stuff lurking in his head without seeing everything else crumbling around him. He'd be happier once he'd found Fin and the Gypsy Trader girl and caught up with Mona.

'Christopher!'

Whoever was calling his name followed it with a sharp whistle, and he looked around until he spotted Lucas Blake, waving at him from a street a little way away. He was tying a tired-looking horse up to a railing.

Smiling, Christopher jogged over. 'What are you doing back?' He was glad to see the Knight – there was something about Lucas Blake that always made him feel better about things. Even the awful secret of his father's betrayal.

'This weather is right out at the city's edge, so there was no point in going further.'

Christopher's heart sank slightly. 'So this is really a Black Storm coming?'

'Take a look around you,' he said, patting the horse's neck. 'What do you reckon?'

Christopher knew he was right; the thunder and lightning were still coming the wrong way round, rain was falling from a clear sky, time had gone funny, and everyone was one breath away from a massive riot. But hearing the Knight say it out loud made his stomach twist.

'Don't you worry, though.' Lucas Blake grinned, and wrapped an arm around his shoulder. 'We'll get it sorted. What would be the point of us if there wasn't trouble to fight?'

'Yeah, I guess you're right.'

'Where are the others?'

'Mona's gone to tell the Regent – she figured out that the trail is leading to West Minster – whoever's doing the attacks is following the flow of the rivers underground, and that's why there's no obvious pattern up here.' He shivered and pulled the sleeves of his sweatshirt down over his hands. It was no longer chilly; this was winter.

'Well done! Once I've got you lot back to the house in Charter's Square, I'll go up to the palace myself and give the Prince's men some support.'

'Don't you ever get tired?' Christopher's whole body was starting to ache from the cold, and all he'd done was a lot of walking.

'I was tired for five years.' Lucas Blake grinned. 'That old rock and roll saying really is true: you can sleep when you're dead. Life's for living, so you have to do as much as you can.'

'You might be right,' Christopher couldn't help but smile back, 'but my feet are still kill—'

An alarmed shriek came from somewhere on their left, only to be cut off as suddenly as it started. A couple of heads turned, but then the people just muttered and carried on their way.

'Oh, that's not good,' Lucas Blake said, already slipping into a sprint.

'Hel—!' It was the voice of a girl, and she was obviously terrified.

The two of them ran in its direction, shoving aside anyone

who blocked them. Christopher's heart was thumping, and the cold air burned his lungs as he panted for breath. It felt like hours, but it was just minutes before they skidded to a halt at the end of a narrow, dirty alleyway that was all but unnoticeable in between the busy shop fronts.

'Down there,' Lucas Blake said, pulling his sword and walking carefully forward. 'I can see someone.'

'Oh no—' Christopher, two paces behind, stopped short at the sight of a pool of ash-blonde hair, bright against the dark ground. 'Oh, *no*!' he shouted, pushing past the Knight and running to the prone figure. He pulled her up to a sitting position and rested her against the wall.

'Anaïs?' He rubbed her cold hands. 'Anaïs, are you okay?'

For a moment her pale blue eyes flickered open and there was a flash of recognition.

'It's me, Christopher,' he said, still rubbing her hands. 'Anaïs, can you hear me? What happened?'

Anaïs smiled, and as she did, crimson-red bled out from her pupils.

'Her hair,' Lucas Blake said, quietly. 'It's changing.'

Nausea gripped Christopher, and the chill he felt was nothing to do with the unnatural weather. It came straight from his heart. The Knight was right: blackness was creeping down from her skull, as if an inkwell had been tipped over her head, changing her silky ash-white mane of hair into coarse, matted locks.

'*What are you doing?*'

Both Christopher and Lucas jumped up, suddenly up on their feet, as two men with torches clambered up through the hatch a few feet away. They were followed by two more, sharp daggers drawn. Gypsy Traders.

'It's Anaïs,' Christopher said, stepping towards them, 'she's been attacked. We need to help her.'

'What have you *done* to her?' The shouting blond man's tattoos were visible in the glow of the torch he carried, and as he grabbed at Christopher's jumper and threw him at one of the Traders behind him, Christopher thought for a moment all the colour had faded, leaving only a harsh black outline. Sharp steel pressed against his throat and a strong arm wrapped round his body. On the ground Anaïs giggled as the tips of her hair were lost to the midnight black.

'Whoa!' Lucas Blake moved forward. '*We* didn't do anything – we just got here.'

'She should never have come up here.' The Trader's voice still had the lilt of water in it, but there was no warmth in its soft tone. It was ice forming on the surface of a lake. '*You* did this to her.' He thrust the torch in Anaïs' direction.

Even the Gypsy Traders gasped: the transformation had been fast, and now their beautiful, graceful princess was gone, replaced by a black-haired, red-eyed creature who drew itself up on its haunches and hissed at them, flicking out a tongue so dark it might have been rotting flesh. The smile on its twisted face owed nothing to the original owner. Despite his own danger, Christopher felt a wave of grief wash over him.

The Trader holding him gripped him tighter.

'You're going *no*where,' he whispered, his breath hot in Christopher's ear. '*You* are going to pay for this.'

'You're coming with us.' The man in front was trembling with contained rage, his words spat out through gritted teeth. 'Francois Manot will deal with you for this.'

'Why don't you let the boy go?' Lucas Blake pulled his golden sword free and held it out, hilt first. 'He's just a kid – just like her.' On the ground, the thing that had been Anaïs pulled herself upright and hissed at them again. Her shoulders were hunched over and her head twitched this way and that. Christopher's eyes moved from her to the Knight and back again. This wasn't good, not for any of them. He thought of Finmere and Mona, probably headed their way, and willed them to stay away.

'Just take me – it's not him to blame; kids just do as they're told.' Lucas Blake stepped closer, holding out his sword. 'Take it. I won't fight you.'

'You wouldn't win if you did.' The Trader grabbed the offered weapon cautiously and stepped back. 'You Knights and your double-edged swords, you think you're so special. Just look at the damage you cause,' he growled.

Anaïs darted past the Knight and scuttled out into the street beyond. One of the Gypsy Traders made a move to go after her, but their leader stopped him. 'We can't take her back like that – Francois would kill us for making him see it.' He swallowed hard, and on his face Christopher saw a mixture of shock, pain and rage – a dangerous combination.

'Just go, Lucas,' he said. '*Go.*'

The Knight didn't even look at him. He moved closer to the blond man in the black leather waistcoat until they were eye to eye. 'Let the boy go,' he repeated. 'You've got me.'

The Trader raised the sword to Lucas Blake's neck and held it there. He nodded at his men and they moved over to the Knight and held him firm.

'Francois Manot will skin you alive for this,' the Gypsy Trader said softly, so close he could have bitten Lucas Blake's nose off.

'Now let the boy go.'

Christopher started to struggle, and his neck stung as the dagger nicked his skin.

'You're a fool.' The Gypsy Trader signalled to the man behind him and Christopher found himself being dragged towards the hatch. 'Why would I let the boy go? A child for a child, that's the Gypsy Trader way. You're a bonus.'

THIRTY

Justin Arnold-Mather sat behind the large desk in the one of the vast halls. He thought things really couldn't have been going much better. The arrival of Simeon Soames had been a nice surprise. He and Levi Dodge had taken some of the Palace Guard to secure their current location. They wouldn't stay at the palace for much longer – he had his eye on a better place – but he would need his army in place to be able to take their next home. Once he was secure, he'd turn his attention to bringing his son into line. Every father needed an heir.

'There're so many of them in my head,' Joe whispered. Although he had abandoned the heavy wig once the hanging had taken place, Joe was still wearing the Prince's clothes, although they were out of place in a way their original owner would never have tolerated. He curled up tighter in the huge armchair a few feet away from the desk. 'I can't cope with it any more,' he whined.

'Yes, you can,' Arnold-Mather said. The Prince's valets were scurrying through the palace, collecting all the literature they could find on the Storyholder's abilities. A large volume lay open on the desk; it wasn't a printed book, but hand-written. He flicked his eyes down one of the pages. 'In fact, you would be quite amazed at what you can do.' He smiled over at the boy. 'You just have to learn to control it, that's all.'

'How?' The word would have been a wail, but Joe clearly didn't have the energy.

'Practise,' Arnold-Mather said. 'And there will be something

in one of these tomes that will help, I am quite sure. Trust me.'
He thanked the valet who had brought him another huge
book and told him to add it to the pile on the desk. The valet
did so, and as he set off again, he gave a small smile, which sat
oddly on a face that looked unused to smiling. Perhaps if the
Regent had given his valets more research time, they might
be mourning his loss slightly more, Arnold-Mather thought
smugly. He turned back to the boy, who was dribbling snot
all over himself, and the expensive leather chair.

'And once they are all gathered, you can stop calling for
them. The noise will ease.' He laced his fingers together. 'You
should be pleased. They are *your* army. This is *your* Rage.'

'I didn't *want* the Rage – I don't *want* all these angry people
in my—' He ran his knuckles hard over his skull, as if he
could somehow get the noise out if he hurt himself enough.
'So many angry and mad—'

'This will be the worst part.' Justin Arnold-Mather really
had no idea whether that was true or not, but a lifetime in
politics was good practice; the lie sounded confident. 'When
the Rage has passed you will feel better.'

The boy in the chair let out something that was halfway
between a sob and a laugh, and for a moment Arnold-Mather
almost felt sorry for him – though not enough to tell him how
to stop his mind calling for an army (a valet had brought him
that little nugget twenty minutes ago; but he'd keep it safely
to himself until they were secure in numbers). The more he
read, the more he realised why the Storyholders were trained
so thoroughly, and kept away from the machinations of the
world. There was so much he could use this boy for – far more
than that fool Golden had ever realised; he had been an idiot
for wanting the stories inside himself. He had learned more
than his other informant had ever managed to discover for
him as well.

His respect for Tova was increasing, even if it was post
mortem. Until today he'd thought her nothing but a foolish

girl, who'd caused trouble for all those around her, but the fact that she had experienced any kind of emotion and not allowed the power inside her to tempt her to use it was quite something. He was relieved she was gone. He could never have made her his little puppet like Joe Manning was. No, everything was just as it should be: Joe had the stories, and he, Justin Arnold-Mather, was now virtually in charge. He allowed himself a tight smile.

The panelled door opened and Simeon Soames strode in. The Knight's forehead was furrowed – maybe part of his brain still couldn't believe that he'd turned sides so easily – but his walk was confident.

'Any problems?' Arnold-Mather stood up to greet the man: Simeon Soames might not be a Knight of Nowhere anymore, but he still needed to be treated with respect. The erstwhile Cabinet Minister understood people; he knew just how to keep them on his side. It was often just the little things … perhaps he should make the young man a general in his new army – maybe even commander of his armies. He'd probably like that.

'No problems at all; more are turning up and we are seg-regating them in terms of skills and housing them in various parts of the palace. When you're ready to move, we should have plenty to get us there.' His frown deepened. 'Depending on how big an army we will be facing. We need to move be-fore the people realise it wasn't Joe who was hanged. They'll come for us after that.'

'I doubt they'll realise before morning. We leave at dawn – it will take that long to finish packing what we need to take. The armoury needs emptying, and these books have to come with us, and we'll need to empty the larders and wine cellars, you know the sort of thing.'

'The doctor from the White Tower has arrived, with all his inmates,' the former Knight said. 'It wasn't him leading the way, though – it was the attack victims, with the black hair and red eyes ...' He tailed off, then shook himself and continued, 'They're not like the others, you know: now they're here they're quite calm. I'd almost say devoid of any kind of emotion. I don't understand them at all.'

'Do they scare you?' Arnold-Mather asked.

'A little.'

'Good. If they scare you, then I imagine they will terrify the enemy. Bring some up: I want to see what they're like around Joe. If they are manageable, we might make them our personal guard.'

'One other thing, about them—'

'Which is?'

'A Borough Guardsman just arrived with a message for the Prince Regent from Mona Savjani. How he got through the crowd I have no idea, because he's old and fat, but somehow he did.'

'What was the message?'

'Whoever has been attacking these people is headed to West Minster, according to Mona Savjani. I thought you should know – these kids, well, I know they're only kids, but they do have a knack of hitting on things that count. I thought it might be important.'

'The thing that created the mad?' Arnold-Mather's brain swirled. 'Yes, that *is* interesting.' He looked up, his eyes sharp. 'Send Levi Dodge with some of the Palace Guard. I want whatever it is brought back – alive, mind. And tell them to be careful. Mr Dodge can look after himself, but I don't want to lose any Palace Guard out of any foolishness.'

'Brought back alive?'

'Oh yes. I have plans for it.' Arnold-Mather slapped the ex-Knight's shoulder. 'I'm very impressed with you, Simeon Soames. When we get to our new location I shall officially make you my right-hand man.'

The young man smiled, then his expression faltered. 'You won't make me go back, though, will you? To The Somewhere?'

Dark clouds passed across his blue eyes, and Arnold-Mather realised why the Rage had taken him so quickly: there was so much fear there.

'I can't Age again,' he continued, 'I can't do that, even for you.'

'You will not have to,' Arnold-Mather said with a smile. 'This is your home now. *I* understand your fear, even if they don't.' He squeezed the man's shoulder. 'Now send Mr Dodge to me, and get back to the preparations. We have a great deal to do, and only a short time in which to accomplish it.'

He watched the young man walk away, the confidence back in his stride, and let out a satisfied sigh. Outside, thunder rolled again, and the small smile became a grin.

'We shall have an army of the mad, young Joe,' he muttered so quietly it was unlikely the teenager could hear him. 'We shall have an army of the mad.'

THIRTY-ONE

'What time is it?' Fin asked.

Fowkes looked at the strange two-faced watch Fin had returned to him. 'Nearly midnight. In both Londons.'

'We've got some visitors.' Henry Wakley peered round the door of the top floor room. 'Benjamin's checking them out, then he'll bring them up. Interesting characters.'

Fin was glad of the distraction. Since arriving back in The Nowhere with Fowkes he'd felt like a bit of a spare part – he'd expected to be heading off to The Circus to meet up with the others, but just as he'd been about to leave, Alex Currie-Clarke had turned up, saying Lucas Blake had gone to fetch them, so Fin should stay put. Despite really being Baxter, it looked like the world was intent on treating him like a kid – he had to admit he found that reassuring. If they were all thinking of him as Finmere, then maybe he really was ...

He pushed the thought away; he couldn't cope with it on top of the more immediate concerns about his friends. He couldn't help but wonder how Christopher would react when he found out that they all knew about his dad. But Christopher wasn't back yet; they'd cross that bridge when they came to it.

'I think we're just about there.' Alex Currie-Clarke was leaning over the small Macbook. 'This system is quite brilliant.' He looked up and flashed a boyish smile. 'Not as brilliant as me – I can make some modifications to make it even more secure – but it's still pretty good. We'll need some rotation of laptops between here and Orrery House, and lots of spare batteries if we're going to run it twenty-four/seven, but that shouldn't be much of a problem.'

'Good,' Fowkes said. 'Good work.'

To Finmere, the gangly redhead had always seemed to be a bit of a fish out of water amongst the Knights, but after watching him figuring out the computer security system Conrad Eyre, St John Golden's main henchman, had installed, he realised he'd made a mistake. Alex Currie-Clarke was a very valuable addition to the team – he might not have Henry Wakley's easy charm, or Benjamin's cool head, but there was no doubt he was a total computer genius. A geek god.

'Amazing.' Harper Jones reappeared through the hidden doorway he'd found in the wall. 'It comes out about fifty feet down the street. We'll have to secure that end.' He looked over at Currie-Clarke. 'Can you rig something up something to cover that far away?'

As Alex told him, 'Leave it with me!' Fin thought how good it was to watch the Knights in action as a group. But he was starting to feel slightly frustrated – he'd got nothing to do, apart from running cups of tea up from Mrs Baker in the kitchen, and not everyone appreciated that. Fowkes had tipped his out of the window and told Fin to go and see what wine there was in the building. Mrs Baker had retorted: 'Andrew Fowkes can wait until dinner for his wine; he'll not be getting a drop before then. Those days are over for that lad.' Her strong words had made Fin giggle, but he'd erred on the side of caution and translated it as, 'There isn't any.' He figured that was the wiser course of action.

Heavy footsteps trudged up the stairs and Benjamin Wakley appeared, followed by a heavyset middle-aged bald man wearing a battered army jacket. Half the buttons were missing and it was done up by a wide leather belt cinched around his waist which left a large V of bare chest visible. He might have been a solid-looking man, but a lot of that was clearly muscle – muscle and scars. His eyes narrowed as he looked at the men around the room before they came to rest on Fowkes.

'You look better than last time I sees you,' he growled, 'but then, you couldn't have looked much worse.'

'Jack Ditch,' Fowkes said. 'Now here's a surprise.'

Fin's eyes widened. The man in the Crookeries Mona used to work for from time to time – but what on earth was he doing here?

'You remember Turpin.' Jack Ditch tilted his head towards the skinny man hovering nervously in the doorway. 'The rest of the boys is downstairs.'

'Fowkes.' Turpin swallowed hard as he said the word. 'Bygones be bygones, an' all that? New beginnings?'

Fowkes favoured him with a sharp glare, and then turned back to the man who was clearly in charge of the band of ruffians. 'But what exactly are you doing here?'

Jack Ditch grinned. 'I allus like to surprise you, Fowkesy, you knows that.' He came forward and leaned on the desk, forcing Alex Currie-Clarke to grab the laptop and shift it safely out of his way. 'I been looking at what's going on out there, and it don't look good. There's a storm coming.'

'That doesn't take a genius to figure out,' the Knights' Commander said wryly.

'True. Even Turpin there knows it, and he was born one roll short of a breadbasket.' He crossed his strong arms across his chest and Fin caught a glimpse of the wide dagger tucked into his belt. It looked like it had dried blood on it.

'But my old mum, wherever she rests, she allus told me to look out for this particular storm – the biggest one, she said. And she said I'd need to pick a side before a side picked me.' He shrugged. 'So here I am. I figured if a drunken waste of space like you's got a team, then that's most likely the one for me and my boys.'

For a moment Fowkes looked shocked rigid, and his jaw

dropped almost to the floor, then he recovered and, grinning widely, he held out a hand. It was the first time Finmere had seen a spark in his eye since Tova's death.

'Welcome aboard, Jack Ditch,' he said, and the two men embraced, slapping each other hard on the back. 'You are just the kind of bloke I reckon we're going to be needing.'

'So, what can we do for you?' Jack Ditch asked once he and Fowkes were seated. 'This weather's no good; the lads need focus. Oh, and I's got some of my streets kids along for the ride too.' He looked at Finmere for a moment. 'We both know as how you don't have to be a grown man to make a difference – and my kids, they're a sight tougher than most grown men.'

Fowkes thought for a minute, then said, 'First off, we need to make this place safe. A look-out system would be good, so we know in advance who's coming, but I don't have Knights to spare – and even if I did, they'd stand out a mile. Your look-outs are second to none, if you think they'll be okay on the streets.'

'Consider it done. I'll get that sorted, and then I'll get the rest inside, if your lot's finished frisking them.' He grinned. 'We'll let you find some of our weapons, to make your lads feel they's doing their jobs – but not all of them. We come devious in the Crookeries – but you'd know that, wouldn't you, Andrew Fowkes?'

As Jack Ditch left the room, Fowkes' smile fell. He glanced at his watch again. 'Simeon Soames should have been back by now. What the hell is he doing?'

Fin was still getting his mind round what had just happened. 'I can't believe *Jack Ditch* is going to help us,' he muttered. 'Mona said he ran the Crookeries – surely if he picked a side, it wouldn't be the good one?'

'Why not?' Fowkes looked up. 'He's a good man. He's fair, and he's honest, in his own way.' His eyes darkened and he looked at the two-faced watch again. 'That's the thing about *good*. It's not always easy to tell from the outside.'

'Time for food!' Mrs Baker bustled in, her apron covered in flour. 'And let's be thankful I made extra because it looks like we've got a houseful. Bread and stew – it ain't much, but it'll see you through.'

No one moved, and she walked over to Fowkes and wagged a finger in his face. 'I don't care if you think you're not hungry; you're going to do as you're told and eat. We can't face what's coming weak, you know that as well as I do.' She pointed a finger at the Commander. 'And don't you think of getting all high and mighty with me – when I say grub's ready, you'll eat. I've got Ted Merryweather's orders on that.' She turned to leave, and then paused in the doorway. 'And Mitesh Savjani and his little girl have just arrived – that nice-looking lad – what's his name? I get them confused ... Henry, that's the one. He just let them in.' She frowned. 'They didn't look very happy. I think she was crying.'

Finmere was moving before he even realised. His heart was pounding in his chest so hard it was threatening to burst out through his throat. *What now?* he thought. He had the *worst* feeling ...

'I sent them to the dining room,' Mrs Baker said as he rushed past her, running for the hall. 'Don't run down the stairs, Fin, you'll fall!'

A second pair of feet followed him, the heavy treads of boots rather than trainers, and Fin didn't have to look back to know it was Fowkes. Of course it was: his best friend from his other life. For the first time he found a mild comfort in that, but it did nothing to ease the dread that had washed over him at the thought of Mona Savjani actually crying.

The wind swept through the long-smashed windows of West Minster Abbey and over the black and white squares that covered what was left of the floor, playing with the plants that flourished between the cracks. Other than that it was eerily quiet away from the noise that filled the streets of London, and George Porter could hear his own breathing echoing through the ruins as he picked his way towards the back of the building. The little stone felt as if it was on fire against his leg, but he had fed so much that it barely drained his strength at all. He felt more human than he had since he'd returned, and he was glad of it – even if he didn't want to think about what he'd had to do to achieve that. He was determined he would enjoy this clarity while it lasted.

There were metal plates embedded in the thick walls, on which were strange carvings, shining like mother-of-pearl in purples and soft whites. He used their own pale glow to pick his way through the broken remnants of a civilisation lost to the other side of the river. Upwards. *He knew the pebble needed him to go upwards, not just to the galleries above, but even higher, into the spire itself. He picked up his pace. Away from the main hall, the smaller rooms were in complete darkness, but his feet led him, unerring, to the tiny door. He opened it and cold air flooded out. He smiled; it felt good against his burning skin. After a moment he placed one foot on the first thick stone step and started to climb.*

Despite Ted's orders and Mrs Baker's best efforts, no one was hungry by the time Mona and Mitesh Savjani had finished telling the story of the Prince Regent's hanging. The scent of the steaming stew was probably delicious, but it made Finmere's stomach churn. Mrs Baker herself put her spoon down and covered her mouth as Mona told them how the crowd had bayed for his blood, thinking he was Joe.

'Terrible,' Mrs Baker murmured. 'What a terrible day.'

'There's more,' Mona whispered, and looked at her father. Fin stared at his friend. Her eyes looked dull, almost lifeless, and her cheeks were blotchy from crying. Fin's hands started to shake and he gripped the sides of his chair to calm himself. If the Prince's hanging wasn't the worst, then what was coming?

The clothcrafter put a gentle hand on his daughter's arm. 'We went to The Circus,' he started softly, 'to meet young Christopher, as the youngsters had arranged.'

'Lucas Blake was headed there too,' Fowkes said quietly. Every minute he looked a little grimmer.

Mitesh Savjani nodded, and his shoulders slumped slightly, as if he couldn't bear the weight of what he had to say.

'I am pleased to see young Finmere here,' he said, 'for to lose him as well would have been too much—'

'As well?' Harper Jones leaned forward, his elbows on the table.

He sighed. 'I get ahead of myself, but I fear the news is not good. We asked amongst the market traders if they had seen the children anywhere, and finally we found one, a man I have known for a long time, who said he had seen a tall boy with a Knight. He remembered them because the Knight was riding Mona's horse with the Prince's livery on it, and he had just tied it up in the street. Mona delivered for this man when she was running around as a child.' His dark eyes flicked round the table and he sighed again.

Finmere didn't like that sigh, not one bit, but his heart was torn between wanting the clothcrafter to hurry up and just spit out whatever had happened, or to shut up and not say another word.

'The man followed them.' Mitesh Savjani was obviously going to go for the first option. 'He was concerned for the horse in all this—' He stopped again, as if hunting for the right words, finally settling on, 'in all this unrest. He said they had been coming towards his shop, but then it looked like they got distracted by something. They ran down an alley.'

The room was silent, apart from the silken softness of his voice. No one was under any illusion that this story was going to end well.

'The man followed them. When he peered down the alley, he saw a blonde girl on the ground.' His voice caught, and he swallowed, before finishing the sentence. 'Her hair was turning black.'

'Anaïs!' Finmere said, and then froze. 'Her hair went *black*?' His heart stopped beating. He had left Anaïs on her own and George Porter had got her. His head was spinning. 'She was *attacked*?'

Mona was crying quietly again and now Fin's own eyes filled, blurring his view of the people around him – but he could barely see them anyway, for his mind was lost in that alleyway, seeing things he wished his imagination would leave alone. Anaïs, turning like those poor people in the White Tower, her beautiful eyes glowing red, her tongue black. And even worse was the thought of her mad and lost …

'Yes,' Mitesh Savjani said, 'so we believe. She ran away when the Gypsy Traders came up through the hatch. She pushed past my friend. Her eyes were red already.'

'The Gypsy Traders? What did the Gypsy Traders do?' Fowkes' face looked as if it had been carved from stone.

'They took Lucas Blake and Christopher down to the rivers, with knives at their throats.' He pushed his bowl of uneaten stew away. 'I am very worried for them.'

'They blame us for what happened to Anaïs?' Now Fowkes was on his feet and pacing up and down the dining room.

'I can think of no other reason for this action, my old friend.'

'But they'll be all right, won't they?' Fin looked from one man to the other. 'I mean, why would they blame *Christopher*? If anyone, they should blame me – *I'm* the one who sent her there on her own; *I'm* the one who should have gone with her.' Tears stung his eyes again. He *was* wrong and this was more proof of it.

'This ain't good.' It was the first thing Jack Ditch had said since they'd all sat down around the table to hear the Savjanis' story. 'Sounds like the Gypsy Traders have caught themselves a dose of the Rage – so not as immune to the rest of the world as they like to think. That ain't good at all.'

'What will they do?' Fowkes asked. 'Where will they take them? We *have* to get them back ...' His voice sounded bleak.

'If I was to put money on it, I'd say as they'll take their revenge the old way.' He pulled a lump of tobacco from his pocket and bit off a chunk. He started chewing it thoroughly, then got up and walked over to the glassless windows. 'And that means they'll pin them out at Traitor's Gate when the tide's low, let old River Times take them.' He tugged the heavy curtain back, leaned out and spat down into the street below. Then he turned back to the room full of people. 'And they'll do it at dawn.' He turned again and peered up at the sky.

Even from where he was sitting, Fin could see that the deeper blue of the midnight sky was turning as the dark greys of those lost hours before the night turns to morning came creeping in.

'And that ain't long away,' Jack Ditch finished.

THIRTY-TWO

He couldn't remember getting down – in fact, he couldn't remember anything after reaching the spire and pulling the stone free from the cradle at its centre. No sword was needed this time; the pebble in his pocket was enough to release its sister from where it had been housed for centuries. The second stone was much bigger than the one he carried, and it was a different shape, chunkier, but it was made of the same pale material, and both looked like they were parts of a bigger something.

He leaned against the wall, holding one stone in each hand, and brought them together. His bones buzzed and the warmth that rushed through him was exquisite. He moaned and leaned his head back against the cold bricks, shutting his eyes, lost in the sensation. The cold and darkness of the night receded … he was in heaven.

He didn't see the man in the Bowler hat creeping forward, or the armed men on either side of him, until it was too late. His eyes flew open just in time to see the stones being wrenched from his grasp; a stinking rag was thrust into his mouth and as cold flooded his body he was dragged into a cage. Every cell screamed out, not at his capture – he was barely aware of that – but at his separation from the stones. It was unbearable.

Justin Arnold-Mather gazed out of the wall of windows in the Throne Room and smiled. Out in the palace yard, men and women scurried to and fro filling carts and carriages. Things that others might think valuable, like gold and silver, were last on his list. The power such things gave you was short-lived; with Joe under his control he was starting to feel there was *nothing* he couldn't control.

The temperature was dropping fast and the Prince's clothes were far too small for him, but he'd found a suitable coat in one of the lavish guest suites. He wrapped it round him, luxuriating in the soft fur lining. He stroked the silky black exterior, and wondered idly what it was made of. Perhaps he should task a valet with digging out any more clothes of this material that might be tucked away in the vast cupboards of the palace. He looked at Joe, sitting scruffily on the throne, and wondered if he should try and make the boy more presentable; people should look at him in awe, not as if he were just one of the mad. Appearances were important, after all—

'We've got him,' Levi Dodge announced as he pushed open the double doors and ushered in the four men carrying the cage. 'He was sitting against the wall of some old church.'

Arnold-Mather looked at the scruffy individual huddled in one corner of the cage. His knees were pulled up under his chin, and his tied hands were looped over the top, as if he were hugging himself, and as the erstwhile politician approached, he let out a long moan. Arnold-Mather thought it sounded like the kind of noise the animal that had originally owned his new fur might have made as the knives peeled him; a desperate, damaged sound.

Then his eye was drawn to the captive's thin hands. 'Well, well, well,' he muttered, as Mr Dodge gestured the other men out of the room, 'he is wearing a Knight's ring.'

'George Porter.' Joe crouched by the cage and tilted his head as if in wonder. 'One of Golden's Knights – we pushed him down a well.' A tear slipped down the boy's dark face, as if this were a memory of a much better time.

'What was he doing at West Minster?'

'He was up in the spire when we got there, pulling these free.' Mr Dodge passed over a small cloth bag. 'We waited until he came down and then grabbed him. It's just a couple of stones.'

'Be careful of saying anything is "just" in this world, Mr Dodge. Your practical nature suits me well, but we are on a steep learning curve here: if this man climbed a spire to get hold of a couple of stones, then they must be important in some way.' He tipped the stones into his palm: both were made of some smooth, pale rock, but they were different sizes. The man in the cage moaned loudly, looking desperate, as Arnold-Mather held the larger lump up to his eye.

'What is so special about these?' Arnold-Mather asked the captive. 'What *are* these?'

The man in the cage strained towards him.

'You want them, is that it?'

George Porter nodded vigorously.

'Then perhaps I will let you touch them – but first, you have to do something for me.' He looked at Mr Dodge. 'Bring in one of the Chancellors,' he ordered, and as Mr Dodge disappeared, turned back to the caged man and said, 'And you must behave, Mr Porter, or you will never see these again, do you understand?'

George Porter mewled, and Arnold-Mather smiled. It would appear that he now had two useful monkeys to do his bidding.

'Let me see,' Joe said, and as he reached out and took them, a surprised smile crossed his face. 'My head is clearer,' he said, sounding amazed as he turned the stones over in his hands. 'The pain – they're actually *stopping* the pain.' Then he gasped and juddered, as if an electric shock had been fired through him, and thunderclaps rolled in waves outside, each clap lasting longer than the last.

Almost automatically, Arnold-Mather turned back to the windows, where he thought he saw just the tiniest black line, cut across the dark grey of the almost-dawn. It looked like a crack in the sky.

'These aren't just any stones,' Joe breathed, 'these are *the* stones. Part of the *one stone*.'

'And I think you have held them enough for now.' Arnold-Mather took them swiftly from the boy's hand and put them back in the bag, ignoring the mewling from the cage. 'What do you mean, the one stone?'

'I don't know.' Joe frowned. 'The words just came to me.'

Outside, the jagged line he thought he had glimpsed on the edge of the horizon had vanished. So it looked like the stones enhanced Joe's powers – but *what* were they, and where were they from? They made the boy more manageable; that he could see for himself – he was undeniably calmer, and he was no longer tugging at his hair and rubbing his head. The valets might know more, and if not, they would probably be able to find out.

Two guards dragged a dribbling figure into the Throne Room, the dainty shoes scuffing against the mosaic floor. The Chancellor's black wig had tilted sideways and the seam of one shoulder of his pink jacket had ripped in the struggle.

'Please,' he was repeating, 'I haven't *done* anything. I'm happy to serve you, you know that.' His eyes darted frantically around the room.

'Good. It is your service I need,' said Arnold-Mather. He looked again at Dodge. 'Untie the prisoner and put the Chancellor in the cage with him. Then let us see you do your thing, Mr Porter.'

'What? *What?* Who is— *What are you—?*'

The Chancellor's desperate pleas were ignored, as were his screams when he realised exactly what was happening to him. Arnold-Mather didn't blame him for screaming – the process was quite horrible to watch, but at least it was relatively swift. At least that's how it seemed from outside the cage. To the Chancellor, it had probably felt a very long time indeed.

*

Ten minutes later, his wig was abandoned on the floor and he was out of the cage, crawling sideways, like a crab, towards Joe. The wispy grey hair that had thinly covered his scalp had grown thick and coarse, and now fell in matt-black locks. His eyes had turned red and as his skin beneath his make-up had paled, so his tongue and nails had turned black. The thing that had been a Chancellor curled up at Joe's feet.

In the cage, George Porter returned to normal and started to cry, long, low sobs that rattled the bars.

Justin Arnold-Mather smiled. 'Gag him again, and bind him. Lock the cage, too.' Once George Porter's wrists were tied securely, Arnold-Mather slipped the smaller of the two stones through the bars into his outstretched hands. 'Ten minutes.'

'Get *away* from me!' Joe sounded disgusted, was shaking the changed man from his foot. As soon as he'd said the words, the ex-Chancellor scuttled away behind the throne, though his mad red eyes stayed fixed on Joe.

Arnold-Mather, studying him, recognised the abject devotion in those alien crimson pupils. 'I think we're finally ready to leave,' he said. He clapped his hands together. 'Mr Dodge, tell Simeon Soames to send a group of our people to keep the Knights busy while we're crossing the city – no one we would care about losing, but enough of them to keep those do-gooder hands full for a while.'

He turned to Joe, who was staring out at the sky. 'Don't look so miserable, boy. It's Christmas Eve: the day we celebrate the birth of a new saviour.' He wrapped his arm around Joe's shoulders. 'And this year, that's you.' He led his little entourage out of the Throne Room and smiled as the Chancellor scuttled close behind. Everything was coming together nicely.

THIRTY-THREE

The Seer had been walking for a long time, and even worn into soft comfort as his boots were, his feet were starting to ache. He figured that was a good thing: if it was time to die, it was a good thing to die with legs aching from taking a good long look at the world. His denim jacket hadn't been done up since the day he'd bought it, and this was no time to start changing habits. Instead, he tried to relish the sensation as the cold wind cut through his shirt. He'd always preferred the feel of the sun on his skin, but if this was truly his last day in the worlds, then he'd far rather the extreme of the cold over indifferent rain.

As West Minster Bridge curved into the mist ahead of him he was surprised to feel a wash of relief. He'd stood amongst the broken statues in the Abbey's garden and watched as the poor mad creature had clambered up to the top of the spire and prised the stone from where it had been kept, safe and forgotten, for so long, and stood in the cold shadows as the men who had been waiting on the far side of the Abbey with their cage and their bad vibes carted him away. The Prophecy was definitely unfolding; there was no doubt about that.

He hadn't enjoyed his walk around the city as much as he'd hoped, although it was as he had expected. He'd stood at a safe distance and watched the mad and the destitute gather at the palace to form a new army. He'd listened as the people bickered and fought with one another, while others – those who would forever be on the side of good, whether they knew it or not – huddled together, watching with confusion and despair. He'd wanted to help them, but this was their journey; his was pretty much done, and the more he saw, the more he felt okay about that. It was time he did one good deed in his life.

He started to walk up the curve of the bridge, his pace the same easy swagger it had been ever since he'd become Billy rather than Arthur Mulligan, a West Coast drifter with a hint of England in his voice rather than the Seer who wouldn't see. He was an escapee from two worlds which were both disappointed in him. He might not have fulfilled his role in many way, but now that he was at the end of his path, he figured everything had happened for a reason: he had become the Seer at a time when it was better for all that the future *wasn't* seen – some things *can't* be changed, even by foreknowledge, they just have to *be* – so what's the point of knowing they're coming?

His feet moved steadily, and he looked down to find himself ankle-deep in the stinking mist that rose up from the river's surface whatever the weather. He was away from the shore now, in that no man's land between the North and the South, and as the white fog curled and twisted around him, curious about this uninvited visitor, only the pale, glowing carvings on the railings let him know that he was heading forward. He was entirely alone with only the lapping of the water beneath and the strange hum of the mist as company, until he reached the peak of the bridge, when he began to feel like he was being watched by the ghosts of the Magi. They had kept this crossing alive, travelling constantly between the two halves of the city, until their final journey, as broken men, when they decamped to the South.

He touched the hand rail. The metal was warm in the icy cold, and he wondered if the ghost of the bridge had embraced him, happy to have a traveller upon it once again. Embedded in the rails was a circular carving, with arrows pointing in both directions, and beneath his feet the angle in the wood was subtly different, tilting slightly down instead of up: he'd reached the midpoint, and the most powerful part of the River Times was flowing not so very far from his feet.

He took a deep breath of the foul air, then reached behind his neck and unclasped the pendant that hung there. He immediately felt strange without it – he had worn it against his skin for a lifetime – too many years to remember. He looked at the beads and the metal that glowed now that it was here, so close to the flow of the water, and allowed a small smile to crack his leathery face. He might not have lived like a Seer, but he would die like one. There were some obligations that you just couldn't shirk; this was one that he'd never even have considered avoiding. He wondered how many of his life choices had ever been his own – or was it all decided at the start? *No!* That was the river, not him, and as he gripped the pendant tightly in one hand and swung his leg over the railing, he pushed that thought away. Fate might carve out paths, but everyone chose their own true destiny, of that he was absolutely certain.

Somewhere in the distance drums began to beat, slow and steady. He steadied himself on the thin metal rail and looked up. Night was turning into day, the scent of dawn cutting through the thick mist that was more concentrated now that the tide had pulled the water back from the banks. He wondered what that day might bring ... then he took one last long breath and closed his eyes. It all had to be exactly as he'd seen it. A moment later he stretched out his arms and fell. The necklace hit the water first and a split second later, the river owned them both.

THIRTY-FOUR

'She's not dead.' Finmere paced across the fresh reeds that covered the floor of the bedroom on the second floor of the Knights' house. 'I mean, we don't know where she is, but she's not *dead*.' He looked at Mona, who was sitting on one of the neatly made beds. 'Once they get hold of George Porter they might be able to cure the mad—'

'That's true,' Mona said. She didn't sound overly convinced, and Finmere wanted to shake her – he needed her to be optimistic. They *both* had to be; anything else would be like admitting they were giving up on their friends, and he couldn't face that. It might tempt Fate.

It was barely ten minutes since they'd left the dining room, their food untouched – after all they'd heard, no one could manage another mouthful – and now Fowkes was gathering men from Jack Ditch's crew who might have some knowledge of the Lost Rivers for a rescue mission. It was all taking an interminable length of time.

'We are going to get Christopher back. And Lucas Blake is with him – he won't let anything bad happen, will he? Maybe the Rage hasn't got her dad – maybe he'll be angry with the Gypsy Traders who took them. Who knows?'

Mona gave him a look that suggested she knew pretty well, and it wasn't anything Fin was going to want to hear.

'And I still don't understand how Christopher's dad knows so much about the Knights and The Nowhere – he can't have got it all from St John Golden. And Judge Brown wouldn't have given him too many details, I'm *sure* of it. And that means someone else must be helping him. It's the only thing that makes sense.' His pacing got more frantic. At least thinking about all these things was better than getting caught up in grief, or worrying about his own sudden split-personality issue. He didn't know how much of his thinking was Baxter's and how much his, but for now he was doing his best to do what Fowkes had suggested and forget everything he'd heard in the Old Bailey. He certainly wasn't ready to share it with Mona yet. Maybe he never would be ...

Mona let out a long sigh. Her concern for Christopher was etched on her face. 'We'll be wasting time if we try to find them underground,' she said. 'It's nearly dawn now.' She chewed her lip and her forehead wrinkled as she went over to the window and pulled the curtain back. 'We need to go to Traitor's Gate – that's where Jack Ditch said they'll take them.'

'Then that's what we'll tell Fowkes. Come on, let's—'

His words were cut off by a shout that started outside and was then echoed through the building: 'Incoming! Twenty or thirty! Armed!'

Fin squeezed alongside Mona and together they peered out of the small window into the frozen air. There were people coming, and they weren't even being subtle about it. Even though night was being pushed aside by day, the group of tattily dressed men wielding swords and axes and a variety of other lethal weapons were holding flaming torches high above their heads as they whooped and yelped with the excitement of the fight to come.

'That's not an army,' Mona said. 'They're just thugs.'

Calls flew around the building and feet thumped up and down the stairs as the Knights hurried to defend against the attack. It was cold enough to sting Finmere's eyes and make them water, but he blinked away his blurred vision and stared at the men and women pounding down the street towards them. Some of them swerved and laughed as they bumped into each other, passing a bottle to and fro and taking long swigs from it. Mona was right: this was no army, capable of taking on the Knights.

'If this is the best Arnold-Mather can do, then we're laughing,'

The small, well-wrapped-up look-out kids scampered along the roofs of the buildings opposite and disappeared into the shadows further along the street, scurrying to safer places, whistling and signalling as they went, tugging their own small arsenal of weapons, mostly slings and stones, from within their coats.

'Jack Ditch's kids could probably deal with this lot on their own,' he said.

'Let's not leave it to them though, eh?' A rough voice cut in as a big hand grabbed Fin and tugged him back into the relative warmth. 'Mind out.' The thickset man pulled a short arrow from the leather quiver on his back. He grinned, revealing glints of metal teeth of every colour filling in the gaps around the few natural ones he had left. 'Haven't had this much fun since the last ruck with the Borough Guard.' He let out a throaty laugh. 'We sent them packing too. No one gets in the way of Jack Ditch's gang.' He winked at Mona. 'That was before your time, lass, when you was nearer one of us than one of them.'

'Well, we're all on the same side now.' Mona smiled at him.

'That we are, love. And ain't it a surprise!' He squinted out the window, ready to fire on whatever command he was expecting.

'Mona.' Fin pulled the girl to one side as more barked orders flew around the house. Grey light was seeping through the gaps around the window. 'It's dawn, Mona,' he said, urgently. 'If we wait until after this fight is done, we'll be too late. Whatever they're going to do to Christopher and Lucas Blake, they're going to be doing it soon. We need to go.'

She paled as she realised what Fin was saying. 'But how are we going to get out? Without going through those people outside?' She pulled her petite frame up as tall as it would go. 'Are we going to fight our way through?'

'We could,' Fin said, 'but I'm really more of a lover than a fighter. I've got a different plan. Follow me.'

He led her up the stairs to the small back room on the top floor. It was empty; the Knights and Jack Ditch's men were clearly concentrating on the lower levels.

'What do you mean, you're more of a lover than a fighter?' Mona's small nose wrinkled. 'That's disgusting. Who would say something like that? Makes me want to throw up.'

'Music reference. Dead guy – don't worry about it.' He fiddled with the wall panels at the back of the room, just as he'd seen Harper Jones do earlier, and finally his fingers found the soft spot. Something clicked inside and a door swung open. 'Voilà.' He gestured like a magician. He'd got quite used to secret doorways in the past few weeks, but Mona's eyes widened. 'It'll take us out onto the street – behind that lot outside, anyway.'

By the time they'd made their way down the dark, narrow stairwell and out onto the street, their smiles had faded. The last of night had been swallowed up by the icy grey of dawn.

'We're not going to make it,' Finmere said, his heart full of dread. 'We have to run.'

Mona slipped her hand into his and they ran.

THIRTY-FIVE

Lucas had tried to talk to Francois Manot, but as soon as the Gypsy Traders had told their leader about Anaïs, even Christopher had realised theirs was a lost cause. In that moment, all the remaining colour had drained from the shaven-headed man's tattoos, leaving only black outlines that made the hitherto magical creatures look simply menacing. Manot might have been fighting the Rage that had the rest of his people in its thrall, but he was lost in that moment, grief pushing him over the edge.

On the drawbridge between water and land he'd drawn his cutlass. Christopher thought that he was going to cut their throats then and there and be done with it, but the old woman stayed his arm.

'Traitor's Gate,' she hissed, spit flying out between the gaps in her teeth. 'The old way.'

Cries of angry agreement went up from those gathered around Manot, and eventually Anaïs' father had put away his knife.

'What happens at Traitor's Gate?' Christopher whispered to Lucas Blake in the boat beside him, but the Knight hadn't had time to answer before he was pulled out of the boat and thrown to the ground at Manot's feet.

They'd left Christopher where he was, and though he'd tried to concentrate on the sparkling water, the beauty of its dancing surface so at odds with the dark thoughts it inspired, he hadn't been able to ignore the sounds of the heavy wooden oars beating into the defenceless Knight. With each thud of wood against flesh, Christopher's stomach had turned over, and he'd bitten down on the inside of his cheek to stop himself crying. This wasn't how it was supposed to be. It was just supposed to have been a stupid bloody adventure ...

Eventually the traders left Lucas Blake. Christopher looked up to see the Knight, who hadn't cried out once, trying to haul himself to his feet. Blood dripping from his mouth and nose, and despite his terrible fear and sadness, Christopher was overwhelmed with a sense of pride. If he was going to be stuck in this situation with anyone, he was glad it was this man. Lucas Blake was someone he could look up to. Fin had Fowkes, Joe – well, now had Christopher's own father – but he had Blake. Two men grabbed the Knight, ready to throw him back into the boat, and as they did, Blake managed to raise his battered head slightly and an attempt at a grin cracked through the pain on his face. Christopher smiled back, through tears he refused to be ashamed of. He had a terrible feeling that this wasn't going to end well, but at least they would not be broken, whatever happened. If Lucas Blake was staying strong, then so was Christopher Arnold-Mather.

An hour or more later he was trying desperately to hold on to that thought. A small boat drifted alongside, carrying a boy of about his own age who was beating slowly on a drum, occasionally looking at the two prisoners in Francois Manot's painted vessel with loathing on his face. Christopher barely noticed; one look of hate amongst so many was nothing. The old woman leaned over the side and refilled her small pail with the sparkling Lost River water. Its pale glitter was almost a match for her mane of long, healthy hair. Grinning malevolently, she scooped out a handful and threw it over Christopher, who gasped as it hit him. It clung to his skin and for a moment he was blinded by the chill, sickly drops. He fought a wave of nausea, and shivered in the cold. His rain felt foggy, and full of creeping dread.

314

'Get used to it,' she snarled, 'it'll be filling your lungs soon enough, this and worse than this.' She crouched beside him, her face so close to his that he could see the pores in her creased skin. 'There'll be monsters in your brains as you drown,' she whispered. 'You can trust me on that.'

She turned her back on him and threw the remainder of the pail into Lucas Blake's face with a bitter laugh.

He gritted his teeth and tried to shake away the water. 'Thanks,' he muttered through chattering teeth and lips that Christopher could see were turning blue, 'I needed cooling down. Bit warm today, don't you think?'

They'd both been stripped of their shirts and shoes before the boats had set off in this grim procession and Christopher's skin was covered in goosebumps. The steady movement of the oars drew them closer to the natural light flooding through the heavy cast-iron gateway that marked where the Lost Rivers flowed into the Times. Between the icy wind and the taste of that awful water in his mouth, Christopher wondered how bad dying could actually be in comparison? *Dying.* Even in this bleak situation, he couldn't really take the word in, not in relation to his own life. He couldn't make sense of the idea of not being there, of nothingness ... He swallowed his panic.

'Raise the gate!' Manot cried, standing completely at ease despite the sway of the water. He looked every inch the leader, balanced gracefully with one foot on the bulwark and one arm holding onto the mast, while overhead the massive sea dragon painted on the sale danced in the chill wind of dawn. His own cutlass was thrust in one side of his belt, and Lucas Blake's golden sword was tucked into the other.

Metal grated on metal, and after a few seconds, the gate slid upwards. The tide was out, and on either side of the Lost River rose sand and shingle banks, clear of both mist and water. Manot leapt into the shallow water and pulled the vessel sideways until it lodged on the sand.

The sails of more Gypsy Trader boats were just visible at the edge of the mist, twenty feet or so away on the River Times, and as the drummer boy's small boat pushed out towards them, other drums joined in, their sonorous beats matching his.

'That's a pity,' Lucas Blake said, quietly. 'I was rather hoping those boats were going to belong to Curran Tugg.'

'I've always admired your optimism,' Christopher said, trying to stop his teeth chattering. 'Now if you could just get your sword back and get us out of here, that would be perfect.'

'I would do, but I'm a bit tied up at the moment.' Lucas Blake favoured Christopher with as much of a grin as his damaged face could manage, and then wiggled his fingers. Christopher was impressed. His own hands were tied so tightly behind his back he hadn't been able to feel them for at least twenty minutes, let alone move them.

Without any warning Christopher was suddenly hauled to his numb feet and pushed to the side of the boat. Lucas Blake was shoved in beside him. Christopher wobbled unsteadily as his legs struggled to hold him up, and he leaned into the Knight, trying to stay standing.

Francois Manot stood several feet away, on the bank of the waterway. Christopher didn't recognise him as the man they'd met before, who'd been filled with a light magic and a fierce sense of freedom. This man in front of him was an angry stranger. They'd never had any chance of reasoning with him.

'Bring them here,' Manot growled. 'It's time for them to meet the Mother River.'

Following Manot's brusque announcement the drum beats sped up slightly, but Christopher's heart was racing ahead of them. Moments later, he tumbled onto the shingle.

*

The icy air burned Finmere's lungs as he panted for breath, but he barely felt it. They hadn't bothered with the back streets this time, instead heading straight down to Times Parade – even though the stench of the mist and the water being so strong there. Fin knew what Mona had been thinking – there were still people out on the street fighting, and they didn't have time to be held up by anything like that. Times Parade was usually clear, and the mile down to the White Tower and Traitor's Gate would be a straight run.

But since they'd snuck away from the Knights' house, the drum beat had got much louder – it was no longer just one instrument but several, sounding out a death-knell across the city – and it looked like everyone in the city who was awake was flooding down to the river to see what was happening. They were all eager to secure a good spot to watch whatever was going on. Though the mist was slowly creeping back towards the river banks and would soon be rolling over the wall and curling around the onlookers' feet, for the moment the stink was bearable, and people were leaning over the wall and peering upriver, trying to see if they could make out the action.

It was strange to see such a wide variety of clothes from different eras, all in one place. Fin recognised some from history lessons and some from the telly series Mrs Baker had enjoyed, and there were some that he thought must be unique to The Nowhere. No one seemed bothered by the differences, though; they were all focused, eyes gleaming with excitement, on the source of the noise. He suddenly realised people were moving around the city much more easily than usual, crossing into different Boroughs than their own, and that disturbed Finmere too. They probably didn't even realise they were doing it.

His feet slipped on the icy cobbles and he fell, dragging Mona down with him. They landed in a confused and pain

317

heap with grit digging into their knees and palms, but no one stopped to help them, or even looked down at them.

Finmere hauled them both up. 'Come on,' he said, 'we're not there yet.' The peaks of the White Tower were visible, but they were still a long way away. Mona didn't need any encouragement; together they weaved their way in and out of the growing throng. What they were going to do when they got there, he wasn't quite sure, but they needed to try *something*, of that he was certain.

The drums increased in speed.

'Why are they getting faster?' he gasped.

'The water's coming in,' Mona said, grimly. 'The drums will stop when the river's reached the banks. They'll be drowned.'

'How much time have we got?' Fin asked the question before he could stop himself. He didn't want to hear the answer.

Mona answered anyway: 'Minutes.' She elbowed her way through a gaggle of women in front of them, and Fin followed in her wake, ignoring the abuse they hurled after them. His skull was pounding with his feet and his skin burned with dread. *Minutes.*

Justin Arnold-Mather could not have been more pleased with the way things were going. Simeon Soames was leading the main procession, a long caravan of men and women with the loaded carts, with a full company of the Palace Guard surrounding the Prince Regent's gilded carriage in the middle. The coach had its curtains drawn against the cold. The occupants were expendable, of course – he might be confident, but he certainly wasn't a fool. He and Joe were following half a mile behind, with George Porter in his cage, guarded by Levi Dodge and two of his men. Dodge had selected the men himself, so they would be quite capable of fending off any attack. And there were the strange stones – he would be curious to see how Joe and the stones reacted if they were threatened. The Knights, or any of the remaining Borough Guard, came for them, they would focus their attention on the leading train; they would not even think about the ordinary carriage ambling along behind. There would be time for pomp and ceremony later. For now, he just needed to get them safely to his chosen base.

Joe had fallen into a deep sleep, his head lolling forward as they bounced over the uneven ground. Arnold-Mather was pleased; the boy would need his full strength if they were going to achieve everything he had planned. If Joe was sleeping, perhaps that meant he was finally learning to manage the stories more successfully ... or was it just the proximity of the stones? The pouch was in his coat pocket, and damned if he couldn't feel some very pleasant heat against his skin from them. On the cart behind, covered with a tattered tarpaulin, was the cage with George Porter, bound and gagged. Arnold-Mather didn't give two hoots what he was doing – he could be sleeping, or wailing for the stones, for all he cared, just as long as he was *hungry*. That was what he needed from the ex-Knight.

A scout brought the not-unexpected news that fighting was underway at the House of Charter's Square. Arnold-Mather knew the disparate band he'd sent had no real chance against trained fighting men, but they had served their purpose: his people were well on their way and there was not a Knight of Nowhere to be seen.

Simeon Soames' route was taking them parallel to the River Time, and some streets in, but even though they had passed over the top of St Paul's and were making their way closer to the east of the city and the Future Blocks at the far end, beyond the marshes, the sound of the drumbeats was clear. Arnold-Mather pulled back the tatty curtain and peered out of the window. His eyes narrowed. Even though dawn was breaking, he had expected more activity around them, especially after the havoc the Rage had wrought throughou` the night. There were people on the streets, he could s that, but they were all far more concerned with scurrying to the steadily increasing beat that was coming from the river-bank, rather than paying attention to him and his army's movements. But these drums might be signalling something dangerous – perhaps an army coming across the river? – and he wasn't ready for that yet.

He called to a man on horseback riding alongside, 'What is that noise? Should we be concerned?'

'Haven't heard that sound for a long time.' The man's once-handsome face had been wrecked by a brand-new burn that ran, still seeping in places, from the top of his head down to his shoulder. His thick, dark hair had been singed off on that side of his head, leaving angry-looking scars distorting his whole face. 'It's the Gypsy Traders,' he told Arnold-Mather, an unpleasant grin on his face. 'They're pinning someone out. It's the old way of justice. They drown people in despair and madness.' He looked in the direction of the steady thump of the drums. 'I'd rather be burned again than face that,' he muttered. 'Poor bastard, whoever he is.'

Arnold-Mather let the cloth drop and leaned back against the rough wooden seat. Joe's head rolled onto his shoulder and he let it rest there. He was in an extraordinarily good mood. So, the Gypsy Traders, whoever the hell they were, were creating another distraction for him. He spared no thought for whoever the drums were beating to the grave, other than a smile that their misfortune was his good luck— But no, this was not *luck*, he reminded himself, absently rubbing his hand against the warm pouch in his pocket, this was *Fate*. It was the *Prophecy*.

He leaned forwards and banged on the wood. 'Let us pick up our speed. There is no point in dallying any longer.' It was time he was on his way.

THIRTY-SIX

It was surreal – that was closest Christopher could come, in his rapidly growing fear and confusion, to analysing his feelings: it was surreal, and it wasn't fair. He'd lost all sensation in his hands not long after Manot's men had stretched him out and locked his wrists in the rusty cuffs that had been embedded into the ground. They'd squealed with disuse as they closed around his skin, but they held him firmly enough, all the same. He wondered if he should have struggled more, but as soon as he'd touched the damp sand and rough stones, he'd been gripped by some sort of lethargy, which washed over him. What was the point of trying to fight the river – how could *anyone* fight it? He'd been doomed since the day he had been born – and all along he had only ever been a bit-part player in other people's stories.

Overhead the day was lightening, though the grey sky was heavy and brooding. The thunder had paused, but it would be back, he had no doubt about that, even if he would never see it. He wanted to cry – he thought he might be crying already … but it was so hard to concentrate. The freezing water was rising to greet them. Now it covered an inch of his skin, and it felt like he was floating, weightless, on the surface of a pool. The mist was like a creeping, nervous ghost, following the water. He was sure he could see strange shapes in it – shapes which sent a chill through him.

'How long will it take?' he asked. His voice sounded odd, muted. The moment the shackles had been fastened tigh

Francois Manot and his men had leapt back onto their boat, and now they were watching with the rest, from a distance. Christopher had almost forgotten they were there. It felt like there was just him, and Lucas Blake, and the river.

'Not long.' They were pinned out only inches apart, but the Knight's words sounded like they were coming from miles away. 'When we're submerged, they will release the cuffs and the tide will take us.'

'I hope it's quick.'

'We'll soon know.'

The water lapped and gurgled around them, and a cold trickle filled Christopher's ear, he almost screamed at the images that filled his head. He swallowed them down. He would not die screaming. He would *not*.

'The Magus said I had until I was thirty-eight,' he said softly. 'I suppose I can conclude from all this that in fact, the Magus knew shit.'

'What?' Lucas Blake moved his head slowly so he was looking at Christopher. He was badly bruised from the Gypsy Traders' beating, and more marks that would never reach their full potential were swelling across his chest and arms. One eye was half-closed, and his lip was badly split.

'The Magus.' Christopher figured there was no point in having secrets now. His dad and whatever he was up to no longer had any bearing on him – nothing did, now. There was only this moment and Lucas Blake. 'He told me I would have died really old. To make you younger I had to give my years.' His memory drifted back to that day in the broken abbey, a few weeks and a lifetime ago. 'He said I would have until I was thirty-eight.' He hiccoughed a laugh. 'Lying bastard.'

'I wish I could give them back.' Lucas Blake's eyes were serious. He sighed, and then gave a little laugh of his own. 'And when I told you that nothing in the future was definite, this wasn't quite what I had in mind.'

There was a moment's silence, an ease in the dread.

322

Christopher could hear his own breathing, harsh in the water.

'I wouldn't take them back – I'm glad I did it,' he said, and he was surprised to find he meant it. He twisted his head to look at the Knight. 'I'm a bit scared,' he said, eventually.

In the water, swollen fingers found his and gripped them. Blake was stretching his arm to the limits. 'I'm a bit scared too,' he admitted, 'but I wouldn't change it either. Thank you, for giving me a taste of life again. It's an honour to die with you.'

Christopher's eyes blurred and his throat tightened, and it had nothing to do with the river. Alongside him, Blake coughed as water flooded his mouth. Somewhere, out there in the world where other people existed, the drums stopped. The river was closing over them.

Christopher squeezed Blake's hand, focusing on his fingers. He looked over one last time while he could.

Lucas Blake grinned, an expression full of the brave devil-may-care attitude that summed up everything he was, had been and could have been. 'Let us be ready,' he said, tipping Christopher a wink.

'Let us be ready,' Christopher answered.

And then the river took them.

The drums had stopped beating at least five minutes before Finmere and Mona finally reached the wall above Traitor's Gate. The mist was curling round their feet, and with nothing left to see, the crowd had dispersed, disappearing back to their homes and their own lives as the new day dawned.

Fin could see nothing of the water, or the boats that had sat and watched as the River Times claimed the Knight and his best friend. Had they gone back to their underground rivers? Did they feel any shame or guilt, or did the Rage still hold them in its evil grip? Fin's eyes burned with tears.

'Christopher!' he shouted as he rattled the locked metal gate. Beyond it he could see old stone stairs leading down the hidden water, and he could hear it, lapping only inches away, as if laughing at his desperate attempt to hold onto a shred of hope. 'Christopher!'

The sound of Mona, sobbing beside him, was the only answer. His hands slipped on the damp metal, but still he struggled to climb it. He needed to get to the other side, to Christopher – this *couldn't* happen, it *couldn't*.

Feet pounded on the deserted street behind them, and strong arms wrapped round him, pulling him down. 'There's nothing we can do, mate.' Fowkes held him tight as he struggled. 'There's nothing we can do.'

Fin tried to pull himself free, but Fowkes refused to let go, despite the kicks and punches the boy rained on him, and eventually the fight went out of him and his shoulders crumpled.

Fowkes hadn't come alone. Mitesh Savjani's turban had skewed in the run and he was puffing and panting like a steam engine, his heavy body more used to fine food than exercise, but he was oblivious to his own exhaustion and dishevelled state as he held his crying daughter.

Fin called out for his friend until his throat was raw, while Fowkes stood beside him, his hand on Fin's shoulder. It seemed to Fin that each time he shouted Christopher's name, another line etched itself into the face of the Commander of the Knights of Nowhere. He could feel those same lines forming on his own young/old soul, and even though he didn't blame Fowkes for what had happened – none of them had got there in time – he couldn't help but feel that somehow they both deserved it.

EPILOGUE

Two hours later, when day had fully broken, the streets of The Nowhere were quiet as its residents slept off what was left of the Rage. A few citizens tried to go about their ordinary business, but there was a hush in the air that hinted that this was no ordinary day. Eventually, the chill breathed black snow that glittered as it drifted through the still air.

Finmere watched it absently. He and Mona had barely spoken a word since Fowkes and Mitesh Savjani had gently but firmly led them away from the river's edge. There was too much to take in – too much had happened to allow him to grieve. He felt completely numb, as if he were watching the world from outside of himself. He wondered if he should close the heavy drapes across the window, but he couldn't bring himself to move, and it wasn't only him who was staring out at the very badly wrong snow. Mona sat on her bed, hugging her knees and looking out at the strange new day, an occasional tear falling silently down her cheek.

Fin missed Joe almost as much as he hated Mr Arnold-Mather. Christopher's dad had fooled them all. He'd killed the Prince Regent, and made Joe make a terrible choice. He focused his grief in that direction. Mr Arnold-Mather knew too much, and someone must have been keeping him informed of events in The Nowhere after St John Golden had been captured. But who could it be? Surely not Ted, nor Freddie Wise. Nor Cardrew Cutler. He couldn't believe it of them.

The door opened and Alex Currie-Clarke came in. 'Mrs

Baker sent me. Here's some hot chocolate.'

Finmere wasn't listening. The snow glinted like shards of diamond in coal, and his eyes widened slightly. Clarity cut through the numbness. 'I think I know who betrayed us,' he muttered.

'What?' Alex Currie-Clarke put the drinks down on a low table. 'What do you mean?'

'Arnold-Mather. I know who's been talking to him. I know who the traitor is.' The snow suddenly forgotten, Fin was on his feet. He pulled his sword free, anger and revenge and the need to *do* something suddenly overwhelming him. 'We need to go to Orrery House.'

'Should we get Fowkes?'

Fin sliced the blade through the air, electricity humming through his arm and feeding the bitter energy of loss that was driving him. His arm or Baxter's arm – right in this moment he didn't care. He looked at the new Knight. 'Are you coming?'

'Count me in,' Alex Currie-Clarke said, pulling his own sword free. 'Let's go.'

Finmere Tingewick Smith's story concludes in the final book in *The Knights of Nowhere* trilogy,

THE LONDON STONE

ACKNOWLEDGEMENTS

A massive thank you to my editor Jo Fletcher who found time to edit this one before heading off to fantastic new publishing pastures. Not enough thank you's for everything you've done for me and my alter ego and I know you'll totally rock with your new line. Plus of course a big thank you to my agent, Veronique, and my friends and family, and all at the Gollancz team.